THE ROYAL CREED

THE RISE OF THE PENGUINS SAGA

STEVEN HAMMOND

Rockhopper Books

This is a work of fiction. Any references to historical events or real locales are used fictitiously. Any other resemblances to actual events, locales, or persons, living or dead, are purely coincidental.

Edited by Michelle Patricia Browne
Cover art by Caner Inciucu
Interior layout by Tanya Adams
Exclusive content at:
riseofthepenguins.net

Dedicated to

My parents; without whom I would not exist.

ACKNOWLEDGEMENTS

Big thanks to Cathy Speiser, for all of your help, support, and general awesomeness. Joy, for always encouraging me, believing in me, and being my best friend. Jesse and Maribel at Grill Masters, for your support, and making delicious writing fuel. And, of course, Buster Dog.

And a special thank you to Deputy/Flight Officer, William Vincent and Deputy IV/Pilot, Mike Sill of the Fresno County Sheriff's Department.

THE RISE OF THE PENGUINS SAGA

DRAMATIS PENGUINIS

Lord Saeson-Basileios Penguin, Ruler of the Misshapen

Aperion-Basileios Penguin, Sovran of the Southern Realm

Mearna-Royal Emperor, Doyenne of the Alliance of Independent Colonies (AIC)

Ceocilus-Royal Emperor, Son of Mearna, Commander

Talus-Royal Emperor, Warlord of Planarseae

Adikos-Royal Emperor, Shadow Warrior

Kiley-King Penguin, Supreme Commander of AIC

Admiral Gregor-King Penguin, Order of Kings

Pìn-Blue Penguin, Spy in service to Kiley

Lavour-Chinstrap Penguin, former commander of AIC

Meuseaux-Chinstrap Penguin

Cryftin-Tawaki (Fiordland Crested) Penguin, caretaker of the Oracle

Lapasia-Hoiho (Yellow-eyed) Penguin, The Oracle

Nok-Rockhopper Penguin

Keerka-Rockhopper Penguin

Leeg-Rockhopper Penguin

Kicki-Rockhopper Penguin, Oracle

Colonel Kairg-Rockhopper Penguin

Lydeck-Rockhopper Penguin

Tretak-Rockhopper Penguin

Pasillas-Humboldt Penguin

Cryzyrky-Adélie Penguin

DRAMATIS PERSONAE

Trofim Grekov-Mercenary, BioCon
Colonel Tyler Jenson-U.S. Military
Keith-Mercenary, BioCon
Thibaud-Mercenary, BioCon
Bryan Turlock-President/CEO GT
Trevor Lawson-GT
Major-General Yulian Utnik-Russian Military
Gina Rosedale-Climatologist
Randy Lee-Photographer

THE ROYAL CREED

CHAPTER 1

Antarctica, Pack Ice Command. One day after the death of the Overlord. Colonel Tyler Jenson stood outside the shattered ruins of PIC, one foot perched on a chunk of ice, pointing and shouting orders over the sound of equipment. Snow-cats equipped with front-end dozer blades pushed dead penguins in to the impact craters, expediently disposing of the frozen corpses. Nearly one hundred personnel consisting of BioCon specialist, U.S. Special Forces, and GT hazmat workers, searched through the carnage, hoping to find living *talkers*, as penguins capable of speaking had come to be known. But the amount of ordnance thrown at PIC and the surrounding area left little chance of finding any survivors.

"Make sure you take several samples of the big ones—what's left of them anyways—to the compound. Turlock's orders," Colonel Jenson said, speaking into a headset. He looked toward the makeshift command center, two hundred meters away, shaking his head. "How the hell should I know? Put them up his ass for all I care. Just do it."

A dozen men dressed in white cold-weather fatigues, carrying packs and weapons, gathered near the colonel while he spoke. Jenson took notice and grabbed a passing GT worker, shoving his headpiece into the man's hands. He faced the group and pulled off his hood. "I'm assuming you've already been briefed, but let me reiterate in case you've forgotten. We're going in here for two reasons. First, you are to find any survivors, penguin or otherwise, and if they can speak, we take them. If they don't, kill them. Second, we need a kill confirmation on one in particular. Though in this mess, it may be difficult," he said, looking at the collapsed entrance.

The powerfully built, strong-jawed squad leader, stepped closer, spiked boots crunching on the ice. "How are we to know which one you want?" he said with a barely perceptible Russian accent.

Jenson stared at the man for a few moments, seemingly gauging what to say. "It will probably be adorned in seal skins. And no, Trofim, it's not the one you're looking for."

Trofim pulled his hood and knit cap off, rubbing his hand across the stubble on his shaved head. *You have no idea what I'm looking for.* He blamed the colonel for the death of his squad…for Alyssa's death. Bad intel cost lives, and from what Tro had learned, it wasn't just the intel. They had been sent in as bait. And people that used Trofim as bait always ended up dead. He stifled a laugh. "After you, Colonel," he said, gesturing toward the entrance.

Jenson looked him up and down. "Why don't you take the lead, Sergeant Grekov?"

Trofim nodded; he hadn't actually expected Jenson to lead the men. "Alright everybody watch your step. The ice might be unstable and we're going in blind. Lights on."

Most of the passages had collapsed under the previous day's barrage, and faint light flowed in from breaks in the once-mighty edifice's crown. Each meter forward they went, the more difficult it became. After careful examination the sergeant found a way through the rubble and the group made their way into the collapsed main hall of Pack Ice Command. The magnificent ice stalactite, which had once bathed the chamber in a rainbow of color, laid in shattered ruin. Wind howled in from a breach near the top of the fortress, carrying pinfeathers of the dead toward the sky. Bodies of dead Royal Emperor warriors who had died in the factious fighting between Antaean and Liutites were scattered about the hall or buried beneath the debris. All of the bodies were checked for life, but no survivors were found.

The men clambered over large chunks of ice, being sure to check behind each boulder-sized piece. The light from the entrance faded only ten meters in, and beams of light pierced the dark recesses of the main hall. Trofim climbed over the debris with the ease and agility of a well-trained soldier. Keeping his light aimed forward, he sat on a hunk of ice and swung his legs over. He heard the cracking before the rumble, powder fell and Trofim dove back over the chunk, intending to tuck and roll. His pack caught, and he landed on his back instead. He rolled out of the way as one chunk fell from above, and sprang up, jumping out of the way of another. The rumble stopped, and he walked through the icy dust and found the rest of his squad. "Is everybody all right?" He acknowledged their affirmatives and looked at Jenson. He hooked his thumb. "There's room to walk on the other side."

They stepped into the main hall, crunching on the shattered ruins of the massive stalactite. Beyond the hall, the arched entrance to the Overlord's chambers remained intact. With all other passages blocked, Trofim led his men down the corridor. He stopped and examined fragments of the bas-reliefs lying on the ground. His eyes shifted toward Jenson, wondering what other secret lay buried in the destruction.

The damage inside the chamber was surprisingly light. The Overlord's macabre trophy collection littered the floor, mingling with dead Royal Emperors. Much of the domed ceiling of the ovoid room had collapsed, revealing a darkening sky. Wind swirled through the rent, uplifting pinfeathers in a spiraling dance to the heavens.

Trofim scanned the area, his light coming to rest on a streak of blood. He traced the crimson path to the body of a Royal Emperor lying across the broken dais of the Overlord, its seal skin cloak draped to the side. Trofim ran to the dais, flipped the stiff body, examining the corpse. So mangled was the carcass that he couldn't tell if it was the one he searched for. He sat back and noticed the flippers lacked the finger-like appendages of the one he had fought. His shoulders slumped in defeat.

Trofim stood to call Jenson to the body, but stopped when he heard an odd sound, like ice grinding together, coming from the rear of the chamber. Weapons and lights were aimed toward the noise in an instant. The icy wall opened, revealing a hidden passage. The men crept forward, coming to a quick stop when a raspy voice came from the darkness. "You do not belong here. This is still our domain," the unseen voice grated.

Colonel Jenson, trailed by Trofim, drew his sidearm and stepped toward the doorway. The men shone their lights inside and jerked in surprise when a penguin hissed at them.

An emaciated-looking, three-foot tall, dull gray penguin slinked out of the passage. Pale yellowish plumage draped down the back of its skull. Large black eyes examined the men with a look of both caution and contempt. The attendant of the former Overlord edged forward, glaring through the light. "You are not welcome here, humans," it said with slow deliberation. "It would be wise for you to leave."

Colonel Jenson leveled his weapon at the penguin's head. "I'm not concerned with being welcome. You'll be coming with us now."

Not intimidated, the attendant crept forward. "This was only the beginning. Even now, as we speak, the Overlord's plans move forward. You have gained nothing."

"Perhaps you would like to share those plans with us? Seeing as how your Overlord is dead," Jenson replied.

The attendant cackled a sickly laugh. "Our only plans are to see you dead, Colonel Jenson."

Jenson's eyes shifted toward Trofim.

The attendant seemed to become gleeful at seeing his unease. "Oh yes. We know of your collusion and treachery. And to that I say again, it will not go unanswered. You and your kind will suffer. And you will die for—"

The penguin's head exploded into a cloud of feathers and blood. Jenson watched the bird's headless body fall to the floor and then holstered his weapon.

Trofim met the colonel's eyes. "I thought we were keeping the talkers?"

"It was uncooperative." Jenson turned to the others, kicking the headless body aside. "Shine a light down the passage. See how big it is."

After an exchange of wary looks between the soldiers, one of the men came forward and stepped into the passageway. "It's a tight squeeze at first, but it looks like it widens out toward the back," the soldier said.

"Do you see any fissures in the ceiling?" Trofim asked, resting his hand on the other's shoulder.

The soldier examined the surfaces. "I don't see any major cracks or damage." He unshouldered his pack and crouched inside. After shuffling for a few meters, he stood straight and walked across a roughly hewn room, coming to an arched break in the wall. "There's a doorway back here."

"Stay where you are. We'll be right behind you," Sergeant Grekov told his man.

No reply came.

"Corporal, did you hear me?" Trofim asked, his concerned eyes falling on Jenson.

Jenson swore under his breath. "Get inside there. And don't leave your packs—drag them behind you if you have to."

Another soldier entered the opening, weapon ready. He reached the back of the grotto but found no sign of the other man. "He's not in here. He must've gone through the doorway."

Grekov shook his head. If one of those scrawny gray penguins survived the bombardment, then anything could have lived. "If he did, he didn't do it willingly." The Russian expletives which followed were terse, but to the point.

"Sergeant, tell the lieutenant to send a second squad here immediately," said Jenson rather calmly. He took a few steps away from the wall, appraising the passageway. "And tell him to send a demolition team. This hole needs to be bigger. And get your soldier out of there."

Sergeant Grekov watched the colonel peruse the Overlord's chamber. Jenson walked about the place with far too much familiarity. *Your soldier,* he thought, continuing to watch him. The statement spoke volumes. These men were nothing but disposable tools to the colonel. Trofim had seen the detachment before. True, death and danger come with the job, but Trofim felt an officer should have some regard for those under his command. Tro put the thoughts aside, he had a job to do. As detestable as he found the colonel, he was his commanding officer. He made the call, and masking his disdain, approached Jenson. "Orders, sir?"

The colonel looked him, seemingly lost in thought. "Keep an eye on that passageway. I don't want anything surprising us."

"What about Corporal Walters?" Grekov asked.

"Who?"

"The missing soldier," Trofim said with accusation.

"Presumed dead," Jenson replied, as if it were an annoyance.

He had to speak up this time. "Sir, with all due respect…I won't give a man up for dead until—"

Jenson wheeled toward Trofim. "Sergeant, we both know what these things are capable of. You better than most. If Watkins is still alive, he won't be for long."

"Walters, sir," Tro said.

"What?" Jenson snapped.

"His name was Walters, not Watkins," he answered, not masking the disgust in his voice. Colonel Jenson was on his list of people who needed to be reprimanded. In fact, he was the only one on the list. When Jenson ignored the correction, Trofim made a point to ignore the colonel. Seeing the other soldier exit the passage, shaking his head, he got to his duties.

After arguing with Jenson over the logic of blasting an already unstable structure, the demolition team left the structure only slightly less stable and with a wider passage. Colonel Jenson reentered the room, and telling Trofim to lead the way, pointed to the widened doorway.

When they arrived at the door Walters had mentioned, Jenson stepped forward to examine the wall and found a small circular opening in the wall. The colonel pulled a wooden dowel from his coat, precisely the correct size, inserted it in the hole, drew his sidearm, and stepped back from the slowly opening door.

Trofim leaned close to Jenson's ear. "That one you killed back there didn't carry a key," he said in a whisper, letting Jenson know it didn't go unnoticed.

"I am aware of that, sergeant. However, you should probably focus on what lies ahead," Jenson said, stepping behind the line of soldiers.

The door slid open, exposing darkness beyond. A soldier stepped alongside Trofim, shining his light through an odd mist. He snapped a couple of light-sticks and tossed them in. The sticks rolled down the passageway, disappearing in the black. "This floor slopes down at a pretty steep angle," he said, ducking his head beneath a low ceiling.

"Can you see anything? Any doors?" Trofim called to the man on point, his voice straining as he tried to keep his footing on the sloped walkway. The mist became thick enough to block the lights, and the air smelled of moisture, odd for a frozen fortress. He knew in his gut that they were walking into a trap. One man was missing already. From his experience at the fight at Forward Command, Tro knew the penguins were waiting for them.

"I think I see a wall a little further down," the soldier finally answered.

The sound of grinding ice filled the narrow passageway, and the squad brought their weapons up. The soldier came to firing position causing his forward boot to give up its tentative hold on the angled ice. He let out a yelp and slid down the corridor until he grunted to a stop against the wall.

"Are you okay?" Trofim called, ignoring Colonel Jenson's swearing from the back of the line.

"Yeah, I mean no. I think I might've broken my wrist," the soldier replied, sounding further away than expected.

"Hold your position. We'll be there in a minute."

The sound of grinding ice began again. "Hurry," the injured soldier shouted. "The wall is giving way. Get me the—" His urgent plea was replaced by a scream, which lasted until it faded into the distance.

Trofim shined his light ahead of him, descending the corridor as fast as prudence allowed, cussing along the way. He reached the opened doorway and peered inside. He saw the floor had given way to a long vertical drop into the abyss. "Baker! Where are you? Can you hear me?" He waited silently for a moment and then pulled off his cap, wiping his brow. He picked up the faint scent of water coming from the open door. They were still on the ice shelf. He hoped the man had a quick death in the Antarctic sea.

While aiming a glare at Jenson, Sergeant Grekov shouted toward his men "That's two. Stay alert, don't get sloppy." He was angry about the loss of two good men, and about the mission. *Find surviving talkers.* To hell with that; as far as he was concerned, they should've blasted what remained of this place into sludge. He just wanted to get paid and get the hell away from Antarctica.

Another door opened, leading to a more level surface. Jenson approached the shaft the soldier had fallen into, pulled the key from his pocket, and closed the door. "It would be nice if I had one of those," Trofim remarked.

"Move out sergeant," Jenson replied, indicating the doorway.

The soldiers filed through the doorway one at a time, flashlights penetrating the darkness. Trofim spotted something. "Hold," he said. All was silent except for the rattling of weapons being brought to position. Something lurked in the distance, a vague form: there, then gone. The other's lights joined his. Nothing.

"This room is huge," one of the men said. His voice echoed inside of the cavern. Trofim hushed the man.

The sound of claws on ice could be heard from somewhere in the room. Lights pointed ahead. The soldiers were rigid with uncertainty, but ready for action.

"There," one whispered, his light reflecting a glimmer.

Trofim spotted it too. Then he spotted another, and then several more. His mind didn't register what he was seeing at first, and then he realized… they were eyes. One by one, hundreds of eyes came out of the darkness. They were in trouble. "Hold your fire. Watch the rear. Let's see what we're dealing with," he said, keeping the men calm. He stole a glance back at the door and spotted Jenson stepping back toward the exit. He didn't have time to think about his hate for the man.

The room started to fill with the sound of muffled clicking. The muffled clicking soon grew into a din. The noise grew louder. Several strange-looking penguins slowly advanced toward the intruders. They weren't normal penguins. Some had white feathered bodies, some were all black, and others were a mesh of gold and black. Their bodies carried elongated flippers which dragged against the ground, while others bore muscular legs, but with stunted flippers. Others had flippers ending in grasping appendages, on stout bodies. Their beaks were short and thick, or long and thin, like the bill of a marlin. The assorted group of hideous penguin faces inched ever closer toward the men.

"Hold your ground. Fire on my mark only," Trofim told his squad. He had years of experience dealing with the strange and unusual, but his resolve nearly waivered at the sight of so many monstrosities creeping toward them.

The ominous clicking stopped abruptly, and the penguins halted their advance.

"Steady," Tro said through shallow breaths.

A low hiss came from somewhere near the back of the room. The hiss became louder. The men shifted while the penguins remained perfectly still. The hissing became an articulated word. "You do not belong here. This is the realm of the Misshapen. Leave now or suffer your fate," the voice rasped and trailed away.

Hearing the voice, Colonel Jenson stepped back into the room. "Your Overlord is dead. His armies are defeated. We will leave when we get what we came for."

After several moments of silence, the voice hissed again, "We do not abide Antaean. He was a fool to make bargains with humans."

Jenson stole a sideways glance at Trofim, who had fixed his eyes on the colonel. "Regardless of your loyalties, you will give me what I came for," Jenson said to the voice.

"What is it that you want—what is the name? Oh yes…Colonel Jenson," the voice said.

Trofim's shoulders slumped, his suspicions confirmed twice. The colonel had been here before, had contact with the penguins, and was in collusion with GT. The other soldiers exchanged looks, realizing the same thing.

"I presume I'm speaking with Lord Saeson," Jenson said. "I was informed that you were dead."

"Apparently Antaean wasn't the only one who was lied to. Tell me what you want and leave here while you still can," Lord Saeson hissed.

Jenson stood silent for a moment. "Where is Aperion?" he finally asked, sounding more brazen.

Now it was Saeson's turn to remain silent.

"If you do not answer me, we will destroy what remains here. So I'll ask again—where is Aperion? We know he is still alive."

"You will attempt to destroy us whether I answer or not. That is your nature," Saeson hissed, remaining out of sight. His tone softened. "But for the hope of my loves and for the sake of their lives, I will take you at your word. Aperion is gone. He left long ago, before the war."

"We assumed that. Where did he go?" Jenson asked with more force in his voice.

"To the Northern Realm. The Northern Paradise, some call it."

"Where is the *Northern Paradise*?" Jenson asked, mocking the name.

"You know where it is—at the end of the world."

"The Arctic? Where?" Jenson asked, sounding slightly confused.

"How could I know this? I have never been away from this place—" Saeson paused, and then spoke in his own dialect, sounding as if he recalled a memory from long ago. "Though there was a time in my youth."

"We need one more thing before we go," Jenson said, interrupting Lord Saeson's reverie.

"Beware of what you seek, Colonel," Saeson said, ignoring the colonel's words. "Aperion is powerful. He is unlike any you have encountered before."

"Your kind doesn't fare well against our weapons," Jenson said with smugness. "We need a penguin that can speak our language. You will suffice."

A loud noise, which could only be construed as a laugh, filled the vast chamber. "Your impudence in the face of uncertainty amuses me, Colonel Jenson. Leave here or suffer the fate of the others who came before you."

Who else has been here? Trofim wondered.

"We're done here. Clean up, Sergeant Grekov," the colonel said.

"The talkers, sir?" Tro asked.

"It's being uncooperative as well. Now follow orders and mop up," Jenson said and then headed toward the door.

Sergeant Grekov looked to his men, doubt etched on his brow. If he didn't follow the orders, he would never get paid. If he did, they might not get out of this alive. *Eliminate the immediate threat first,* a voice echoed in his mind from long ago. "You heard the colonel. Let's light this place up," he said to his men as he pulled out a flash grenade.

"You don't have to do this, sergeant," Saeson said. His plea was answered by consecutive detonations of M-84 stun grenades.

CHAPTER 2

The shooting began. Indiscriminant gunfire brought down everything in its path. The misshapen penguins howled as the bullets tore through them. Several seconds of sustained gunfire later, Trofim called for the men to cease fire. Nothing stirred. He twisted toward Jenson. "Orders, sir?"

Jenson stood outside the doorway, shielding his eyes from the sergeant's light. Before he could answer, the mournful wail of Lord Saeson erupted. "My loves. You have killed my loves!"

Trofim felt a chill climb his back. This wasn't going to be good. "Reload. Reload and retreat," he shouted. The low rumble of grinding ice vibrated through his feet. He wheeled around and saw Jenson with the key out, his expression smug. *Betrayed.* He fired, peppering the wall, but Jenson ducked behind the closing door and disappeared. Trofim made a dash for the door, but it was too late. Another soldier jammed the barrel of his gun into the hole, hoping to trigger whatever mechanism operated the door. Nothing happened.

"You will suffer your retribution, humans!" Lord Saeson bellowed. "Kill them. Kill them, my loves!"

"Backs to the wall," Grekov ordered. "Don't let them get behind us."

The sound of scurrying clawed feet came at them from every direction. The soldiers scrambled for position. Beams of light sprayed forward, spotting dozens of penguins pouring through unseen recesses. They stood no more than two-feet tall, with thick black bodies and white wings. Jagged serrations ran the length of their long, narrow bills. The men opened fire. The first line of attackers fell, but more followed. An unyielding, seemingly endless stream of attackers came at them.

The first man dropped, brought down by the multitudes, as he tried to reload. With beaks abnormally agape, using their bills like steak knives, they carved through layers of clothing and flesh. The bloodcurdling screams reverberated through the chamber, but his squad mates were busy with their own battles. The jagged-billed penguins slashed at the man until he stopped moving, then joined the others.

After sweeping gunfire in front of him, Trofim found a brief reprieve. In the faint light, he spotted new forms coming out of an opening doorway. These were much larger, standing nearly four feet tall, with broad, elongated beaks perfect for stabbing. Their heads were supported by thick necks, and their solid, wingless bodies were covered in ecru plumage, resting on stocky, powerful legs. Trofim took a sharp breath at the sight.

Seven men remained standing, nearly all were wounded. They were all low on ammo and were starting to sweat beneath their gear. "Choose your targets. No wasted shots. We can still get out of here." He hoped for reinforcements, but his gut told him they were on their own. They had heard too much. Jenson had found the opportunity to silence them. If they got out of there, Jenson would have a huge payback coming. *If?* Trofim reprimanded himself. He would not accept ifs. The only *if* that existed was if he would have a bullet left to put in Jenson's head. He felt the weight of his knife against his hip. But who needed a bullet?

The lancers halted their advance. Trofim looked around, not knowing what would come next. The sound of grinding ice lifted his spirits. Had he been wrong about Jenson? He looked back at the door expectantly and realized the sound hadn't come from behind them; but from the side. The lancers had just been a diversion. He shined his light on the doorway and spotted several horrifically malformed penguins of various sizes. Some had gnarled, twisted beaks, adorning severely angled heads, while others crawled on wings and feet. "What is this place?" *This is hell*, his mind answered back. Gunfire erupted.

CHAPTER 3

Undauntted by piles of their dead comrades, the penguins continued attacking. With the human combatants distracted by the onslaught of new attackers, the lancers charged forward. In less than a minute five men were impaled by the thrusting beaks. Trofim could only watch when the final man fell beneath a swarm of assailants. All of the misshapens' attention were now on him. Last man standing once again. He stepped away from the wall, drew his Colt and eight-inch knife, and like his battle at Forward Command One, prepared for a final fight.

They all came at him at once. Trofim swept gunfire ahead of him; killing fourteen birds with fourteen shots. Saving one round, he holstered his pistol and braced for the onslaught. When the first penguin reached him, his knife separated its head from its body. He slashed and stabbed, disemboweled and decapitated at a blinding speed. A pain in his right calf told him of an enemy to his back. Without taking his eyes off of the bird he had by the neck, he lifted his injured leg and felt the satisfying crunch of a penguin skull beneath his boot. He plunged his eight inch knife into the body of another bird, then nearly bisected the creature.

Undeterred by Trofim's brutality, the penguins rushed him. The press of the attackers was proving too much, and several beaks found their target. Trofim fought harder; killing those he could, but he was soon overwhelmed, falling to the blood-stained ground. A loud penguin call sounded, and the attacks stopped.

Trofim Grekov scooted against the wall with knife in hand, exhausted and bloodied. The scattered lights of the dead soldiers cast dancing shadows on the ceiling. The chattering penguins parted as Saeson approached. He sheathed his knife and laid his tattered hand on his pistol.

Saeson stayed in the shadows. The shadowy figure presented a vague reminder of what he had faced at the outpost. He estimated it to be nearly six-feet tall and half as wide. He kept his pistol holstered, waiting to see what came. He could just shoot it, but he knew that would seal his fate. Best to stay alive until all options run out. "What do you want? Why don't you just kill me? Get it over with," Trofim demanded through ragged breaths.

"You are a great warrior, human," the form hissed. "You have fought bravely. You need not die."

Trofim heard the faint sound of grinding ice, followed by the skittering of several more clawed feet. "Show yourself."

A low, stuttered, hiss came from the shadows. "You humans are so duplicitous. I know your thoughts." The spectral form came closer, but kept its distance. "I am Lord Saeson, ruler of the *damned*, those deemed unworthy by Antaean. I command the underworld, and you are now mine."

Trofim had seen enough Royal Emperors to know that they were not to be trifled with, and this thing was more than a Royal. "The Royals are dead. Release me or you will share their fate," he said with more confidence than he felt. If he did manage to get free, he would see this place razed to the ground. Hell, that was probably going to happen anyway. Jenson had gotten what he had come for. The thought of the colonel triggered a flare of anger.

"The Royals are of little concern to me. However, you are not in a position to bargain. You will be made to serve me, or you will die," Saeson said, creeping ever closer.

Lord Saeson came in to view. The scattered beams of light cast shadows on the intimidating form. His estimates were correct—Saeson stood a full six-foot tall, his large body supported by stout, powerful legs, terminating in long claws at the end of splayed, webbed feet. Wide, elongated wings dragged against the floor at his side. His head supported a broad yet long, narrowly tapered, curved, karambit-like beak. Yellow-gold plumage draped from the top of his head to his shoulders.

Tro knew there would be no escape this time. This thing would kill him; if not now, then soon. The bombs would drop before long; he was wounded, and surrounded by hostiles. He had been defeated by a penguin for a second time, and he wouldn't allow a third. He thought of Alyssa, a true friend. She might have been more, had he the courage to open his heart to her before she died. "I'm sorry, A-bomb," he whispered, smiling at the thought of her nickname. "We're all as good as dead anyways, Saeson. And I will not be made a servant." He pulled his gun and placed the barrel to his head.

The last thing Grekov saw as he pulled the trigger was Lord Saeson swinging a massive flipper toward him.

CHAPTER 4

"Let's go," Colonel Jenson ordered the first soldier he saw exiting Overlord's chamber.

The faint sound of gunfire drew the man's eyes to the rear of the chamber, and he looked to the colonel questioningly.

"There's nothing that can be done," Jenson answered the unspoken question. "I have what we came for, and the others have sacrificed themselves for the information. Let's make sure their sacrifice is not in vain."

When he crawled out of Pack Ice Command, he saw a man in an orange jumpsuit with a fur-lined hood and amber goggles on his face walking toward him. Jenson tensed. "Damn it. I don't need this now," he muttered. The man approached Jenson, removing his goggles and cold mask, revealing darker skin and a chiseled jawline. He stared at the colonel without saying a word. Jenson gritted his teeth and spoke. "There may be a small problem."

"How small? Or should I ask, how big?" the man said.

"I assure you, Mr. Turlock, it's nothing that wasn't entirely unexpected. If Vance hadn't been so eager and exercised patience, this would've never gotten out of control."

Bryan Turlock, the new President and CEO of Global Tech/Global Threat Environmental, whose cockiness made the former CEO, Vance Lyons, look like a timid school boy, was not the kind to put up with those he saw as beneath him. Colonel Tyler Jenson was beneath him. Turlock, who matched Jenson's height and carried an aura of being just as able as the colonel, took no offense. "Colonel, there is no need to become defensive. If your predecessor, Colonel Maycotte, were here, he would likely say there is no blame. We all are here to achieve the same ends. And we are nearly there. Now, what type of problem have *we* run into? Tell me, please."

Jenson wondered if Turlock was attempting some kind of vague threat when mentioning Maycotte's name. If so, it didn't work. After all, the colonel had ordered the strike to kill Maycotte. Turlock's condescending tone made him consider pulling off a similar stunt. Jenson began walking toward his helicopter and Turlock walked with him. "As you know, we expected some resistance. But it will be dealt with. The problem is that we are dealing with Saeson. I believe you were briefed about this particular abomination?"

"From what I've been told, Saeson is the passive one. Did you get a talker?"

"No. His malformed or misshapen attacked. My squad got separated. I'm presuming all parties are dead. But before the attack, I learned something you might find interesting." Jenson hung the words out like bait on a hook.

"And what is that, Colonel?" Turlock asked impatiently.

"He confirmed that Aperion *is* alive," Jenson said.

The CEO stopped. "We suspected as much. And where is Aperion?" Turlock asked, sounding impatient.

"Could be anywhere. But he's not here. If he were, I doubt that I would have survived to tell you this."

"That doesn't do me any good, Jenson," Turlock growled.

"I have an idea, but in the meantime, I would suggest the penetration ordnance I asked for so we can blow this place to hell."

"No. That's out of the question. Recent events notwithstanding, we still have to exercise a small bit of caution," said Turlock. He looked at the ruins of Pack Ice Command. Its battered form made it more ominous. He turned his attention back to Jenson, looking at him from the corner of his eye. "Where is the Russian? I need him elsewhere."

"He was lost in the confrontation with Saeson. That is why we should do what I said, and blow this—"

"Don't think of yourself as invaluable, Colonel. Whatever information you're holding can be found by other means," Turlock said, turning to walk away.

Jenson gave the man a few steps, then spoke, "You're right, Bryan. I wouldn't want to make the same mistake as Vance Lyons."

Turlock made a move as if he were going to reply, but instead, kept walking to his chopper.

Jenson watched the man until he boarded his helicopter and continued watching until he was in the air. Satisfied that his point had been made, he called out to some nearby soldiers, "Get PDMs in and around that entryway. I don't want anything coming out of there...anything." He stared at the entry for a moment, nodded, and turned away.

CHAPTER 5

Congealed blood covered Trofim's eyelids, making them difficult to open. He awoke in a dimly lit room. Faint yellow light broadcast from somewhere unseen gave the impression of the first light of day. He scanned the ovate chamber. The haziness of the walls played tricks on his bleary eyes.

Feeling an ache, Trofim gingerly touched his forehead. He felt something firm pasted along his head that wasn't a bandage or congealed blood. He resisted the urge to pick; instead, he tried to remember how he got here… wherever here was. His first inclination was that he was in a hospital, but there were no monitors and no sterile smells. In fact the room smelled opposite of sterile, but he couldn't place its origin. He lifted his head to sit, but couldn't find the strength and flopped back onto his bed. *Bed,* he wondered. It was somewhat soft, conforming to his body like no other bed he had ever been in; and it was warm, a nice contrast to the surprisingly cold air of the room.

Trofim closed his eyes. He remembered the penguins and the fighting. He remembered putting the gun to his head. "Am I that bad of a shot?" he jibed at himself, trivializing his attempted suicide. He recalled the hopelessness, the others dying, everything except pulling the trigger. He remembered a cold hard slap just as he was about to pull the trigger. He realized that he wasn't in a hospital; he was still in the penguin stronghold.

"I lost twice today."

He lay there wondering about the day. He thought of killing Colonel Jenson, but saved it for later. He thought of Alyssa, as he had every day since she'd died. He thought about how long he had been unconscious. He tried to look at his watch, but his arm felt like aspic; a lifeless, gelatinous blob, refusing to budge. He was sure he had been out for no more than a few hours. He brought his top lip over the bottom, and feeling a full growth of hair, realized he had been there much longer.

"This is stupid. I got to get up." Trofim continued to talk to himself, trying to stay awake. He attempted to rise once more, but fell back, exhausted by the effort. "I can do this. I *have* to do this. Come on Tro, get your lazy—"

"Do you ever shut up?" a quiet voice said harshly, cutting off his self-motivation.

A wave of adrenaline kicked in and Trofim sprang to his feet. He spotted a penguin sharing the bed with him just before an ocean of dizziness overtook him. His legs turned to *lapsha*, sending him back to the bedding.

The penguin let out a sigh of relief when he heard Trofim's unconscious breathing. "Thank the Ancients, now I can get some R and R—whatever an R and R are."

CHAPTER 6

"**L**ord Saeson, you have done well. See to it that the human remains alive. He will prove useful."

"Yes, *my Lord*. He is in the infirmary, sharing quarters with the Gentoo," Saeson said with a touch of animosity. "He takes space from those he wounded."

"The loss of your loves is regretful, but it is necessary that the enemy of our enemy lives."

"Then why did we not take more? Greater numbers could lead to greater success. Or perhaps you wish to emulate Antaean and make a fool's bargain?"

"Mind your place, Saeson. Your life was mine to save, and it is mine to take if I so desire. If you had acted more quickly, the human called Jenson would be dead. But as it stands, these circumstances will prove sufficient. Best that he is killed by one of his own. The human has been betrayed, and he is dangerous. Talus can attest to that."

"My apologies, Lord Aperion. My life is yours—a fact you will not let me forget, even if I wished to," Saeson replied, lowering his beak in deference.

Aperion walked across the small, dark chamber. He stood a head taller than Saeson, and carried a large and formidable beak. A pelican-like pouch, hung below the serrated beak. A long black crest of feathers surrounded the top of his head like a dark crown. His coloring resembled an Adélie penguin more than a Royal Emperor. "The events which have transpired have done so at my whim. With Antaean dead and his remaining warriors scattered, I will assume my rightful position as Sovran of this realm."

"*Sovran* and mighty Aperion, had you killed Antaean when I suggested, you would have controlled his warriors."

"My naïve and simple-minded brother, do you not know Mearna? The warriors had imprinted on her. Only Liutites had a chance to kill her, and she played him like a fledging toying with a squid. No, it was best that it turned out as it did. Mearna will seek me out. But these are waves best left for another tide. Now you must see to the recovery of the human and his Gentoo cotenant. If the human is to survive, he will need to be recovered before the others leave our territory."

"If Talus doesn't kill him first," Saeson answered.

"The Warlord will do nothing more than gloat. Talus is under control."

Lord Saeson stared at Aperion with forced patience. He didn't press his brother further, and changed the subject. "I do not know if the human will survive our healing methods. It is vulnerable to the cold. It has been in the infirmary for many days already and shows little signs of recovery."

"The Ancients knew of this time, Lord Saeson. The Oracle spoke to *me*. These are events which must transpire if we are to survive. We are the true descendants of Theosidon; the Basileios, not Antaean. We are destined to subjugate the Royals. They betrayed Theosidon. It is in their nature to lust for power, and as it had been in ancient times; their lust for power is their undoing. Mearna knows she cannot hope to control the clans without me, and yet she will plot my murder. But you, dear brother, so lost in caring for your misshapen, failed to see what I have seen."

Aperion walked to the other side of the room and let out a quick shrill call. A doorway opened, and he stepped into the corridor, turning to look at Saeson. "When the human has recovered his strength, see to it that he and his companion are allowed to escape. I am confident that the human will kill the Colonel Jenson, and that the Gentoo will serve his purpose as well. I have work to do now, brother. I will find my queen, and we will have our peace. Fulfill your destiny here, Lord Saeson. May the currents let our paths cross again one day."

Lord Saeson watched Aperion depart. He heard the distant splash when Aperion reached the sea below PIC. The Sovran would follow the under ice trails to the open ocean and attempt to bring the Royal Emperors under control, find his queen, and conquer the clans. Saeson surveyed Aperion's chambers, dark and empty. He missed the sunlight. He had spent too long in the gloom. But that would change soon; now he had command of Terra Australis, the Southern Land, with no Royals to stand in his way. "Let him seek out Lapasia; the Oracle will keep her secrets, and I will keep mine." Saeson made a low rumble in his throat and the door to Aperion's chamber closed behind him.

"You should've let me kill him," a voice said from the shadows.

"General Talus, you know better. Aperion must play his part, or this will all crumble."

CHAPTER 7

ISLA FORTUNA, a small uninhabited island near Cape Horn: Mearna and Ceocilus came ashore and flopped on the rocky ground.

"I haven't swum this far since the Trials," Ceocilus said through ragged breaths.

Mearna lay still for a few seconds before pushing herself upright. "Get up. The others may be coming ashore. We need to show them strength," Mearna admonished her son.

"Do you think many have survived? The waves were larger than I have ever seen," Ceocilus asked.

"Of course they did. The lesser clans have to hunt to survive. We have gone soft, sitting in the luxury of Pack Ice Command. Don't underestimate them, or you'll end up like Antaean," Mearna said.

Ceocilus stared at his mother. "I have never underestimated them," he said evenly.

Mearna eyed her son. The swim had been arduous. Racked by sixty to ninety foot waves near the cape, there had been times when she doubted whether or not she would survive. The long, circuitous journey to avoid Naval ships had taxed her strength. "We will rest here for a few days. If Commander Kiley and the others do not arrive during that time, we will think of another plan."

"What is our plan now? Go to the North? And what then?"

"We will seek out—"

"Good of you to join us," a voice cut in from higher up on the shore. "We were beginning to wonder if perhaps the humans or a squall had taken you."

Mearna and Ceocilus snapped their heads toward the newcomer.

"Commander Kiley," Mearna said. "We were just discussing you."

"I suspect that's true," Kiley said, not masking his suspicion. "We have been waiting for days. I was about to give up hope."

"Hope is not one of your strengths, Commander. Have the other warriors arrived?"

"Yes, M'lady. Just yesterday. However, Commander T'Cuh-ka took the Magellanics and left for the Straits shortly before you arrived. He seems to have lost his spirit for battle. Which is just as well; the Magellanics lacked commitment. I wonder if he or Cuh-trük was their leader," Kiley said derisively.

"The Magellanics paid a heavy price for Antaean's blunders. Neither he nor Cuh-trük can be blamed if they chose not to follow us. The Overlord's foolishness has cost us another ally."

"Humph," Kiley snorted. "The Kings achieved victory at South Georgia and Sandwich Islands."

"Yes, Commander, a victory against an overwhelming force of thirty humans cannot be dismissed," Mearna spat.

Kiley narrowed his eyes. "A victory against the humans, regardless of their numbers, is still a major victory. And we had no weapons," he added looking at Ceocilus.

"If you say so, Commander," Mearna said, ending the debate. "What word have you from Pack Ice Command? Did anybody survive?"

Kiley hesitated. "T'Cuh-ka briefed me on the battle of Pack Ice Command. Most of the forces, on both sides were destroyed. The humans' attacks from the sky were devastating."

"What of Liutites and the Chinstrap?"

"Before I get to that, I would be reticent if I were not to tell you that I have received a message from the Order of Kings."

Mearna stared at Kiley. She was not in the mood to hear about the Order right now. "Your Order has swum against the tide for too many years. It seems the Magellanics were truer to the cause than the Kings. But as much as I loathe to know, let's hear it, Commander."

"At the command of His Highness, King Elinthaw, and by the direct order of Admiral Gregor all King penguins are to be immediately withdrawn from the forces of the Penguin Defense Alliance," Kiley stated sharply.

"Well this puts us on a different path. Apparently the Order will stand idly by as the humans continue to wreak havoc on those who are defenseless," Mearna snapped back. As much as she hated to admit it, the Kings were a necessary part in her plans. "Tell me something I want to hear, Commander. I am beginning to feel like our ambitions will lead us nowhere."

Kiley remained quiet, listening to her approach the edge of a tirade. When it seemed she was approaching Liutites' famous lack of control, he interrupted. "M'lady, the Order of Kings has said to withdraw from the PDA."

"So you have said, Commander," Mearna said, her irritation rising.

"M'lady, the Penguin Defense Alliance no longer exists. We are now the Alliance of Independent Colonies. I cannot obey their demands because of the impossibility of the demand," Kiley said with a smugness only a King penguin could carry.

Mearna looked at Ceocilus, then back to Kiley. This King's lust for power nearly equaled that of a Royal's. This could be beneficial. "Commander Kiley, are the forces of the King's still at our disposal?"

"Yes M'lady, as are the Chinstraps, the Adélie, the Macaroni, the Gentoo, and my new allies, the Humboldt. With the Chinstraps and Adélie driven from their homes, our numbers rival that of the PDA at its peak," Kiley said proudly.

Mearna felt reinvigorated by the news. She meandered to the crest of the shoreline and saw several hundred Royal Emperor warriors gathered in the interior of the island. Now she wasn't just reinvigorated, she felt almost giddy with the promise that these forces represented. She could hunt down Aperion, find the queen, and destroy the line of Basileios penguins once and for all.

"There is more, M'lady," Kiley interrupted her visions of grandeur.

Mearna cringed at hearing the title, *M'lady*. She would have to change that. *More?* she thought. What else could top this?

"There is the issue of Liutites," Kiley told her.

Her body deflated. "Yes Commander, go ahead."

"We have on good account that Liutites is dead."

Now the day had gotten even better. Mearna's eyes glinted with joy. She would have loved to have seen his demise. A multitude of possible endings for Liutites filled her imagination. "How do you know this?" she asked cautiously.

"T'Cuh-ka said he spoke to the Rockhopper, Nok, who was present and assisted Lavour in killing him. Apparently Nok, Lavour, another Chinstrap, along with the Gentoo Leepoh, killed Liutites. And if you don't mind me expressing my own bit of good news, that oppressively annoying General Leepoh died during the fight as well," Kiley said with a touch of glee.

"What about Lavour?" Mearna asked, hoping he had died during the fight as well.

"He and the other Chinstrap have gone their own way. He resigned from the AIC, as has Nok," said Kiley.

Mearna mulled over the information. The Rockhoppers could be brought back in line; she would see to that. Everything had worked out perfectly, well nearly perfect, if Lavour had died. But if he truly resigned from the AIC, then he had been marginalized. Good enough, she thought. "And what of the all of these soldiers we have at our disposal? I don't see many around," she said, surveying the rocky landscape.

"Yes, M'lady. I have sent a large contingent, namely, the Macaroni, toward the Island of Bokis, New Zealand, as the humans call it. I guessed that since we have previously attacked the western coast, the humans might be looking for us along that route. I believe we should attack a few areas far from there to pull the human's eyes in that direction, allowing us to continue northward along the western coast."

Mearna eyed Commander Kiley, knowing he was as well versed in duplicity as herself. It was time to give Kiley what he desired. "You have done well, Kiley. Perhaps you should command the Order. But leadership of the Order of Kings notwithstanding, it is time you have been given the title you so abundantly deserve. Will you pledge your loyalty to me, and perform and carry out orders as Supreme Commander of the Alliance of Independent Colonies?" Mearna waited for Kiley's decision. She had no doubt that he knew she had ulterior motives, but she also knew a King's pride, and that no King, not even during the Great Auk Wars, had attained such a lofty position.

Kiley scrutinized Mearna, his eyes showing her two could play catch the squid. "Yes, M'lady. I will obey your command so long as you see me fit to carry out your orders." He gave a high-beak salute and waited for her to speak.

"Then by the authority bestowed upon me by the wisdom of the Ancients, you are now Supreme Commander of the Alliance of Independent Colonies. Your first order is from this day forward, to address me as Doyenne," she said, happy to be rid of the title *M'lady.* "Gather our fellow penguins for the proclamation."

After the Doyenne's announcement of the new Supreme Commander, during which several of the Royal Emperor warriors expressed their doubts about being led by a King, Mearna called Ceocilus aside. "We need to have a discussion…a *private* discussion. There are things you need to know, which I have not yet told you," she said quietly in the language of the Royal

Emperors.

"Is this about Lord Saeson?" Ceocilus asked conspiratorially.

"Partly, but this goes beyond him. You need to know this in case I am taken to The Great Sea."

"You are not going to die, Mother. Not anytime soon," Ceocilus said.

"No one knows their time, Ceocilus. This journey has made me feel my age. Youth has fled my body."

"Youth may have fled your body, but your mind is as sharp as shark's tooth."

"A sharp mind can't out swim a hungry Orca. But enough of this. When the others leave, stay behind and I will tell you what you need to know. The fate of all Royals rests in what you will learn."

^^^

After Mearna and Ceocilus departed, a Little Blue penguin emerged from a crag in the rocks and quickly scurried away.

Under the cover of night, the Blue penguin approached Supreme Commander Kiley. "Ah, Pín my friend. What news have you brought me?"

Pín chattered on for nearly a minute, adding flourishes of obscenities to emphasize certain points.

"The fate of all Royals?" Kiley mulled over the information. He had heard rumors of the one called Saeson, but like most, he dismissed it as nothing more than stories to frighten hatchlings. "You have done well. I will uphold my promise and see you safely taken to your home. Until then, stay out of sight. If the Doyenne or her offspring know you survived, they'll kill you."

Pín grumbled something in the Blue penguin dialect and shuffled away.

Kiley watched the penguin walk away, happy to keep the Blue in indentured servitude; he was too valuable a spy to let go. "The fate of all Royals," he said again. Now this was something he needed to know more about.

CHAPTER 8

"Open the room. The human has rested long enough," Lord Saeson said to a misshapen standing guard.

The rush of fresh air caused both of the room's occupants to stir.

Trofim's eyes fluttered, trying to focus on his surroundings. "How long have I been asleep for this time?" he said to no one. He had vague memories of being fed some paste-like substance and given fresh water, but they seemed more like a dream.

"Not long enough," a voice came from the left of him.

"Oh yeah…penguins," Tro replied, recalling where he was. He lifted his head, finding it easier to do so than on previous attempts. Through his hazy vision, he saw a large dark form. His first thought was to stand, but prior experience taught him not to. "Lord Saeson, I presume?"

"You are correct," Saeson answered, his voice coming in a crackling hiss. "What are you called, human?"

"I've been called many things, none of them too polite," Tro answered.

"Hah!" his penguin roommate blurted out. "We're both on the same iceberg there, friend."

"I'm not your friend," Tro replied.

"After all of this time we've spent together? That's a wound that will never heal," the penguin said.

"Enough of this!" Lord Saeson shouted, rushing toward the prone man. "You live because of me. It would be prudent of you not to mock your savior. What is your name?"

"No sense of humor," Trofim said to his roomie, then tried to focus on the dark, enormous shadow looming over him. "My name is Trofim Grekov."

"Tell me Trofim Grekov, why did your commander abandon you?"

Trofim felt his body temperature rise. He hadn't given the colonel a thought during lapses of consciousness. "A death wish, I suppose."

"I am confused, Trofim Grekov. Why would any being wish to die?"

"I don't think he wishes to, but he's going to." Trofim felt the first sense of vigor in a long time.

"I believe your hunt may be postponed for a time. You do not yet have the strength to carry out your quest. And we may have need of you." Lord Saeson spoke in a calm tone, carrying a hint of threat.

Trofim sat up, his head swayed, and his bedding pulled him back down. "I won't be this weak forever, Lord Saeson. You can't keep me prisoner for long."

Saeson walked toward the exit without turning back. "You are mistaken, Trofim Grekov. You are not our prisoner, you are our servant. Now rest—food will be brought to you soon." Lord Saeson exited the room, the door falling shut behind him.

Tro got up and stepped toward the door, but it closed before he got there. His body swayed, and the room began to spin. He put his back against the wall to ease his descent. Sliding down, he noticed his clothing didn't feel like fabric. On closer inspection, he saw that he wasn't wearing clothes, but was covered in a thick yet flexible crusty casing. He scratched at his cocoon, trying to discern its origin. "What is this stuff?" he said, picking at flakes.

"Hah," his penguin not-a-friend bleated. "It's what is keeping you from dying."

Tro strained his eyes to see the penguin and noticed a great blotch of the substance across the penguin's chest. "Okay, penguin. I take it you were injured too. But what is it?"

"It's many things, or so I've been told. But it's mostly what your kind calls guano," the penguin said, not concealing his mirth.

It took a few moments for what the penguin said to sink in. And when it did, Trofim sprang to his feet. "Shit? I'm covered in shit?" The motion proved too much for his body to handle. He spun and passed out on his pallet.

The penguin looked at his, unconscious roommate. "Hah! And you're lying in it too. Good sleep, Trofim Grekov."

CHAPTER 9

Colonel Jenson and another officer exited the helicopter when the skids hit the ground. He walked with purpose toward the door of the GT compound, formerly operated by Dan Alcorn. "Keep up, Major Dremmel," he shouted to the man trailing him. The man hurried to catch him. When they reached the door Colonel Jenson motioned for Dremmel to wait outside. The major threw up his hands in exasperation.

Jenson pushed the door open, slamming it shut behind him. "When will your crew be done?"

"Colonel Jenson. I'm sorry, but you weren't expected," Bryan Turlock said, motioning to a group of reporters sitting around the common room. "I was just about to brief these people about the accident here at the Global Technologies Antarctic facility. I had them flown in so they could see for themselves. Is there some insight you would wish to provide?"

Jenson glared at Bryan. "No. But I'd like to listen, if you don't mind. This should be interesting." He walked to a table behind the press.

Bryan gave the colonel an equally hard glare. "That won't be a problem, Colonel. In fact, you might find that you may learn a few things. Now, before we were interrupted, I believe it was the British Free Press who was going to start us off."

A lithe man sitting toward the rear of the group of ten people cleared his throat. "Yes. We have all heard the reports coming from the Falklands about some sort of chemical disaster. GT has holdings in the British territory. What do you know about this?"

"Mr. Hutson, is it? I cannot answer because I haven't seen the supposed disaster nor have I been briefed. Like you, I am thousands of miles away from the situation in the Falklands. I've heard the same reports you have. I can only comment on what I know."

After an exhaustive ten minutes of dancing and sidestepping questions, Bryan Turlock let out a heavy breath. "Okay, I'll let you in on the truth. Really, the whole truth. What happened here is quite simple. My predecessor, Mr. Lyons, uncovered an ancient species of penguins who were both intelligent and ambitious. Our company, Global Threat Environmental, does the dirty work our energy and weapons branch cannot. In this particular situation, we needed to find a way around the Antarctic treaties so that we could exploit the abundant natural gas, coal, and oil reserves buried in this pristine landscape. Mr. Lyons made an accord with the creatures and the United States government to cause an interspecies war of sorts, which would allow us to bypass the treaties."

Colonel Jenson stood up and appeared to reach for his side-arm, but Turlock raised his finger toward him.

"GT furnished the penguins with armaments, these steel beak covers," he said, fishing a sharp inch-long object from his pocket, holding it up for all to see. "And the penguins attacked. The U.S. Armed Forces were obligated to protect their citizens in the region. Unfortunately, so were the Russians, French, British, Japanese and so forth," Turlock continued. "Unfortunate as well, the penguins were a bit overzealous in their work, and thousands of people lost their lives. This war spilled over to the Falklands. I admit this has gotten far out of hand. But we do have a contingency plan to deal with the local fauna. Understand this. The treaties are now void, and we are now in a war for resources with the aforementioned nations. There are trillions of dollars buried beneath this frozen land, and I have my shovel. Any further questions?"

The group of reporters sat in silence for nearly half a minute. "Are you telling us that the tabloid reports of penguin attacks are true?" an American reporter asked.

"Quite true. And you can also quote me as saying that the United States military ordered several missile strikes which were designed to eliminate the threat. Again, unfortunately, we have on good account that large factions of the penguins are still alive. Ludicrous, I know. But all true."

"Mr. Turlock, will you please be straight with us?" the American asked.

Bryan Turlock said nothing for a moment. "You're right. I will be. But first, if you don't mind staying seated, I will bring in someone who can clear up this mess for you. Colonel, will you accompany me, please?" he said. Jenson was all too eager to oblige.

Once outside, Jenson spun toward Turlock. "That was some stunt, Turlock. Why did you—"

"Best get your man," Turlock interrupted as they walked toward a helicopter. Jenson motioned for the major, the pair watching him trot towards them. "This whole idea of freedom of the press has gotten out of control. People really don't need to know everything. That's one thing you and I can agree on. The press plays on people's fear; that's how they earn a living. True, there's some real scary stuff out there. You've seen it, or at least know of it. But it doesn't affect people's daily lives."

"But you just told an entire press corps the truth," Jenson said.

"They don't want the truth, Colonel. They want the sensational, but grounded in their idea of reality. Those mercs in BioCon, they've seen things that would make grown men wet their pants. And we both know the formal press doesn't want to know about it. It's left for the tabloids. Global warming, killer asteroids, pandemics, and terrorist attacks are about as much as the public can handle. If they knew half of what the select few know, there would be panic in the streets. The simple-minded fools would cause riots. There'd be chaos, and you know it."

"Then why? Why did you tell them?"

"Because it doesn't matter. Most of the press can be bought, but there's always one ethical one in the bunch who thinks the people *must* be told the truth—somebody who fancies himself to be a superhero, standing up for truth and justice and all of that bullshit. Then he has to be silenced. Take that paleontologist in Chicago; she wouldn't keep quiet about the data. And where is she now?"

Jenson kept a blank face.

"That's right. I know where she is. But do you think all of those happy lovers splashing their feet in Lake Michigan know her corpse is encased in cement not thirty yards from shore? Right…it's best that they don't."

"Is there a point to this? I'm sure you didn't just call me out here to explain your views on freedom of the press."

"Indeed Colonel. To be honest, I didn't want to call you out here at all. But, I have to do what I'm told…from time to time," Turlock stopped walking and turned to face the GT base. "What I've done today is a great service to the *freedom of ignorance*, if you will. Inside that building are the top ten investigative reporters who have the wherewithal or ethics to not accept bribes or give in to threats. All of their phones and devices have been disabled. A fact, I'm sure, they're just now beginning to realize. And what I have here," he reached in his pocket, "is a detonator. For ignorance, Mr. Jenson."

Bryan Turlock thumbed the trigger, and the entire compound erupted into a ball of fire. Major Dremmel dove for cover, but Colonel Jenson only watched the spectacle with an unreadable expression. Debris splattered around. Jenson looked at Turlock, who returned a half-cocked smile. "Let's go, Major," he said, boarding his helicopter.

CHAPTER 10

Randy kissed Gina a final time and watched her go through security at John Wayne Airport in Santa Ana, California. The look in both of their eyes carried both longing and fear. After Antarctica, they just wanted to be together, but life got in the way.

"Call me as soon as you get off the plane," Randy shouted. The last light of the setting sun shone through large windows, shimmering off of Gina's sandy blonde hair. She disappeared from sight. Annoyed people standing in line looked back at him. He didn't care. He only cared about Gina, and he hated seeing her go. Odd phone calls and suspicious vehicles raised their paranoia over the past weeks. Colonel Maycotte had told them both that they were lucky to be alive. Randy took it as leftover paranoia from surviving Antarctica, but Gina took it as something different.

Randy, overcome by his sudden emptiness, stepped back towards the line. "I love you, Gina Rosedale," he yelled, drawing more angry looks. A second later his phone buzzed. He read the text: *I love you too, Red. Now be quiet or you'll get arrested.* The message was punctuated with a smiley face which put a smile on Randy's.

Randy threw his bags on the ground, happy to be free of the weight and was about to grab a taxi when two men approached him. "Mr. Lee, your ride is this way," the stranger said indicating a black car. A third man picked up his bags with ease and walked to the car.

Randy thought about trying to run, but thought better of it. As he walked toward the car, he messaged the license plate and what type of car he was getting into to Gina. Noticing that the men weren't overly concerned about him texting put him slightly at ease. *Well,* Randy thought, *if they were going to kill me, they've had plenty of other opportunities before now.* He knew they were caught up in something they didn't want to be in. Things weren't making sense. Upon landing in Los Angeles, they visited the GT office to collect their pay, along with the bonus Lyons had promised. The representative for GT informed them that there were no records of either them or Lyons working for the company. Randy hoped to get some answers now.

"After you," a man said, seeing Randy hesitate to get in. The man followed Randy and took a seat facing him. Another took the seat between Randy and the door.

Once the car began moving, both Randy and the man facing him began to speak. "I'm sorry," the other said to Randy, "go ahead."

"Okay. You know me, but I don't know you," Randy said, doing his best not to sound intimidated.

"True, Mr. Lee," the other said.

When the man said nothing else, Randy persisted. "What is your name? And why the chauffeured ride?"

"Very well. I suppose it would be rude of me not to introduce myself. My name is Bryan Turlock. I am the CEO and President of Global Technologies, Global Threat, GT, and so forth. And you are here because I need to know of your time spent in the compound in Antarctica…the penguin compound."

"You'll have to excuse me, but I don't know what you're talking about. I'm just a wildlife photographer, and I've never heard of penguins living in a compound. Or at least, one that's not a zoo," Randy said with a blank expression.

"Very admirable of you, Mr. Lee. You hold true to your word, and are keeping silent. But let me assure you, I *am* the CEO of GT and I know what happened to you and your lovely lady friend while in Antarctica. I also know about the photos you took. So there's no misunderstanding on your part, here," Turlock reached in his pocket and handed him a business card and ID. "I'll need that back," Turlock said, taking both out of Randy's hands.

"Okay. So let's say you are who you say you are. I've already told Colonel Maycotte and Vance all I know," Randy said, sitting back and trying to appear relaxed. He wasn't. This Turlock was worse than Vance Lyons.

"That may be true. But it's what you might not know, maybe something you overheard. Something you dismissed. That's what I need."

Randy looked at Bryan, puzzled, and then looked at the man sitting next him who kept his eyes forward and face expressionless. "Forgive me for being a little slow. Are you asking me if I forgot something?"

"You'll have to excuse me; I can be somewhat cryptic from time to time." Turlock leaned forward and clasped his hands together. "I believe that you told all that you do know to Mr. Lyons and Colonel Maycotte. But they aren't alive anymore."

Randy sat upright at hearing of the colonel's death.

"And to be honest," Turlock continued, "you weren't the only one who has been to the penguin compound. But being as how most of them are dead, I need to know more about what you saw while being held captive."

"Honestly, Bryan. May I call you Bryan?" Randy said.

"No," Bryan replied.

Randy cleared his throat. "Honestly, Mr. Turlock, I think I've told all I know to the others. And I mostly heard squawking and clicky noises. Only a few actually spoke to me."

"And I believe you, Randy. The trouble is—I haven't heard it. And the only person left who has is an associate of mine and he is being difficult to work with. We need to know all we can and share information if we are to prevent further loss of life. The tragedies in Antarctica, the Falklands, and other places could have been prevented if we had known more. As we speak, war between Great Britain and Argentina has become inevitable, and China is posturing, making claims to Antarctica. As I said, this could have been avoided. So, regardless of my predecessor's ambitions, we need to stop this."

Turlock paused and stared at Randy. A light seemed to ignite in his eyes, and he continued. "The penguins at the compound were eradicated. There are those who are hell bent on seeing the rest of the penguins, not just the…what are they? Oh, yes—Royal Emperors. Not just seeing the Royal Emperors dead, but seeing all species eliminated to prevent this type of thing from happening again. Personally, I think that would be a terrible tragedy. But there is little I can do to prevent it unless I have all of the information available to me. And you were there."

Randy wasn't surprised to hear that most of the penguins had been wiped out. He knew their fate from the time he learned of the attacks. Despite his promises to his Chinstrap friend, Meuseaux, there was nothing he could do to help. He only hoped that Meuseaux had somehow escaped the killing. He decided he would do what he could to prevent further deaths for either people *or* penguins. "What can I do?" he asked.

Turlock smiled. "Before you start from the beginning, tell me what you know about Aperion."

"Aperion?" Randy replied. "Sounds Greek."

"Yes, more true than you know. Did you, during your time there, ever hear anything about a creature named Aperion or Saeson?"

"No. For the most part, my only contact was with a Chinstrap who had escaped from being sacrificed to leopard seals."

"Sacrificed? Interesting." Turlock appeared intrigued, but seemed to catch himself from following up on the question. "I need to know whether you know where the penguins may be headed. There was a large group which separated from the others before the bombing of the compound, but the satellites lost track of them."

Bombing? Randy thought. *Of course they bombed them.* He thought of Meuseaux and the others he had met. The Gentoo who was happy to find out his offspring was still alive. He thought of the coincidences which had brought them all together; the fact that he had a love for penguins, and he had saved the lame Gentoo's life. Randy had always been a dreamer. He believed fantasies weren't beyond reality, and believed that coincidence was less likely than fate. "All I know is that they believed that there's a paradise in the north. I don't know where, though. Maybe Greenland?"

"What makes you think they would go to Greenland?"

"Because the Great Auks, a penguin-like bird now extinct, used to live there."

Turlock smiled a satisfied smile. "The north, you say? I think, maybe, you can start from the beginning now. Tell me what you know about Antaean and the other Royal Emperors. You can leave out the part about the Chinstraps; they don't matter."

Randy was happy to leave out the details about the Chinstraps. He was also happy to know that Bryan Turlock was wrong—the Chinstraps mattered quite a bit.

CHAPTER 11

"How can I sleep if you don't shut up?" Trofim yelled at his roommate.

"How can I shut up if you don't sleep?" his roommate yelled back.

Trofim let out a sigh of disgust and attempted to stand up, but as soon as he stood, waves of dizziness overtook him, and he had to sit. He had noticed the overwhelming stench of ammonia in the room, and determined that as the cause of his dizziness. He also wondered how long he could breathe it before it caused brain damage. He looked at the Gentoo and guessed it had been in there far too long.

Trofim rolled off of his pallet and began doing push-ups. The cleaner air lingered near the ground. With his wounds mostly healed, he was getting anxious and going a little stir crazy. Fortunately, the Gentoo slept a lot while Tro was awake. He hated to admit it, but the penguin did help pass the time. He considered being nicer to the bird. It didn't seem to mean him any harm, but it was hard to be nice to creatures that had killed a couple dozen people he knew. However, he was happy that the deformed penguins had returned his clothes to him. He was free of the body cast of guano and who knows what else. "The first thing I'm going do when I get back to civilization is take a long, hot shower," he said to himself.

"And what is so uncivilized about this place?" the Gentoo asked.

Tro sighed. "Listen, *friend*," he said.

"Hah! So we're friends now?"

"No!" Tro said adamantly. "Let me start over. Listen, *penguin*—"

"I have a name," the Gentoo interrupted again.

"I don't care. And this place isn't what I would call 'civilized'."

"What would you call it?"

"Just because you made a big nest in the ground and called it home doesn't mean that you're civilized," Tro said between grunts.

"Do your big nests built on the ground make *you* civilized? And this is not my home. I'm stuck here, just like you, friend."

Trofim let his body fall to the floor. It had never occurred to him that the penguin might not be there on his own accord. "Are you a prisoner or something?"

"Something," the penguin answered.

"Now you decide be un-talkative, not while I'm trying to sleep." Trofim sat cross-legged and looked at the Gentoo, who was lying in an unnatural supine position. "What is the something?"

"That's what I am trying to understand. I'm a penguin, and human-speak is not my natural way of speaking, so I might get a word wrong. I'm not sure what I am. To be truthful, I'm not quite sure how I got here."

"Were you injured during the bombing?" Trofim asked.

"No. A big penguin decided he didn't like me too much and gave me a poke with his beak."

"You have that effect on penguins too?"

The Gentoo did a double-take. "Apparently I do. Which reminds me; we had things under control before you started bombing us. Bombing; is that the right word?"

"Technically, it was a missile strike, but you can call it bombing. But, when you start killing people, bombs usually start falling."

"Doesn't that make the things you blowup want to blow you up?"

"Not if they no longer exist. Trust me, you blow up something the right way, it doesn't want to fight anymore," Tro said, getting a little irritated again. "Did it make you want to blow us up?"

"Bah! Penguins don't have things to blow things up with. But if I did, Orca would be first to get blown up…or maybe seals. When I was younger, and just swimming along the shore, a pod of Orca tried to eat me. I swam this way and swam that way. I swam under them and around them. Orcas are smart, but not as smart as they think they are smart. I swam in and out of their pod, and as I leapt out of the water for a breath, I spotted it: a boat. The Orca saw it too, and they knew what I had in mind. I went straight for it, but I didn't get there. They stopped me. I said they were smart. But as a penguin, if you stay relaxed while things are trying to eat you, you have a better chance of not getting ate."

Trofim laid back and let out a heavy sigh, thinking about finding a way out as the Gentoo continued to ramble on about his skill in evading predators. If the penguin wasn't here by choice, then he might be able to use him to get out. His thoughts drifted away toward the pleasant thought of killing the colonel. From there, as they always did, his thoughts went to Alyssa, to the day she died: killed by a penguin. Not a penguin like the babbling Gentoo, but a large, vicious penguin with the capacity to kill a man. At least he had killed it, or hoped he had. The truth was that he never knew what happened to the *Big Bastard*, as he came to know it. A sudden rise in the penguin's voice snapped Trofim from his thoughts.

"…and then I leapt onto the boat. Fortunately, the Orca didn't tip the boat over. They knew where I was. So there I was, on a boat and saved by humans. I was young then, and hadn't seen what a human could do to a penguin; otherwise, I might have stayed in the water. So I would definitely blow up the Orcas." The Gentoo went silent, as if lost in thought. "On second thought, I would blow up a few seals. Definitely seals."

"I wish I could blow something up right now," Trofim said, looking at the Gentoo.

"Some appreciation. I regale you with stories of cleverness and bravery and this is the 'thank yous' I get? Have you ever had something try to eat you? I bet not. Humans don't live in the water."

"There are plenty of things out of the water that will eat you too," Tro said. He decided to start playing nice. He was alone, and maybe, just maybe, this penguin might be of use. But first he had to be its friend. He didn't trust the bird, but a single penguin was easier to deal with than an army of them. "I'll tell you my tale of something trying to eat me. I got called for a job in Canada—"

"What's a Canada?"

"It's a place. Far north of here," Tro answered, trying to shut down his irritation again.

"North? Is it covered in ice?" the Gentoo was intrigued, and with a great effort, pushed himself upright.

"Parts of it."

"Before you continue, I have to ask; is there a place like here in the north?"

Trofim looked at the penguin. They all seemed to be obsessed by notions of the north. First Lord Saeson had said Aperion had gone there, and now this one. He'd play along. "Yeah. Though not as big. Why?" he asked.

The penguin sat quietly before answering until Trofim cleared his throat. "A legend among penguins about a land of ice. The Northern Paradise, some call it. I doubted it existed. Maybe it does."

"I wouldn't call it a paradise. There's a lot more people up there than there are down here. For now, anyways."

"Just as well. I wouldn't want to go there, even if I could," the penguin said.

"I'll tell you what, penguin. You help me get out of here, and I'll take you to that paradise or wherever you want," Trofim offered.

"Bah! I said, I don't want to go there. But another human told me of a place I'd like to go. I'll tell *you* what, human. I'll help you get out of here if you'll take me there."

Trofim let the Gentoo think it was his idea. He didn't know where the penguin wanted to go, but it didn't matter; once he was free of here, he would ditch the bird. "Okay. Deal. Tell me, what's your name?"

"Now you want to know. When you find that I'm indispensable."

"Indispensable? I thought you had trouble with English?"

"Not as much as you."

Trofim laughed. "True. Well…tell me your name. You were so eager before."

"Leepoh."

"That's it? Leepoh?" Trofim snorted. "It's different from the others I've heard. Not very…noble."

If Leepoh was offended, he didn't show it. "And what names have you heard?"

"Antaean, Aperion, Saeson," Trofim recited.

"Bah! They're just bloated gas bladders of names and penguins. Is your name really Trofim Grekov?"

"Trofim Alexander Grekov," he answered with pride.

"Hah! That's a beak full of rotten squid right there, if I ever heard one. Why would you give yourself a name like that? Speaking of squid, I could sure use more than a mouthful right now. Do you like squid? Did I ever tell you about the time I ate a squid that tried to eat a friend of mine?"

"No," Trofim cut him off. "But I'm sure you will."

The sound of grinding ice spared Trofim the tale. The door opened, and he noticed that both he and Leepoh took in deep breaths of fresh air. *It's not just me, then,* he thought.

"Eat," a misshapen penguin said. Another dumped a load of ice-fish from its pelican like beak to the floor by Leepoh.

Trofim twisted his face. "I am *not* eating that."

"You didn't mind while you were recovering," Leepoh said between mouths full of fish.

"I didn't."

"You did," Leepoh replied.

"How come I don't remember this stuff?" Trofim said quietly. *Maybe the smell is giving me brain damage.* The fresh air rejuvenated him. He considered attacking the penguins and making a break for it. When he stood, his pack hit him in the chest, flung in from the dark corridor.

"Eat, human," Lord Saeson said from the hall.

"His name is Trofim Lakakarguh Geekoff," Leepoh said with indignation.

Ignoring Leepoh, Trofim scooped up his pack. When the door shut, he examined the wall for key holes. Finding none, he sat down, pulled off his outer gloves and opened his pack. "Interesting. Why would they give this back to me?" Inside the bag, he found rations, a small butane stove, a utility knife, spare gloves, and everything else he packed before the mission, minus weapons. He wasted no time in ripping open his rations.

The two quietly enjoyed their meals. After watching Leepoh swallow the last of his meal, Trofim broke the silence. "Where would you like me to take you?"

"Randy told me of a place. A place called Califorka. My fledgling is there," Leepoh said, sounding somewhat optimistic.

Trofim hadn't expect Leepoh's answer. It was one thing to think of these birds as intelligent, but strong family bonds were something else. "California is a big place. Maybe if I can find this Randy, he can tell us where your kid is. Did he say anything else about where he lives?"

"He said a facility. All I know is that it's at a place called Califorka. Do you know the place?"

"I have a good idea where the facility is. But first we have to get out of here."

CHAPTER 12

Trofim popped open the blade of the knife. It wasn't much to look at, designed for opening cans and other more menial tasks, but he had killed with less. He raised an eyebrow at Leepoh, whose stomach was rumbling loudly with digestive noises. "Are you sure you should have eaten all of that? Your stomach sounds like it desires revenge."

Leepoh looked at Tro through half-opened eyes. "Hah! I think you underestimate the appetite of a Gentoo. The noises you hear are calls for more."

Trofim shook his head. "You act like you're starving."

"I haven't eaten this much since before I got here. In fact, I haven't eaten this much since I ate the squid that tried to eat my friend. That reminds me, I was about to tell you about that before Lord what's-his-beak showed up."

Trofim fished a sewing kit out of his pack and began mending the rents in his clothing while ignoring Leepoh's tale of bravery and hunger. When he finished his sewing, Tro lit the small stove, attempting to warm his hands. Feeling the tingle of blood flow, he extinguished the tiny flame and leaned back just in time to hear Leepoh conclude his story.

"Impressive, was it not?" Leepoh asked.

"Yes, it was not," Trofim answered, drawing a glare from the Gentoo. "Listen, penguin. I have a feeling our chance to go will be here soon. Just do what I say and follow my lead."

"You've been here before?" Leepoh asked.

Tro stared at the bird. "Well, no. But I can't—"

"And you want me to follow your lead? Hah! Listen to me, human friend. Once we get out of the lower areas, I can show you a way out that few penguins know of. Well maybe more than a few, but I'm sure of few of those few are in more than a few pieces after a few of your bombs. So maybe there really are only a few penguins who know of the way. Maybe fewer."

Trofim dragged his hand down his face. "Do you have a point?"

"I have a few points. I'll show us the way out." Leepoh took a serious tone for the first time, which caught Trofim off-guard. "Once we get out of this room you'll have to follow me. I had the not so pleasurable pleasure of coming down here once before and I think I can get us out. But you can't kill anybody. If you do, I don't think Saeson will allow you to live a second time."

The last thing Trofim wanted to do was trust a penguin, but he didn't have many options. "Okay. You actually do have a point," he conceded. "I don't think we'll meet with much resistance. Its seems they want us to leave. But if that's true, I don't understand why they don't just open the door and let us go."

Leepoh appeared to be pondering the question. "Think of it the way Saeson thinks. If you had a prisoner who you wanted to escape, for whatever reason, and that prisoner, who happens to be you, had killed several penguins, what would the other penguins think if you let you go?"

Trofim wasn't sure how to take the Gentoo when he spoke with reason. Even if it was somewhat muddled. "I suppose you have another point. I'm sure he has his reasons. He said as much just before…" Trofim's thoughts drifted away, toward something unseen.

Leepoh studied Trofim, waiting for him to finish talking. He looked at the door. "We have a visitor," Leepoh said, his voice unusually tense.

Trofim picked up on the Gentoo's change and palmed his small blade.

The sound of the slow grind of ice filled the room. Tro looked to his roommate, noticing the Gentoo's body stiffen. Leepoh seemed to know what was waiting on the other side of the door, and Trofim guessed that the bird wasn't happy about what was there. When the door finally opened, Trofim shared Leepoh's feelings.

"So it is you," Talus, the Warlord of Planarseae said. He stood calmly, brandishing a club in each hand.

Trofim sprung to his feet, stumbling as he did. "You son-of-a-bitch!" He gripped the small blade tightly and rushed forward.

Talus hissed and brought the first club up, easily blocking Trofim's stab, then swung the second, catching the man on his left shoulder.

Trofim spun through the blow and landed a kick in Talus' midsection, driving him against the back wall of the corridor. He shifted his grip on the knife and went in for a killing stab. A large beak swung in from the hall and caught Trofim in the throat and chest. The strike sent him stumbling back. He caught his foot on the bedding, and his backside found the icy floor.

Leepoh went to Trofim's side, but he pushed him aside. He stood ready to attack again, but Lord Saeson's huge frame filled the doorway.

"You will not attack my guest," Saeson bellowed. He entered the room, followed by two razor-bills. Talus stayed behind the lord of the misshapen.

"This isn't your fight. This is between me and him," Trofim said, pointing to Talus.

Talus hissed a laugh from doorway. "In your condition, it wouldn't be much of a fight. In fact, I'm a little disappointed. On our previous encounter, your kick actually hurt. What happened to the warrior who bested me not so long ago?"

Cryzyrky stepped close to Talus, raising her one flipper. "This is not the time to taunt him, Warlord. He is still weak," she said. Talus only grunted.

"I'm still capable of killing you," Trofim snapped. "If your guard will step aside, I'll show you." He glared at the Warlord, Alyssa's killer.

Memories of that day poured through his mind, darkening his thoughts. Trofim looked at his captors, judging what it would take to kill them before he got to the Warlord.

Seeing Trofim's body tense in anticipation for another attack, Leepoh stepped between him and Saeson. "What is the meaning of this?" he said, speaking in human talk for Trofim's benefit. "I thought you meant for us to recover, and you bring *Talus*, of all penguins? His insanity is only surpassed by Liutites. Or was. So I guess he's the insanityest now."

"General Leepoh," Talus said. "I'm surprised to find you in league with this human. Do you know how many penguins he has killed? He is quite the murderer."

"Do you know how many Royals I killed?" Leepoh said. He stood tall and firm, not backing down.

Talus laughed. "You don't have the Alliance to assist you this time. Am I to take it you are challenging me? I haven't killed anything in quite some time, and I am more than ready to end the drought."

"Bah!" Leepoh blurted. "The last time I saw you, you were killing seal pups. I'm not a seal pup."

"You have courage, General. A bit misguided, but I admire that in a penguin. Even if I have to kill you, I do admire your courage. The Ancients will be glad to have you in the Great Sea."

"None of you are killing each other," Saeson interrupted.

Trofim gently nudged Leepoh aside. "I appreciate your help, but I can handle this." He glared past Lord Saeson. "What do you say we finish this? Talus, is it? I've been wanting this for a long time."

"There will be no more fighting," Saeson commanded. "Talus, you have your confirmation. Now be gone."

Trofim made another move, but was met by Saeson's large flipper. The thought of killing Saeson crossed his mind, but he reconsidered, certain that if he did, a thousand freakish penguins would be on him in an instant. No, he had to stay alive; if not to kill Jenson, but to kill the *Big Bastard* too.

Trofim stepped back, practicing his calming exercises, keeping his knife at the ready. "So what is your purpose for this? Why bring him here? You knew what would happen."

"He wanted to see if you were the one. Know this, Trofim; no creature has ever bested Talus in combat. Not human, seal, or penguin."

"Know this, penguin. I'm not leaving here until I kill him."

"Did I say you were leaving here? Do I need to remind you that you only live because of my mercy?"

"No. In fact, it seems to be something you're quite proud of. It's been my experience that only the powerless remind others of what power they attain." Trofim barely had time to flinch before an elongated flipper met him across the face, sending back to the floor.

"Your insolence will get you killed. My mercy only goes so far," Saeson spat. He looked at Leepoh. "Keep your friend under control, or I will let the Warlord do as he wishes to the both of you."

Leepoh looked from Trofim to Saeson and back again. "Did you hear that, Trofim? He knows we're friends."

Trofim let out a quiet growl. The Gentoo had a strange way of both infuriating him and calming him, but it didn't change the fact that Alyssa's killer was standing only feet away. He looked at Saeson and relented for the time being. He crossed his legs, pocketed his weapon, and took a deep, calming breath. The time would come.

Talus looked in, surprised to see Trofim being compliant. "You've taken the fight from him, Lord Saeson," he said in penguin dialect. "I commend you. But if I were you, I would be wary."

"You got what you came for, Talus. You are dismissed," Saeson said.

"Very well. Cryzyrky, let's go."

"Cryzyrky?" Leepoh said. "I didn't see you back there. Still hanging around with that featherhead?"

Cryzyrky marched into the room. "I find it difficult to believe that Saeson had the compassion to rescue a penguin such as you. It would have been better if you were left to die."

"Bah! Such words. I can't remember, but doesn't your name mean 'unwanted'? Or does it mean 'one and a half'? Or 'seal bait'?" Leepoh asked, waving both flippers at her.

Cryzyrky glared at Leepoh. "And I believe your name means 'a Skua's ass'."

"Hah! How'd you know?"

"Cryzyrky, leave the traitor to his fate. There will be another time," Talus said from the hallway.

"Traitor? Traitor?" Leepoh cried, trying to sound as indignant as he could.

Cryzyrky, like so many before her, grunted with annoyance and left.

"We will meet again, Trofim," Talus said. "Very soon."

Trofim remained sitting, a calm face hiding his hatred. "I am looking forward to it, Talus." He let a smile creep across his face, knowing that he would get the opportunity to finally kill him.

CHAPTER 13

With the Warlord gone, Saeson sent the others away as well. The door closed, leaving him alone with Leepoh and Trofim. Trofim looked at Leepoh, who did his best impression of a shrug.

"What will you do if you leave here?" Saeson asked.

The question surprised Trofim. That damned Gentoo had been right. "*If* I leave here, I'll hunt down and kill Jenson. Before I leave here, I'll kill Talus."

Saeson studied Trofim. "I would prefer you not to kill Talus, but I am certain he will seek you out, and his fate will be his own."

Trofim remained unreadable, determined not to excite Saeson any further. He only nodded.

"Now you will learn the truth." Saeson looked at Leepoh, who kept his beak closed for a change. "Your Colonel Jenson and a man called Lyons are the instigators of this war between our kind. They interfered in a conflict they knew nothing about. The Royals and Basileios have kept one another in balance for a thousand generations. I am a Basileios. Talus is a Royal, but Talus has no loyalty to his kind.

"In the time before man, the Royals, known in the old tongue as the K'tha, desired power and conquered the Southern Sea. But that was not enough. Their ruler, Thelios, attempted to conquer the North and was thwarted by what you call the Auks. For a generation, they fought. We, the Basileios, known then as the Cu-kisc, rose up and defeated the K'tha. The clans were freed and peace was restored.

"The seas grew warm, and the clans declined. Over generations, the Cu-kisc and K'tha declined as well, and were thought lost, as so many others had been. But both survived, kept secret on the Island of Kosk'kor. The way of Miaska—the Taker—, brought hunger and disease to the island until all were gone and only two clutches of eggs remained. An Ak'k'kray-ta, what you know as Emperor penguins, named K'K'ro-klayk and her mate K-uh-ke, saw to protecting the clutches."

Trofim rolled his shoulders and stretched his neck. Saeson's speech was causing his patience to ebb, as long-winded explanations often did. He desperately wanted to stand up and throttle the history professor and leave its twitching body behind. Instead, he took another calming breath. The lesson could be useful. He looked at Leepoh, who seemed to be rapt.

Saeson continued, ignoring Trofim's impatience. "The eggs were hatched. It was hoped that by rearing the young together, that there would finally be peace between the Cu-kisc and K'tha. But the Great Light came, and K'K'ro-klayk was killed, leaving the burden to K-uh-ke."

"Antaean hatched first, followed by Mearna, and they were followed by Treodon. The Royal bloodline was secure. Aperion was next, and then I. Within the span of a week, it became apparent that Antaean was as his ancestors, and that no amount nurturing could eliminate his need for violence. While K-uh-ke was away, Antaean convinced Treodon to kick the two remaining Basileios eggs from the nest, and they were thought lost. However, when K-uh-ke returned, he found the eggs. One was incubated. The other was given to Cryftin, a Tawaki, a crested penguin of uncertain breeding, and secreted away. He is the caretaker of the Oracle, Lapasia, a Yellow-eyed penguin."

"Don't the Yellow-eyes have a name?" Tro asked, finally taken in by the history.

"Yes, but it cannot be translated to your language," Saeson answered. "The egg was hatched, a female Basileios named Akronas. In time, Antaean betrayed and killed K-uh-ke, and we were left alone. Aperion found this place and we took shelter. But Antaean arrived soon after. The rest is as you know it to be."

Trofim and Leepoh exchanged glances. "Did you know all of this?" Tro asked Leepoh.

"Bah! The truth is rarely true. What happened to Akronas?" Leepoh asked.

Saeson clicked his beak, as if debating whether or not to answer. "Aperion and Akronas were mated. But all of their offspring were sterile. A deal was made between Aperion and Antaean. Aperion took the females produced by Mearna and Treodon, and between them hatched those who are known as the Misshapen. Antaean saw that those who could prove useful continued to breed. The others were sacrificed to the Phocids. The Kaurochs were put to labor, expanding Pack Ice Command. The others remained loyal to me, and I refused to allow them to be put to Antaean's designs."

"Why not kill this Overlord?" Trofim asked.

"The Royal Emperors breed and mature much faster. We were vastly outnumbered. With the alliance of the clans, we had no hope of victory. Antaean attempted to kill Aperion, but Aperion escaped. The passages were closed in an attempt to starve us out, but we found other means to survive. Know this; I have no desire for war. I only desire peace. Aperion craves a kingdom and revenge on the K'tha. Jenson knows this, and he aims to prevent Aperion from putting an end to his plans. The war will continue as long as the K'tha survive. Only Aperion can end the war, and for reasons I do not know, Jenson and others want it to continue."

"But why did—"

"No more questions," Saeson interrupted. "Jenson must be stopped. And to that end, you will be allowed to escape. Be prepared; the time is coming." Lord Saeson abruptly turned to leave. "I will tell you that Talus fights for no one other than himself. He will attempt to stop you. What you do with that is your own choice." Saeson said no more and left Trofim and Leepoh to their thoughts.

"And I thought *I* talked a lot," Leepoh said. "Remind me to take a nap the next time he comes in here."

Trofim stood and stretched his stiff legs. "Just be ready when our time comes."

"Hah! I was hatched ready. Ready for what, I don't know. But ready for something. Lots of somethings. Lots of wiggly somethings. Squids and fishes most likely. Do you like squids? That is the right word, right? Squids? I can never be too sure. I heard they were called calamar or kal'mar."

"You know Russian?" Tro asked, hearing kal'mar.

"I never rush in to anything, unless it's time to eat squids."

Trofim ignored Leepoh; he had heard enough babbling penguins for the day. "Just be ready."

CHAPTER 14

"Why didn't we meet the others at Isla Fortuna?" Meuseaux asked Lavour as they bobbed in the rough sea of the Southern Ocean.

"We've been through this, Meuseaux. Isla Fortuna is not a safe haven. T'Cuh-ka is smart enough not to have lingered there. Besides, we're better off on our own. The humans will be looking for large groups of penguins," Lavour said, riding the crest of a wave.

"Still, I'd feel a little safer if we had more eyes around us."

After being pulled down by the huge wave, the two Chinstraps swam back to the surface. "With all of the things you've escaped from, I'm surprised you're so jittery," Lavour said, taking a gulp of air.

"Escaping Phocids, booms, and maniacal penguins is one thing; having my body dashed against an unseen rock or being eaten by a shark is another. I'd just like to see a shore again…or a horizon," Meuseaux shouted, paddling hard against another wave.

"When was the last time you saw a shark? And if you do get dashed against a rock, at least you'd find the shore you want so badly."

Another wave took the pair of Chinstraps under the water once again. "That's not very reassuring," Meuseaux said, coming up for air. "And no, I've never actually seen a shark. Toothfish, Phocids, and Orca are bad enough. African penguins talk about them, and I would prefer not to push my good fortune."

"I'm thinking Humboldt squids are worse," Lavour quipped.

"There you go talking about that squid again. And that just reaffirms my point—you escaped because of Leepoh and Nok and a hundred other penguins."

Lavour quieted at hearing Leepoh's name. He had only known the Gentoo a short time, but felt like he had known him for a lifetime. The pain of loss threatened to rise up and swallow him like the sharks Meuseaux spoke of.

Meuseaux looked at Lavour and shook his head. "You didn't force Leepoh to go in there with us. He made his choice. You didn't kill him; Liutites did. And Leepoh still fought even as he lay dying. You should honor his sacrifice instead of blaming yourself for it. It's *not* your fault, Lavour. Focus on where you're going, not where you've been. "

Lavour didn't want to hear Meuseaux. After leading the assault against the Royal Emperors, he felt Leepoh, Mevoule, and a host of others were his burden to carry. "Enough talk, Meuseaux. We need to get through this storm before we get dashed against a rock."

Meuseaux watched his friend dive beneath a wave. He sighed, took a deep breath, and followed.

Through two nights of storms, the seas finally eased to the point where they could focus on something besides fighting the waves. In the breaking daylight, a relatively calm horizon appeared before the pair. Pale orange drifted across the sky, chasing away the last gray of night. Lavour faced the western sea line, letting the swells lull him into a tiny bit of relaxation. Meuseaux surfaced and joined him in staring at the seascape. "Not much out there," he said, jarring Lavour from his thoughts.

"There's plenty out there; we just can't see it yet," Lavour said without looking at him.

"Well there's not much to eat around here, either. I'm not sure how much longer I can go without eating."

"We'll just swim a little longer. I'm sure the light will bring some food to the surface."

"I hope so." Meuseaux paddled over the crest of a swell, turning his head back in the direction they had come. "I've never been this far north. The water feels different."

Lavour looked at his friend. He recalled his first foray north, during the war. The water did feel different, foreign, like seeing a new island for the first time. They were a long way from home, but home no longer existed. The Overlord had seen to that. The thought of home brought on another feeling of guilt. He had lived through so much, and so many hadn't. "Let's see about getting some food, shall we?" he said. Meuseaux happily agreed.

After hours of finding nothing, the Chinstraps once again met at the surface. "This place is a wasteland," Meuseaux said. "There should at least be some krill."

Lavour shook his head. "I don't know. I've never been this far from land. Maybe the wide sea doesn't have much to eat."

"I'm telling you, the water feels different. That has to be it," said Meuseaux.

Lavour ducked back below the surface and swam, trying to get a feel of what Meuseaux was talking about. He resurfaced ten meters away from Meuseaux and called him over. "You know, I think you're right."

"Well thank you for the confirmation," Meuseaux jibed.

"It's a little warmer. Maybe that has something to do with it?"

"What do we do? We can't go without food for much longer and who knows how far we are from the shore now?"

"Let's go a little deeper. We're bound to find something."

Down they went, searching the darkness, hoping to find something… anything. On their third attempt, they heard a faraway noise; a distant warble, quiet at first, but growing louder. The warble was joined by another, and then another. They continued to listen, and the noises grew louder. The warbles turned to whistling bellows. The penguins looked at each other and quickly swam to the surface.

"Do you know what that was?" Lavour said through excited breaths.

"I sure do," Meuseaux said, equally excited. "Whales. And where there are whales, there has to be food. How far away do you think they are?"

"It's hard to say. But it's coming from the northwest," Lavour said, looking to the sky, checking the position of the sun. "We'd better hurry; they swim pretty fast."

"Not as fast as a hungry Chinstrap."

Lavour and Meuseaux swam with as much speed as they could muster, gliding through the water like tiny torpedoes. When they got close to where they guessed the whales would be, they were no longer singing. The penguins stopped, floated on the surface, and scanned the horizon.

"Where are they? Why did they stop?" Meuseaux asked.

Lavour looked above and below the surface. They sky had turned into a haze of gray. Knowing that humans hunted the creatures, his anxiety rose, thinking there might be a ship nearby. He spotted something in the distance. At first, he worried that his suspicions were correct. Then several more things appeared in the distance, and he recognized them right away as the flukes of Humpback whales. "Do you talk with your mouth full?" he asked Meuseaux.

"I try not to."

"Maybe whales don't either. There they are," Lavour pointed with his beak. "Let's go. But be careful; we don't want to end up in the mouth of one of those things."

Meuseaux hesitated. The thought of accidentally becoming food while eating curbed his enthusiasm.

Lavour noticed his hesitation. "Come on. We've been through worse things than scavenging a meal from a whale."

"While that may be true, I would prefer not to meet my end in the belly of a whale."

"So you would rather meet your end by starving?"

Meuseaux looked at Lavour, and then to the whales. "Good point. Let's eat."

The Chinstraps swam near the whales, keeping their distance and watching in wonder. The enormous beast swam beneath a large school of small fish, shooting bubbles from their blowholes, sending the fish toward the surface. One by one, the whales took turns taking huge gulps of panicked fish.

"We'll stay back and catch the escapees," Lavour said, watching the spectacle.

Meuseaux nodded. He watched gulls swoop in, snatching meals. "Do gulls fly far away from shore?" He asked, pointing to the birds.

"I never paid attention," Lavour said. He watched the gulls and wondered the same thing.

"There might be land near," Meuseaux said.

"Maybe. But let's worry about one thing at a time."

Lavour and Meuseaux darted in close to the feeding whales, nabbing fish after fish. They ate until their stomachs could hold no more. The whales finished their meals and paid the tiny penguins no mind as they swam past and disappeared into the depths. The duo floated on the surface with distended stomachs and tired eyes in a post-feast lethargy, listening to the squawking of bickering gulls, the sea nearly lulling them to sleep.

"We should really find the shore. It would sure be nice to find a quiet patch of rocks to take a proper nap on," Meuseaux said, sounding dazed.

Lavour opened his eyes and stared at the horizon, watching the gray sky reflect on the glimmering surface. His gaze followed the gulls taking flight and disappearing in the east. Something caught his eye amongst the white caps; a fleeting glimpse. Being uncertain about what he had seen put him on alert.

Sensing his friend's apprehension, Meuseaux perked up as well. "What?" he asked, following his gaze.

Lavour remained quiet, not pulling his eyes from the horizon. "I don't know. I thought I saw something."

"Something? A good something or a bad something?" Meuseaux asked with apprehension.

"Probably just one of the whales," Lavour said, his confidence not matching his words.

The pair stared intently into the distance. Meuseaux's head twitched. "Did the something have a big top fin?"

"Yes," Lavour said quietly, fear creeping into his voice.

Both remained motionless. The air thickened, tightening their chests, threatening to suffocate them. A large black dorsal fin surfaced one hundred meters away, followed by a spray of water. The Chinstraps looked at each other. "Orca," they said in unison.

"Head east," Lavour shouted. "The gulls went that way. It's our best hope."

Lavour and Meuseaux sped away. They dove and breached the watery plain, taking big gulps of air before diving below again and again. They didn't dare look back; instinct told them the Orca followed. "It's getting closer," Lavour shouted to Meuseaux as they flew from the surface.

Lavour felt something bump against his foot. He knew that the jaws of the killer whale were ready to bite down and drag him in for a meal. He pumped his flippers harder and felt the drag of the water ease as he put distance between him and his pursuer. He pulled his flippers hard, hoping against hope that he wouldn't feel the deadly bite. He broke the surface for another gulp of air and saw the Orca surface beside him. He looked at the creature. Their eyes met; deep, dark eyes of death staring back at him, matching his speed, taunting him. Lavour broke hard right with Meuseaux following.

The Chinstraps kept their course, with the Orca once again tailing them. After several minutes, the Orca appeared to their right, this time looking at Meuseaux. "What's it doing?" Meuseaux asked in a panic, breaking to the left.

"I don't know," Lavour answered, soaring over the surface. "Playing with his food."

Again, the Orca appeared on their left, forcing the Chinstraps to the right. "It's wearing me down," Meuseaux cried. "I don't how much longer I can do this."

"Just keep swimming," Lavour urged his friend. When he broke the surface, he spotted land. "Land…dead ahead."

"Please don't say dead," Meuseaux barked between breaths.

The Orca fell in behind the penguins, putting on burst of speed, nosing at the Chinstrap's feet. They spotted the island a hundred meters away and pushed themselves harder, the killer nudging their feet.

The Orca eased back, but stayed close. The land grew closer; fifty meters, twenty-five meters, ten. "We're gonna make it!" Lavour shouted.

Meuseaux was about to agree when felt the head of the Orca press against his feet. Lavour saw his friend rise into the air, riding the mighty Orca's head like an amusement park trainer. Meuseaux flew the remaining distance to the shore and landed unceremoniously on the coarse sand. The Orca came to a rest on the shore a meter away from Meuseaux, the top half of its body out of the water.

Lavour hit the beach just feet away and scrambled to Meuseaux's side. He wasn't going to let his friend go without a fight. The Orca looked at Lavour, let out a spout of air, and wiggled back into the sea. Lavour urged Meuseaux to his feet. "Get away from the shore!"

The pair ran further inland and collapsed on the sand, exhausted, but happy to be alive.

CHAPTER 15

After lying on the beach in silence for several minutes, Meuseaux spoke. "What do you suppose that was all about?"

"I have no idea," Lavour answered. "I thought you were a meal for sure."

The Chinstraps got to their feet and surveyed their surroundings. White sand stretched out in a circular path for a quarter mile. Half way around the arc, large jagged spires jutted out of an otherwise barren landscape. Terns and gulls squawked noisily, squabbling for position on the spires. "Where do you suppose we are? I've never seen an island like this," Meuseaux said.

"You're asking a lot of questions I don't have answers for. But my biggest question is, why that Orca didn't eat you?"

"It was just playing with us. Or maybe it didn't know what we were, and wasn't sure what to do."

"I always thought Orca bit first and asked questions later."

The two started walking toward the spires, leaving their questions behind. They traveled no more than a few meters before spotting a solitary dark figure standing halfway between them and their destination. They stopped and watched the form walk toward them. "What now?" Lavour said. He had had enough adventures for one day, and wasn't in the mood for any more.

"It's a penguin," Meuseaux answered, happy it wasn't another predator.

"I think it might be a Rockhopper."

"It looks a little big to be a Rockhopper. I don't think Rockhoppers live on this side of the ocean."

"Neither do Chinstraps, but here we are."

"We don't live here."

"We're alive here. After that Orca incident, I wouldn't mind staying for a while," Meuseaux said.

"Shush. Here it comes."

The penguin waddled up to the Chinstraps and came to a halt. Lavour sized up the other. It stood a couple inches taller than a Rockhopper, with a similar yellow head crest. Three small white stripes adorned the cheeks on side of its red beak, and a robust frame told Lavour it wasn't a Rockhopper. The newcomer stared at him with red eyes.

"Hello," Lavour finally said when the other stayed silent. He looked at Meuseaux, who carried the same confused expression.

After another moment of silence, the penguin spoke. "Chinstraps. I expected one, not two. But since when does a Chinstrap travel alone? Apparently never," the penguin said in a gruff tone, continuing to inspect the pair.

"Are you alone?" Meuseaux chimed in, taking exception to the comment.

The penguin looked at Meuseaux. "We are never alone, Meuseaux," he said, then turned and walked away.

Meuseaux looked at Lavour and back to the retreating penguin. "Hey. How do you know my name?" he asked, running to catch up with the other, with Lavour following.

"I know many things, Chinstrap," the other said without breaking stride. "I know you, I know Lavour. I know where you come from and where you are going."

"That's a fine trick, stranger, because we don't even know where we're going," Lavour said. He wasn't sure what to make of the odd penguin, and the Ancients know he had seen his share of odd penguins over the past year or more.

"Stranger?" the penguin replied. "You came to my atoll. You should think twice before calling me a stranger."

"We were being pursued by an Orca. We didn't come here by choice," Lavour snapped.

The other penguin stopped walking and faced Lavour. "Ceatak? Oh, he's harmless enough. He was just having a little fun," the penguin said through a laugh.

"Almost getting eaten isn't much fun," Meuseaux said, feeling every bit as agitated as Lavour.

"If he wanted to eat you, he would have."

"You talk like he's a familiar," Lavour said.

"Walk with me," the penguin said, heading to the shore.

Standing near the water, he made several odd chirps. Within seconds, a fluke appeared on the surface. Lavour and Meuseaux stepped back. Several seconds later, the Orca sprang from the water, its head resting on the beach. The Chinstraps darted away, stumbling on the sand and falling over one another.

The penguin shook his head. "When you're done acting like frightened fledglings, come here. He's quite safe."

The Chinstraps exchange glances and took a few cautious steps back toward the other.

The crested penguin turned his back on the Orca to urge the timid Chinstraps back down to the shore. Behind him, the Orca opened its jaws wide. "Watch out!" the pair cried in unison.

The other ignored their pleas and began to laugh again. "He'll close his mouth soon enough." He faced the Orca. "Quit that; they're a little more faint-hearted than most." The Orca closed its mouth and lowered its head.

The pair stood in awe of the spectacle. "We're not faint-hearted," Meuseaux said. "We've just never seen an Orca that wasn't a mindless killer."

"Mindless?" the other spat. "An Orca is far from mindless. Maybe the fish and squid think you're mindless."

"I am when I'm hungry," Meuseaux replied.

The penguin chuckled again and took a few steps closer to the Orca, looking it in the eye. "Ceatak, were you trying to eat my guests?"

The Orca uttered a few clicks, and Lavour swore he saw it shake its head. He looked at Meuseaux, wide-eyed.

"Well, there you have it; he said no. And unlike penguins and men, Orcas don't lie." He looked back to Ceatak and thanked him. The Orca lifted his head and wriggled back into the sea. Swimming away, Ceatak slapped his tailfin, dousing the trio of penguins with the splash. "He thinks that's funny," the penguin said, shaking the water away.

With water dripping from the tip of Lavour's beak, he stared at the penguin. He was dealing with a penguin of a different sort. He had never heard of anyone making friends with an Orca. That would be akin to having a Phocid as a pal, and he was reasonably certain that would never happen. "All right, you know us, but we don't know you. What's your name? And how do you know who we are? And to be honest, I don't know what clan you come from."

"So many questions, Lavour. And I must say, I'm glad you dropped that silly title of Commander. It's not befitting of a penguin to exalt himself above others."

Lavour nodded his head. It was a title he was happy to be rid of.

"My name is Cryftin. I am a Tawaki. The humans call us Fiordland penguins or some silly name. In the ancient speak, we are Kutak-uh. Though I prefer Tawaki; it flows from the beak much easier. I dream the dreams of the Oracle. She is my source of knowledge."

"The Oracle is a myth," Lavour said. He, like many other penguins had heard the legends of an Oracle, but dismissed them as fiction.

"So have many been led to believe. Antaean would have had us think her dead. The Oracle's visions told him of his end if he pursued his course.

She told him of another who would lead the penguins to peace before the end time. Antaean left in a rage and sent his minions to destroy us. But the Oracle had foreseen his treachery. I urged for us to go, but she told me the sea would save us. And she was right. When Antaean's minions approached, the Great Wave followed. The Great Wave pulled Antaean's forces to the bottom of the sea and together, Lapasia and I rode the crest of the wave and were deposited here. I had little reason to doubt her before, and I have no reason to doubt her now."

"You rode a wave all the way here?" Lavour asked doubtfully.

"I never said where we started from."

"So the Oracle is real?" Meuseaux interrupted.

"As real as you or I," Cryftin answered. "She has expected Lavour's arrival for some time."

"She didn't know I was coming? I thought she could see the future," Meuseaux scoffed.

"Your fate has been in flux for some time. The future is never set. Chaos changes our paths. Like the wind catching a raindrop, it takes us from where we could have been to where we are. You, Meuseaux, have been buffeted by the wind of chaos, and your course has changed many times." Cryftin eyed the young Chinstrap. "At times, resilience can change your fate…as you well know."

"I'm sorry, Cryftin, but I don't believe in fate," Lavour said. "When you put your faith in destiny, you deny responsibility for your actions. It was suggested that I was the one who would lead us to peace. And for a time, I almost believed it. In the end, thousands of penguins died under my command. Old friends and new; Mevoule, Leepoh, Natoo, Treeg and so many others; was it their fate that they died? No, it was their belief in some half-cocked story about destiny…my destiny."

"We all share the same fate to travel to the Great Sea. From the day we are hatched we begin our journey to the end. Some die young, some die old, but none can escape. Your friend Leepoh, he knew this."

"And Leepoh met his fate because of me."

"No. Not because of you. We all make choices. Who are you to think the end of one's life is your responsibility? It is the choices we make that guide us either expediently or methodically to the Great Sea. Some choices are foolish. Antaean's choice to ally himself with the humans was foolish. You are not to blame for his war. However, the choice to stand against evil, tyranny, injustice, regardless of the outcome, is never foolish. If you do not believe in fate, you believe in neither life nor death."

"Fate," Lavour said coldly. "Lannera, Mevoule, Leepoh, my own fledgling; they met their fates." Lavour turned his back on the old Tawaki and stared at the sea. The weight of his burden made him tired…angry. He took a step toward the water, and the Orca's fluke appeared. Lavour grumbled and turned back to face Cryftin.

"Remove your ballast, Lavour. Before it drags you to the seafloor," Cryftin said in a calm voice.

Lavour replied with a long, exhausted sigh.

"The Oracle awaits you."

"Is seeing her my fate?" Lavour asked.

"No. It is your choice."

CHAPTER 16

Lavour and Meuseaux followed Cryftin to the spires. "It's late, and you are weary from your journey. Rest here, for you will need your strength if you choose to speak with Lapasia," Cryftin told Lavour. The Chinstraps craned their necks to see the top of the structures. From a distance, they had appeared to twist toward the sky, but on closer inspection, they saw the irregular formations were actually the remnants of a great colony of coral, grave markers of forgotten lives. The white and ecru monoliths were, at places, as wide as the atoll itself. Lavour stared at the formations and wondered what the past few months, or years, really meant. He had gone from an anonymous penguin living his life, to a conscript in the PDA, to commander and rebel, and back to being anonymous in the span of two years.

After the war, he had been certain of one thing: that any appearance of someone fulfilling a destiny was nonsense, and that the world was governed by sheer coincidence, if anything at all. Now he wasn't so sure. But then again, he wasn't so sure about Cryftin. He could have gotten his information from any number of defectors from the war. Lavour's mind drifted to the war. Lost in thought, he closed his eyes and fell into a deep and well-deserved sleep.

Seeing Lavour fall asleep, Meuseaux walked to the structure and examined the rough and porous surface. The sun had nearly set, and the gulls quieted their squabbling. "Your friend carries quite a burden," Cryftin said from behind Meuseaux, causing him jerk in surprise.

"You're sneaky for an old penguin," Meuseaux said, regaining his composure.

"You don't live to my age by splashing about, or by being unaware," Cryftin said, giving Meuseaux a slight reproach.

Meuseaux looked at Cryftin from the corner of his eyes. "I thought I was safe here," he said a tone to match Cryftin's.

"A penguin is never free of danger, especially now. But there is no need to blame what cannot be changed."

"Tell that to Lavour."

"Lavour wants to change what can't be changed. Because of that, he feels powerless, which leads to his feelings of guilt and anger. If he decides to see Lapasia, he will get a few answers, but he will also find new questions."

"How does she know what will happen, or what has?" Meuseaux asked.

"When Ceatak chased you, could you feel him behind you, even though he didn't touch you?"

"He touched me plenty when he shoved me onto the shore," Meuseaux snorted. "But yes, I could almost feel his jaws. It's saved me more than once."

"That is your instinct. Knowing what *could* happen before it happens, even though you have never experienced it. Now imagine an instinct of the greater world around you. I believe that is how she knows. Some have said it is a gift from the Ancients. They said Lapasia is a vessel of the Ancients; others said that she's mad. But it matters very little. She has what most do not. The tern flies and a penguin cannot, yet we are all of the same kind. She is what she is supposed to be."

Meuseaux considered the old penguin's words. It was commonly accepted by most penguins that the spirits of long dead penguins guided their actions, and those spirits were guided by the Elemental Spirits, The Creators. Living in Antarctica, he had heard stories of Huhellsus, The

Great Shaper or Spirit of wind. "Are the Ancients real?" Meuseaux asked.

Cryftin stared at the darkening sea and let out a long breath. "Everything that you keep in your heart and in your mind is as real as you and I. Remember that, Meuseaux, and use care on what you carry with you."

Meuseaux had no reply and no more questions. The answer wasn't what he had expected, but it was more than what he hoped for.

Cryftin ambled up the beach toward the coral structure. "You're safe for the time you are here. You should sleep as well, Meuseaux. Tomorrow will be a longer day than today."

CHAPTER 17

The morning sun broke through the haze, chasing lulling seabirds from their roost, sending them squawking in search of their morning meal. A cold breeze caressed Lavour into the waking world and freed him from dreams of lost friends and days he longed to forget. He found himself alone, in front of the coral monolith. It loomed over him like a future he couldn't avoid. The voices of Meuseaux and Cryftin exiting the surf brought him to full alertness.

"You're awake," Meuseaux said, sounding annoyingly cheerful for someone who had experienced as much horror as he had. "I was beginning to wonder if maybe you were pretending to sleep to avoid going on a morning feeding run because of Ceatak."

"Leave him alone now, Meuseaux. Sleep can be the best cure for things that ail the body and spirit," Cryftin said. "Sometimes the best answers can be found in dreams."

"Do you ever say anything that isn't a lesson?" Meuseaux snipped.

"A lesson can only be taught to those willing to learn," Cryftin quipped.

"Apparently not," said Meuseaux, approaching Lavour. "Get up, before this old bird starts spouting off something about a lazy penguin having a lazy mind or something."

"I'm up, if only to avoid another lecture," Lavour said, ruffling.

Cryftin wagged his flipper at the Chinstraps. "Youth is wasted on the ignorant," he snorted and walked away, shooing gulls off of the beach.

Lavour watched Cryftin march away, muttering complaints. He walked to the shoreline, stopping to stare at the breakers.

"You don't have to be afraid," Meuseaux said from behind. "We really should consider having an Orca as a friend. Ceatak chased big shoals of fish right to our beaks. It's almost as easy as the troughs back at Pack Ice Command."

"Where's the fun in that? It is the pursuit of our meals that keeps a penguin's mind sharp. An easy meal can make one lazy and fat," Lavour said, none too serious.

"Curse the Ancients; now you sound like that Tawaki. This is worse than the learning center," Meuseaux said, walking away. "And go eat. The headmaster said you'll need a full belly today,"

"I'm going to need more than a full belly," Lavour muttered to himself. He took a few steps into the sea and saw Ceatak's fin break the surface. He took a couple of more tentative steps, doubts creeping in to his mind. *What if that isn't Cryftin's pet swimming out there?* He couldn't tell the difference, and he wouldn't know until it was too late. Lavour cast his worries aside went in search of breakfast.

Swimming through the water with nothing more to worry about than catching a meal, Lavour felt almost normal for the first time in a long time. It had been too long since the sea felt like freedom rather than an oppressive avenue between trauma and trouble. The cool water reinvigorated him, giving him the feeling he had long forgotten: just being an anonymous penguin swimming in the nothingness of the sea.

Lavour swam and darted, snatching stray fish. He recalled his first few plunges when he and Mevoule swam side by side, both scared and wary, but neither admitting that fear. The thought of his dead friend didn't cause pain, but rather, happy memories of childish games. They would dare each other and close their eyes to see who had the courage to keep them closed the longest. Remembering his friend, Lavour closed his eyes and swam.

The thrill of it sent waves of excitement through his body, followed by apprehension when his adult mind urged him to use sense. He ignored the adult and swam hard and fast.

When prudence and the need of air got the better of him, Lavour opened his eyes, flew to the surface, and grabbed a big gulp of air. When he dove below again, he saw a large shadow ahead of him disappear into the darkness. Probably Ceatak, coming to taunt him again. He stopped swimming and let his body slowly float downward, trying not attract attention. The form swam back toward him. *Is it Ceatak?* A surge of doubt flowed through his body. *It's what I get for having fun.*

He let himself drift in the tugs of the current. After another minute of watching the shadow swim, he decided that he could either wait to see if it was Ceatak or make a dash for shore. *If it's not Ceatak, I'll be food.* Or he could face his fear and see what swam in the shadows. None of the options sounded particularly appealing. He chose the third and swam straight toward the creature.

He swam forward, and within seconds noticed the tail fin swooshing left and right, not up and down like an Orca's. *Bad choice.* Lavour made an abrupt U-turn and made a dash toward shore. He zigzagged, hoping to keep whatever it was off of him. He thought of Meuseaux's sharks and wanted to take a look, but he didn't want to know what they looked like from the inside. He paddled hard and banking right, felt the swoosh of the enormous creature swim past him. He caught a glimpse of what pursued him. It had to be a shark, he was sure of it. Lavour swam up and porpoised to find land. He spotted the shore and knew what he had to do.

The shark turned and sped toward him, and he responded by speeding straight toward the shark. Lavour put on a burst of speed, intending to swim over or under the beast at the last moment, but he never got the chance. A blur of black and white smashed into the shark like a torpedo into a Zodiac. Lavour had to make a quick dive in order to avoid the thrashing of bodies. He surfaced and turned to watch the spectacle. The water churned and foamed as the monstrous creatures engage in life and death combat. The shark's head broke the surface, gaping jaws silently reaching out, trying to bite something. The Orca tore into the shark with its own powerful jaws, ripping chunks of flesh away. In moments, the mighty shark succumbed to the attack.

Lavour decided that he should probably get to shore in case the Orca wanted dessert. By the time he reached the sand, gulls were shrieking and fighting over Ceatak's leftovers. Lavour walked up the beach and found Meuseaux and Cryftin waiting for him.

"Did you find anything to eat?" Meuseaux asked, laughing.

"I think I lost my appetite," Lavour said. "And you know, I really wonder about your sense of humor sometimes."

"It's a good thing Ceatak didn't lose his appetite," Meuseaux said, not being able to stop poking fun at his friend.

"I'm glad you got a good laugh out of me almost being eaten once again," Lavour said, not humored. "I'm glad those sharks don't live close to where I do, or did; otherwise, I think we'd have a few less penguins."

"Kar-kara usually don't come around here," Cryftin said, "and when they do they're usually weak, like the one you encountered."

Lavour snapped his head at Cryftin. "Weak? Weak! That's what you call weak? I'd hate to see a strong one."

"You were never in any real danger," Cryftin said. "Ceatak was waiting for the right moment to ambush the poor thing."

"Poor thing," Lavour huffed, walking away. "That *poor* thing was going to eat poor me."

"Pity the strong, for they carry the weight for us all," Cryftin added.

Lavour shook his head in an exaggerated, less-than-serious way. Despite the attack, the swim and sense of freedom he had felt had been invigorating. For the first time in a long time, the future didn't loom so large or seem so bleak. "Where is this Oracle? I have things to do," he called back to the sage.

"Then you have decided?" Cryftin called after him.

"I have chosen," Lavour said, not stopping to look back.

CHAPTER 18

Cryftin and Meuseaux joined Lavour at the foot of the coral monolith. A narrow passageway marked the entrance, and the acrid stench of bird droppings offended Lavour's nostrils. "The Oracle doesn't get many visitors, does she?" Lavour said, trying to shake the smell away.

"It's not so bad on the inside," Cryftin said. He carried the same light nature as Lavour. His tone turned serious. "Remember you will face many obstacles on your journey to see Lapasia."

"I've faced many obstacles over the past two cycles. What's a few more?" Lavour put on an air of bravado to mask his doubt. His list of obstacles was long: sharks, mad penguins, deadly seas, explosions, fire, guns, and carnivorous squid. He had faced it all, and against the odds, he had survived. While he still doubted things such as fate, except for in Cryftin's terms, he had come all this way and ended up in a place where maybe, just maybe, he could get some answers and find a purpose to it all. "Is there a certain path I should take?" Lavour asked, stepping into the mouth of the cave.

"Like all things, the direction you choose is your own," Cryftin answered.

"Always full of helpful answers," Lavour muttered. "See you on the other side, Meuseaux."

"Be careful, my friend," Meuseaux called out in a pensive voice.

"Your friend will be fine," Cryftin said. He turned from the cave and looked to the sky. The ever present haze hid the blue, like drapery obscuring the world outside of a window. Cryftin wasn't looking for the beauty of a crisp blue sky; he sought the time and their place in time.

He closed his eyes, and Meuseaux stared at him curiously, but remained silent, not wanting to disturb him from whatever piece of riddled advice he was conjuring.

Cryftin's eyes opened with a start. He looked to Meuseaux, eyes wide. "The days are later than I thought. How could I have let myself get lost?"

Concern crossed Meuseaux's face. "I don't understand. Lost?"

"Yes. I mark the days according to Lapasia's sight. I'm old, Meuseaux. Old and stupid." Cryftin began to pace along the beach. "When Lavour emerges, you must leave immediately."

Meuseaux's concern turned to fear. He matched Cryftin's nervous pacing. "Why? What's wrong?"

Cryftin plucked at a few loose pinfeathers on his chest, avoiding eye contact.

"What aren't you telling me?" Meuseaux demanded.

Cryftin looked at Meuseaux and hesitated a moment longer. When Meuseaux opened his beak to ask again, Cryftin spoke, "Aperion is coming."

"Aperion? He died a long time ago."

Cryftin steadied his gaze on Meuseaux. "There are some who you believe dead, but who have not made the journey. Aperion is very much alive, and with Antaean dead he seeks his own empire. He comes to find his queen."

It took a moment for Meuseaux to digest what he had been told. What did he mean by *there are some*? He was certain that Liutites was dead; he had killed him. "His queen? Here? There's only you and the Oracle…" Meuseaux's voice trailed away as realization dawned.

"Yes, Meuseaux. She knows where his queen is and she knows what will happen when he finds his mate. An Oracle is forbidden to lie. If she does, she will spend eternity in torment. She will die before she tells him. And that is why I have been a stupid old fool. Lapasia marked the day of

Aperion's arrival. The day she spoke of is tomorrow."

Again, Meuseaux had to let the words sink in. "Why the worry, though? If Aperion kills the Royals, then we'll be the better for it."

"No, Meuseaux. There is one among them who can turn the tide. But if Aperion sires his kind, we will all suffer."

"Who's the Royal? Can't we just get him to take care of Aperion?" The magnitude of what he had been told was beginning to weigh on Meuseaux. All of these prophecies of doom and destined penguins was really just too much. It made him want to follow Lavour's path of apathy.

"Lapasia would not tell me who it is for fear I would say the name and Aperion would know. All I know is that Lavour still has a part to play."

"But why—"

"Ask nothing else. The answers will only lead to more questions," Cryftin said abruptly. "Now we can only wait and hope Lavour emerges soon." The old Tawaki sat down and closed his eyes. The conversation was indeed over.

Meuseaux watched the sea. Across the white caps, he saw the fluke of Ceatak the Orca as he played happily with a belly full of shark. "Why doesn't he sic Ceatak on Aperion?" he said quietly. "That thing just killed a shark; surely he could take down a penguin, even if it was big and angry and in need of a mate and the stuff of legends."

"Ceatak will try. He will not succeed," Cryftin said quietly.

"I thought you were asleep or meditating, or transcending to a higher plane or something?" Meuseaux said. No reply came, and Meuseaux let out an exasperated breath, returning his gaze to the sea.

CHAPTER 19

Lavour took slow and cautious steps through the darkness, finding that the passage opened into a wide path. As promised, the stench of bird droppings dissipated and was replaced by the smell of seawater. Dim light from the overcast sky shone through fissures in the ceiling, casting shadows onto the craggy gray walls, lending to the idea of predators lying in wait.

Lavour clambered over the uneven ground, crunching on flakes of coral and the occasional dried gull skeleton. He examined the remains to make certain they weren't penguins. He pushed the idea of ambushing monsters from his mind and pressed forward. Every half minute, he heard the gushing spray of seawater from somewhere ahead but beyond his sight. The room narrowed, leading to a roughly hewn corridor.

Further in, the ground turned smooth from countless years of salt-water and wind buffing the stone. Mist sprinkled Lavour the further he traveled, following a gentle curve. The cavern moaned in anticipation of each burst of sea-spray. Lavour expected to find a breach in the walls at the end of the tunnel where the surf had broken through. Instead, he found a hole in the ground as wide as two Chinstraps were tall. Within seconds, the wind began to moan, and the water pushed through the hole like a geyser, dousing everything within, nearly knocking Lavour off his feet.

Lavour searched for another passage, something he had missed. Finding no other way, he doubled back, certain he had missed something along the way. He reached the chamber, finding only the fissures, which were too high to reach and too narrow to fit through. Feeling befuddled, he returned to the breathing cavern and watched the repeating spouts of water.

He closed his eyes, deciding on his next move. Cryftin said he would face challenges, but deathtraps were more than challenges. He had to go down the hole; it was the only way. He hem-hawed about, scratching at the stone, hoping another answer would present itself. He stared at the hole and braced himself. He timed the intervals and when the tunnel inhaled, he fell to his stomach and slid down the hole.

The surface, worn smooth through the ages, made Lavour descend much faster than he had anticipated. Moments into his descent he felt the push of air coming back toward him, his timing had been off. He closed his eyes, bracing for the impact. The moment before the collision, the bottom dropped out from under him. He felt himself pushed into a wide expanse, tumbling through complete darkness. The current shoved him upward and just as quickly as it had begun, it began to pull him back. He fought against the tug, but found himself caught in a vortex. He lost all sense of direction and desperately searched for a foothold. His flipper brushed against something solid. Rock. It had to be rock. He fought harder, his strength ebbing.

The swirling came to a sudden stop. Lavour looked around and found himself in a shallow pool. Feeling like a fish caught in a tide pool, he fumbled and felt his way along the edge until he found an upward slope. The push of air and water returned. With no time for caution, he scrambled out of the pool and flopped to the ground, hoping he had found a high enough purchase. The water surged into the pool, and retreated at his feet. He let out an exhausted breath. "Challenges, my tail feathers; that *was* a death trap."

"Death is a trap from which none can escape, Lavour," a strange, grating voice echoed from somewhere unseen.

Lavour got to his feet in an instant. Only then did he notice a dim light emanating from a gap in the wall far to his right. "Who's there? Are you the Oracle? Lapasia?"

"Answers to many questions. Too many questions for a Chinstrap, I say," the voice said, sounding a bit more distant.

Lavour walked toward the light. "Is it wrong for a Chinstrap to have questions? We all have doubts from time to time."

"Some more than others. Come, Lavour."

The voice wasn't pleasant, sounding shrill, like the calls of skuas as they fed on penguin chicks stolen from unwatchful parents. He made his way across and through the darkness, keeping his eyes focused on the light and suppressing a curse each time he stubbed his claw against unseen obstacles. He entered the gap in the wall wide enough for three Chinstraps, and into a room as magnificent as anything he had seen while at Pack Ice Command. Diffused light glimmered through opaque walls of pearlescent coral, bathing the interior in a myriad of violet, peach and cerulean. Bright white light radiated through thinner sections of the coral window. Lavour wondered if he had died along his journey and gone to the Great Sea.

Lavour surveyed the area in wonder. The beauty of the chamber made the difficult passage worth the effort. He spotted Lapasia, the Oracle, standing on a pedestal made of a whale vertebra. Lapasia stood on her plinth, pale yellow eyes focused and unblinking, fixed on Lavour, as still as a statue. "You are Lapasia?" he asked tentatively, breaking the silence.

The Yellow-eyed penguin said nothing at first. Lavour looked around, thinking he had made a misstep of some sort.

"I am," she said.

The Oracle quivered and stared at the colorful ceiling. Lavour followed he gaze, then returned his attention to her. He had seen a Yellow-eyed, or Hoiho, only once before, at the Great Gathering just before the war. She was white breasted, with gray feathers on her back, transitioning into a pale-yellow and gray head with a stripe of dull yellow wrapping to the back of her head. His examination of her distinct plumage was interrupted when she spoke again.

"Like all living things, your life has been marked by tragedy and success," Lapasia said. "This is the way the Ancient ones, the Elders, have determined for us all to live."

Great, another lesson on the Ancients, Lavour thought. *I can get this from any common elder penguin.*

"A common elder can only tell you what they believe," she said.

Her statement shook Lavour. *Had to be a coincidence. She can't read my thoughts.*

"There are no coincidences, Lavour. Everything which transpires has purpose, good *or* bad." She hopped off the bone, nabbing a tiny crustacean scurrying across the ground as she landed. "If you believe that all things are coincidence, then you believe you only live by chance. You are here. I am here. The coral died here. These are not coincidental." Lapasia once again looked to the ceiling, and seemed to be lost in a trance.

Lavour said nothing and looked around the expanse to find an escape route if needed. The penguin's shrill voice and her lapse into different mental states frayed his nerves.

"Your part in these times is not over," she said.

Lavour's head perked up. This was different. Now she'd said something of interest. "What if I want it to be?" he asked.

The Oracle's head snapped toward Lavour as if he had spoken a blasphemy. "What you want is irrelevant. You cannot change the tide, it flows whether you want it to or not." Her tone turned harsh, almost angry.

"And what will happen? More death, more war, more betrayals?" Lavour asked, his voice flavored with accusation. "I will not take part in killing again."

"Yes, Lavour of Kentaksa," she said, referencing his place of birth. "All of what you speak of will transpire and more. You may or may not kill again. But you cannot escape what you must do. You live because others sacrificed themselves for you. And you will make sacrifices so that all shall live."

"Sacrifices?" Lavour spat. "I've made sacrifices. Why is it up to one penguin? Why do *I* have to make more?"

"It is not up to you alone. You will make allies…friends where you will not expect them. They will make changes as well, but not without you. We are, all of us, facing a crosscurrent which will decide our fate. Not just you and I, but the clans, all penguins. Many will be lost. If you flee, you will only aid the currents of change and the end will be hastened."

"Are saying that all penguins will die?" Lavour shuddered at the thought. How could every single penguin die?

"They may. If Aperion lives, all will die." She looked away once more, staring at the unseen. Her body stiffened and her eyes grew wide. "We must all make sacrifices," she said. Her voice had changed from a grating call to quiet, almost forlorn. Her body slumped. She raised her head, looking at Lavour with pitiable eyes.

The sudden change unnerved Lavour more than her high-pitched cackle. She had seen something, or her intuition, as Cryftin called it, had told her something. The Chinstrap stood stiff as the Oracle walked toward him. She stood and stared, her beak nearly touching his. Lavour forced himself to breath.

"Lavour," she said in a whisper. "Fate draws near. You *must* find those who can bring this to an end. Your allies will be few, but they will be powerful. Old friends will aid you. Enemies will become friends. Allies will become enemies. But remember, this is not destiny. Our only destiny is to journey to the Great Sea. The choices you make, the choices I make, and the choices of others will determine the final outcome. A ripple on the surface can change the course of a wave."

"But why me? If it's not destiny, then why does it have to be me?" Lavour began to feel the familiar weight of burden press him into the ground.

"You are not alone, Lavour," she said, her voice turning soft, almost motherly. "You, me, all of us are not single entities. The sea carries us, brings us together for a time, and the sea carries us apart. You have the strength, the calm that others need to steady their fears. And when you fear, your friends will give you strength…if you allow them to. You were hatched at a time of chaos, and the Ancients gave you strength for your time. Remain steadfast, and the course will run in our favor."

"So the prophecy—"

"There are no prophecies…only possibilities," Lapasia snapped, turning away. She picked up a stone from a pile and cast it aside. "Every choice we make alters the future." She took another stone and tossed it aside. "Every action has an effect." She continued to toss the stones, leaving one. "Until you are left with only one outcome."

Lavour looked at the stone and at the new pile, trying to find a lesson in a heap of rocks. "But there's another pile."

"Only because of my actions. If I did nothing, the pile would have never been."

Lavour's head spun with a hundred questions. "How can I know which choices to make? Which will be the right ones?"

"You can't. Trust yourself and those closest to you, and the path will open." Lapasia closed her eyes and trembled. "It is the seventh cycle, and the southern waters run further north than in a hundred lifetimes. Follow them, and when the time comes, return. May the Spirits of the Ancients strengthen your swim."

Lavour still had questions, but Lapasia tucked her head into her chest, indicating she was through. He looked around the cavern, hoping to find another exit.

"The tide is low. Your path is safe," Lapasia said, answering his unspoken question, and then tucked her head once again. "Go now, don't delay, or it will lead to the end," she added, her voice muffled and low.

Lavour took one last look at the beauty and left the room. He went to the pool and found it empty. It was then he spotted a natural walkway to the bottom. "I couldn't have waited until low tide to begin with?" he muttered, leaving Lapasia to her visions.

CHAPTER 20

Lavour exited the caves to find Meuseaux and Cryftin waiting for him. Meuseaux stared at him anxiously while Cryftin never took his eyes off of the seascape. Lavour said nothing and walked straight to the shore. Meuseaux hurried behind, calling after him. "Well?" Meuseaux asked.

Lavour kept his thoughts to himself at first, but then he recalled Lapasia's words. "I have a feeling Lapasia is in danger."

"And so is Cryftin. Aperion is coming," Meuseaux said. The fear in his voice told Lavour all he needed to know.

"Aperion is real. I thought they were just stories—a specter from legend."

"I heard a lot of strange things while at PIC; about the under realm and about Lord Saeson's Misshapen. I dismissed them most of the time. But the Overlord had his secrets. What I would like to know is, why didn't Antaean or Liutites just kill him? If he was a threat, that is."

"They probably thought they could use him or Saeson for some other purpose. Maybe they tried and failed. Did Cryftin tell you about him?" Lavour kept his eyes on the sea. The water looked different. Ominous, as if it were a living thing, harboring menace, with the intent to destroy everything he knew and cared about.

"He told me some," Meuseaux answered. "He said Aperion might kill them."

Lavour looked at his friend. He liked Cryftin, and didn't want to see more penguins he cared about die. "Lapasia said we should leave here immediately. I'm thinking we should stay and protect them."

"And if we all die? What then?" Cryftin's voice cut in.

"At least we will die for a purpose," Lavour said. "I won't just swim away knowing your lives are in danger. I can't."

"Neither can I," Meuseaux said. "We've taken down big penguins before; we can do it again."

"No, Meuseaux. No, you can't. And neither can you, Lavour. You are not strong enough. Lapasia is not a fighter, and I'm far too old to be of any help. Whatever the outcome, you must be away from here."

"But surely, you don't want to die? We can help; buy you time or something. I won't allow it," Lavour said, despite Lapasia's warning.

"I admire your resolve, Lavour. Many do. That is why you cannot flippantly give your life away. You will be needed to bring the war to an end. Lapasia told you so. She told me so. And no, I don't want to die. But I will not allow Aperion to find his queen. I will do what I can to prevent it. You must leave…soon."

"Who is this Aperion, that he can't be beaten? I'm sure we can wear him down and have him follow us to the sea, where Ceatak can finish him off," Lavour said, sounding like a pleading child.

"Aperion is large. He is bigger, stronger, and faster than any penguin you have encountered. As you are in size compared to an Emperor, so is Antaean compared to Aperion. If you confront him now, he will kill you. He will kill Meuseaux. And he will kill me and the Oracle. Had Lapasia been alive when his mate's egg was hidden, we would have known. We would have destroyed the egg. We would have destroyed them all. We thought we were safeguarding the future. We didn't know we were harboring our doom."

"We?" Meuseaux asked. "You were around when Antaean was hatched?"

"I told you I am old. I was once a member of the Council of Thrace," Cryftin said proudly, yet with a hint of sorrow, "chosen by the clan elders to govern the affairs of penguins of the realm. We settled disputes, and all clans obeyed our decisions. And then the Royal we saved seized power and dissolved the Council." Cryftin stopped talking and surveyed his surroundings. "That is all you need to know. There is another who knows the stories. And though he could take a short tale and make it longer than a swim around the world, he holds much knowledge. When you meet with him again, ask him to tell you about Thrace."

"Again?" Lavour asked. "I know this penguin?"

"Do not be certain of what you think you know," Cryftin said. "Remember this; Aperion is mad for power and mad in faculty. However, none of that will matter if you do not leave here now. Go, and remember what the Oracle has told you. You are the wind that will help change the current."

"I won't leave until you are safe," Lavour said, planting his feet firmly in the sand.

Cryftin sighed. "The choice is yours, and if you choose to stay, then you choose to die. And if you choose to die now, all will follow."

Lavour's body slumped. He had carried the burden of the death of thousands, and the thought of the responsibility of a million more was more than he could bear. *There are no prophecies, only possibilities*, he reminded himself. But if one of those possibilities led to the end of penguinkind, then he would do his part to prevent it, as would Cryftin and Lapasia. "I hope to see you again," he said to the old Tawaki.

"Perhaps in another age," said Cryftin. His body sagged with relief. "Be safe, yet bold. Find the son of Antaean."

Meuseaux jerked his head. "I thought you said—"

"I said many things. Now go."

The statement added more questions to Lavour's mind, but it was a clam to crack open at another time. "Goodbye," Lavour said.

"Farewell. Ceatak will be along soon. He will see you safely away and then go to his fulfill his duty. Remember us and stay the course," Cryftin said, then abruptly turned away.

Meuseaux joined Lavour at the ocean's edge, cold water lapping against their feet. "Did the Oracle tell you the future?" he asked.

Lavour contemplated the question before stepping into the surf. "No, Meuseaux…she didn't."

CHAPTER 21

Trofim awoke from a fitful sleep to find Leepoh standing over him. He nearly reached up to grab the penguin by the neck until he realized who he was. "Don't do that. You could get hurt," Tro said, getting to his feet.

"You were talking. I talked back, but you didn't insult me, so I guessed something was amiss," Leepoh said, sounding concerned. "You were asleep but saying things. And you say *I* talk too much. At least I keep my beak shut while I'm asleep."

"I didn't know I talked in my sleep," said Tro.

"How could you know if you're asleep?"

"I must've been dreaming." Trofim shivered and scrunched his eyes, tying to wake up. He pulled out his pocket knife and began shaving ice off the wall. Cupping his hand below, he caught the flakes and put them in his mouth, letting the ice dissolve.

"What's an Alyssa?" Leepoh asked, watching Trofim scrape at the wall.

Trofim spun around and glared at the Gentoo. "You never mind that. Keep your nose to yourself."

Leepoh looked around the room. "Where else would I keep it?"

Trofim shook his head and returned to gathering shavings. "I meant, mind your own business." The close quarters were making him stir crazy, and seeing Talus had put him even more on edge. He stepped to the far side of the room and relieved himself in the small penguin-sized latrine. Finishing his work, he started his workout routine by doing squats while holding his pack above his head.

"You know, that smells really foul," Leepoh said, snorting.

"Yours doesn't exactly smell like daisies either." He stopped his workout, withdrew his knife, and tried to stick it in the door seam, as he had done several times before, hoping to trigger a mechanism.

"What's a daisies?" Leepoh asked.

Trofim looked down at the bird who stared back with earnest eyes. There was a lot the penguin didn't know, couldn't know. Feeling exhausted from the brief workout, Tro let himself slide to the floor and sit closer to eye level with the Gentoo. "Daisies are flowers. Some smell nice. They grow on plants. Have you ever seen a flower? They come in different colors. Daisies are yellow…and white and pink, I think. Maybe other colors too. Hell, I don't know."

"Yellow? Yellow. I might speak your talk, but I think I still have a few things to learn. What's a yellow?"

Wanting to keep his mind off his predicament, Trofim decided to educate the penguin. "Yellow is almost like the color of your beak. Some of you have yellow head feathers."

Leepoh's eyes opened wide in understanding. "I've seen flowers. I've always called them 'smell funny things,' not daisies. My Rockhopper friend has yellow head feathers. When I see him again, I'll call him daisies."

"I'm sure he'll appreciate that." Hearing that Leepoh had friends and the desire to see them brought on a twinge of guilt over his plans to ditch the bird. *What am I thinking? He's a penguin; he can swim or walk to wherever his friend is.* He listened to Leepoh go on about how he couldn't wait to see his friend Nok and about how he'd be surprised to find out Leepoh was alive.

Watching him and getting to know him, Trofim felt compassion for the bird. He dismissed his feeling as something akin to Stockholm syndrome, and reminded himself that these things were capable of killing. But the damned things had emotions just like people. He cursed himself and got on with telling Leepoh about things he might not ever see. For the first time since the day Alyssa died, he found himself enjoying somebody's company. He felt a new twinge of guilt for enjoying a bit of life, but deflected the thoughts by delving deeper into conversation with his friend.

The two talked for hours. Trofim even began to replace irritation with amusement at hearing many of Leepoh's tales, which almost always ended with him eating something. Trofim educated Leepoh on human culture and life, and Leepoh taught Trofim about penguin history, religion, and even politics. The conversation turned back to flowers and dreams, and Trofim slipped back into stoicism.

Leepoh tilted his head and stared at Trofim in silence for a bit. "Who is Alyssa?" the Gentoo asked with uncharacteristic trepidation.

Trofim was about to reprimand the Gentoo, but caught himself. He faced the wall, scratching the back of his head. He let out a long sigh and looked back at Leepoh. "Alyssa..." He said with a deep breath. "Alyssa was a very dear friend. She was...she was a joy to be around. No matter what we went through or what kind of hell we faced, she had a way of making me smile. She made me happy." He smiled and turned away, scratching at his thick, scraggly beard.

"Was she your mate?" Leepoh asked, doing his best to sound empathetic.

Trofim snorted a laugh. "No. No, nothing like that. Maybe one day, she could've been. I don't know. Stranger things have happened." He looked down at Leepoh. His mood darkened, almost becoming a physical thing. "Talus killed her. She died trying to save me, and I couldn't save her. And I promise you this—I will kill that son of a bitch before we leave here."

Leepoh, in one of the few times in his life, was at a loss for words. He studied his friend's face, trying to put the expressions to the words and emotions. He lowered his head, his eyes watching the ground as he examined his thoughts. "Revenge is never what you think it will be. Sometimes it destroys you as much as the one you sought vengeance on.

Sometimes it kills you."

Trofim stared at the bird with narrowed eyes; angry at first, but realizing his words rang of a little truth. He was about to reply with a philosophy of his own when the door began to open. Trofim pocketed his knife and prepared for whoever or whatever might enter this time.

They stared at the doorway, waiting. Nobody came. They looked at each other. Trofim stepped to the entryway and peered around the corner. The dark hall appeared empty. "I think it's time to go," he said. He stepped back in and slung his pack.

Leepoh looked down the corridor, mimicking Trofim.

"Do you see or hear anything?" Trofim asked, hoping the animal's keener senses could pick up something his couldn't.

"Nothing," Leepoh said, and walked out the door as if it were an everyday thing. "This way. And you'd better keep up—I don't want some wingless human slowing me down."

Trofim let an exasperated breath. "You know, you don't actually have wings. They're flippers," he whispered, fishing through his pack for his remaining glow stick. He snapped it and threw it down the darkened hallway. Leepoh looked back at Trofim, giving him a questioning look. "I want to see what's ahead. I don't like surprises."

"Bah!" Leepoh blurted. "A surprise would surprise me. I don't think Lord Fat Beak is capable of surprises. A surprise requires foresight and cunning. What Saeson lacks in cunning, he makes up for in stupidity."

Trofim picked up the glow stick and tossed it down the next passageway. In the dim glow of green light, Lord Saeson stepped out of the shadows. "You were saying, Leepoh?" he said looking down at the surprised Gentoo. Lord Saeson loomed tall over the diminutive Gentoo, fixing him with a cold glare. "In spite of your comrade's opinion of me, I am quite capable of foresight *and* cunning," he said to Trofim, keeping his eyes on Leepoh.

Trofim looked at Leepoh, who appeared as if he was about to say something that probably shouldn't be said, and stepped between the two.

"Never mind him. You know as well as anyone that his mouth moves on its own accord."

Saeson continued to watch Leepoh and let out a laugh. "Unfortunately, I know it all too well," he said turning his attention back to Trofim. "Unfortunately as well, he is necessary for you to leave here. His notorious curiosity has finally served a purpose."

"You know I think I'm being insulted. And I should know. I've been insulted by Rockhoppers, Chinstraps, Macaroni, Adélies, Magellanics, Blue, Emperors—"

"I couldn't imagine why. Clamp your beak," Trofim said, wrapping his hand around Leepoh's beak, thus putting an end to another prolonged spiel. "I'm assuming you're not here to stop us?"

Lord Saeson stepped away. "Your Colonel Jenson plans to kill Aperion. Only Aperion can stop the Royal's advance. We need the colonel to die."

"Jenson will die. I promise you that," Trofim said. He felt his hatred for the man resurface, and with it came his desire to kill Talus. "Though I'm not—"

Lord Saeson raised his flipper to stop him. "If the opportunity to kill Talus presents itself, then you may take it. I will not interfere. But know this—your time for escape is limited. Once you are found gone, I will have to sound the alarm. Your weapons will be found—if Leepoh takes you on the correct path."

"The correct path?" Leepoh exclaimed, a little too loudly for the other's taste. "You forget who you're talking to. I've known my way around this place when Diutes was a fluffy ball of stupid. We'll take the correct path all right. And we'll be taking it now! Come along, Trofleem."

Trofim followed Leepoh, doing his best to silence the verbose bird. He was glad he'd have his weapons back, knowing he'll need them if he encountered Talus. He would be a happy man if he could kill both Jenson *and* Talus. He could care less if Jenson planned to kill Aperion, whoever that was. Good riddance to the lot of them. They had killed several good men, and if he could have, he would have killed every last one of them for doing so. He watched Leepoh scurry ahead, happily trundling along. Well, maybe not *every* last one of them.

CHAPTER 22

"We need to get through this hole. It looks a little little for you," Leepoh said, peering over a pile of rubble. The path Leepoh led them on had been relatively clear until they started upward. Cracks and fissures crisscrossed the walls; anterior chambers had collapsed upon themselves. Here and there they passed the remains of dead penguins of different sorts who had sought refuge in the lower reaches, only to have the ceiling collapse on them. An occasional ray of light cut through the darkness, illuminating obstacles and more of the dead, but giving them the hope of a long-awaited freedom.

Trofim fought off waves of dizziness and fatigue. Being stuck below ground for an indeterminate amount of time with a diet consisting mostly of cold fish, and the occasional ration, had left him deficient. He hadn't put much thought into a balanced diet while in captivity, but the exertion highlighted just how badly off he was. Trofim looked at his clothes as if for the first time, and noticed how they seemed to hang off of his leaner frame. "I don't think I'll have a problem fitting through there. I need to rest, though." He sat on a boulder size block of ice to catch his breath.

It seemed like they were travelling much higher up than they had down when Colonel Jenson led them to Lord Saeson's chamber. Leepoh explained that the infirmary was on the lowest level of Pack Ice Command. After hearing about the Overlord's opinion of damaged penguins in a previous discussion, it made sense to have the wounded or ill kept from Antaean's reach. The past few months had been a whirlwind of discovery, heartache, and brewing hatred. That son of a bitch Jenson had known all along what they were facing. Hell, by all accounts, he had even set the whole thing up. Now, if he could just find his promised weapons, he'd climb out of this hell and hunt the bastard down.

"Hey, person," Leepoh called. "Come get your things and let's get out of here. You're slower than a whale stuck in ice."

"Things?" Trofim said, getting to his feet suddenly, which brought on another wave of lightheadedness. "What things? My weapons?"

"Yes. Your noisy things and your stabby thing," Leepoh said, motioning with his beak to the hole.

"Why didn't you say so?" Trofim said, crawling into the narrow space.

"Why would I say 'so'? Does 'so' mean I found things?" Leepoh asked in confusion.

"No, it means get off your ass and come over here."

Leepoh looked at the block of ice. "I thought you were sitting on ice, not an ass."

Trofim laughed. The penguin reminded him of himself after leaving Russia, when he tried to learn the colloquialisms of other cultures. "It's just an expression," he said through grunts, reaching for his weapons.

"Hah! I understand now. Trofim, get off your ass and get moving. I thought I heard someone call an alarm," Leepoh said casually.

"You know what? Just never—wait, an alarm?" Tro asked. A burst of adrenaline coursed through his body. "When did you hear an alarm?"

"When you sat on the ass."

Trofim cursed, hoping that the Gentoo wouldn't pick up on that bit of vulgarity. "Why didn't you say so? I mean…never mind. Let's get moving." He grabbed his Colt and rifle, useless except as a bludgeon without any rounds, and spotted his knife. He snatched it up greedily, feeling the heft, glad to have his equalizer in hand. He looked back and saw Leepoh walking toward him, his two-foot frame small enough to walk mostly upright in the narrow chasm. Had it been an earlier time, he would have reached back and lopped off the Gentoo's head without a second thought. But, as unlikely as it seemed, he considered him a friend. "Come on. Don't fall behind."

"*I'm* waiting on *your* ass," Leepoh said.

"Will you just forget I ever said that word…please."

"What word?" Leepoh asked.

"You know what word," Trofim said, trying to avoid getting caught up in one of his verbal marathons.

"Is it 'ass'? Do you want me to forget ass? Ass, ass, ass, ass-ass. How can I forget an ass if I'm not sure what an ass is?"

Trofim rolled onto his back and gave Leepoh his best 'shut up' stare. "You need to be quiet now, Leepoh," he said in his best patient and parental voice.

Leepoh stared at Trofim and whispered, "ass."

Trofim grunted and continued crawling.

The two crawled and walked respectively for what seemed like an exorbitant distance until coming to a space big enough for him to stand. Trofim stood, stretching tired and tight muscles, while Leepoh inspected the path ahead. Trofim took a closer look inside his pack for a stray bullet or two. Finding none, he strapped his blade to his side and joined Leepoh in the inspection.

Trofim examined the cavernous but dark and rubble-strewn room. It seemed a testament to the strength of its construction to have withstood the amount of ordnance dropped on the structure, but Trofim suspected they didn't want to destroy it completely. Whatever the reasoning, the occasional trickle of falling ice told him it wasn't very stable and they probably shouldn't linger any longer. "So which way?"

Leepoh looked at Trofim, then at three different possible paths. He took a step toward the right, hesitated then took a few more confident steps toward one of two on the left. "It's this way," he said.

"You didn't look so sure," Tro said, seeing Leepoh's trepidation.

"Bah! There're three paths, but only one way to go. This is the one way. Now move your—"

"Don't say it," Trofim interjected quickly, before Leepoh finished his thought.

"What? I was going to say move your head."

"I doubt that. Why would—" Trofim let out a grunt as he hit his head on a low-hanging stalactite. He rubbed his head and glared at Leepoh.

"Don't give me the angry eyes. I tried to warn you," Leepoh said, heading down his chosen path. "I swear to the Ancients, I don't know why you don't want to listen to me. I guess it must be a specieses thing. A penguin can't be as smart as a human. No way that's possible. Well I'll tell you what. No, wait. I'll tell you what later. Whatever a what is. Something ahead of us smells of guano."

"Where ahead?" Trofim asked, unsheathing his knife.

"Outside ahead," Leepoh said.

"What do you mean? We're almost out of here? Why didn't you tell me?" Trofim asked incredulously.

"I did tell you. Do all humans have such a bad remembering thing?"

Trofim ignored the bait and ran ahead. The light was growing stronger, and the prospect of finally being free of hell propelled his tired legs. He exited the passage into the wide expanse of freedom, and was immediately struck across the chest with something solid and painful, sending him flailing to the ground, losing his knife in the process. He looked up to find Talus standing over him.

"I could hear that Gentoo's babbling from here to the sea. It's a wonder the whole compound isn't here to greet you," Talus said, drawing back his club for another strike.

"See? I told you I smelled guano," Leepoh said, jumping back when Talus swung at him instead.

CHAPTER 23

Leepoh had already ducked back inside the passage before Talus' bludgeon struck the ice. The distraction was all Trofim needed to get to his feet. He scanned the ground, and spotted his knife two meters behind him. It was too far away, and Talus had returned his attention to him.

Talus, armed with a club in each hand, intended to make this fight a short one. He swung wildly at Trofim, alternating blows left and right, and it was all Trofim could do to avoid the strikes. "Fight, human! Where is the warrior I admired on that day? Is your strength *and* courage gone?"

Trofim refused the bait. He had no weapons, and the journey had taken a good portion of the strength he did have. He watched Talus' eyes glint with satisfaction of an upcoming kill. Trofim remembered the look. Trofim's eyes narrowed, and a sneer crossed his face.

Talus' eyes widened at seeing Trofim's expression. "Ah. There's the fight coming back to—"

Trofim cut him off with a well-placed kick to the midsection, sending the Warlord flying off his feet. With the penguin temporarily incapacitated, he took the moment to survey his surroundings. In the diminished light of approaching night, Trofim saw a precipice two meters to his left. Nearing the precipice, he saw his knife glimmering and bouncing up and down. It took a moment for him to realize what he was seeing. The one-winged penguin was taking his knife toward the cliff.

With little time left before his knife would be lost, Trofim took a gamble. He un-shouldered his rifle and pointed it at Cryzyrky. "Stop. Or I'll kill you both."

Leepoh, had busied himself with pecking at Talus, tormenting the Warlord while he attempted to right himself. He stopped his harassment and turned to see what Trofim was yelling about.

"Does that one understand what I'm saying?" Trofim asked Leepoh, taking a step closer to Cryzyrky.

"Do you?" Leepoh asked the Adélie, who answered with a nod.

"Leepoh, take the knife and bring it to me." He kept the weapon trained on the penguin.

"Drop it," Leepoh said in penguin dialect.

Cryzryky looked at the gun, then at Leepoh, and let the knife fall from her beak. "You're an idiot."

"Idiot? Bah! Do not under estimate me or my idiocy," Leepoh said, picking up the knife.

"The human is using you. As soon as you serve your usefulness, he will either kill you or abandon you to your fate," Cryzyrky said.

Leepoh took a couple of steps and put down the knife and faced the Adélie. "You're wrong," he said with all seriousness. "He's my friend. He's taking me to see my fledgling. As soon as he kills Talus, we're leaving this place and not coming back." Leepoh picked up the knife and headed toward Trofim.

Talus got to his feet and watched the exchange. "Cryzyrky is correct, Leepoh. The human will betray you. They are all liars."

Leepoh dropped the knife at Trofim's feet. "I knew plenty of penguins who were liars, too."

Talus eyed Leepoh and then Trofim. "In fact, I believe he is lying right now. I believe his weapon doesn't work," Talus continued to say, switching to English for Trofim's benefit. "If it did work, he would have killed us by now." Talus began walking toward Trofim.

Trofim's bluff had been called. He shifted his aim toward Talus, who didn't flinch. Tro swore under his breath. Talus raised his bludgeons and prepared to strike. There was no time to grab the knife. "Bang!" Trofim shouted, making Talus flinch. He charged forward and crosschecked him under the beak with his rifle. Talus tried to swing his clubs, but didn't have the chance.

The two fell to the ground with Trofim on top of the penguin. He gripped Talus' beak with his left hand and began beating him in the head with his right. Over and over, punch after punch, Trofim pummeled the Warlord.

Cryzyrky ran to Talus' aid. She leapt at Trofim, scraping her beak along his face. Trofim batted her away, which gave Talus the chance to strike. The Warlord lifted his head to stab him, but Trofim landed another fist. No matter how hard or how many times he punched the penguin, the damn thing wouldn't die. His punches were getting weaker. He punched the penguin once more, nearly collapsing on top of him. He decided to make it easy on himself and just cut the damned thing's head off. He rolled off of his opponent, stumbled to his feet, and shuffled toward the knife. Reaching for his weapon brought on waves of dizziness. He had to finish this now, while he still had some strength. "Leepoh, keep the little one off of me. I'm going to kill the big bastard."

"I don't know what a bastard is. Maybe you should just kill Talus."

Trofim shot Leepoh a look he had become all too familiar with.

"Some humans," said Leepoh.

Trofim lurched toward Talus. The Warlord was still lying on the ground; his head to the side breathing heavily. Trofim shifted his grip on the knife. It seemed almost anticlimactic for him to kill him this way, but he didn't give a damn about dramatic endings. It was time to kill the son of a bitch. He stood over the bird, the darkening sky still holding just enough light to catch a gleam in Talus' eyes. "Now she'll be avenged," Trofim said, lifting his blade to strike.

"The dead know nothing of vengeance. They are simply dead," Talus said, bringing his bludgeon around and striking Trofim on the knee, making him drop to the ground.

Trofim rolled away from the second strike, cussing himself for not rushing to kill his enemy. The pain in his knee fueled his anger. He watched Talus struggle to his feet. He clutched his knife and moved in. There would be no hesitation this time. He raised his blade like a hammer and sliced down. The attack cut into the Warlord's seal leather vest, but missed flesh. Trofim brought the edge back, and Talus could only raise a flipper in defense.

Talus howled out in rage when the knife cut into his left flipper. He swung his right, catching Trofim in the side. Trofim brought his blade back for a sluggish strike, which Talus had no trouble parrying. The combatants circled one another, eyes burning with a warrior's fire. Talus jabbed and swung at Trofim, trying to keep him at bay. His flipper dripped blood, hanging to his side, as useless as his swollen left eye.

Talus called out to Cryzyrky and the Ancients for help.

"Get out of the way," Cryzyrky said, hearing Talus' call. "How dare you betray your kind?"

"'Kind' isn't a word I'd use when talking about Talus," Leepoh said. "There's no such thing as a loyal Royal. So back off, Seal Bait, and let them have it out."

Cryzyrky glared at the Gentoo. She attacked, rushing him, attempting to drive her beak into Leepoh and finish the job Liutites had started.

"Ah!" Leepoh exclaimed, slapping at the enraged Adélie. "It's unbecoming of an Adélie to become so unbecoming."

Cryzyrky tried to stab Leepoh again only to be slapped away. "Do you ever shut up? Just shut up!" Cryzyrky bull-rushed Leepoh and drove him into the wall. She bit and pecked at him, trying to find a way to silence the Gentoo for good.

"There are nicer ways of asking, you know," Leepoh said, driving his beak into the side of Cryzyrky's neck. The Adélie retaliated by biting onto Leepoh's. "I heard this is courtship for some penguins. Are you trying to ask me something, Cryzyrky?"

Cryzyrky withdrew her beak and glared at Leepoh with unbridled hatred. "Uh-oh," he said. She struck him hard with her flipper.

"Shut up! In the name of the Ancients, shut up." Cryzyrky began to attack Leepoh again, but another call from Talus stopped her. She turned to him and saw that he was in trouble. She wouldn't let him die.

Trofim slashed at Talus, narrowly missing his throat and putting an end to the fight. Talus struck back, delivering a harmless blow to his shoulder. Trofim stepped back and caught a flash of white in his peripheral vision. Realizing it wasn't Leepoh, he stepped in and kicked. He felt the satisfying weight against his foot and caught a glimpse of Cryzyrky's white breast before she disappeared over the precipice.

Talus watched his friend disappear into the night. His rage turned almost palpable. He swung at Trofim repeatedly in a half-blind, frenzied assault of pure violence. Trofim ducked, bobbed, and weaved, letting the Warlord wear himself out. The attacks slowed, and he struck once more, which Trofim batted aside.

Now it was time finish this. His strength had left him, but he wouldn't need much to run his knife into Talus' gut. He leaned in, practically falling against the Warlord, grabbed Talus by the back of the head, and plunged the knife into his midsection.

Talus looked down at the knife, then back at Trofim. "You fight well. You truly are my equal. You did your best, and you should be commended."

Talus brought up his club, and Trofim felt his hand lift with it. He swore he had felt the blade go in, through bone. He looked down and saw his knife stuck in the Warlord's bludgeon. He spat a curse, and tried to wrench the knife and club from Talus' surprisingly strong grip. His hands were weak and cold, and he found himself in a life-or-death tug-of-war.

The two yanked back and forth, each knowing that whoever wrested the weapon would win the battle.

Talus let loose with his bloodied flipper and slapped Trofim in the face. Trofim winced but held fast. Frustrated by his own feebleness, he let go of the weapon. The shift in momentum caused Talus to stumble back and lose his grip on the club. Both watched their weapons tumble through the air, the glint of steel highlighting their trajectory over the edge of cliff.

Trofim and Talus looked at one another. "Well, go get it," Trofim said. He kicked Talus in the chest, sending him over the edge.

Trofim collapsed to his backside, gasping for breath. Leepoh came to his side. "Thank you for all of the help," Trofim said without looking at the Gentoo.

"Help? I didn't help. I had my beak full of that Cryzryky. I think she wanted to be my mate. That, or she wanted to kill me," said Leepoh.

"I think I know which one," Trofim said. He sat silently, taking inventory of his injuries. He leaned up and looked over the edge, but could see nothing in the darkness. "I loved that knife."

"A friend of mine used to come to this spot. There was more of a spot back then, though." Leepoh looked over the edge, then back at the hole they exited from. "Saeson's minions are still looking for us. Better get off the ass and get moving."

"Please quit saying that. It's not right," Tro said between grunts of pain, getting to his feet.

"Quit saying what?"

"You know what. Just stop."

"I can't stop if I don't know. What is it? Is it ass? Why do want me to stop saying ass? There, I've stopped. Ass."

"You didn't…never mind. Say it all you want," Trofim said, following Leepoh down a rugged path.

"Bah! You take away all of the fun. Ass."

CHAPTER 24

Aperion's ability to swim was matched only by his ability to kill. He could swim twice as far and twice as fast as a common penguin. Too long he had been under the feet of Antaean, kept at bay by the Overlord's multitude of warriors, stuck in the tomb of the underworld. If only he had gotten a second chance to find Antaean alone and unguarded, he would've torn Antaean's head from his body and made a meal of what remained. Aperion was a survivor. And while his brother, Saeson, may have been averse to resorting to such things, Aperion was not above consuming other penguins to survive.

Many a time had a newcomer to Pack Ice Command gotten lost, only to find his way into one of the many waste chutes leading to the lower reaches. Food was food, no matter how you came across it. Rather than making the treacherous swim below the ice pack to feed, where air holes could disappear within a day, a stray Macaroni penguin made a tasty and nutritious meal, unless his brother Saeson got to the wayward traveler first.

Now, Aperion was unencumbered, free to swim the sea and assert his will. He snatched fish, squid, whatever he could find. What was too big to consume, he killed for sport. He dove deep, retraining his lungs, pushing them to their limits, feeling the burn as his body cried for air, taking pleasure in the pain. His hatred of the Royal Emperors fueled his body as much as the creatures he passed. The next step towards revenge was nearing. Lapasia and her mouthpiece, Cryftin, knew where his queen had been hidden. The thought of it angered him beyond reason. If she was dead, then all would suffer.

Aperion surfaced, riding the ocean swells, scouting the horizon. Night would come soon. If he didn't find what he was looking for now, it would mean another day at sea. He knew he was close, and swam on. He rode the swells, ready to give up for the night and swim blindly toward his destination. He looked below the surface, beseeching the Ancients to guide his way. When he raised his head, he saw it. Not land, but birds returning to roost for the night.

He tracked the birds, following them to his future. He and his queen would at last be together. Aperion thought of his offspring and building an army of loyal sons and daughters, and he thought of finally ridding the world of the Royal Emperors, the K'tha.

Lost in thoughts of the future, he almost didn't see the Orca until it was too late. He twisted away. Conical teeth scraped against his foot, letting him know how close *he* had come to ending up a meal. The speed of the attack created cross-currents strong enough to spin him around. Aperion scanned the water, trying to find his attacker in a darkening sea. He floated, paddling slightly to change his view; eyes wide in preparation for the assault he knew would come at any moment. He narrowed his eyes and saw a flash of white against the inky black of the deep. The white turned to a shadow against the dark. The Orca was coming for him.

Aperion pulled himself through the water, prepared, swimming toward his assailant. He would not back down. He carried no instinct to flee; yearnings for violence told him to attack and kill.

The combatants swam toward one another at speed, bridging the gap in seconds. Aperion spotted the white chin of the Orca a moment before he saw the fleshy pink maw open to take hold and make a swift kill of him. Aperion tucked his flippers, spun onto his back, and dove beneath the attack, dragging his beak along Ceatak's soft white underbelly. The Orca twitched in a spasm of pain and caught Aperion with a thrust of his fluke, sending him tumbling, like a sea urchin caught in the surf.

When the world made sense again, Aperion spotted the Orca coming from beneath him. He considered another headlong charge, but prudence interjected. He chose a circuitous route for the next attack, banking in a tight curve, trying to outmaneuver his foe. The Orca couldn't match his severe turns, and Aperion found himself with a clear attack on the killer whale's side. He darted in, plunging his beak in the Orca's side. Ceatak thrashed wildly and greeted Aperion with another swipe of his tail.

The hit sent Aperion flying over the surface of the water. He floated for half a second before he came to his senses. When his vision cleared, he spotted Ceatak, jaws wide, coming at him. Aperion pushed away, thrusting hard with his powerful flippers, but it wasn't enough. The Orca caught him by the tail and began to drag him down. He flapped hard against the downward pull, but Ceatak's strength proved to be too much. He took him down like a fish running with bait. With his back pressed against Ceatak's body, there was little he could do. The Orca had caught mostly tail feathers, so he pinned his flippers against his side and waited.

Aperion's patience paid off when his tail started to budge. The feathers tore away, leaving Ceatak with a mouth full of plumage. Aperion flapped hard, wanting to head to the surface for air, but having had his tail feathers plucked, his pride wouldn't allow it. He turned on the Orca, came at him from behind, and latched onto the whale's tale with his serrated beak.

Ceatak thrashed his tail, trying to shake the weight of the penguin off, but Aperion held tight. He held the tail for nearly a minute until he felt his beak start to slip away. He had tired the Orca, but it would take a lot more to drown the beast. Aperion let loose of the tail and thrust himself over the dorsal fin. When he passed over the Orca's head, he jabbed his beak into the blowhole.

Ceatak thrashed and twisted away, trying to slap the penguin with his tail once more, but Aperion had already swum away. The Orca surfaced, spouting blood from his blowhole. He had done more than asked, and turned away from the atoll.

Aperion surfaced a good distance away from Ceatak, turning back for a moment to see if the Orca had followed. Satisfied that he had deterred the beast, but disappointed in not getting the kill, he scanned the horizon. Night had fallen and a sliver of a moon showed itself between the clouds. The Basileios penguin swam ahead until he spotted a dark formation in the distance. "There you are. Now I will have my answers."

CHAPTER 25

Aperion felt the reassuring firmness of solid ground for the first time in uncounted days. The sand crunched beneath his weight and he felt the sting of air against his wound. The Orca had taken a little more than feathers. His legs felt the strain of his bulk and although the fight had been invigorating, fatigue haunted each step, threatening to pull him to the earth. He ruffled his feathers and the effort caused him to fall to his stomach. Rest was not such a bad idea.

Aperion opened his eyes and scanned his surroundings, trying to gauge how long he had slept. He spotted the faint glow of the waxing crescent moon, hiding behind a thin layer of clouds. He berated himself for giving in to his body's weakness. Unconscious and in the open, he could have fallen victim to any number of threats, not the least of them Cryftin, if he'd had the courage to attempt such a thing. The lack of such made him wonder if they were even on this spit of land. Or perhaps Lapasia had a premonition of his coming and fled. Or worse yet, they could be dead. He blocked out the voices telling him he had failed already and walked toward the most likely place to find them; the coral monolith.

Aperion walked across the dark beach with no fear of predators. The coast had no smell of Phocids. When he reached the structure, he studied its surface, dragging his flipper across, feeling the coarseness while searching for a gap hiding in the shadows. He found it. The cavern's moaning breeze carried the smell of seawater and guano. He examined the opening. It would be a tight squeeze, but he could fit.

He looked in, and a voice called from behind. "You will not find what you search for in there," Cryftin said from a distance.

Aperion spun around, spotted the Tawaki, and charged forward. He crossed the distance with such speed that Cryftin had little time to react. He struck the Tawaki with his enormous beak, sending him to his back in a blink. "It appears I have found something out here."

Cryftin shook the cobwebs from his head, getting to his feet. He stood unflinching before Aperion. "I believe it was I who found you," he said, ducking beneath another swing. "Tell me something. Do all Cu-kisc greet strangers in such a manner? Perhaps Antaean was wise to discard your eggs. Such impolite behavior."

Aperion swung at Cryftin with his flipper, and this time Cryftin couldn't avoid the strike. "Antaean is dead and you will join him soon if you do not mind your beak," he spat. He walked over to the prostrate bird and placed his foot on his chest. "Where is the Oracle?"

"Such treatment of your elders. No wonder your egg was abandoned," Cryftin said, gasping for breath.

Aperion's foot pressed harder. "Where is she?"

"How did your encounter with my friend the Orca go? He's very protective, you know," Cryftin said, this time through a wheeze.

Aperion reached down, took Cryftin in his beak, and flung him against the coral. "It fled before I could kill it. He was not as protective as you believe." He approached Cryftin as he stood and pressed him against the wall. "Now, I will ask you just one more time. Where is the Oracle?"

Cryftin looked at Aperion with half open eyes. "That sounds like a question for an Oracle," he coughed out.

Aperion stepped away, letting Cryftin fall to the ground. The Tawaki wasn't going to talk. "I have a feeling she is in the cave," he said. He looked down at Cryftin, waiting for a response. When none came, he took him in his beak and squeezed.

"The Ancients will curse you, Aperion. You and your kind are doomed to extinction. The Cu-kisc were supposed to balance the K'tha, not conquer the races. If you continue to swim in this current, Miaska the Taker will see to your demise."

Aperion bit down, breaking Cryftin's spine, and tossed him to the ground. "And I will see to yours."

"Then you have chosen your fate," Cryftin whispered.

Aperion took Cryftin's head in his beak and bit. He spat out the old penguin's head, stepped on the body, and entered the cave.

CHAPTER 26

Lapasia shuddered. "Cryftin," she said. The wind moaned through the cavern, heralding Cryftin's departure to the Great Sea. Fate had come to her lonely atoll, and she could do nothing to stop it. She closed her eyes and swayed with the rhythms of the seas. She could attempt to flee, but her pronounced age would only allow her to live until the next tide. Her head bobbed and stuttered as she sought another outcome. Like all visions before, they led to the same end. Beyond her looming death, she saw the myriad of fortunes for all of the clans, for individual penguins, and disturbing images she could not comprehend. She saw the multitude of destinies for Aperion. His rule was not certain. Her body went rigid. The end of her time in this realm drew near; she was at peace.

Lapasia stood motionless on her pedestal. Aperion had already passed through the tunnels, and her last vision of him becoming trapped and drowning did not come to pass. She opened her eyes from her trance of narrowing possibilities and waited for him. Only the slightest traces of light could be seen in her chamber. Ripples on black water danced in and out of sight. The diffused glow of a weak moon shone through the thinnest window of the coral ceiling; tiny sparkles of sand winked at the darkness. Aperion broke her serenity, emerged from the pool, and sought her out in the blackness.

"Oracle," Aperion's voice echoed through the cavern. "I seek answers.

You will give them to me." His head swiveled, his time in the darkness of the underworld assisting his search. He spotted Lapasia and approached.

Lapasia hopped down and circled Aperion. "The currents of the future and of the past spin in eddies of possibilities. Speak your question or leave."

Aperion let out a derisive snort. "Answer me directly and I will leave. In fact, I would have you in my court if you are forthcoming."

Lapasia closed her eyes and began dipping up and down as if she rested on the ocean's surface. She stopped as suddenly as she started. Her eyes opened slowly. "Do you think you can deceive an Oracle? You will not have a court. If you do not alter your path, you will be taken by fate long before. The paths of your life are controlled by you."

Aperion towered over the Yellow-eyed penguin, trying to intimidate her with his bulk. When that didn't work he resorted to threats. "I don't think I can deceive one, but I can kill one. First, you will answer my questions."

Lapasia answered his threats with silence and an unimpressed stare.

Aperion growled in frustration. "Where is my queen? Does she still live?"

"Whether she is alive or not matters little. If you do not rid yourself of ambition, your end will bring the beginning of the end."

"Don't speak to me in riddles. Answer my question plainly, or I will make your journey to the Great Sea painful and long. In fact, much longer than your friend outside. Where is Korè?"

Lapasia made a show of rising and falling, as if she were in a trance and sought the answers, when in truth, she already knew. "North."

"This I know already. Is she alive? And if she is, is she north of the Great Eastern Sea or the Greater Sea here?"

Lapasia swooned again, this time in an actual trance. In her waking dream, she once again saw the possibilities. The undercurrents of potential outcomes had diminished, and all but one led to Aperion's death. She searched for the impact of a lie if she chose to send Aperion in a different direction, and the end result shocked her, pulling her out the spell. "She is in the realm of the Greater Sea. But heed this warning—she, like you, will die long before your hopes come to fruition. You will not go to the Great Sea. You will be cast into Cayaske, the land of endless beach with no shore. Mahak-chig-rantoo, the Guardian of realms, will see that—"

"Enough of this!" Aperion turned away and paced the ground. "Tell me how this death will occur."

Lapasia put aside all pretense of searching the currents and answered as plainly as Aperion had requested. "A penguin or a man. A piece of the sun or a fall from a cliff. An Orca or a land Phocid. If you stay on this course, the paths to Cayaske will be multitude. In the sixth season, you will know and you will see." Lapasia went rigid and watched Aperion approach, his dark coat catching glimmers of pale light. "Killing me will not change your fate. It will only freeze your destiny in the deepest ice, far from the thaw."

"If killing you won't change anything, I don't have to worry about angering the Ancients, and you won't answer anybody else's questions." Aperion speared Lapasia through her body and let her slide off to the ground. He stood over her, satisfied with his work.

Lapasia felt the embrace of the currents. In her mind, she saw her spark of light. The light travelled across the seas and mingled with another, a youthful light, far away and safe. Her knowledge passed on, and Lapasia drifted back to the world of the living. She opened her eyes for a final time. "You cannot destroy the Oracle. You have failed, Aperion." Her body twitched in a final vision. Her eyes sprung open. "We have been…" She fell into the Great Sea before Aperion struck again.

CHAPTER 27

Ceocilus traversed the rocky beach until he found his quarry huddled with a group of Chinstraps. The perpetually gray skies held the promise of another day of drizzle to dampen the morale of the Alliance. He used his driftwood staff to keep from slipping on the round wet rocks. He warbled, and the Chinstraps dispersed. "Supreme Commander Kiley, the Doyenne wishes to speak with you at once."

Kiley eyed the Royal Emperor. The thought of reprimanding him for a breach of etiquette crossed his mind, but Ceocilus stood a foot taller and carried a big stick. He reconsidered. "I'm surprised. It seems her meditations take precedence over all else these days."

"The Doyenne seeks the guidance of the Ancients. Perhaps you should follow her lead and be more respectful."

"The Ancients," Kiley scoffed. "If one has to commune with the Ancients daily through obsessive meditations, while ignoring all else, then no thank you. I'll share company with them when I'm dead, not while I'm still alive."

"Don't let the Doyenne hear your blasphemy; she might rescind your rank."

"I didn't hear you disagree," Kiley said. Ceocilus didn't respond.

The pair climbed over a rocky outcrop to one of the few sheltered areas. In a crag amongst the rocks sat the Doyenne of the Alliance, Mearna. The trickle of small stones brought her eyes up. "Supreme Commander Kiley, I have heard rumors that a group of Chinstraps have given in to the breeding cycle," she said. It was an accusation of Kiley's leadership, not a question.

"Yes, Doyenne. We have lingered here for so long that they have taken up residence and nested," Kiley said, returning the accusation.

Mearna stared at Kiley for several heartbeats. "Kill them. This is not our home. We have a long journey before we find home. Then, and only then, will they nest."

Kiley's eyes shifted toward Ceocilus. "Doyenne, if we kill them, it could cause disloyalty to the point of rebellion. The Chinstraps outnumber all other clans five to one. We would lose a large portion of our forces, as well as our lives."

"Am I to understand that our Supreme Commander fears the Chinstraps?" Mearna said, standing to look down on Kiley.

"No, Doyenne. But it would be ill-advised to repeat Liutites and Antaean's policies concerning the lessor clans. It would be best to abandon them to their fate. The humans will invariably find them and *they* will eliminate them."

Kiley did not like the look in Mearna's eyes. Over the course of the past weeks, she had become reclusive, reminding him too much of Antaean. He looked to Ceocilus, who remained stoic and unreadable. Kiley matched him, waiting for a response.

"The Ancients have spoken. The humans will come, as you have said. The waters have been overhunted. It's time to leave." She sat back and closed her eyes once again. "The Royal Emperors have been ordained to rule the oceans, to lead all of penguinkind into a new prosperity. Antaean ruled with a stone beak. I shall not repeat his error."

She has gone mad, Kiley thought. She had just ordered the murder of two-hundred Chinstraps, and now she's saying she won't rule like Antaean? And speaking with the Ancients? The Royals were no more ordained to rule than a Gentoo. If any clan could rule with absolute sovereignty, only the Kings had the strength of numbers, the strength of will, and the mental stability to govern the masses.

Kiley studied Mearna. Had Ceocilus not been there, he would've driven his beak into her throat, and then they would see who had the right to rule. He would take absolute command of the alliance and bring them under the control of the Order of Kings. But now was not the time. He still had much to learn. If Aperion was still alive, then perhaps he would eliminate the problem of Mearna for him.

However, it was time to see how far he could push her. "Doyenne, during my time at PIC I heard rumors of the Basileios, Aperion, and the so-called Lord Saeson. Do they still live?"

Mearna's eyes snapped open, and she sprang to her feet faster than Kiley thought possible. "Whether Aperion lives or not is of little consequence. His queens are dead, and the Basileios clan will end with his death. I would presume that Lord Saeson was killed during the attack. We left so that the Royals would survive. Our creed demands that the Royal Emperors shall rule. The Ancients have willed it to be, and so shall it be."

Rule? It shouldn't have surprised Kiley. Mearna had finally shown herself to be no different than the others. She presented herself as a benevolent ruler, but her contradictions betrayed her. "It's unfortunate that Lavour hadn't the chance to inform the masses of our ordained departure; our following would have been much larger. Be that as it may, I will rouse the masses we have and we will set to sea by morning."

Mearna watched Kiley, then abruptly looked toward the sky. "Morning may be too late, Supreme Commander. We will leave at nightfall."

Kiley and Ceocilus followed her gaze. Kiley's eyes widened, and he scrambled to the top of the rocks. "On your backs…now. Everyone on your backs."

Within a minute, the entire Alliance scattered and fell to their backs, showing their white stomachs to the sky, trying to camouflage with light gray stones. The jet screamed overhead and the penguins stayed perfectly still. A half million eyes stared at the sky, wondering if they had been spotted. A minute later, Kiley got to his feet. "Tonight then, Doyenne."

Kiley trundled over rocks to inspect his forces and give the orders. Ceocilus joined him, giving the Supreme Commander no time to speak to Pìn. A knot formed in Kiley's gut; the deal with Mearna had become increasingly one-sided. To further his doubts, he spotted two Royal Emperor Shadow Warriors, trailed by a limping Rockhopper coming to shore.

The Shadow Warriors spotted them and approached. "Where is Mearna?" the lead Warrior asked Ceocilus.

"The *Doyenne* is not taking visitors," Kiley answered before Ceocilus could speak. "What business do you have with her?"

The Shadow Warrior cast his dark gaze on Kiley. "What business is it of yours, King?"

"I am *Supreme Commander* to you, and you will address me as such. It is very much my business," Kiley said, unflinching before the intimidating creature. Kiley looked down at the Rockhopper, who lifted his head before finding a small stone very interesting.

The Shadow Warrior kept his gaze on Kiley for several heartbeats, then looked to Ceocilus. "Where is she?"

Ceocilus looked at Kiley and spoke first. "This way," he said. Ceocilus lead the Warriors away without as much as a second glance at Kiley.

Kiley fumed at being dismissed by Ceocilus and the Shadow Warriors. "So this is what it has become?" he said quietly. He stopped the Rockhopper as he passed. "What is your name? Where did you come from?" The Rockhopper looked wide-eyed at Kiley, but said nothing and scrambled behind the three Royals.

After the group disappeared from sight Kiley spoke. "Pìn, see what you can find out about our visitors."

The Little Blue penguin scurried from between a pair of large stones, chirped at Kiley, and dashed to the next rock to follow.

"The secrets you keep, *Doyenne*, will be the secrets that kill you," Kiley whispered.

CHAPTER 28

"Your failure is unacceptable, Lydeck. It would have been better for you to have died at your colony. In fact, death may be the best thing for you now," Mearna growled. She stepped forward, and Lydeck shrunk back. She turned her eyes on the Shadow Warriors. "However, it was not the first time Antaean's elite force has been bested by a group of Rockhoppers."

Lydeck perked up, looking like a penguin who found hope that he wouldn't be skewered. "Doyenne. It is Doyenne, isn't it? Forgive me if I'm mistaken. The Rockhoppers—"

"Did I say you could speak?" Mearna's eyes bored into Lydeck, extinguishing his flicker of hope as quickly as it had come. She returned her attention to the Shadow Warriors. "How many of you survived? Tell me that you are not the only two who survived."

"We were vastly outnumbered," the lead Shadow Warrior said. "The idea was folly. A battle against the Rockhoppers in their warren was a plan doomed to fail. However, if the Rockhopper had succeeded in killing a single fledgling, the outcome may have been different. Or if he had secured the alliances he had promised, it wouldn't have come to a fight."

"Forgive me for not understanding. Perhaps I heard you incorrectly. But how does the life of a single fledgling determine the success or failure of securing an alliance or conquering a colony?" Mearna listened to the prolonged explanation without really hearing it. Her thoughts were elsewhere. The Atlantic no longer mattered, she didn't care about the north, and the Pacific was too vast to ever hope to control. Antaean and his foolish alliance with the humans had cost them. She had to find Aperion and kill him. And there was only one penguin who would know where he could be—Lapasia. "Send word to your fellow shadows lurking in the depths. Tell them to join us. We leave at dusk. Go, before I change my mind and have you executed for your intolerable failure." The Shadow Warriors hurried off and Lydeck began to follow. "Not you. You stay."

Lydeck faced Mearna. He closed his eyes and waited for her beak to end his life.

"What to do with you? Why those fools allowed you to live is beyond me. But, others have seen you, so I can't kill you here. It might inspire some half-cocked rebellion." She towered over the Rockhopper.

"Doyenne, my life is yours if you would, in your mercy, allow me to live," Lydeck sputtered.

"I have no *mercy*, Rockhopper. However, unlike Antaean, or worse, Liutites, I am not without reason. I am in need of an aide. You will do my bidding without question. Whatever I say, whenever I say. Do otherwise and I will tear you apart, bit by tiny bit, until the last thing you see before you die is a bloody pile of your pieces. As you said, your life is now mine. Do you agree, or should I just kill you now?" She took a step toward Lydeck, opening her beak as if getting ready to take a bite.

"I am yours. I will do what you ask," Lydeck said. He bowed his head in submission. "But I did not come away entirely with nothing."

Mearna eyed Lydeck, thinking he was trying to save himself. "Tell me, Rockhopper, what did you come away with?"

"An Oracle. There is an Oracle at the colony."

Mearna pondered the information. She would've been too old to make the journey. "She could be many places, but we would've known if she was there."

"But, M'lady, I—"

"You will address me as Doyenne, or you will not speak again." Mearna's eyes glinted with the hope that Lydeck would make the same mistake twice.

Lydeck bowed his head. "Yes, M…Doyenne. But if I may be allowed to speak."

Mearna glared at the Rockhopper. "It appears you already are."

"Yes, M…Doyenne. It's just that I don't believe it to be a ruse. All of my maneuverings were either undone or blocked before they could be fulfilled. I put plans into motion that only I knew of, and yet, they were countered. It was uncanny. It is the only way they could have known—I spoke to no one."

"It doesn't take an Oracle to see stupidity. This is the last I will hear of it. You are dismissed until needed." Mearna sat back and closed her eyes, appearing to fall into her meditations.

When Lydeck had gone Mearna's eyes snapped open carrying a disturbing gleam. "Ceocilus, see that the Supreme Commander is properly rousing the forces. When the Shadows return, tell the captain that I need to speak with him. I have a small task for them to…execute."

CHAPTER 29

When Ceocilus went to perform his duty, Pín slipped out from his hiding spot and went in search of Kiley. He darted in and out of crags, careful not to be seen. The trouble of not being seen by thousands of eyes was daunting, but over the course of several weeks, he had found the best hiding places. Sometimes those places were in plain sight. There were so many squabbling penguins on the tiny island that most paid little mind to the Little Blue penguin in their midst. In fact, the only penguins he made a point to stay hidden from were the Royal Emperors and the Kings. He found the Supreme Commander engaged in conversation with Ceocilus. And like any good spy, he crept to within earshot and eavesdropped on the discussion.

^^^

"They will be ready to leave before the sun sets. I have informed those who have chosen to nest that they will no longer be under the protection of the Alliance. They understand the dangers inherent in their decision," Kiley said.

Ceocilus surveyed the rocky landscape, taking in the gray surroundings, which seemed to meld with the gray sky. "The Chinstraps will be hard-pressed to survive in this environment. This terrain is better suited for Rockhoppers or Gentoo," he said, with unusual empathy for a Royal

Emperor.

Ceocilus' tone caught Kiley off-guard. Was that compassion coming from Mearna's offspring? Maybe he could use that compassion to sway him toward another way of thinking. It was no secret that the Royal Emperors thought of other penguins as the lesser clans. In fact, the only Royal he had ever heard without that mindset was the Warlord of Planarseae. But even he was as bloodthirsty as a starving Phocid. "The Doyenne's solution to the Chinstrap's breeding habits seemed a bit extreme, don't you think?"

Ceocilus snapped his head toward Kiley, giving him the impression that he should have started with something a little more subtle. "The pressures of leadership can drive a penguin to extremes. She seeks to emulate her predecessors," Ceocilus said, turning his head back toward the darkening sky. "But it would be prudent for you to mind your words. Your words betray your thoughts, Supreme Commander. Do not let your beak swim ahead of your mind."

Kiley took the mild rebuke in stride. "Her predecessor's actions cost a million penguins their lives. I hope that won't be the case with her."

"We have learned from the mistakes of the past, Supreme Commander. Our only goal now is to kill Aperion before he leads us all to our doom." Ceocilus gripped his staff tightly, clearly uncomfortable with conversation.

Kiley watched Ceocilus tense. "The Doyenne has become unclear in her plans. If we truly are pushing northward, my idea of sporadic attacks to the west would only serve to put the human eyes elsewhere. While they look to the southwest, we should be able to swim north unfettered." When Ceocilus failed to respond, Kiley pushed on. "So Aperion is a real threat? He is only one penguin, how can he be a threat?"

"Antaean was only one penguin. Lavour was only one as is Mearna. As you know, most penguins only want to live their lives and care little for conquest. But the masses can be made to follow. You tell them of a threat, whether real or perceived, and they can be convinced. I believe that the Doyenne truly has the best interest of penguinkind at heart. But she, no, all of us, are now penguins without a home. The human threat is very real. Aperion, given time, could easily amass the forces needed to see his desires come to fruition."

"And what are his desires?"

"Dominion over all penguins. Endless war against the humans. Conquest of the north, and possibly retaking the south."

Kiley stepped back. "I don't see how retaking the homeland is such a bad thing. However, war with the humans is upon us. They will hunt us, and we will hunt them. It is the new reality."

"All we can hope for is peace. War with the humans is folly; they are too great a foe to ever hope to defeat." Ceocilus paused and stared at the waves breaking against the shore. "I have heard stories that their numbers are equal to the krill in the sea. They are insurmountable."

"The krill can be devoured," Kiley said.

"The krill are defenseless," Ceocilus snapped. Again, he paused and narrowed his eyes at Kiley. "Whatever your motives are, they would be best served to not expand this war. Your orders to attack the island nations of men have been countermanded. Messengers have been sent to recall the forces."

Kiley bristled at the news. "Perhaps I should talk with the Doyenne to find out just what authority, if any, I have in this alliance."

"Mearna is the authority. You can ask her if you wish, but I would advise you to swim carefully. She is not to be trifled with. She is as powerful as Liutites and twice as cunning as the Overlord ever was."

"If you don't mind me asking, why are you so forthcoming? This could be seen as a betrayal of her confidence."

Ceocilus checked his surroundings. "I seek to renew the Council of Thrace. Then, and only then, will we have a chance at peace. The humans know our secrets now. Perhaps we can reach an accord and broker a peace for all involved."

"The council no longer exists. Antaean saw to that. They have all been killed or died of age, their laws died with them," Kiley said. He was old enough to remember the dissolving of the council and how Antaean had *restored* order in creating the Penguin Defense Alliance. He also remembered how quickly the Order of Kings bought into Antaean's ideals without so much as a second thought, thinking they would achieve equilibrium with the Royals. But, like so many others, they soon found that equality among the clans was not in the Overlord's plans. While restoring the council might sound like a grand idea, it would be a hot day in Planarseae before he would see a Royal Emperor on the council.

"Not all are dead. I know of one who survives. Perhaps there are more," Ceocilus said. He turned away, leaving no doubt that the conversation was over. He began to walk away, but looked back to Kiley. "See to it that your spy conceals itself with more care. If the Doyenne were to spot him…the consequences would not be to your or his liking."

With Ceocilus gone, Kiley searched the rocks until he found Pín's most likely hiding place. "What did you learn today?" he said to the rocks.

Pín climbed out of the crag and chattered on while Kiley listened with strained patience. "Ah, well, the Rockhoppers will never be brought back into line. That colony in particular is far too independent, and I seriously doubt there is an Oracle there. From the stories I've heard, there can be only one. No, who we need are the Magellanics. But I doubt that T'Cuh-ka will be joining any more alliances." Kiley looked down at the tiny Blue penguin, letting the air thicken between them. "You are fortunate Ceocilus is proving to be unlike his kind. Otherwise you might not have had the chance to eavesdrop on my conversation. You best take care, or you might find your value to me more trouble than your worth."

Pín babbled on indignantly for a good minute. All the while, Kiley watched him with eyes devoid of expression. "No," Kiley finally said, stopping the rant. "You are not released. I still have use of you."

Pín chirped a little more.

"I doubt that would be very wise of you. A Blue penguin alone in the open sea would make a nice snack for any number of creatures. Go hide amongst the others and ready yourself; we leave at nightfall." Kiley dismissed the Blue with a wave of his flipper.

Pín scampered away, muttering Blue penguin curses at Kiley.

CHAPTER 30

Trofim clambered over the rough terrain, stumbling over unseen obstacles, while Leepoh hopped over them with ease. He was about to comment on Leepoh's lack of warnings, but the Gentoo had been relatively quiet for a change. And after donning his cold weather mask and enduring a half hour of questions and jokes that only a penguin would understand, Trofim wasn't about to do anything to get the loquacious bird babbling again. As it turned out, Tro's caution was for naught.

"If you could stay on your feet for longer than a few hops, we might be able to get out of this cold before we die," Leepoh said, easily avoiding the next rut in the ice.

Trofim didn't see the rut, and once again found himself on all fours. He fixed the Gentoo with a hard glare. "It would help if you could give me a little warning. You are closer to the ground." The statement was only half true. He was exhausted. The fight, the escape, and the cold had taken their toll. To make matters slightly worse, his knees were badly bruised from numerous falls, and stiff from his numerous years of abuse. He got to his feet and tried to rub the pain away.

"Bah! If I warned you about every nook and crack, I wouldn't stop talking."

Trofim was so astounded, he had a hard time articulating his thoughts. "You never stop talking. At least you would be saying something worthwhile."

He ignored Leepoh's never-ending retort and pressed on. He had to get to the base he hoped was still there. He had several frost nips, but frostbite was becoming a real concern for him. He didn't have a plan B if the base was gone. His best hope would be to seek shelter back inside PIC and hope that Saeson's minions wouldn't find him. But with the constant chattering of his companion, he had little hope of that.

The pair traveled onward, each step becoming more labored for Trofim. He thought that even Leepoh might be succumbing to the cold, because his babbling had all but ceased. They approached a large pile of unnatural-looking blocks of ice, and Leepoh stopped. "What is it? Why'd you stop?" Trofim asked, cautiously walking ahead.

Leepoh hopped up to Trofim's side. "There are humans on the other side of this."

"What are you, a clairvoyant?"

"No, I'm a penguin."

"No. I mean…you know what? Forget it. How do you know there's someone there?"

Leepoh cocked his head back and forth. "I can hear them. Can't you hear them?"

Trofim pulled off his head gear and listened. He couldn't hear a damn thing other than the wind. The penguin's hearing ability would be a useful skill, if could just find a way to make the penguin useful. While he couldn't hear the people around the debris, he was certain he could see them. "Stay here. I'm going to take a look."

Leepoh, never being one to take advice, followed. Tro didn't have to look back to know he was there and swore his favorite Russian expletive, following with an admonishment of silence, interlaced with more obscenities. He cautiously climbed over jagged chunks of ice, each seemingly teetering on the edge of crumbling and falling from their precarious position.

When he reached the top, he peered over and saw floodlights in the distance. He heard the hum of generators in a fenced compound two hundred meters away. Three mobile command and housing units sat in the center of the compound. To the far right, he spied a helicopter, sitting on a landing pad. He found his way out; now to find a way in. He caught the movement of a patrol. There were only two men, but they were armed. In any other circumstance, Trofim wouldn't have a problem taking care of the patrol and gaining access to the compound, but he was exhausted, malnourished, and all he had was the small pocket knife. He would have to think of another way.

He studied Leepoh in silence for a minute and considered his options while the Gentoo nervously looked back and forth. If he brought the penguin with him, whoever was inside would likely take him and perform one experiment after another on the bird. It was also likely that whoever was there wouldn't expect to see another person, especially him. If there were any members of the B.C.U still there, he'd be fine. If Jenson was there, he would have to cut the colonel's throat, snap his neck, and do several other things to the man. That would create a few problems. No, the penguin would have to stay behind. It was never his intention to take him where he wanted anyways.

Trofim continued to stare at Leepoh, who met his gaze and stared back. He was sure the penguin would be fine on his own. *Hell...it's a penguin.* They lived there.

He was about to tell the Gentoo a lie when he realized he couldn't. True, he was annoying as hell, but he seemed more human than most people he knew. And as much as he hated to admit it, he liked the damned bird. He was like a parrot who could get his own crackers. He would do what he could, but for now, he had to get inside the compound.

"Okay, penguin. You'll have to stay somewhere out of sight. I don't think it would be wise to take you in with me."

Leepoh straightened and puffed his chest in pride. "I do well in a fight. Did I ever tell you about the time I spent in the Falklands?"

"You've told me more than I care to know about a lot of things," Trofim said.

Leepoh's beak went agape, like he was affronted.

"Listen, I don't know what their attitude toward your kind will be. They could shoot you on sight…or worse. Do you see that helicopter to the right of the building?"

"I have no idea what a helkatoter is," Leepoh said without a blink.

Trofim sighed; trying to keep in mind the language barrier, though he was sure Leepoh had deliberately mispronounced the word. "It's the big thing over there," he said, pointing.

"Oh, the helkapotter."

Trofim ignored the mispronunciation. "When you see it start to move, you move. Get there quickly. That's our way out and your way to California."

"Will the others see me? I need to eat."

"I'll create distraction." Tro's accent began to thicken, and he forced himself to stay calm. There was no time to meditate, and he doubted the penguin would remain quiet long enough for him to even attempt such a thing. "Are you ever not hungry?"

"Are you ever not breathing?" Leepoh quipped.

Tro raised his eyebrows at the question. "Just do as I say for once. And stay sheltered, out of the wind."

Leepoh nodded and appeared to be taking the situation seriously. "How are you going to get inside?"

"I'm going to walk in." Trofim started climbing down the fractured ice.

"Sounds sound. Move your ass."

Tro stopped and put his chin in his chest while taking a deep breath. "Why did I ever say that word?"

CHAPTER 31

Trofim felt vulnerable walking in the expanse between PIC and the compound. The smooth ground carried only hints of depressions from craters. Unshielded by the remnants of Pack Ice Command, the wind tore at the tatters of his coat, stabbing like an icicle through the thinner layers, making his trudge across the field much more laborious. He was no stranger to brutal winters, but the cold of Antarctica was an element to itself. The prospect of warmth within the buildings filled him with urgency. Thoughts of a warm blanket, proper food, and even the use of a suitable restroom was nearly enough for him to put aside his ambitions to kill the colonel—until he thought of Jenson's smug face while sealing him and the others in that tomb. No, he'd kill him as soon as he saw him.

As he approached, Trofim studied the fencing surrounding the compound. Cameras were mounted at each corner of the hundred meter chain-link fence line. They weren't defending against human incursions; that much, he was certain of. There were no loops of razor wire adorning the tops. He briefly entertained a more furtive entrance to the complex, but seeing the patrol step out of a makeshift guard booth stationed at the gate told him he had already been spotted.

The two men stood with weapons cradled in their arms, waiting for Trofim to approach. Trofim staggered forward and stood before the men on wobbly legs. "Who are you? How did you get here?" one of them, a tall man with broad shoulders and an unlit cigarette seemingly frozen to his thin lips, asked through a heavy French accent.

"Just let me through, frog," Trofim said, his own accent as thick as the man's.

The man glared at Trofim in silence before he snorted a laugh. "Trofim Grekov. I would kill any other man for the insult. What are you doing out here? I thought you were dead."

"That's only half-true, Thibaud. I could use some food and water. How about opening up?"

"You look like you could use a lot more. Sorel, open the gate and get the medic to attend to this babushka." Thibaud put his arm around Trofim to keep him standing.

Trofim laughed. "I didn't think a French peasant would know what that means. But today, it may be true. Tomorrow? Not so much."

Within a minute, a pair of medics came rushing toward them and took Trofim in their arms. He let himself be half carried across the yard, nodding or shaking his head to a series of questions that were coming at him much too quickly. He scanned the grounds, taking mental notes of the layout. He took special notice of the shadows between two buildings, where a small, fenced pen held some of the odd penguins he had encountered below PIC.

The door opened and a flood of warm air embraced Trofim. He could scarcely recall when anything had felt so good. Aromas of food, disinfectant, oils and the musk of breath assaulted his senses. It was a good smell, a very human smell, and one he hadn't realized he had missed. He tried to walk forward, but his legs felt like sacks of wet flour. Then he was on the floor. The world became a spinning blur, and the next he knew, he was laying on what seemed to be a gurney, while somebody was pulling off his boots.

Trofim's vision cleared in time to see Thibaud's face looming over him. "Jesus, Tro. You smell as bad as you look."

"I must've died and gone to hell, because all I see is the devil's ass looming over me," Tro rasped through a cough. He tried to laugh, but a surge of prickly needles washed over his skin as the warm air touched him. He gritted his teeth through the pain and tried to collect his thoughts. "Jenson," he said. "Is Colonel Jenson here?"

Thibaud gave him a quizzical look. "I don't know who Jenson is, Tro."

"He was the commander here. Is he still here?" His body matched his tense voice.

Thibaud studied Trofim while shaking his head no. "I recognize that tone. The last time I heard it was in Columbia. You have some issues with this man, then?"

Trofim let his body be lifted and rolled as the medics stripped his clothing. "You could say yes." A medic pushed on a bruised knee. "That hurts," he said, and then looked back at Thibaud. "Is he here?"

"No. I've only recently arrived, so I can't tell you where he would have gone to."

"Can't or won't? Don't pull the chain with me on this one. I need to know; he got a lot of us killed. A-bomb, Millerton, Padre, and a list of others. I need to settle the score." Trofim's voice was calm, but it carried menace.

Thibaud took a step back. "I don't know him. But if I find him, he might pay well for this information," he said, trying to ease the tension.

"No amount of money would be worth what I would do to you." Trofim's eyes squinted with humor rather than malice.

"I do not doubt that, my friend. But it is as I said. I don't know the man. But there is someone lurking in the doorway who just might." Thibaud turned to the door. "Get in here, you Irish pig."

A thick pale skinned man with deep gray eyes stepped in. Shocks of red hair partially hidden beneath a well-worn herringbone Donegal cap matched a beard which did its best to mask a burgeoning grin. When he saw Trofim, the grin burst into a boisterous toothy laugh. "Tro! You Russki bastard—I thought you were dead."

Trofim's laugh matched the man's, and the two embraced. "Lies, Keith. All lies. Good to see you're still here."

"Aye. By the gods, you stink, man," he said, pulling away. "How? You've been gone for damn near three months."

Trofim's brow scrunched. "That long?" He went silent, trying to come to grips with the lost time. The thought of lost time fanned his hatred.

"Aye. It has been. How'd you do it? Did anyone else survive?"

"No. No one else. I had some help, but we'll talk about that later," Trofim said, cautiously eyeing the medics.

The medics paid him no mind, cutting away the last of his undergarments. They laid a blanket over him for warmth and dignity.

"I'll be needing a few things from the pockets before you burn those clothes," Tro said to them.

"Well, if anyone could survive, it would be you. This is a strange one, isn't it? I never thought we'd see something on such a scale. Christ, who'd a thought wee little things were capable of such?"

"We've seen plenty things that shouldn't be, haven't we?"

Keith nodded his head. "I heard ya asking for Jenson. So what are ya needing him for? He do something he shouldn't ought've?"

"You got that right. Keith, the man locked us inside and left us to die. He has…what do the cowboys say? He has a reckoning coming."

"You're not a very good cowboy, Trofim."

"And you still look ridiculous in that ugly hat. They ought to burn it with my clothes."

"That's me lucky cap you're talking about. I've had it for ten years now." Keith took off the Donegal and looked at it with pride. "Now, about Jenson. He left not long after you died."

"I'm not dead, Keith."

"Aye, well, ya smell it. He might have gone to the States, but I couldn't tell ya where. And if truth be told, I don't know if Jenson is his proper name. Ya know how these jobs are. Ya can't tell who's who. But we get a nice salary. And speaking of salary, I'm 'bout to be leaving here in a day."

It was what he expected to hear. Most of the contacts for jobs had false identifications. It was a way for governments or corporations to disavow any knowledge of what was really going on. A name could easily disappear and sometimes the person attached to the name disappeared as well. Trofim hoped that wasn't the case. He wanted the honor of making whoever Jenson was disappear. "The U.S., you say? I shouldn't have trouble tracking him there. Where are you headed next?" he asked, watching the medic insert an I.V. needle.

"I can't tell ya much, but it's somewhere in the Mojave or there abouts."

"You go from one extreme to the other, don't you?"

"It'll be welcome for about a day, I'm sure, after this frozen hell. I will say it has something to do with a strange lot living underground. Indian legends and what-not. My kind of work. Working the mines as a lad as I did." Keith stepped aside for a medic as he rolled an EKG device between them.

"I'm sure you'll find no coke in the desert. Who's running this place?" Trofim winced while the medic rubbed an abrasive on his chest to ensure the EKG leads would adhere.

"A regular, a major named Dremmel. If ya ask me, he's a bit of a flunky. Probably put in place because he's easy to agree." Keith watched a blood pressure cuff being put on Trofim's arm. "Listen, I'm gonna let the medics do their work. Don't do nothing stupid while I'm gone. I know your propensity for causing trouble and leaving a place you don't wanna be. Hell, if ya wasn't in such sorry shape, I'd take ya with me tomorrow."

"I'm naked. What trouble can I cause?"

"That's when ya do yer worst. Just let the doctors do their thing. I'll see 'bout getting ya some gear. I'll be back."

Trofim watched Keith leave. He was one of the few people in the business that almost always spoke with sincerity. His thoughts drifted from the matter at hand and landed on Alyssa. He shook his head. He had to stop doing that and focus on the present. He felt himself start to fade to sleep only to be interrupted by questions on how he managed keep from being frost-bitten and an assortment of other questions. He gave vague answers, as usual and managed to stay awake until he was covered in heated blankets. His last thought was of that damn Gentoo before he finally gave in to sleep.

CHAPTER 32

Randy Lee sat alone in his apartment in San Luis Obispo, California. It was the first day he hadn't heard from Gina since they parted at the airport. He had sent several text messages with no reply. He tried to convince himself that she was just busy or had her phone turned off, but a tickle of doubt planted itself in the back of his mind. She had told him about her own encounter with Bryan Turlock, and had described him as having an air of duplicity with a streak of menace. Randy just thought he was an asshole. But whatever the man was, if he hurt Gina…that was a thought he wouldn't entertain.

Nervous energy buzzed through Randy. He turned on the TV, sat down, got up and turned the TV off. He checked his phone for the hundredth time, grabbed his camera bag, and headed to the door. He strolled along the walkway between drab ecru single-level units, absently checking the camera's battery, and looking toward the nearby grove of eucalyptus trees. He detoured toward the parking lot to retrieve his tripod from his car when his phone began to ring. He fumbled through his coat pocket, his ringtone blaring loud enough to echo off of stucco walls. He checked the number only to see 'unknown' displayed on the screen. He hesitated to answer. The only unknown number he had been receiving was from a tabloid asking for information on what took place during his time in Antarctica. He had no idea how they knew he had been there.

He pocketed the phone, discouraged once again. The phone rang again. "Damn it," he said. This time the screen said *My Love*. It was Gina. He hurriedly answered the phone. "Gina."

"That's probably the goofiest ring tone I have ever heard," Gina said.

"What? That's Al Hirt's 'Java'. A classic." Randy scrunched his brow in confusion. "I don't—wait, what?" realization dawned. He spun around, searching and hoping. Then he saw her leaning against the hood of a car with an amused, self-confident, and beautiful smile. He stuffed the phone in his pocket and ran to her.

"Hey Red," she said as he neared.

"It's strawberry blond."

"Shut up." She took hold of him and kissed him; a long, deep kiss to make up for the time apart.

When she pulled away, Randy stood with his eyes closed, not moving, lost in her presence. His eyes slowly opened, and he saw her face inches from his own. "I love you," he whispered.

"I love you too," she said in a husky, quiet voice. She cleared her throat. "Out for another adventure?"

"What?" he asked and then remembered his camera bag hanging off his shoulder. "No. No more adventures, please. I was just…well I hadn't heard from you and…I guess I got worried and was trying to take my mind off of you."

"You don't want to think of me?" She asked, cocking an eyebrow.

"Yeah. I mean, no. What are you doing here? Why didn't you tell me you were coming?"

"You never know who might be listening these days. And there's also this law against using your phone while driving in California. So…surprise!" She threw her arms out and gave him a big cheesy smile.

Randy took her in his arms for another hug and kiss. "Let's get your stuff. How long are you staying for?" he asked, being lead to the back of her car.

"That depends, really."

"On what?"

"How long you'll have me here." She watched for his reaction out of the corner of her eye.

Randy stopped and looked at her. "How does forever sound?"

Gina locked her eyes on Randy, and rubbed her hand through his hair and down the back of his neck. "Actually, that sounds really good." They kissed again, as if it were the first and last kiss they would ever know. The moment was broken when Randy's phone started ringing once more. "Provided you change that ringtone."

Randy fished his phone out. "I love this song. Sometimes I won't answer just so I can hear it play." He looked at the call ID again and dismissed the call.

"Nobody important?" She gave him a questioning look.

"Ah, I've been getting weird calls. A tabloid keeps calling me, wanting my story about Antarctica and asking for pictures. I told them I didn't know what they're talking about. But they're being persistent. To be honest, it's been a little rough. I haven't gotten any photo jobs since I've been back. I had a blog I used for my business, you know, for freelance work, but it got taken down, and every time I start a new one, the same thing happens. I don't think it's a coincidence. I think somebody wants to make sure nothing slips out."

"It's good that you didn't accept the offer. I didn't feel safe at home anymore."

"Did somebody threaten you?" Concern crept into Randy's voice.

"No. Just weird stuff."

"Weird how?"

"Well, for one thing, I started that Krav Maga class, and on the second day a new instructor showed up. He wanted to teach me things, different techniques, advanced stuff. And he asked me a lot of questions, like if I've had any firearms training. He even offered private lessons at no charge.

I've learned that if something is offered free, then there's a catch. Nothing's free."

"I don't know. You're young, beautiful. Pretty women get a lot of offers for free things, don't they?"

"This wasn't an offer for a drink from a creeper at a club. This was from a creeper at the gym. When I asked why, he said he noticed my natural ability. Whatever the hell that means. I'm telling you, I was floundering in that class. There's no way I attracted anyone's attention unless they were looking for who didn't belong. And then things got creepy, well, creepier. Military vehicles parked down my street, black cars. I was afraid to use my phone, and I knew if I told you, you would panic."

"I'm not that much of an old woman, am I? I mean other than the house coat and slippers. I don't go about panicking."

Gina looked at her phone, then showed it to him. "Sixty-four missed calls today?"

"Okay, so I worry…a little. But what you said about not being impressive. You single-handedly infiltrated that, that fortress; shot with accuracy; rescued your old lady; and fought off huge, angry, mutated penguins. That's pretty impressive. Maybe somebody noticed that?"

"Meuseaux helped. I just want normal back. I haven't been able to find a job. It's like I don't exist or somebody doesn't want me…us…to go back to normal."

"Meuseaux led you there; you did the rest. We'll do our best to have a normal life, even if the new normal is creepers, and unmarked cars, and being jobless, and eating beans and ramen every day. You're here now. I think we'll be better off together. At least I won't blow up your phone like a scorned stalker anymore." Randy closed the trunk, grabbed a few bags, and led her to his apartment.

Gina set her suitcase, duffle, satchel, handbag, and daypack on the floor while Randy looked at the two bags he carried with shame and quickly stacked them on the others. "Welcome. *Mi casa is su casa*. Or something like that. That's about the extent of my Spanish." He scratched his head. "Well, let me show you where everything is. This is the living room… obviously. That's the kitchen…even more obviously. The door on the left is the bathroom; to the right is the laundry, slash linen-closet. Straight ahead is the bedroom. It's not much, but it's cozy."

Gina examined a large media shelf full of CDs, taking in his eclectic taste. She looked around the fastidiously clean apartment; not what she expected from a single man, but not surprised. She walked into the bedroom, which was only a bedroom in name by virtue of the fact that it did contain a bed. In nearly every other square inch were stacks of various photography books, books about penguins, and a whole slew of science fiction and fantasy novels. Magazines of the same ilk intermingled with the books, and where there weren't books, the remaining space was taken up by photography equipment and a small desk with a laptop and printer. The walls were adorned with photos, and her eyes came to rest on a section of wall which was clear of all but one photo: a picture of her in Antarctica. In the photograph, the wind swept her hair and she wore a sardonic, but almost shy smile, with a perfect blue sky as the backdrop. She stayed silent, staring at the picture. She looked back at Randy, who had his hands in his pockets, looking every bit a bashful boy. "Stalker," she said with a smile.

Randy smiled. "That's my favorite picture. I love it…the subject, anyways."

Gina wrapped her arms around Randy and was about to kiss him when his phone alerted him to a text message with the sound of braying penguin. "You're very popular," she said, giving him a kiss on his forehead.

He shook his head in disgust and read the message. "It says there's a package at my door." The two exchanged worried glances. "We need a dog," Randy said.

After looking through the peephole, Randy cautiously opened the door. He looked around to see if anyone was near and grabbed the package. His name was scribbled in black marker on the small box. He picked it up and gave it a small shake.

"If that was a bomb, we'd both be dead, you know," Gina said, peering over his shoulder.

"If someone wanted to blow me up, they probably wouldn't do it in a crowded apartment complex." He placed the box on the coffee table. Gina's statement made him think before opening it. What if it was full of anthrax or some other kind of lethal toxin? He fished out his pocket knife and looked at Gina. "Wait outside. Take my phone. If something happens, take it to the police. They can probably trace the calls."

"Sorry, I'm with you now, and I ain't leaving. You probably didn't expect such a clingy girlfriend, did you?"

Randy was about to protest, but the expression on Gina's face told him no amount of debate would change her mind. "Okay. Fine. I don't mind clingy, just don't follow me when I use the bathroom. You might change your mind about me." He stuck the blade in the box and slowly dragged it across the tape. He pulled back the flap, wincing as if expecting something to pop out. When nothing happened, he pulled at the other flap with a little more daring. When no pops or smoke or spring-loaded snakes sprung out, he removed the contents: a folded piece of paper accompanied by ten one hundred dollar bills. "This is a nice surprise."

"Read the note. What does it say?" Gina said, ignoring the cash.

Mr. Lee, We've had one brief phone conversation, but you have refused to answer all further attempts to contact you. My name is Malcolm Lowe; I am an investigative journalist at The Alliance Examiner of NPL news Inc. It is of the utmost urgency that you speak with us. First, let me say that Miss Rosedale is of interest to certain parties, which I am not at liberty to name. With the exception of having her identity slowly disappear, she is quite safe. You, on the other hand, are not. You have been deemed expendable by another party. Your only hope of ensuring your safety is to make what you know public. While I cannot promise that it will ensure your safety with any certainty, being in the public eye can help. To be honest, this is not a purely selfless offer. I am hoping to shine the light of truth on the incidents which took place in the southern hemisphere. You and your photos are our only connection, as I cannot approach Miss Rosedale. As you well know, you have found yourself in the middle of events which will have and are having global consequences. You can help save countless lives and help prevent the eradication of a species. Please accept the cash advance as an offer of good faith. If you accept the offer and have the courage to come forth, place the empty box on top of the recycling dumpster on the north end of the complex by two p.m. tomorrow. If your answer is no, please be environmentally conscious and place the box inside.

Randy and Gina looked at each other in silence. The perceived threat was no longer perceived. Randy felt nauseous and somewhat faint. The world spun around him, and any hope he had of having a normal, quiet life had just disappeared as fast as the hope arrived. He sat on the chair and leaned heavily on the table, the weight of what he read becoming more than he could carry. Gina saw his face go pallid and grabbed a bottled water. She sat down next to him and took his hands. "So what're we going to do?"

Randy closed his eyes and absorbed the warmth of Gina's touch. Her hands buoyed his resolve. He fought back the urge to retch, picked up the water, guzzled it down, and slammed it hard on the table, like a cowboy in a saloon asking the keep for another round. "The first thing we do is get that dog." He stood with as much vigor as he could muster and felt his wooziness return. "But before that, I think I need to go lie down."

CHAPTER 33

Trofim shot awake. A dim lamp shone in the corner casting shadows in a room full of medical equipment. He looked at his heart monitor; blood pressure and heart rate were fine. He tugged at his I.V. and sat up. A pile of clothes sat on top of a chair to his side. Keith or Thibaud must've brought them in while he slept.

A low voice called his name from outside the door. It was a familiar voice, a voice that couldn't be. Trofim's head spun and he laid back. The door opened, and Trofim's heart began to race. "Alyssa?" He closed his eyes. "It can't be. You're…you're dead."

"I'm not Alyssa. She's dead."

Trofim was confused. He put his head back on the pillow, his body felt like jelly. He felt the not-Alyssa fumble with his arm and pull the I.V. out. Unpracticed hands shot a wave of pain through his arm, and the adrenaline sent a shock through his body. Alyssa melted away and Keith came into view. "What's happening to me?" he mumbled.

Thibaud entered the room and quietly closed the door behind him. "Get your gear on," he said, tossing the clothes on to Trofim's stomach.

"What's going on? Why are…" he paused as a wave of dizziness washed over him. "What the hell is going on?" he asked, a little too loud for the other's taste.

Keith put his hand over Tro's mouth. "Shh. Quiet, lad. Just get dressed.

Here, let me help you." Keith propped Tro up and began putting the first layer of socks on him. He handed him his undergarments and realized there was a problem: a catheter. "You want to do that? I like ya and all, but I'd prefer not to be touching you in those places."

Tro looked down and realized Keith's dilemma. Something happened while he'd slept. He calmed himself, reached down and pulled the cath out without a flinch. He pulled up his shorts, nearly falling out the bed from the effort. Thibaud braced him. "Will one of you tell me whass going on?" Trofim slapped his own face, trying to snap himself out of the drunk-like stupor.

Keith stepped back in, helping him with the form-fitting under layer of clothing. "I was keeping an eye on you. Thibaud here was watching the medics. After what you said about that Jenson fella, we felt it was right. The Frenchy is a might good at surveillance. We've had the communications equipment monitored since we set up here."

"It's what I do," Thibaud chimed in.

"Anyway, the medic was talkin' to your colonel. He wants you dead, Tro. But the medic wasn't game ta do it."

Hearing Jenson's name brought up a hot flare of hatred from the pit of Trofim's stomach. "Where is he? Where is that sonfabish?"

"He might be coming here…or worse. The point is, he gave them orders to keep ya drugged up 'til he got here. But I'm not sure he's coming. He might have something worse planned."

"Worse?" Tro asked, while Thibaud removed the heart monitor leads. Tro stopped him. Even in his hazy state, he knew the medics would be monitoring him from the other room. "They'll know."

"No worries. You can say Thibaud and I gave 'em a taste of their own medicine. It'll be daylight soon. We gotta get movin'."

"How many do we have? Men, that is." Trofim stood and it took both men to catch him.

"Just the three of us. The others are mostly regular military," Keith looked at Thibaud. "And Sorel wasn't up for the game."

"Meaning?" Trofim said, trying to keep his chin off his chest.

"He tried to stop us. I think he was that Jenson fella's watch dog. We stuffed his body in a foot locker," Keith said, as casually as if he were talking about the last football match. He continued to help Tro get dressed. "Now let's try getting ya on your feet."

Trofim stood; his knees buckled, and he was once again caught by the others. "I need something to eat. Food will help."

"Ya gonna have to do better, Tro. We got provisions, but if ya eat something now after having nothing proper for who knows how long, you'll be crappin' from here 'til next Tuesday. And today's Wednesday."

Trofim looked at his cold-weather face mask and placed it on his head. "I'll deal with it."

Thibaud disappeared and returned less than a minute later with a bit of bread and water. "Here, this will help."

"Thank you. Good to see somebody has a bit of compassion." Trofim greedily shoved the bread in his mouth. It felt like a holiday feast. Even though his jaws quickly tired, having nothing so firm to eat in quite some time, he continued until it was gone and sucked down the water just as quickly. He stood once again. His legs trembled, but they held. Keith and Thibaud reached for him, but he nodded and waved them away.

Thibaud handed Trofim a pistol. "Are you well enough to use this?"

Trofim gave him a *did you really just ask that*, look and Thibaud put up his hands in defense. "What are we up against? How many men are here? Do you have clearance to use the chopper?"

Keith leaned in. "About forty men. Like I said, they're regular military. Most of 'em think we're regular too. Not bad fellas, and I'd like not to hurt them if'n it can be avoided. We don't have any more clearance than the lot of 'em, but that's no problem. Thibaud's a fair pilot if you haven't got your wits about ya. I was hoping we can jus' take the bird and fly away without any trouble."

"When do we not have trouble?" Trofim stopped and leaned against the wall, the room seemed to swirl around him. He closed his eyes to let it pass. "What about you, Keith? Your next job? This might put your ass outside."

"I doubt it'll be assin' me out, if that's what you're meaning. Hell, we've done plenty we shouldn't ought've and still went to the next. Otherwise, we'd all be outta work."

Trofim scooted and stumbled behind the others as they moved down the hall. His stagger caught the attention of two soldiers sitting in the common room and watching a movie. "Hey, is he all right?" one asked while standing.

"Yeah. Just taking him out for a bit of fresh air. I think the cold will help," Keith said, keeping his eye on the other, who was looking at them suspiciously.

"Did the medics clear it? He doesn't look much better than he did when he came in."

"Yeah…yeah. Too much Dilaudid; they said the air will clear his head." Keith looked to Thibaud, who gave him a subtle *shut-up and let's go* gesture.

The other man stood. "Who checked out his gear? I wasn't notified." It was the quartermaster, and he took his job very seriously.

Thibaud let loose of Trofim and walked toward the quartermaster. "It's my spare gear." His dark eyes stared down at the man, threatening him not to ask any more questions.

The quartermaster didn't pick up on the threat. "That man is a foot shorter than you. If you took anything without authorization, there'll be hell to pay," the man huffed and began to walk toward the hall.

Thibaud's shoulder's slumped in resignation, and he nodded toward Keith, who stepped in front of the man. "Now, ya needn't be checking on that, lad."

The other soldier stepped toward the two just as Thibaud took the quartermaster in a choke-hold. Keith spun on the other and delivered a chopping blow to the side of his neck, followed by a downward kick to his knee. The man shouted out and was silenced by a hard uppercut, which sent him sprawling over the furniture. He saw Thibaud dragging the quartermaster backward while keeping the choke-hold and a few seconds later the man's body went limp.

"No trouble, huh?" Trofim asked, leaning against the wall.

"They weren't no trouble," Keith said. "Thibaud, you get to the chopper and get 'er prepped. Tro and I will clean this up. How long will it take ya?"

"If it's fueled; no more than five minutes…I hope."

"Tro and I will be there in four. Hop to it, laddie." Thibaud ran out the door without a reply. "Now we wait and listen. As soon as we hear those blades turnin', that's when we go."

"Shouldn't we give him some cover?"

"Not in your condition. Speaking of which, I stuffed some grenades and the like in your pack. So be careful," Keith said, patting Trofim's pack.

"You couldn't find me a tac-vest?"

"You're on drugs, ya know?"

"I'm fine. Let's get the hell out of here."

Keith was about to argue some more, but a man's voice stopped him.

"What the hell happened out here?" The voice came from a large man, whose frame filled the hall.

"Ah crap," Keith said. "Burger."

"Burger?" Trofim asked.

"Yeah, Burger. Look at 'em. He's a big, dumb pile of meat. This could be the trouble." Keith stepped toward the meat man. "We just had a bit of a tussle. Nothin' to be concernin' yourself over."

Burger stooped down at the first unconscious man. "It looks like more than a tussle. He needs a medic." He stood and began to walk back towards the medic's quarters.

"I said, ya needn't be concernin' yourself over this." Keith turned to Trofim. "We best get goin'."

Burger's eyes shifted between the two men, narrowing in suspicion.

"Wait here. I'm calling the sergeant."

"That's the trouble when ya deal with heaps a meat; they just don't listen," Keith said to Trofim, turning his attention back to Burger. "Now I said ya needn't be concernin' yourself. I can't let ya be talkin' to nobody."

Burger's face reddened, and he stepped toward Keith. He took Keith by the front of his coat and shoved him against the wall. "And you're gonna stop me?"

Trofim casually leaned against the wall and watched and waited for the oncoming spectacle.

"I suggest ya take your hands off me, laddie. That is, if you'll be wanting to use them again."

The veins in Burger's forehead throbbed, and his lip curled into a sneer. "That sounds like a threat. Are you threatening me?"

"Ya see, Tro. Dumb as a box a rocks." He gave Trofim a cheesy grin and a thumbs up, then quickly jabbed it into Burger's eye. Burger howled in pain, and Keith repeated the action with his other hand. The big man stumbled back, his hands pressed against his eyes. Keith caught him with three quick left jabs, followed by a hard right. Burger stumbled, but didn't go down. "Damn, the man *is* made of nothing but meat. I've taken down bigger brutes with less."

Trofim remained posted against the wall, arms crossed. He nodded in the direction of Burger, who was charging blindly at Keith. Keith turned back just in time to brace for the impact. Tro stumbled across the room before the men crashed through the thin modular wall. Trofim leaned against the sofa, watching the scuffle, waiting for the inevitable back up. Within a few seconds, others came pouring out of the back hall.

The wall broke a second time as Keith and Burger tumbled back into the central room. Burger stood, hands raised, squinting through half-blinded eyes. Keith got back to his feet. He feinted with a left and followed with hard kick to the big man's groin. Burger let out an *oomph* noise and Keith followed up with another kick to the groin, followed by two more.

He didn't hear one of the other soldiers screaming for him to halt, and he finally dropped the man with an elbow strike to the side of his head. "Aye, he was some can of piss, eh, Tro? When all else fails, a kick in the bollocks, I say." Keith reached to the floor to retrieve his Donegal.

"I said stand down and put your hands in the air," a harsh voice called from the hall.

"I hope he has a brother," Tro said, watching Keith ignore the shouts. "If not, that's the end of his bloodline."

"This is your last warning," the man said again.

"I was hopin' we'd be able to get out of here without resorting to violence," Keith said. "Is yer head clear enough?"

Trofim nodded and scanned the armed men standing at the entrance to the hall. Each stood shoulder to shoulder, weapons drawn, but only the speaker had his gun on them. Tro pulled his gun and squeezed off three shots, tagging the talker in the knee, the man to his left in the in the shoulder, and the final man in the in the shoulder as well.

Keith grabbed their weapons, and retreated, facing the fallen men in case one thought about being a hero. "Now that was nice shootin'. Maybe you are a cowboy."

"No, it wasn't. I was trying to kill them."

A commotion coming from the back of the building made Keith's focus return. "It's time to scatter."

The two ran out of the building and came to a sudden stop. The entire complex was lit up with security flood lights. Keith looked at Trofim. "Daylight's come early."

CHAPTER 34

The first of the soldiers ran out of the other buildings, scanning the compound, searching for a target, unsure of what they were looking for. They had been told about the penguin attacks, but with the exception of the capture of a few Misshapen who had found their way above ground, there had been no attacks, no excitement, and definitely no action. When the alarm sounded, they were up and dressed in full gear within minutes, and hurrying toward the doors with itchy trigger fingers ready to be scratched.

Keith casually strode toward the first man, a sergeant whom he knew as well as any others, which was by name and rank only. Keith looked back to Trofim, who was nowhere to be seen. "There's a bit of trouble in A barracks," he said, putting on an American accent.

The sergeant started to go, but looked at Keith questioningly. "I thought you were Irish?"

"Aye, but I can talk like a Yank when I have ta."

The sergeant called his men and they rushed to the barracks. Keith looked around for Trofim. He was about to go when he spotted Tro running from between the two buildings. "Where'd ya get off to?"

"Distraction. Let's go," Tro said through heavy breaths. He stumbled off toward the helipad without looking back.

Keith was about to inquire further, but saw what kind of distraction

Trofim had created.

Several Misshapen appeared from around the corner, taking tentative steps at first but becoming bolder when they saw the open ground before them. The creatures ran toward the fence. Prevented from going further, they began clawing and biting at the fencing. The guards outside of the fence, who were already alerted to a disturbance, spotted Trofim and Keith making their dash for the helicopter. The lead guard fired into the crowd of penguins, which fled from the gunshot. With the gate cleared, the man shouted for them to halt. When they ignored his command, the man leveled his weapon and fired.

Keith hit the ground, and Trofim ducked for cover behind the last building. Trofim looked at the helicopter and could make out Thibaud flipping switches, going through preflight checks. The blade tie-downs had been removed. All that remained was for Thibaud to engage the rotor clutch to start the blades turning. The panel door was open, waiting for the two to jump inside.

Keith crawled next to Trofim and stood. "The bastards are shootin' at us," he said sounding surprised. He peered around the corner and spotted the group of Misshapen headed their direction. He fired a burst toward them, which sent the frightened creatures back the way they came.

"I shot three men. Did you think they wouldn't shoot back?" He looked across the thirty meters between them and the helicopter and considered making a break for it.

Keith seemed to read his thoughts. "Don't do it. Not yet. The blades need to be turnin' before we go."

Shouts of men returning from A-barracks and shooting at the penguin escapees told them there wasn't much time. Trofim looked around the edge of the building and saw Saeson's Misshapen scurrying toward the open gate. They were so fearsome when he encountered them in the depths of PIC, and now he saw them for what they actually were: frightened animals with very few adaptations to live in this harsh environment. They'd probably die on their own. He almost felt sorry for them. The guns fell silent, and Trofim signaled for Keith to keep his eye on the back of the building.

A megaphone squawked. "Trofim Grekov. This is Major Dremmel. I have been in contact with Colonel Jenson. Stand down, and he promises you your safety."

Hearing the name sparked Trofim's hatred once again. "Let us leave and I promise you your safety," he shouted back. "They work for Jenson too?" he asked Keith.

Keith shrugged, then shook his head in resignation. Things were about to get bloody.

"That's not possible. This is your final warning. Stand down now, or we will be forced to open fire," the major said.

Trofim twirled his finger in the air at Thibaud, and the rotor began to turn. He looked at Keith, who crouched and looked around the building, picking his targets. "Are you ready?" he asked. Keith gave a thumbs up.

Movement near the rear of the building caught Trofim's eye. The time for talk had passed. He brought up his weapon and fired two quick bursts. He saw two men fall, and the compound erupted into gunfire.

Keith fell to his stomach and sprayed gunfire across the field, dropping six men, who were scrambling for cover. The wall above him burst into splinters, and he rolled back to cover. "This is a fine spot ya got us in," he said, standing and leaning against the wall.

Trofim said nothing. Familiar waves of fatigue washed over him, threatening to make him fall. He shook his head trying to clear the foggy tendrils attempting to steal his consciousness. He looked up and shot out the flood light directly overhead. He took aim at each of the nearest lights and shot, while Keith praised him for his good thinking.

Keith continued to take shots at the advancing soldiers, cussing with each one he took down. "They're gonna try ta flank us. I'll cover ya. Get to the chopper."

Trofim was about to argue when the wall behind erupted with gunfire.

He grunted and hit the ground. He spun around, ignoring a burning pain in his left arm, and emptied his weapon into the wall. "Empty!"

"Wee bit busy," Keith shouted back over the sound of his own weapon. He was doing his best not to kill the men, even though they weren't returning the favor. A soldier broke toward the gate under covering fire, and Keith took him down with a single shot to his thigh. He ducked as several shotgun blasts came from inside the building.

Trofim drew his pistol and emptied it into the wall. He pulled off his pack, grabbed a grenade, and pushed it through a breech in the wall. "Run!"

Keith dashed for the helicopter, one hand carrying the bag and gun, and the other pulling Tro to his feet. The wall exploded, and bullets peppered the ground and whizzed past their heads. The wheels were already off the ground when they dove through the door. The helicopter buzzed the fence, and they flew into the early morning sky, dawn breaking behind them.

Trofim closed the door shut and stared out the window. He could see the lights of vehicles racing toward the base from the entrance of PIC. In the pale light of morning, he spotted the tiny dark figure of a penguin against the featureless sheet of white, standing halfway between the compound and icy ruins.

"Run," Trofim said in a whisper, his face pressed against the glass. "Get the hell out of there."

"What's that you said?" Thibaud asked from the cockpit.

Trofim looked back watching the dark speck disappear into the distance. "Nothing," he answered.

CHAPTER 35

Leepoh saw a man running to the machine; even from a distance, he could tell it wasn't Trofim—too tall. His instinct told him it was time to go, and he strode across the ice with the casual confidence of a penguin who had escaped the journey to the Great Sea on several occasions, even before the war. However, his casual confidence waivered when more flood lights sprang to life and uncertainty tugged at his feet, forcing them to stop. He stood and watched men run about. Leepoh considered making a casually confident retreat. Then he spotted Trofim and decided he'd wait and see.

After a minute of waiting and seeing, he could no longer bear the weight of anticipation, and began a direct, albeit slow, walk toward the compound. Then the penguins were set free. At first, he admired Trofim's altruism, but at seeing some of the escapees being gunned down, he reconsidered. He recognized the penguins as Lord Season's Misshapen. He tried to be indifferent. His feelings toward them were fear and repulsion at best, but when he heard the sound of their fear, he relented. The gate opened, and the Misshapen made their escape from the compound.

Gunfire between Trofim and the other men caused a general panic among the birds and Leepoh let out a long sigh and called out to the frightened penguins. They came to a stop, looking around in confusion. Leepoh shook his head and called out again. "Over here, stupids," he said.

After what seemed to be an inordinate amount of time, especially in his impatient state, the waddle of Misshapen finally came to him. "Do you know how to get to Saeson?" Leepoh asked. The Misshapen squawked in confusion. Leepoh stared at the birds, and he felt his impatience and budding frustration soften. These poor things, although adult, were like fledglings; simple-minded and lost without their father figure to guide them. Leepoh thought back to when he had overheard Saeson refer to them as his *loves*, and realized that they were nothing more than babes, bred to exaggerate their most fearsome appearance, but at the cost of a strong mental capacity.

Leepoh tried to remember what little he knew of Basileios speak. He knew most of the other clan languages, even some from clans that no longer lived. But whereas the others resembled one another, mostly only differing in the emphasis on certain clicks or guttural vibrations, Basileios was its own distinct dialect, more akin to that of Blue penguins. He did his best to communicate what he could, pointing toward PIC and hoping they would get the gist of what he had said.

After a few minutes, the Misshapen seemed to understand and headed away in the direction he had pointed. One, a near albino, three feet tall, with only nubs for flippers, but a fearsome wide and serrated beak, stopped and let out a loud honk of a noise at Leepoh, then tapped his beak against Leepoh's and continued on his way. Leepoh guessed the gesture meant gratitude and hoped it didn't mean they were pair-bonded for life.

The Misshapen moved quickly across the ice, and Leepoh found himself worrying about them. He briefly considered abandoning his quest to find his son; he felt certain that he was safe and beyond all of this war nonsense, and what would he do once he got there? But he knew Trofim would be waiting for him, and didn't want to risk the human's life. Trofim said he was his friend and friendship meant more than anything to Leepoh. He looked for the Misshapen, but they had already disappeared. "We need to set things right," he said to the darkness. "Antaean was just the beginning."

The first hints of daybreak appeared on the horizon, and Leepoh watched the humans fight. He heard snowmobiles approaching and then he saw the helkakotter rise into the air like a gull on a thermal. He watched it, disbelieving what he saw. The gunfire stopped, and the helicopter flew overhead. For a brief moment he thought it would land and he would have to run to it, but it didn't. It kept flying. He heard the approach of the snowmobiles and the shouts of men, but he didn't take his eyes off of his escape retreating into the burgeoning morning sky. "He left me," Leepoh said. He looked at his surroundings, men to his back and right of him; Talus was probably still alive and lurking around PIC to his left. The sea too far to walk to on his own; he would starve or freeze before he got there. There was no place to go. "Bah!" he said, and began walking nowhere in particular.

CHAPTER 36

"Is the transponder off?" Keith asked Thibaud, who replied with a scowl. Keith took a seat next to Trofim who sat quietly, almost sullen. He cut a strip from a spare shirt in his bag and began to wrap Trofim's wound. "We really made hames out of that one, didn't we, Tro?"

Trofim looked at Keith, and at the back of Thibaud's head, then pulled on a headset. "We have to go back."

Thibaud heard and turned back. "We're not going back, Tro." His voice carried a heavy seriousness that insisted it wasn't up for debate.

Keith looked between the two men. "Ah, he's jus havin' a bit of a lark. The boy's been through a lot."

"I'm not joking. Turn it around now." His voice was deadly serious and anyone who had ever spent time in his company knew that the term 'deadly serious' was literal.

Keith rested his hand on Trofim's shoulder, and with the sincerity of a friend lowered his voice, "Now, why would we do something as half-cocked as that? We only just escaped with our lives."

Trofim locked eyes with Keith. "I made a promise." He hesitated, knowing how it would sound. "I promised the one who helped me escape that I would take him with me."

"An' who'd ya make that promise to?" Keith asked, sounding as though he had already guessed the answer.

"Leepoh," Trofim said. "I'd be dead if it weren't for him."

"Who's Leepoh? It's a queer name if I ever heard one."

Trofim tensed, trying to contain his impatience and cursed before answering. "It's…he's a penguin. I owe him my life and my word. He'll die otherwise."

"I think the medication is havin' an ill effect on yer head, lad. They's the ones that's been killin' people, ya know?"

Trofim's thoughts swirled. He had planned to leave him behind anyways. But he had helped him escape, helped him in the fight against Talus. His thoughts turned to Alyssa. What would she think if he didn't keep a promise? Would she have thought less of him? He tried to shake the thoughts, but his gut told him that there was a purpose for their meeting. Something more, something intangible on the edge of conscious and sensible thought. Trofim felt his patience ebb. "Turn it around," he said. The menace in his voice was real.

"We're not going back," Thibaud said. "I'm flying, I decide where we go, and it's not back there. Don't ask again."

Trofim leapt from his seat, pulled his gun, but stopped short of putting it against Thibaud's head. "I'm not asking. Turn it around…now." He leveled the gun at Thibaud.

"It's a goddamned penguin, Tro. You're going to shoot me over a penguin?"

"No. I'm going to shoot you because you won't do what I'm asking."

"C'mon now, Tro. We needn't get upset. Put the gun down," Keith said.

"We have to…*I* have to go back. Take me back. Set me down someplace close. I'll find my own—"

Thibaud banked the helicopter hard to the right, and Trofim fell against the door. He leveled the flight and followed up by pulling back hard on the yoke, which sent Tro tumbling to the back. Ignoring Keith's tirade of cussing, he leveled it once more and banked to the left. By this time, Keith had caught hold of the restraint, preventing more of his own tumbling. Trofim wasn't so lucky. Thibaud brought the helicopter back level and looked back at Tro, who was trying to pull himself up. "Don't ever pull a gun on me again."

Trofim staggered to the rear seat and buckled himself in. "I won't… unless I intend to use it."

Keith scowled at both men and fastened himself in as well.

After a few moments of silence, Thibaud looked back at Trofim again. "Now, tell me why this penguin is so important that you would threaten a man who has saved your life on more than one occasion?"

Frustrated with the unusual feeling of being defeated again, Trofim stared at the deck. "It's a talker. I believe it can give us information that could save lives. A faction of these creatures escaped. He could lead me to them."

Thibaud stared out at the brightening sky, but said nothing.

"More people will die," Trofim added.

"Turn it 'round," Keith said before Trofim continued. "If'n Tro has a hunch or something more…" he paused and looked at Trofim. "Then we should just do it. He's got a bit of sight in him, and a good deal of smart too."

Thibaud grunted in frustration and turned the helicopter around. "Now you listen—both of you. I'm not dying for a damn bird. If the thing is gone, whether killed or caught, I'm leaving…with or without you. I'm not staying for a fight. I got a job in Germany that will pay enough for me to… well, it'll pay good enough. And in the meantime, Tro, you're gonna tell me what I don't about all of this."

"Ooh-la-la. Do you have the mademoiselle waitin' for ya back in Francé?" Keith asked in the worst French accent either of them had ever heard.

"Something like that. Just never mind," Thibaud said.

Keith was about to prod Trofim to jibe Thibaud further, but saw the downcast look in his eyes. "Oh. Sorry, lad."

Trofim pulled his eyes up and stared beyond the window. After a few moments of listening to the steady thrum of blades, he pulled his shoulders back and lifted his chin, and began to tell them everything he had learned during his time in PIC and about his conversations with Zach Millerton.

CHAPTER 37

The deep blue sky melted into a light violet over a blossom of yellow-orange. Leepoh stood and watched the approaching snowmobiles. He braced himself; they weren't going to take him without a fight. He guessed that there wouldn't be much of a fight if they used their guns. "If the Ancients are real, this would be a good time for one of them to show themselves," he said. The thought made him remember the stories of the Ancients his father told him in his youth. One story came to mind, a tale of Cuasan, the Prince of the Underworld; Lingus, a Gentoo Elder; and the Ancient Trickster, Calophus. It was a tale that all penguins knew, or should have known. It involved playing dead to trick death, and it saved many penguins from the jaws of seals. With that in mind, Leepoh simply fell to his back and waited and hoped. Any ideas of fighting to his last breath or giving his enemy what for were gone. What good was it to fight if the only outcome would be to receive a hole where one wasn't needed?

The hum of engines came closer, and Leepoh forced himself to remain calm. He waited and listened. The engines thrummed, but remained a good distance away. He heard the motors quiet to an idle, followed by the shouts of men. He heard the rattle of a metal gate opening. His curiosity almost got the better of him, but he forced his head to stay down. He worried that they were sending more troops out to scour the area. If that were true, they would find him and take him, or shoot him, or have him for a meal. None of the options sounded particularly good to him. The engines roared to life again, but only briefly. Within a minute, the engines went silent, once again followed by men shouting and the clank of the steel gate.

Leepoh dared to lift his head to see what he could see. "Hah! Thank you, Calophus!" he blurted. The men had either not seen him or ignored him. Leepoh guessed that the human soldiers had bigger squid to catch than a dead penguin after Trofim's ruckus. He escaped another potential death, but with the sun rising, he would be spotted in an instant if he got up and tried to make a break for cover. He could try to belly-slide away, but his black feathers would give him away in a second. "I guess I could lie here and wait to freeze to death."

With little else to do but stay where he was, Leepoh's thoughts drifted to Mee'oni, his fledgling in the far off land of Califorka. While Leepoh never really gave much credence to the reality of the Ancients, the parables had proved their worth on several occasions. The fact that the human called Randy had taken his son away, in essence saving him from a short life of hardship. Then several seasons later, he crossed his path again as a captive at PIC, and again when the Alliance went to confront the Overlord. He couldn't help but think that, perhaps, greater forces were at work. He thought about his mentor on the Council of Thrace, Cryftin, and what he had said during his lessons on the Great Giver. '*You think you control the direction of your life, but you are wrong. It is the current which directs us; it takes us to the unknown; we follow it to live and it brings the unforeseen; it is a greater force than our will which causes one another to swim together for a time, only to have the flow pull them apart or swirl in an eddy to be seen time and again*'. Leepoh knew he was caught in an eddy of his own.

He heard the vague churning of helicopter blades on a fast approach. He stayed on his back and tilted his head back until the top of his beak touched the ice. Looking from his upside down point of view, he spotted the helicopter. "Well how about that for coincidence?" Leepoh said aloud. "If that isn't Trofim Geekov coming back for me, I'll lay an egg." He looked around, checking to see anybody had heard his proclamation.

"I guess I should get ready for action." While still lying on his back, Leepoh began flapping his flipper-wings like a child making snow angels. He rolled to his stomach and shook his tail and prepared to get to his feet. The thumping blades grew louder. He knew he wouldn't have much time. The men Trofim had fought would hear the helicopter too. Before he stood, a thought occurred to Leepoh. *What if it isn't Trofim?* The idea brought on doubts and worry. "Then I'd have to lay an egg? How can I lay an egg? It's not natural. It can't be done." He stayed put, wanting neither to be seen nor shot, nor to lay an egg.

As he lie still, another thought occurred to Leepoh. *If it is Trofim and he thinks I'm dead, then I'll be dead for sure.* The helicopter approached and he had to make a decision. "Bah! Life's not worth living if you're not afraid of dying." He got to his feet and made a dash for the descending helicopter.

CHAPTER 38

Thibaud piloted the helicopter with the skill of an experienced aviator. He brought it in low and fast. The three men were reasonably certain that the personnel at the compound wouldn't be expecting them to return. The element of surprise would be theirs, but not much else. If the penguin was still alive, *and* hadn't fled, *and* remained where Trofim had last seen him, they would be exposed.

There wasn't much a plan to put in place, so the men engaged in conversation for the five minute flight back. Trofim told Keith and Thibaud the condensed version everything he knew about Colonel Jenson's and GT's motives, the bypassing of the treaties, and what he knew of the penguin's intent. It was enough to make Keith's blood roil, but Thibaud remained passively neutral. Even though Keith and Thibaud were angered at being misled by their employer, none, including Trofim, had any desire to be involved in an international conflict.

"And the dispute in the Falklands has erupted into a full-scale war between Great Britain and Argentina," Thibaud said.

Trofim thought about the possibilities. It seemed the world was headed toward a global conflict, with penguins being the catalyst; maybe not the catalyst, but the scapegoat. Their participation had been kept hushed by all parties. Some governments knew of the threat—, the U.S., Great Britain, Russia, China, France and probably a few more—, but each of those nations blamed their losses on one another as the excuse to go into Antarctica. Drilling and mining were coming to the South Pole, and the riches to be found would lead to territorial disputes. That would lead to war. "I don't care about the wars. I only want to find Jenson, kill him, and go away. I'm done with the fighting, I'm done with jobs, I'm done…end of story."

Keith met Trofim's eyes. "How ya gonna live? Killin' boogey-men isn't a marketable skill ya know?"

Trofim turned away and looked through the cockpit window. "We're almost there," he said, ignoring the question.

"They're gonna know we're comin'. We'll have to drop in quick, find your bird, and scoot out. Presuming he's still there," Keith said, checking his gun.

Trofim stared out the window, looking for any sign of Leepoh. He was risking not only his life, but the others, on nothing more than a promise to a penguin. If things went to hell, he'd give himself up before letting the others pay for his actions.

"Is that your bird?" Thibaud asked. He had spotted a black spot against the ice lying motionless. "I think we're too late. He looks dead."

Trofim strained his eyes looking for movement or any sign of life. Seeing no sign of life or any other penguin nearby, his heart sank. He was too late. "Okay. Let's go. He's dead." He sank back in his seat and berated himself for ever leaving him behind in the first place.

Thibaud pulled back on the yoke and banked right. Trofim watched as a few men came out of the buildings with weapons ready, only to lower them. His eyes drifted to Leepoh, silently apologizing for his death, when he saw him suddenly stand and start running toward them. Adrenaline surged through Trofim. "He's alive! Set it down."

Thibaud recited several French expletives, brought the chopper around, and put it down fifty yards away from the running penguin.

"Cover," Tro said, throwing the door open. He leapt from the platform and dashed toward Leepoh. He covered the distance with speed and slid to the ground, snatching up the fifteen-pound bird. He got to his feet in an instant and began to sprint back. He heard the crack of gunfire and vaguely heard Keith telling him to move his ass. He hoped the Gentoo wouldn't go into another excessive recitation of the word. Clouds of dusty ice swirled around the helicopter as his ride began to lift. He tossed the squawking penguin inside and dove in behind him, while Keith continued to keep the soldiers pinned down with bursts of fire.

Thibaud pulled the helicopter back hard left, sending the occupants tumbling. He leveled the flight, opened the throttle, and made haste away. Keith scooted into his seat, rubbing his neck and cussing Thibaud and his flying skills. The pilot snorted a laugh and insulted Keith's masculinity.

Trofim righted himself and looked down at Leepoh, who was still lying on the deck. "Are you all right?"

"Ay, no worse for the wear," Keith answered while rubbing his neck, which drew a look from Tro. "Oh. Ya meant the bird."

Leepoh blinked a few times. "I have been jostled."

"He sounds like a wee parrot," Keith said with a laugh. Both he and Thibaud had been briefed on the penguin's ability to speak, and in their line of work there was little that could surprise or shock them. Still, they couldn't help but to be intrigued. "Tell me, wee thing, how long have you been able to speak?"

Still on his back, Leepoh looked back and forth between the two men. "Can you help me off my ass?"

Keith let out a large guffaw. "I like him already," he said through his laughter.

Trofim let out a long sigh. "Yeah. He picks up on words and uses them… excessively. So just mind what you say."

Trofim helped Leepoh to his feet and then to the seat next to the window. Leepoh stared out the window. If he was marveled at the sights he didn't show it and took in the scenery with the casualness of an experienced flyer. He turned his attention back to Keith. "I've been able to speak since I was hatched," he said, cautiously eyeing the weapon in Keith's lap.

Keith followed Leepoh's eyes. "Oh. I guess I won't be needin this." He pocketed the magazine and stowed the gun below the seat. "Ya could talk like a man since ya was a baby?"

"Hah! I learned how to speak human after I was fledged."

"And he hasn't stopped since," Trofim quipped.

"Scoot," Keith said, pushing Trofim aside to sit next to Leepoh. "I wanna hear what he has ta say."

"He has plenty to say. Leepoh, tell him about your squid hunting," Tro said, and Leepoh started in at once.

"Pardon me, I don't mean to break up your *rassemblement amical*, but we can't make it to Dumont d'Urville," Thibaud said. "I think we will have to aim for Bellingshausen station. Do you think your comrades will shoot us out of the sky?"

Trofim tightened his lips. Bellingshausen, the Russian military base, would be on full alert. Could get tricky. "They might. They're no friends of the Americans. Let me talk to them on the approach." It was all Thibaud needed to hear, and he went back to not paying attention to the conversation.

Tro laid his head back. His body felt like a soggy *pirozhk*, and his head felt even worse. He closed his eyes, listening to the droning of the blades and the equal droning of Leepoh and Keith babbling on about their feats of daring. The combination created white noise capable of lulling an insomniac to sleep. Before sleep took him, Tro's lips parted into a crooked smile with the thought of Leepoh meeting his match in verbal drivel with Keith. His smile quickly faded, and he fell into a restless slumber.

∧∧∧

"Tro, wake up." Trofim heard Keith's voice coming from beyond a door. He stood and slowly walked toward the voice. Broken glass littered a narrow hall, windows blown out by something that escaped his memory. Cullet crunched beneath heavy boots. He lifted his hands, knuckles battered and bloody. He had been in fight. He couldn't recall who or what he had fought, he just remembered punching. *"Trofim."* He heard the voice again. It wasn't Keith. It was a woman, familiar, but he couldn't place the voice. *"Trofim, don't."* It was Alyssa. What did she mean by don't? How could she even be with him? *She's dead.*

He was where he should be; where he had to be, to set things right—to finish it. He reached for the doorknob, brass-coating flaking and dull against a blonde wood door. His hand hovered, feeling the cold metal a hair's breadth from his fingertips. No more hesitation. He turned the knob and pushed the door. He found him. His quarry sat in an armless paisley Darby chair, wearing a tattered navy blue suit. His face had been beaten severely. Blood stained his white shirt. Trofim's eyes followed the path of blood down until they rested on the shotgun aimed directly at his chest. "Trofim," Jenson said, and fired.

Trofim sat up with a startled gasp, his restraint keeping him pinned to the seat. He looked wide-eyed at Keith, who was hovering over him, his hands gripping his shoulders.

"Christ, it's like wakin' the dead," Keith said.

Trofim looked around in confusion, and his eyes met Leepoh's. The Gentoo stared at him, unblinking. They held each other's gaze for a heartbeat. Trofim scrunched his brow, and Leepoh turned away without saying a word. "What's going on? Where are we?" he asked, turning his eyes back on Keith.

"We're approaching King George Island and we're low on fuel," Thibaud said from the cockpit.

Trofim climbed into the copilot's seat and put on the headset. When he found the proper frequency, he was greeted a barrage of threats and Russian profanities. Trofim spat out a few of his own choice words, and the conversation ended.

Thibaud waited for an answer and had to ask when none was forthcoming. "Keep your heading," Trofim said.

Keith leaned into Leepoh. "Thibaud's not much of a talker, but Tro makes him look like a gabby lass. Trofim there is a rock. He keeps the world at a distance. I'm guessin' he'll be even worse now."

Trofim shot a look at Keith, telling him he wasn't in the mood for any shenanigans.

"That reminds me of a story," Leepoh said.

"Is it a long story? We're landing in less than ten minutes," Tro said, climbing from the front.

"Bah! I don't know what a ten minutes is, but it's not long."

"I can't wait," Tro said, falling onto the seat.

Leepoh began without further encouragement. "There was a penguin who was born with tiny, thin flippers. He couldn't swim as fast as the other fledglings, and the others taunted him and called him names. Every time they came to shore, they would complain that Skinny Flippers, that's what they called him, they complained that he slowed them down, and that they would all get eaten because of him. Skinny Flippers would walk along the shore through a line of torment. 'Skinny Flippers, Skinny Flippers, swims like a stone. Skinny Flippers, Skinny Flippers, leave us alone.' Skinny Flippers was so hurt he stopped his swimming lessons, and sat on the shore and watched as the others would swim and frolic in the surf. But still, the others would tease him when they returned. He got angered by their words and walked a long way down a rocky shore until he could walk no further. He looked around and found a tiny rock, and Skinny Flippers picked it up with his skinny flippers and threw it to the ground. He got an idea. 'I know,' he said, 'I'll build a wall to keep them away.' He picked up another stone, the biggest he could pick up with his skinny flippers, and set it beside that one. He kept at it and soon he had a tiny wall."

"But the others came and continued to taunt him with their mean words, and Skinny Flippers kept building his wall. And then he built another tiny wall behind him. And then another to his side and another to his other side, and the tiny wall surrounded him. Before long, Skinny Flippers discovered that he could lift bigger rocks. He piled the bigger rocks on top of rocks and still more rocks. After a season of building his walls, his flippers had grown large and powerful, and he was able to lift almost any stone he wanted. By the time winter had come, he had built a fortress so big and tall that no one could reach him, and he would never feel any hurt ever again. He looked at his powerful flippers and stone walls and said, 'now no one will ever call me Skinny Flippers again.'"

Leepoh stopped talking and stared at Keith and Tro.

Trofim looked at the Gentoo, waiting for more. "That's it? What happened to the Skinny Flippers? Did he go back and show them all how strong he was?" Trofim said, nudging Keith while laughing.

Leepoh stretched his own flippers out and slapped them against his body. "No. He didn't build a door, so he starved to death."

Trofim's jaw hung open, and Keith burst into laughter. "That story is worse than Russian fairy tales. It's the worst story I've ever heard," Tro said, climbing back to the cockpit.

Keith continued to laugh and jibe Trofim, while Leepoh sat in an odd silence and watched Trofim. Keith finally settled down when Thibaud told him to shut up. They were making their approach.

Keith sat back and put on his serious face. "You know, bird, that was a fine lark...a fine one. But I don't think your friend liked it much."

"Bah! He thinks too much."

"Or maybe not enough," Keith said.

Trofim looked back, his lips a line through his beard, eyes narrowed. "I can hear you," he said.

Keith nudged Leepoh with his elbow and nodded toward Trofim.

Leepoh looked at him curiously and mimicked the gesture with his flipper. "We mustn't get his drawers in a bunch; he's killed more things than I can count, and for a lot less reason than givin' him cheek."

Leepoh stared at Trofim who had turned his attention to barking at someone on the other end of the radio. Thibaud set the helicopter down without incident. When the blades stopped turning, four men covered the exits, weapons ready.

"Listen to me," Trofim said to Leepoh. "Stay in here. Get under the seat if you can. If anyone sees you, don't speak—just make your squawking noises." Leepoh was about to reply, but Tro cut him off. "This isn't a game. I won't let them hurt you, but you have to do your part. Do you understand?"

Leepoh nodded his head and squawked, and Trofim sniffed a laugh.

Keith watched the exchange and saw the genuine concern in Trofim's eyes. He leaned in close to Tro and whispered. "Ya know, ya should stop actin' a caffler and listen to yer friend's story. He's wiser than most men I've met."

Trofim breathed a laugh. "He's wiser than one, for sure."

CHAPTER 39

Trofim slipped out the door, spotted the gun trained on him, and immediately raised his hands. Keith and Thibaud were directed to stand by Trofim when they exited the chopper. "Where is the Major General?" Trofim asked in his native tongue, sounding both impatient and angry. The guard pointed to his right. He spotted the intimidatingly large man walking toward them and let out a sigh of relief.

The man stood, staring down at Trofim with an intensity that would make most men feel inadequate. After several seconds, the man's hard face broke into a wide smile and he let out a boisterous laugh. "Trofim, you *shluha vokzal'naja*, you look like you crawled out of a yak's ass. You have been around the Americans much too long." He took Tro by the shoulders and shook him bodily, followed by an embracing hug.

Trofim returned the hug. "Yulian, good to see you. You're not as big as I remember."

"And neither are you." He squeezed Trofim's shoulders. "It looks like you've been starved."

"More true than you know," Trofim said. "Now call off your *devochki*; I would like to introduce you to my companions."

"That might be true for some, but they fight with great heart. That's why I chose you so long ago," Yulian said, waving the soldiers away.

"You chose me because I could kill better than most."

Yulian turned, looked Trofim dead in the eyes, and pushed his meaty index finger into his chest. "No, Trofim. I chose you because your heart is stronger than any man's I've known."

Trofim pulled his eyes away to his companions. "Keith, Thibaud, this is Major General Yulian Utnik. I have known him since I was young man." In the presence of Yulian, his accent returned more easily.

"*Dobroe utro*," Yulian said, gripping each of the men's hands firm and strong. "If you are a friend of Trofim Grekov, then you are welcome here."

"And good morning to you, Major General. Merci," said Thibaud.

"Ah! You're French? My first love was a French girl. My family vacationed in France one summer. I was thirteen, she was twenty-two. She was beautiful, but she did not know I existed. I carried her in my heart until the day I married the Baba Yaga."

"I'm Keith." He extended his hand. Keith was nearly Yulian's size in height, but not in bulk.

Yulian took Keith's hand, noticing the slight bruising from his fight. His eyes went to the helicopter and back to Keith, who just smiled and looked at the sky. He looked at Trofim while laughing and noticed him swaying. "It looks like our friend could use a meal, or perhaps a dozen meals. Let's go inside, and we will discuss what brought you here in a stolen helicopter over food."

Trofim looked back to the helicopter, hesitated, and then followed Yulian. The glance didn't escape the major general's notice. "Did you leave something behind, my friend?"

Trofim exchanged stoic looks with Thibaud and Keith. "We'll talk inside."

Yulian studied Trofim as they walked. "Nothing dangerous, I hope."

"No. I promise you, there is nothing dangerous aboard. I give you my word," Tro said as they approached the door.

Yulian nodded and gripped Trofim's shoulder. "You are the only person alive whose word I will take as truth." He led the group down the main hall, showed them the lavatory, and took them to the mess hall. "The food is not so good. But it is hot and filling." He shouted to the cooks to prepare the food and took a seat at the head of a long table.

Several minutes of idle conversation ensued, until Yulian demanded the food by yelling at the cook. After a heated exchange, he turned back to his guests. "A man could starve waiting on that *mudak*." The cook brought out steaming bowls of *lapsha*, and as he set them down Yulian threw up his hands. "I asked you to bring food and you bring us this?" The cook, not knowing English, ignored the comment.

Trofim snatched up his spoon and began eating at once. He winced at the flavor, but his hunger overcame his taste-buds, and he ate the food with zeal.

Yulian laughed. "I was going to warn you that his *lapsha* taste like the back side of a mule. How anyone can make chicken and noodles taste this bad is beyond me."

Several courses of bad cuisine later, Yulian leaned back in his chair. "So tell me Trofim, are your friends involved in the same work as you?"

"Yeah," he answered through a bite of bread. "I've known them for some time. They're not so bad."

"Ah thank ya, Tro. That's the best compliment I've had in a dog's age," Keith said with a laugh.

"Did the Americans hire you? This mess has their footprints all over it," Yulian said, his face becoming serious.

"You know we are not allowed to say who our employers are," Trofim said, matching Yulian's tone.

Yulian nodded. "I will respect that. Don't worry, my friend. But I know there's a private party involved. The Americans don't typically use the type of helicopter you stole. But it seems we are all thieves these days. After the purge, as some are calling it, the French never returned to several of their stations. We beat the other nations to the spoils." He looked at Thibaud, who, as per his nature, said nothing, only moving his head in slightest of gestures to indicate he didn't care.

"So tell me, Trofim, what made you leave in such haste?" Yulian gave him the fatherly look that he remembered from when they'd first met, years before. Trofim hesitated. "I can't help you if I don't know what to help with."

Trofim looked at his companions who gestured for him to go ahead. He looked at the cook, who was then chased out of the mess hall by another of Yulian's boisterous and insulting commands. Trofim took a deep breath. He was at Yulian's mercy. There was no other way out of Antarctica except through him. He wondered if they would've had fuel enough to reach the French station if they'd had this kind of luck. Yulian Utnik of all people, the man whose life he saved years before, and had guided him to a new life. Perhaps there were no coincidences.

Trofim told him most of what had happened. From his first encounter at Forward Command, to Jenson's betrayal within PIC, and finally, the shootout at the American base, all the while with Keith adding adjectives and vulgarities for what he called 'color'.

When Trofim finished, Yulian sat rubbing the stubble on his broad chin. "From what you told me, I do not believe this Colonel Jenson is truly military. He may be more….or less. But I can see why you want to kill him. If I could be truthful, I would like to kill him myself for what he has done to you. Now…" he paused and looked at each man sitting around the table.

Trofim braced himself for whatever was coming next. He knew from experience that whenever Yulian began a sentence with *now*, it meant things were going to be his way or not at all.

"You will rest here for a couple of days. Trofim, you need to recover. And don't argue. It will do you no good and it will do you no good to go on your quest in this condition. I will see what I can do about arranging transport to Ushuaia. Though I am limited. From there, I'm afraid I can't do much. I can never repay my debt to you, Trofim, but I hope this will count as a sizable payment."

Trofim met Yulian's eyes. "I never held you in debt, otets."

Yulian bowed his head. "In the meantime, I should like to meet this bird of yours."

"He is not my bird. He is very much his own bird," Trofim said.

CHAPTER 40

Ceocilus touched the shore first, followed by Mearna, Kiley and an assortment of other penguins. Night had fallen and one by one the penguins came ashore and fell to the sand. The journey had been arduous. Several near misses with naval ships, mistaken landings on wrong islands, and an encounter with a pod of Orca nearly disheartened some of the leadership. Only Mearna's totalitarian command and determination kept the group cohesive. To keep that cohesion she relied on Ceocilus' unwavering support. She resolved that once Kiley outlived his usefulness, her son would supplant the King penguin as Supreme Commander. But before that could happen, she had to find the Oracle.

Mearna approached Ceocilus, proud and tall, carefully hiding her fatigue. Her advanced age had begun to show itself on the expedition. She contained her ragged breathing. "Ceocilus, see to the organization of squads. We will begin the search at first light."

"Yes, Doyenne," Ceocilus said with a salute. "But if I may ask a question. Why not begin the search tonight? If Aperion arrives before—"

"If Aperion arrives now, it would be to his misfortune. No matter how powerful he is, he would be no match for our forces." Mearna shifted her eyes and sighed. "And I would like to lead the search, but I need to rest before I do."

Knowing better than to press the issue, Ceocilus agreed. "Of course.

Rest would do all of us some good." He saluted and left Mearna to her recovery.

Mearna watched Ceocilus leave, and then a thought scratched through her tired mind; the Oracle would have known they were coming. "So where is the Oracle's keeper, Cryftin?" She sighed. The wrong island again.

^^^

Ceocilus was no more than two minutes into his task before Supreme Commander Kiley beckoned to him from up the shore. He took a breath. If Kiley wanted to have another discussion about Mearna's leadership, now wasn't the time. Kiley chirped another call to him, this time in the ancient language, which made Ceocilus' feathers tingle with alarm. He looked to see if Mearna had heard, and was relieved to see she had already fallen asleep. He marched up the sloping sand to find Kiley pacing on the top of a small dune. "What is it?" Ceocilus asked, trying to keep the irritation from his voice.

Kiley's beak parted as if he were about to say something but changed his mind. He began walking up the atoll instead. After several steps, he turned back to Ceocilus and urged him along. "This way."

Ceocilus reluctantly followed. "What is so important that you dare to use the ancient talk? It is reserved for emergencies only and for the elite. If Mearna had heard…"

"And the Supreme Commander is not elite?" Ceocilus refused to take the bait, and Kiley continued. "If Mearna had heard, then she would know what a fool's errand we are undertaking."

"If she had heard, we would both be in for a seal's gnashing."

Kiley made a derisive snort. "The Kings have been speaking the ancient language since time immemorial. The Order is no longer subjugated to the Royals. We can choose our path."

Ceocilus took several steps before speaking. "And you can choose a path your order doesn't want you to take."

"Even though the Order of Kings are now independent of the Royals, it doesn't mean that they don't lack foresight." Kiley shuffled through the sand for several steps before continuing. "But this is irrelevant. In fact, it all might be irrelevant." He stopped and looked down.

Ceocilus let his gaze follow Kiley's and spotted a curious movement on the ground. A dark patch on the sand appeared to moving on its own accord. He leaned in for a closer look and saw that the movements were tiny crabs. He took one in his beak and promptly dropped it. "What are these things?"

Kiley took a step closer to Ceocilus. "The question isn't so much what they are, it's what are they eating?"

Ceocilus gave Kiley a cautious look and scattered the crabs with his beak. He studied the crab's feast for a moment and let out a tired sigh. He only needed to see the remnants of yellow head feathers to know that they had arrived too late. He took a step back, and the crabs returned.

"The rest of the body is over there." Kiley caught Ceocilus' eyes. "We have to assume that the Oracle is dead as well."

Ceocilus paced around the skeletal remains. "Who else knows?"

"Just me," Kiley said, scanning the area.

"And your spy?" Ceocilus followed Kiley's gaze to see if he could spot Pin.

"He hasn't arrived yet," Kiley said, trying to hide a hint of concern.

Ceocilus stopped his pacing. "We'll let the Doyenne rest and inform her in the morning."

Kiley eyed Ceocilus suspiciously. "And if she finds out on her own. What then? Her stability has been marginal at best lately." He stepped in close to Ceocilus. "What about the Rockhopper?"

"What about him?"

"He might have been telling the truth. Mearna herself said that there can be only one Oracle. Once she finds out, she will order us to the Rockhopper colony. I don't think that would be wise."

Ceocilus stepped away from Kiley, keeping his eyes on the coral structure. After a few seconds, he turned back to Kiley. "Not long ago you were complaining about not having enough food, and now you want to stay?"

Kiley shifted nervously. "I never said I wanted to stay here. But the Rockhopper colony Lydeck came from lies close to the King's territory. I'm certain they know by now that I have disregarded their orders."

"Fear in a commander is not a desirable attribute."

"It's not fear. Do you really want another war between the clans? The Kings know the islands well; if we were to become engaged in a conflict with the Order, what's left of this coalition would crumble. And when the Doyenne's alliance finally falls apart, this Aperion will come in and destroy what remains."

"Perhaps that would be best," Ceocilus said.

Kiley hesitated before speaking. His eyes locked with Ceocilus'. "And what of Aperion?"

"We kill him and put an end to these wars forever."

"A noble plan. I will do what I can on my end; you see to it on yours."

"But without the Oracle, Mearna has no hope of finding Aperion." Ceocilus stepped toward the shore and scanned the juts of dead coral. "Are you sure your spy hasn't arrived yet?"

"If he has, he hasn't shown himself to me. Why?"

Ceocilus didn't answer. He continued to stare at the shadows between the coral. "When or if he arrives, bring him to me. We need a spy to find a spy."

Kiley became instantly alert. "Where?" he asked, following Ceocilus' gaze.

"He was hiding in the shadows a moment ago. Too big to be Pìn."

"Is Mearna keeping her eye on you?" Kiley asked, stepping toward the shadows they watched.

Ceocilus gave Kiley a doubtful look. "Stand guard over the remains. I'll rouse the Doyenne before the sun." He walked away without another word.

∧∧∧

Kiley watched Ceocilus leave. He returned his attention to the dark crags near the ancient coral, watching, hoping to catch sight of Pìn. There was something there; he could almost feel a presence returning his stare from the black. A whisper of a chirp from behind gave him a slight start. "Pìn," he said, hiding his relief. "I feared you were eaten by a gull."

Pìn chattered a fury of expletives and blasphemous oaths at Kiley for even suggesting such a thing.

"Settle yourself. I have work for you to do." Kiley cut off the next tirade about not getting a chance to rest before resuming his servitude. "Go to that coral formation. Someone has been lurking in the shadows. See what you can find."

Pìn looked at the dark spaces, then back to Kiley, letting out a few quiet chirps.

"It's safer than staying out here in the open, where Mearna can find you."

Pìn continued to mutter profanity about Kiley's parents while hopping toward the nearest crag.

The Supreme Commander ignored the noise. "Who has been watching us? Or the better yet, who do I have to kill?"

CHAPTER 41

Lydeck jumped back when Ceocilus' gaze fell on him. He stayed motionless, pressing his white stomach against the coral, certain that the Royal had spotted him. When he heard no footfalls crunching across the sand in his direction, he let out a deep breath. He peered around the outcropping and made out the form of Supreme Commander Kiley, standing as still as a stone.

He was sure he heard them mention *the Rockhopper* during their conversation, and had no doubt that meant him. And like nearly every other discussion amongst the AIC hierarchy he had eavesdropped on, they mentioned Aperion. It was obvious that Mearna and her lackeys feared Aperion. Lydeck limped further into the moaning cavern, contemplating what he had heard. "Whoever this Aperion is, he's a threat to her." He heard the subtle clink of broken shells behind him and stopped. He listened intently, but the steady drone of the wind muffled any more noise.

He nestled into an area relatively free of debris and let his mind drift to the events that had brought him to this place. Nok and his band of noble warriors had undone all of his work back at the colony. "And Tretak...I hope I never see that penguin again," he grumbled quietly. His toe ached at the thought of her. He let out a breath and stared into the darkness.

"So this was the home of the Oracle? What a dreadful life. Living alone in some desolate cave. This place is more suited for some ne'er-do-well like

Tearsk, rather than a penguin with that kind of power." The thought of Tearsk made his innards quiver. The more he seethed, the more he hated the young Rockhopper. He retraced his steps from the colony to Isla Fortuna and his deal with Mearna. "I went from being the elected Commander to servant in a moon's cycle." As he stewed in his hatred for Tearsk and every other Rockhopper at the colony, a dreadful realization came to him. "I told her about the Oracle." An icy chill ran up his spine. Only a beak full of others knew about it, and once she found out this Oracle was dead, she would kill him to make certain he told no one else.

Lydeck sprung to his feet and began pacing, sliding on centuries of debris with each nervous hop. Fear swam through his body. "I have to leave," he announced to the emptiness. He forced himself to slow down. He had to think this through. "Where would I go? I can't go back to the colony. They'll kill me if I ever show my crest there again." He considered going alone to the north. But a lone penguin in an unfamiliar sea would end up as a meal before long.

In his haze of panic, inspiration struck him. He lauded himself for his cleverness. "Aperion. Aperion is the answer. But how to find this creature?" He thought about all he had heard while eavesdropping on Ceocilus and Kiley. They had seemed keen to keep what they knew from the Doyenne. *They don't trust her,* he thought. He had no doubts that she didn't trust them, or certainly, at least Kiley.

Lydeck slunk to the entrance of the coral monolith and stared out at Supreme Commander Kiley. "I'll use Kiley to find Aperion. But first I have to tell Mearna of his betrayal…whether he plans to or not" He remembered an old penguin adage, *Sometimes, in order to escape a seal, you have to swim straight towards the jaws.* "Now to go wake the beast."

Lydeck stepped outside, keeping a careful eye on Kiley standing only a few meters away. He took another step but froze mid-stride, his foot hanging a fraction above the ground. A quiet clatter above the wind came from behind. "That wasn't natural," he whispered. He crept back inside, squinting toward the darkness, trying to see what hid in the traces of broken moonlight. He moved forward, fighting to keep his mind from filling the darkness with lurking predators and villains.

He scanned the chamber, straining to see any movement. He was about to dismiss his fear on paranoia, when his eyes came to rest on smooth object out of place on jagged rubble. Only the faintest of light caught the odd roundness of what appeared to be a penguin, trying to hide in the dark. He initially thought it might be the body of the dead Oracle, but corpses don't move gravel. Lydeck's heart pounded.

He considered leaving whoever it was to their own devices, and nearly did, but he couldn't recall if he'd been speaking his thoughts aloud or not. He had found a way out of his mess and wasn't going to let anyone stop him. Lydeck moved toward the shape in the dark, cautiously, he didn't know what he had to face.

Whatever hid amongst the rubble didn't move as he approached. The dark played tricks on his eyes, and he lost sight of his quarry. Lydeck continued to half hop toward the spot. He took another lame hop and landed on something soft. The soft lump screeched and skittered away. Lydeck fell back and caught a glint of light tracing the small penguin fleeing deeper into the cave. He cursed, struggled to stand, and took in after the intruder.

He followed the sound of small feet tripping in the darkness. Whatever it was, it was definitely not a fledgling. The sound of the footfalls disappeared when it entered the narrower passage. Lydeck slipped to a stop. The moaning wind tested his resolve. Sea spray from deep in the tunnel warned him to take the chase no further.

It's just wind and waves, he told himself. He followed the curved and narrowing path until the force of the wind and sea-mist forced him to stop. The surf retreated and the wind turned to a whisper. He knew the little penguin had to be there, just out of reach and sight. Another quiet moan of air began to grow. Lydeck braced for the push and spray. The channeled energy of the surf threatened to knock him back. He pictured himself being dragged through the tunnel to an unseen death. When he felt like he could no longer resist the pull, the wind and water retreated.

Lydeck shook the water from his feathers and turned to go back; deciding that whoever he was pursuing must have been sucked into the void. The wind began to grow once more, signaling another surge. With it came the distinguishable sound of tiny footfalls trying to outrace the surf's advance. Lydeck swung his flipper when the steps neared and struck the fleeing penguin harder than he intended. He heard a chirp of protest and pounced on where he guessed the penguin might be. He landed on the penguin, who continued the indecipherable protest.

The concentrated surf battered the two, threatening to haul them both away. Lydeck had no choice but to stand to keep from being pulled to his death. The moment he stood, the small penguin made a dash for freedom. Lydeck tried to slap it once again, but the tiny penguin ducked and ran. Lydeck grunted and took after it.

Lydeck entered the wider chamber and listened for the crunch of debris. All was still but for the continuous labored breaths of the sea. "He couldn't have gone far," he said, straining to see in the faint glow of moonlight. He moved his head in a slow swivel, hoping to catch sight of the uninvited guest. He scanned each shadowy nook until his eyes finally came to rest on the penguin. His eyes smiled with satisfaction.

Rather than advance on his prey directly, Lydeck took a roundabout route. He hobbled over piles of ancient bones and flakes of stone until he stood between the other and the only sure way out. Now was the time for the direct approach. "I see you. You can't escape. Now, tell me who you are and what you're doing in here?" Lydeck waited for a reply. Receiving none, he moved a little closer. "There really is no need for this foolishness. Did someone send you here?" he asked, being answered again with silence. "This will have to turn ugly if you don't answer."

Lydeck had had enough of playing the subservient role. He had been blamed for the murders of other penguins, so why not actually do it this time? He half-hopped toward his victim, firming his resolve, letting the hatred of all life's inequities he had endured buoy his strength. A sudden rattle of tiny rocks, followed by a string of heated chittering snapped him out of his murderous haze. Lydeck stared at the small penguin standing with a splash of moonlight glinting in his angry eyes.

Pìn boldly marched up to Lydeck, laying a barrage of untranslated profanity on the Rockhopper.

"Stop your babbling and use the common language," Lydeck demanded. When Pìn continued to harangue Lydeck, he pushed the Blue penguin to the ground, eliciting a more vehement onslaught of vulgarities. "I don't understand your savage talk. Speak Common, before I lose my patience."

Pìn quieted, stared at Lydeck, and shook his head while turning away.

"It's not wise to turn your back on me." Lydeck struck Pìn, sending him flailing against the wall. "Now, we'll try this once more. Why were you spying on me?"

Pìn got to his feet while scanning the dark, searching for an out. He looked at Lydeck and uttered the only Common phrase he could speak.

Lydeck didn't appreciate having his head likened to guano and struck Pìn again. "If that's all you're going to say, then I have no more use for you." He slapped Pìn back down as he tried to stand.

Pìn scurried back to his feet and made a dash for freedom before Lydeck could deliver the next blow. He leapt over a small heap of stone flakes and tripped on the bones of a dead gull, sending him back to the ground.

Lydeck was on him in an instant, landing with his full weight on the smaller bird. "Not very smart. I had my doubts about killing you, but those doubts are gone."

Pìn lifted his head and pecked Lydeck on the neck. Shocked by an assault from such a diminutive foe, Lydeck stammered for a threat. Finding none, he grunted, took Pìn's flipper in his beak and began to drag him toward the tunnel.

Pin issued insults and protest while being dragged over sharp rocks and rough stone. He fought to free himself, but Lydeck had him firmly in his grip. The Rockhopper bit down a little harder each time he tried to resist.

Dragging a penguin who was half his own weight proved to be more taxing than Lydeck had planned. By the time he reached the point where the waves funneled through, he was spent. He flung Pin forward and rested against the cool, smooth stone. Lydeck shouted above the moan of the approaching surge, "I hope this teaches you a lesson. You shouldn't put your beak where it doesn't belong."

Pin replied with a weak chirping insult.

"But you know what they say, lessons are wasted on the dead." The violent jet of wind and water hit Pin, knocking him forward at first, but then dragging him toward the abyss. Lydeck listened to one final indecipherable torrent of insults before the Little Blue penguin disappeared into the nothingness.

Despite his exhaustion, Lydeck felt unusually light after following through on his first premeditated murder. He had no lingering doubts or remorse. He felt liberated. He hopped and limped toward the exit feeling rather smug and confident about his accomplishment. "Where was I? Oh, yes. Time to inform the *Doyenne* about her Supreme Commander's treason."

CHAPTER 42

Lydeck skulked toward the sleeping Doyenne, ducking behind dozing penguins, and staying out of sight of curious eyes. He poked his head over a prone King and scurried a little closer. He crossed the distance between himself and Mearna's outer ring of Royal Emperors. He moved across the few empty spaces of beach, falling to the sand, feigning sleep, each time a Royal twitched or snorted in its sleep.

The trek was taking excruciatingly long, and he had difficulty keeping his mind on the task. His thoughts wandered back to the small penguin. Had he known that killing a penguin would come so easily, he would have gotten rid of Nok's son himself, and not left it to the ineptitude of that failure Ki-ok. He tried not to dwell on the past, but his fear and paranoia had cost him his chance to become Commander. He shook the thoughts away. He wouldn't make the same mistakes. Now, all of his plans would depend solely on him.

Lydeck squeezed between a pair of Shadow Warriors and his body quivered with revulsion. It was the two who had survived Nok's attack and abandoned the fight. He refocused once again, and crept the remaining distance to Mearna. He looked around, trying to find Ceocilus, knowing he was rarely far from his mother. He scanned the moonlit beach and spotted him some distance away, standing on the ocean's edge, staring out at the breakers. He let out a sigh of relief and leaned close to Mearna's ear.

Lydeck parted his beak to speak, and Mearna's eyes popped open, startling him enough to send him backwards.

"If I thought you had the courage or strength to attempt an assassination, I would kill you. In fact, I should kill just to be rid of the nuisance," Mearna hissed.

Mearna made no attempt to do so, giving Lydeck the courage to approach once again. "My humble apologies for disturbing your slumber, Doyenne. But as your servant, it is my duty to inform you of what could be an attempt to betray you."

Mearna made an exaggerated effort to look at Lydeck. "And who would be fool enough to attempt such a thing?"

Lydeck looked at his bad foot, slowly etching a line in the sand. "The Supreme Commander, Doyenne…and Ceocilus."

Mearna stared at the Rockhopper with unreadable eyes. Lydeck did his best to stand bold under her glare until she barked a laugh. "Tell me, where did you come about this information?"

"I overheard their conversation. They discussed the possibilities and have expressed doubt in your leadership." Lydeck stepped back in case she lashed out.

"I'm sure half of the Alliance has doubts over our direction. Neither Ceocilus nor Kiley has the power to muster a rebellion. Now go away, before I lose my patience."

Lydeck bowed away then lifted his beak in salute. "Yes, Doyenne. My mistake." He took a step away and turned back. "However, I found it odd that they would withhold information from you. Such as the Oracle being dead."

Mearna rose, her full frame looming over Lydeck. "If you are lying to me, I will drown you in the surf."

The satisfied glint in Lydeck's eyes faded to worry for a moment. He had heard about Mearna's disturbing proclivity of standing on insubordinates in the shallows allowing only the tops of their heads to break the surface, giving them a prolonged and tormenting execution. He had never actually seen it happen; it could've been a rumor, but Lydeck wasn't keen on testing the rumor. He forced the satisfaction back to his eyes and bowed to Mearna. "I assure you, Doyenne; I swear on my honor. I am telling the truth."

"You have no honor, Rockhopper. You live only by my grace."

Lydeck bristled inside. *If you had followed through with your promise, we would have had control of the island and not be out here in this desert of water, chasing dead mystics,* he thought, being careful not to think it aloud. "Yes, Doyenne. Be that as it may, you need only to see for yourself. The Supreme Commander is standing guard over the body of…Cryftin, I believe they called him. The Oracle's caretaker, I presume?"

"Cryftin," Mearna spat. "Whatever his fate, I'm sure it wasn't brutal enough for what he deserved."

"If you speak it, then I am certain it is true," said Lydeck, feigning subservience.

"Your opinion is of no consequence," Mearna snapped. "Disappear into the masses. If what you have told me is the truth, then you might be rewarded."

Lydeck backed away. "By your grace, Doyenne." After Mearna roused her guards and waddled away, Lydeck wedged himself between a pair of sleeping Gentoo, eliciting grumbling complaints. A general disturbance caught his attention. He lifted his head in time to see Ceocilus rush past to catch his mother and couldn't help but feel proud of his work. "A grain of sand, and I will soon have my pearl."

CHAPTER 43

Pin fought against the pull of the tide, using every bit of his energy to keep from disappearing into the unknown. He bounced from stone wall to wall more than he swam, each collision edging him nearer to unconsciousness. In the few seconds since being tossed into the vortex, his emotions flipped between fear and anger, and back to fear. He had nearly reached the point of resigning his fate to whatever might come when the pull of the water eased. The remaining seawater raced past Pin, depositing him on a smooth and steeply angled stone.

Pin shifted his weight in an attempt to stand and slid a little further down the tunnel. He scraped his beak along the stone to slow his descent. Coming to rest on a gentle rise in the tube, he laid on his back in relief. He scanned his surroundings; nothing but blackness in either direction. The wind began to push upward once again and he braced himself for the next onslaught.

The water caught Pin and forced him back the way he had come. His first thought was that he would be smashed against the rocks. His second was that he would land at the feet of Lydeck, who would make sure he wouldn't survive a second time. He tumbled through the darkness, calmly awaiting his fate. He slammed against the tunnel wall and felt the water soften. He found himself in an expansive pool with dull light easing through translucent walls. He quickly swam to the edge and scrambled out, feeling the tug of the water on his feet as it began to swirl back down the tunnel.

Pìn lay on the gravelly ground, catching his breath and fighting against passing out from shock and fatigue. Several minutes passed, and he decided that lying on the ground wasn't the best way to avoid any unseen dangers. Getting to his feet he noticed an odd smell, a smell he was too familiar with—the smell of death and decay. He immediately became alert. Sounds heightened and his eyes widened to catch any movement, but the repetitive gasps of the sea and the faint light nearly negated any caution. He came to the conclusion that if he couldn't sense something near, than neither could the something. He followed that with another thought: if there was something in here, it lived here, and would know he was here. Pìn forced himself to stay calm and slow his racing thoughts. What could a monster eat stuck in a cave like this? He concluded that it ate wayward penguins who got sucked into its trap. Pìn chirped profane remarks about his predicament and got to the task of searching the cavern for a way out.

Pìn walked about, scanning the darkness until his eyes came to rest on the large vertebrae. He recognized it immediately as a bone of huge beast and came to a quick halt. If something could make a meal of such a thing, then what would it do to a tiny penguin? He hoped it would see him as too small to be a worthwhile meal.

The smell of something dead grew stronger when he approached the bone. It didn't take long to find the source. Pieces of an unfortunate penguin were scattered on the ground. He carefully examined the parts, trying to determine what sort of penguin it had been. He recognized the body immediately as Hoiho. They lived near his home. He scanned the area once more, keeping alert for anything that would lead him to a similar fate.

Stepping back, Pìn looked to the translucent ceiling, trying to determine when the sun would rise, when his eyes caught sight of an odd protrusion on the top of the bone. He knew it was something he probably didn't want to see, but his curiosity and training as the Overlord's spy compelled him to gather as much information as he could. He circled the vertebrae and found a heap of detritus piled against the back. Guessing it had been used a platform of some sort, Pin climbed up. When he reached the top, he immediately wished he hadn't. A small penguin head laid on the edge, dead eyes peering forward.

Having gone this far, he decided to investigate further. It was without a doubt the Oracle. The display might have been shocking to some, but he had spent two years in service to Overlord Antaean, and the Overlord regularly displayed trophies such as this in his throne room.

Pin hopped down and did a cursory scan of the rest of the chamber. He didn't need to look any further to know what had happened. During his years at PIC, he had heard the stories of Aperion and Lord Saeson living in the dark underbelly of the compound. And though he had never gathered the fortitude to investigate the lower reaches, he had seen the misshapen on more than one occasion. He had even seen the pitiable Kaurochs being forced into submission by their Royal Emperor handlers. He knew that Aperion had been here, Aperion the unredeemable and cannibalistic beast from the shadows, and if Antaean and Liutites were considered mad, then Aperion was a fathom deeper in the sea of insanity than the two combined.

Pin made his way to an alcove in the far wall of the room and found a nest lined with feathers. He took a cautious step into the nest. It was soft, warm, and inviting. He lay down, his eyes growing heavy while listening to the steady rhythm of the waves. His eyes drifted toward the rear of the natural antechamber and it was then that he realized he could hear the ocean from that direction as well. Thinking it had to be an echo, he ignored it for a moment until he felt a light breeze coming from the same place. Curiosity drug him to his feet once more, and he followed the breeze to the narrow end of the nest-chamber. A shaft leading up, sat at the end of the room. It was narrow, but wide enough for a penguin. He looked up the natural chute, spotted easily negotiable ledges leading upward, and followed them.

The shaft terminated at a high ledge a few meters above sea level. Pin quickly scampered out, disturbing several nesting gulls in the process. He looked back, the passage looked like nothing more than a nondescript hole in the ground. He easily hopped down to the shore and looked back up. It had been too easy. It was an easy escape route, not unlike the small spy tunnels that had crisscrossed Pack Ice Command. Pin wondered why the Oracle hadn't used it. She could have easily escaped the brute and saved herself. He dismissed the question. Pin had his freedom. Now he had to decide how to use it.

CHAPTER 44

Supreme Commander Kiley paced around Cryftin's corpse, awaiting the return of either Ceocilus or Pìn. Pìn had been gone too long for his liking. After catching a glimpse of a penguin crest scurry out of the cave, trying to stay hidden in the shadows, he felt a twinge of real concern for Pìn's well-being.

His pacing came to an abrupt stop when he spotted Mearna's large frame waddling uneasily across the beach, headed in his direction. "Betrayed. Ceocilus has betrayed me," he said with equal parts hatred and resignation. Kiley looked around for a possible escape route if it proved to be necessary. He looked at the remains, kicked the crabs away, and considered burying the evidence before the Doyenne arrived. He spotted Ceocilus hurrying to catch his mother. Kiley wouldn't hide the evidence; if he went down, he'd make certain Ceocilus followed.

Mearna approached and slowed her already sluggish pace. She stood in front of Kiley, framed by her Shadow Warrior goons. "Is there something I should know, Supreme Commander?"

She addressed him by rank, which sent a small eddy of relief through Kiley. She hadn't decided to have him executed yet. He looked to Ceocilus, who stood at a distance, watching the scene with caution. "Perhaps; perhaps not, Doyenne. We discovered the body of a dead penguin. Due to its advanced state of decay, we are unsure of which clan it belonged to." He made sure to say 'we' to implicate Ceocilus.

Mearna strode forward, not taking her eyes off of Kiley. She looked down and inspected the remains, paying close attention to the remaining head plume. "Why wasn't I informed immediately?"

Kiley began to speak, but Ceocilus stepped in. "Like the Supreme Commander said, we were unsure of the clan. I asked Supreme Commander Kiley to stand guard until dawn, thinking it best to let you rest. It is clearly not Lapasia, unless I have mistaken her race."

Mearna stared at Ceocilus for several heartbeats. "No. This is not the Oracle. This was Cryftin." She took a few steps away, turning her back on the four others. "If he is dead, then I am certain she is as well. Our journey has been for naught."

"Doyenne," Ceocilus spoke, "we can't be certain of that yet. We will conduct a full investigation at daybreak."

Kiley interrupted before Mearna could reply. "I agree with Ceocilus. There may be a chance she's alive. There's a cave, she could have hidden and escaped from whoever did this."

"No. She is dead. I have on good account that another Oracle has come into being. Lapasia is dead; we have no more need to stay here. You will rouse our forces at dawn, and we will head to sea by midday."

Kiley wanted anything other than to head back toward the Kings territory. He had no doubt that he would be executed for treason if they were to find him. "If I may, Doyenne. I still think a proper investigation is in order. It may not be in your best interest to abandon the search based solely on hearsay."

Mearna turned to one of the Shadow Warriors. "You were there; do you believe that the Oracle was at the Rockhopper colony?"

The Shadow Warrior bowed his head. "It seemed to be an earnest statement, spoken by a youth, ignorant of the gravity of what he said."

"You see, Supreme Commander? Shadow Warriors do not lie. The Oracle is there. We will find her, and when we do, we will find Aperion."

Mearna turned the Shadow Warriors. "Find the Rockhopper. Kill him. He is of no more use to us."

"Gladly, Doyenne," the lead Shadow Warrior said, enthusiastically rushing away to find Lydeck.

Mearna looked between Ceocilus and Kiley. "I am faced with a conundrum. Lapasia must've known about this other Oracle. Therefore, she did one of three things. She could have told Aperion her whereabouts. And knowing Aperion's sadistic nature, he may very well have tortured the information from her. Another possibility is that she lied to him. But from what I understand, an Oracle is incapable of dishonesty. Or at least, she is bound by the Ancients to speak truthfully. Therefore, Aperion may still be heading north."

"But we don't know that Aperion has even left the homeland," Kiley said. "He could—"

"No, Supreme Commander. Aperion leaves a trail of death. This is evidence enough," she said, indicating the skeletal remains. "The other possibility, and most likely, is that Aperion killed her before she could answer, or because she wouldn't. So he is likely still heading north under the assumption his queen is there."

"So which direction do we go?" Ceocilus asked.

Mearna looked at her son and then to Kiley with an unpleasant gleam in her eyes. "Both."

"Both?" Kiley said. "I don't how that would work. We need to decide which direction and go that way." He had no desire to face the Order of Kings with diminished numbers behind him.

"It will work, Supreme Commander. We will divide the forces. You will take half of the Alliance and make your way north. You will make several blatant coastal attacks along your journey, drawing human attention away from the south, and perhaps attract Aperion's attention. This was your idea to begin with, if I'm not mistaken?"

Kiley said nothing. Sending out decoys was all fine and good as long as he wasn't the decoy.

"You will be Commander of the Northern Alliance. Seek out Aperion. If by some small chance you find him, kill him, and then you may return south." Mearna continued to stare at Kiley. "And Ceocilus will be commander of the southern forces. We will find this new Oracle."

Supreme Commander Kiley stared at Mearna. She had found out about their plans, however tentative they were, and she separated him from Ceocilus. She had beaten him. "As you command, Doyenne," Kiley said, barely masking his disdain.

"I'm glad we agree, Commander. You will take contingents of Rockhoppers, Kings, and Gentoo with you. You have your battle; now, don't disappoint me." Mearna nudged Ceocilus to come with her.

Kiley shared a look with Ceocilus. It was up to Ceocilus to end her reign now. He briefly considered attacking Mearna, killing her and ending his troubles. He would convince the Order of Kings that that was his plan all along and he would be seen as a hero. But, Ceocilus wasn't ready. There would be no way he would stand idly by while Kiley murdered his mother. Now, if he could only find Pin.

CHAPTER 45

Lydeck heard the commotion of the Shadow Warriors pushing and shoving sleeping penguins in their search. They were looking for him, he knew it. He had given Mearna information and now she was going to make sure he wouldn't share that information. He had known the risks, and they were about to prove too much.

Lydeck sat still, his heart beating fast. He had to think of something quick. Shadow Warriors were beyond negotiating. They were single-minded assassins, and they were coming for him. Lydeck got to his feet and staying low, scurried between larger penguins. He looked to the ocean. Escaping to the sea was not an option. With moonlight beaming on the wet sand, he'd be spotted in an instant.

He surveyed the beach, trying to formulate a plan. Then he found it. He slinked to where a large group of Rockhoppers were sleeping huddled together. He circled the outside of the huddle, searching for what he needed. He poked his head up and spotted the dark figures inspecting where he had been. He continued circling the group until he found his mark: a Rockhopper sleeping with its foot untucked. It was a female, but he doubted the Shadow Warriors could tell the difference.

He leaned in close, his beak inches away from the exposed foot. He opened his beak, and the Rockhopper shifted in her sleep, causing a wave of semi-conscious complaints from her neighbors. Lydeck waited for the grumbles to die down and leaned back in. For a moment, he almost felt a twinge of guilt for what he was about to do. *Better her than me*, he thought. He could hear the groans of complaint from sleeping penguins and knew the Shadow Warriors were getting closer. No more time to waste. He took an exposed toe in his beak, clamped down hard, and spun his body, inflicting as much damage as he could on the unsuspecting Rockhopper. The Rockhopper yelled out and tried to pull away. Lydeck held tight as long as he could and released the toe.

The huddle awoke in a cacophony complaints and expletives. Lydeck moved away as the mass of Rockhoppers berated his victim for disturbing their slumber. He ducked into a group of roused Kings, hiding in the crowd until he got a safe distance away from the chaos.

He watched the Shadow Warriors march across the beach, taking up positions on either side of the Rockhoppers. The Shadows ordered the Rockhoppers into a lineup. They stood shoulder to shoulder, demanding the meaning to the intrusion. Several Royal Emperors came to the Shadow Warriors sides and after a brief conversation, the lead Shadow began to walk down the line, inspecting each Rockhopper top to bottom. When they reached the female Lydeck had maimed, they examined her foot. There was a brief, but heated exchange of calls before the Shadow Warrior forced her from the lineup. The Royal Emperors stood between her and the Rockhoppers. In an instant, the Shadow pierced the Rockhopper through her neck and chest with two savage stabs. The mob of Rockhoppers pressed forward, but any thoughts of retaliation were quickly suppressed by the Royals.

Lydeck stared, wide-eyed, awestruck by the cold lethality demonstrated by the Shadow Warrior. He shuddered, knowing it could have been him. "Too bad for her," he said to himself, without a hint of sincerity. He watched a minute longer and spotted Ceocilus rushing to the scene. He lost interest, slipping away into the waning darkness, plotting his escape from the atoll.

CHAPTER 46

Ceocilus arrived on the scene and examined the dead Rockhopper, then turned his attention toward the Shadow Warrior. "This was uncalled for," he hissed.

The Shadow Warrior stepped closer to Ceocilus, glaring, his eyes carrying a glint of satisfaction and menace. "It was the Doyenne's orders. Perhaps you should take it up with her."

Ceocilus took a step closer as well, meeting the other's glare. "It would be wise for you to mind your tone when speaking to me."

"I answer only to Mearna, not her fledgling."

Ceocilus growled, puffing his chest, prepared to strike if necessary. "You seem to think your status with her grants you immunity. I promise you it does not. Tell me your name so I can inform her whose corpse I will leave for the gulls."

The Shadow Warrior looked Ceocilus over. Though not fully mature, he carried the size of his father, Antaean, and it was enough for the Shadow to reconsider his posturing. "I am sure the loss of her fledgling might cause the Doyenne an unneeded distraction. With that in mind, we will continue our discussion another time." He turned his back on Ceocilus and walked away.

Ceocilus was tempted drive his beak into the base of the Shadow Warrior's skull, but an attack from behind would be a coward's way. "I asked your name, Shadow."

The Shadow Warrior turned his head, his black coat gleaming in the moonlight. "Adikos," he said. "Remember it, fledgling."

Ceocilus considered rushing the insolent warrior when Kiley arrived, interrupting the dispute. "Making friends, Ceocilus?"

Ceocilus spun toward the King, his body feeling the rush of an impending fight. Something he hadn't experienced since his training at PIC. Seeing Kiley take a step back, he steadied himself, letting out a long breath. "I usually don't want to kill my friends."

"Are allies included in your list of things not to kill?" Kiley joked, trying to ease the tension.

"If you're referring to the Shadow Warrior, he's not an ally." He looked at the crowd of distraught Rockhoppers and lost any feeling of humor he had gained. "He killed one of our own. It appears that the Overlord's influence still prevails in our ranks."

Kiley looked at the dead Rockhopper. "Why would they kill this Rockhopper? Was he provoked?"

Ceocilus gave Kiley a look, telling him that he should know why.

The Supreme Commander approached a grieving Rockhopper. "Tell me what happened here?"

The Rockhopper shot a look at Kiley and quickly settled himself when he saw who was speaking to him. "That, that *thing* killed my mate. That's what happened."

"Do you have any idea why? Tell me in detail so I can get to the bottom of this and have him brought up on charges," Kiley said, trying to give an appearance of still having authority.

The Rockhopper went into a lengthy report about the incident, after which Ceocilus leaned toward Kiley. "I believe the Doyenne's pet is behind this."

"Could he have something to do with the separation of our forces? If he overheard our conversation…"

"Without a doubt. Mearna needs us…for now. Keep an eye on your wake during your swim north; I wouldn't put it past her to send an assassin." Knowing the Rockhopper's vindictive nature, he turned his attention to the group. "I promise you, this will not go unanswered. It will take time. Any ideas of retaliation will just make it much more difficult."

A murmur of anger and distrust buzzed through the group. The Supreme Commander stepped in to quell the growing rage. He lowered his head to the lead Rockhopper. "Plans are in motion," he said in hushed voice. "Keep it amongst yourselves. Know that they will not go unpunished."

Ceocilus stood with his back against first pale light of dawn. He surveyed the atoll, watching the multitude of penguins begin to awake. They had lost everything. It was time for change once more. They needed to return to their unassuming lifestyle before they were all pushed into extinction.

He watched Kiley mill about the groups, informing them of his push northward. He feared that extinction might come regardless of their path. Ceocilus had learned the truth from the elder members of the Resistance. The truth that his father, the Overlord, had made alliances with the humans, the enemy he had sworn to destroy. He also learned that the war was nothing more than an end to the means, a purge, a culling of the so-called lesser clans, so that the Royal Emperors would no longer have to compete for the diminishing resources. But unlike his father, and by all appearances, his mother as well, Ceocilus had a conscience to do what was right for all concerned. And if that meant removing the Doyenne from power, so that they would no longer pursue whatever warped vision she had, then so be it.

CHAPTER 47

Supreme Commander Kiley calmly strode on the shoreline, addressing each of his commanding officers. "Admiral Welsy, you will be commander on our coastal assaults. Our mission is to strike and fade. We go ashore, hit the humans hard, with our full strength, and retreat to the sea. Each raid will take place near dusk to allow our escape."

Welsy cleared his throat while looking at the surrounding commanders. "Sir, what do you hope to accomplish by such raids? The humans will undoubtedly seek us out. We have nothing to gain by these strikes and it will likely draw needless attention on our journey north. It will lead to unnecessary losses."

Kiley looked to the other commanders, asking them all if they felt the same way. Nearly all did. "I appreciate your concerns. Your devotion to the wellbeing of our members is admirable." He paused and looked around the beach conspiratorially. "With the Doyenne's forces away, I can finally speak freely. Our mission is the first phase of a multi-pronged plan set in motion by myself and Ceocilus. Our intent is in fact to draw the human's attention."

The news caused a stirring among the officers. Welsy spoke up. "Sir, are you suggesting that we should be decoys…bait?"

"If you will let me continue, Admiral Welsy." His tone didn't match the politeness in his words. "The Doyenne is fixated on finding an Oracle.

Now I know most of you have by now heard the stories about Aperion, so I won't elaborate. Why she is so intent on finding him is of little consequence to our plans. But, rumor has it that he too is heading north. But again, that has little to do with us and our plans. We will continue north and carry out these raids to draw the human's attention away from the southern forces, allowing Ceocilus undivided attention to undermine the Doyenne's authority and take control of the alliance."

"And what good will that do us?" Welsy asked.

"We will proceed north for a season, at which point we will return south posthaste, take control of the alliance, and end the Royals' dominion once and for all."

Once again Welsy spoke up. "Why not follow them now and take control?"

Kiley tried to mask his irritation. Welsy was not unlike a younger version of himself, constantly questioning the leadership and their motives. Kiley answered with forced patience. "We can't hope to accomplish our goals with the Royal Emperors backing Mearna. Ceocilus is key. He will demand loyalty from them, and only he is capable of such a thing. We'll let him do the hard work of inciting another rebellion, if it comes to that. We will swoop in like a petral stealing a snowbird's catch, and we will once again have control of our homes."

"I hope this works. I, for one, look forward to returning to our homes and seeing the beaches brown with youthful feathers," Welsy said.

"As do I. When we reunite with the Order of Kings, our task will be made that much easier." Supreme Commander Kiley looked at his officer corps. Not the best there had ever been, but the best of what he had. "Our first stop is the Galapagos. I have allies there who I hope will join our struggle. You are dismissed. See that your respective companies are to sea immediately."

The officers went to see about their duties. Kiley stopped Admiral Welsy before he got away. "Admiral, come here for a moment. We need to speak."

Welsy hesitated before approaching Kiley. "My apologies if my question were out of line, sir."

"No, no, no. It's understandable. With what we've been through, I'm surprised half of contingent hasn't defected."

"I would never—"

"I know you wouldn't. You're a King. We are a proud and dedicated group. That's why it is only natural in these unnatural circumstances we find ourselves in, that we ascend to the role of leadership. And that, Admiral Welsy, is why I asked you to stay behind."

"I'm not sure I understand, Supreme Commander," Welsy said, the apprehension in his voice obvious.

"With the Doyenne taking half of our contingent southward, I find myself without a second. I think you would be a perfect fit for Commandant." Kiley watched Welsy wrestle with the idea of a promotion.

"I gladly accept, sir." Welsy lifted his beak in salute.

"Very good, Commandant. See that you find a suitable replacement for your position. Dismissed." Kiley watched the young King scoot away, filled with obvious anxiety over his new responsibilities. Supreme Commander Kiley let out a satisfied breath. First Mearna, with her brutal and stupid order to kill a penguin in plain sight of the alliance, carried out by an equally stupid brute, the result of which practically ensured the Rockhoppers being open to rebellion. Now Welsy, the only King this side of the Strait of Magellan with a glimmer of independent thought was now devoted in service to him. There would be no one to stop him now. Not Ceocilus, not Mearna, and if the Order of Kings refused to acknowledge his authority, King Elinthaw would be shown that like all things old, his way of thinking would die with him.

Kiley walked to the water's edge, but hesitated before going in. He scanned the coastline, searching one last time for Pin. Finding nothing, he lowered his head and fell into the waves.

CHAPTER 48

Pin watched the multitude of penguins head to sea. He nestled in his nook, safe from any eyes. He really was free. He spotted the Supreme Commander leave. It almost appeared as if Kiley would miss him. He knew better, though. Kiley had been his master, a fact he'd held over Pin on most days. He was not unlike Antaean—a bully to the smaller things. Though he did have to admit that there was one large difference; Kiley wasn't a murderous wretch like the Overlord. Pin's thoughts fell back to seeing his friends murdered by Antaean. He could do nothing but stand and watch, and hope that he wouldn't be next. The horror of seeing their lifeless bodies tossed across the room, stuck with him. He would never forget.

He had to figure out his next move. He considered staying on the atoll; there was plenty of food. He could live the rest of his life as a hermit, far away from wars and trouble. But that wouldn't do. He had to find a way home. He firmed his beak and stood bravely against the sea. Home was where he belonged, and home was where he'd go. He hopped down, set to go, when movement caught his eye. He fell back into cover and watched. A bouncing yellow head plume attached to a limping Rockhopper scurried to the shore and swam away, headed towards Kiley's group.

Pin watched the waves for a moment longer then hopped to the beach. He knew it was the Rockhopper who tried to kill him. He considered going after him, but knew it wouldn't do any good. He walked toward the opposite shore, pausing to look at Cryftin's bones, picked clean by the crabs, which, in turn, were picked from the beach by the seabirds. He continued to the south shore and found the deceased Rockhopper. Pìn chased away the scavengers and examined the body. The gulls returned as quickly as they'd fled and chased Pìn away.

So much needless death. He shook his head and stepped into the cold water, feeling the dying waves lap at his feet. He took a few more steps. The strength of the surf increased, pushing against his body. He pondered the meaning of it all. The vile always seemed to hold power. He took another step against the surf and remembered an old adage taught to him by an old Blue penguin long ago: *The surf may be chest-deep to you, but to others it is as deep as their feet.* He correlated the lesson to the dead Rockhopper. He had been around enough to know the work of Royal Emperors. To the Royals, her death was insignificant, probably an object lesson to instill discipline, but for her mate, it was the end of the world.

Pìn sighed. He fell backwards and let the waves carry him to shore. He didn't have a plan. He didn't know what he could do to stop any of the insanity; he only knew he had to do something. For now, that something was wait. The penguins might come back this way. The cold current ran directly through this strand of beach. The Rockhopper might have Aperion in tow, if Aperion didn't eat him first. He didn't know how he would deal with that; he would jump down its throat and choke the beast to death if he had to, but he would do something.

He got to his feet, strode across the guano speckled sand, and kicked at the clumps for allowing him to have a conscience.

CHAPTER 49

Trofim double-checked rations and armaments while listening to Leepoh and Yulian discuss a myriad of topics, with Keith chiming in. It was the first time in a long time that Trofim felt any sense of ease. He even let himself laugh when the Gentoo corrected Yulian's English. The days he had spent at Bellingshausen Station let him regain some strength, and he'd even put on some weight, in spite of the awful food.

Tro walked around the Mi-38 Russian helicopter. He examined the extra fuel tanks necessary to make the flight to Ushuaia, Argentina. It was a large helicopter, not inconspicuous in the least, but Yulian had decided that it was best-suited for Trofim's needs. He would refuel in Argentina and be able to head to parts unknown to lay low, the better to figure out his best course of action in the hunt for Colonel Jenson.

Thibaud approached Trofim and handed him a large knife, not unlike the one he had lost during his fight with Talus. "Yulian said you looked naked without it. The quartermaster or supply chief, or whatever they call him, handed it to me on the way out. So…there you go."

Trofim unsheathed the blade immediately. He swung the knife, getting a feel of the heft. He raised it against the sky, reflecting sunlight into Yulian's eyes. The other offered a gesture as if to say it was nothing, and Tro gave a salute with the knife in return. He turned his attention back to checking supplies and felt Thibaud staring at his back. "What do you want to say, friend?"

"That intel we got on Jensen is two days old. He might not be in Peru by the time you get there."

"I don't expect him to be."

Thibaud exhaled. "Then why go? He knows you're alive now. He'll be expecting you."

"I hope he is. He caught me off guard the last time, this time he won't be so lucky. He will be nervous, maybe cocky, thinking I can't get to him. He'll be wrong. And I will kill him." Trofim patted his knife to show just how he will do the job.

"Provided we don't get shot out of the sky on our journey, there is also the fact that killing an American officer carries harsh penalties of its own." Thibaud looked down and stepped aside as Leepoh pushed his way past him like a little general. He was about to say so, when Yulian spoke from behind him.

"The Americans wouldn't dare shoot down a Russian helicopter. It would be an act of war, and they don't have their pieces in place yet to begin such a fight," Yulian said. "And Tro, my friend, this colonel answers to someone else, a man by the name of Bryan Turlock. The American who runs GT. I find it strange that the military answers to a corporation."

"It's America. That's the way they do things," Trofim said, looking down at Leepoh, who seemed to be trying to figure out the conversation. "And from what we already know, it seems GT has been calling the shots from the beginning. I don't find it strange at all."

"Not at this point in the game," said Thibaud. "They usually set the goals and back off to let the military handle the rest. GT is deeper in this than anything I've seen before."

"And I just received word that Jenson's location is unknown. He's no longer in Peru. He could be headed back to America, or even back here. You might be crawling into a deeper pit than you can climb out of," Yulian said, resting his hand on Trofim's shoulder.

Tro looked at his friends. Thibaud carried a serious, but unreadable expression; Yulian, looking at him with the eyes of a mentor and surrogate father; and Keith sitting on a crate, scratching his head under his donegal, remaining oddly quiet. Trofim placed both hands on Yulian's shoulders and gave them a firm squeeze. "*Otets*, if we don't know where he is, then I'll wait. I'll find a quiet island and train until I hear something. I'm not going to rush in and get myself killed. I'm going to finish this, and then I'm out. I need to…I just need to stop."

"Once we hit Ushuaia, I'm done. I can't help you," Thibaud said.

Trofim turned his embrace to Thibaud. "I know. You've done enough already. I owe you a great debt."

Thibaud gripped Tro's forearm. "You won't know where I'll be to pay me back. After that job we did in Australia, let's just call it even."

Trofim let out a small laugh at the memory. "Keith will be in America. If I need any help, he'll be around, and I still have the connections with BCU."

"I'll be in a hot stinkin' desert, that's where I'll be. An' it's a far cry better than this place. Then again, maybe not. It's the high desert in California. I'd say that place is like an armpit, but I wouldn't insult an armpit like that." Keith stood and looked at the landscape. "I might just miss this place. I'm trading the blissful scenery of ice and sea and mountains for brown hills, brown water, and brown air. Aye, but it pays well."

Yulian raised an eyebrow at Keith. "You know, Trofim…I miss those days of freedom. I should like to do that once more before my time ends."

"You should go with Keith. I'm sure BioCon won't hold any hard feelings," Tro said, looking at the clear blue sky.

"And go AWOL? And spend my life in a Russian prison? No, I would like to return home one day as well. Though I don't know why." Yulian paused and released a long heavy sigh. "I am shackled to a desk now. I'm too old and slow for that kind of work. Besides, I can help you more from here."

"We should go," Thibaud said. "I want to be there by nightfall."

"Take care of my helicopter. I'm not so sure we made a fair trade," Yulian said, smothering Thibaud's hand in his. He turned to Keith next. "Have fun in California, my friend. Enjoy the sunshine and bikinis."

"The only bikinis I'll be seein' there is me own briefs."

"I didn't need to hear that," Thibaud said, climbing into the helicopter.

Yulian squatted down as close to eye-level with Leepoh as he could get. "You take care of Tro. He needs to be looked after. And don't you worry, there's people working to set the world right. You'll have your home again."

"Bah! When you've had a lot of friends who have been eaten, it's never right." Leepoh looked for a boost from Trofim. Receiving one, he climbed into a makeshift travel crate.

Trofim blocked out the sound of Leepoh and Keith arguing over who should be in the box and faced Yulian. Suddenly feeling like he would never see the man again, he found himself at a loss for words. The sound of the helicopter coming to life let him hide in his silence.

"They are expecting you in Ushuaia," Yulian said, freeing Trofim from saying goodbye. Yulian took him in a firm embrace, which was returned by Trofim. He kissed him on the cheek, patted him on both shoulders, and stepped back, watching him close the air stairs. He got a safe distance away and watched the helicopter begin to rise. He caught sight of Trofim's face appear in the cockpit window just before the blades kicked up enough dusty ice to block his vision. "*Proschay moy syn*," Yulian mouthed. "*Proshaiy.*"

CHAPTER 50

The helicopter touched down just after sunset on the outskirts of Ushuaia. Thibaud let Trofim land since it would be his helicopter and he needed to get the feel of it. A partially-lit helipad cornered by three guard towers made the landing somewhat difficult, but he had landed in worse conditions. The landing hadn't made him nervous, but the lack of any personnel meeting them on the pad did. It had been his experience that if someone didn't have anything to hide, they usually didn't. Trofim and Thibaud looked at each other, both feeling a certain wrongness about the area.

Trofim climbed into the back and began loading weapons. Keith followed suit without asking questions. "Turn off the interior lights," Tro barked to Thibaud, fishing out night vision binoculars. He scanned the surroundings from the port windows, moving to each one down the line.

"What do ya see?" Keith asked.

"Nothing." He ditched the night vision for a thermal scope. "I got movement. Two armed personnel twenty meters left of the north tower. Don't see anything in the…wait. Possible RPG in the east tower." He jumped to other side. "Three SUVs…Chevy Suburbans, parked fifty meters down the south road, likely armored."

"What do you want to do?" Thibaud asked, slapping a magazine into a sidearm.

"Let's just take off," Keith said. "Maybe we got the wrong place."

"No, this is the place. We're low on fuel. Not enough to get us to Chile," Thibaud said.

Leepoh stepped out of the crate. "Is this all you humans do is fight each other? I swear to the Ancients, I don't know how you conquered the world."

"You need to stay in your box, penguin," Tro said. "I didn't take you all this way just to get shot."

"Bah! I didn't come all of this way to stay in a box, either."

"Just stay in there," Trofim said, not masking his protectiveness of the bird.

Leepoh picked up on Trofim's tone and stepped back inside. "A bite or two of fish would be nice, if I have to stay in here."

"We can't stay in here all night," Thibaud said.

Trofim continued to scan the perimeter. If there was anybody out there with bad intentions, they wanted him. Tro wasn't willing to put his friends in harm's way again. He surveyed the compound once more and spotted someone walking to the helipad. "You two stay here. Someone is coming."

"I'm not letting ya go out there an' gettin' shot up," Keith protested. Thibaud said nothing.

"If they wanted us dead, we would be dead already. Just stay here." Without any further discussion, Trofim slung his weapons and tossed Keith the thermal scope. He lowered the stairs, and poked his head out. His head didn't explode, it was safe so far. He casually walked down the steps, keeping his eyes moving, watching for potential threats. He took a few cautious steps toward the man at the edge of the pad, when the other called his name through a thick Russian accent. *That's a good sign*, he thought.

"Trofim Grekov," the man called again. "Welcome," he continued, speaking Trofim's native tongue.

"Not much of a welcome," Trofim said, keeping the conversation in Russian and, looking at the towers.

"They're aiming at your friends down the lane who say you are a criminal, wanted for murdering thirty men in Antarctica."

"It wasn't thirty. You spoke to them?"

"Yes. I told them I know nothing of your alleged crimes, and reminded them that this base houses Russian diplomats. And any act to try to take you by force would be an act of war."

"What did the American look like?" he asked, though he already knew the answer.

"Tall, pale skin, blue eyes. Red cheeks. I take it you know him?"

"Yes. And I'm going to kill him." Trofim looked toward the helicopter and gave the all-clear signal. Keith and Thibaud exited armed to the teeth.

The other fixed him with an examining look, followed by a nod of approval. "I apologize for my rudeness; I am Iosif. Yulian said you will need to be refueled. Feel free to use the facilities while you're here."

The four men walked to the nearest building, making introductions. Once the door closed behind them, Trofim spun toward Keith. "Jenson is here. His men are parked down the street. How long do you have before you make your connection?"

Keith checked his watch. "'Bout an hour. What's your plan?"

"Thibaud?" Trofim asked.

"I have to be at Malvinas Argentinas Airport in thirty minutes."

"Perfect," Tro said. "Iosif, is transportation arranged for him?"

"Yes. I have a car waiting in the garage. Tell me what you're planning. I need to know whether or not I will be expecting visitors from the police."

"Thibaud, leave the main gate in ten minutes. Does that give him enough time to get there, Iosif?"

"Yes, yes. The traffic is light this time of day." Iosif waved a soldier over and informed him to escort Thibaud to the garage.

Trofim looked at Thibaud. "When you get to those vehicles, stop for thirty seconds. If you can see which vehicle Jenson is in, tap your brakes to indicate which one. Arouse their suspicion and leave. That's all you have to do."

"I was hoping to leave under better circumstances, but it seems the better circumstances await me at home. It has been good working with you. You will not be forgotten." Thibaud shook Trofim's hand and allowed himself to be escorted away.

"Keith, you do what you do best. Create a…what's the word? A ruckus. Get their attention after Thibaud leaves."

"A ruckus is what I do," Keith said with a joyful exuberance, heading toward the door. "I got just the thing."

"Iosif, show me to a back door," Trofim said, unshouldering two automatic rifles, removing three frag grenades; he double checked two pistols, holstering them in his tac vest, and securing flashbangs.

"First tell me what you plan to do. I can't take this lightly, this country is in a state of war with Great Britain and they can make things difficult for us, if whatever you're planning on goes awry."

Trofim began to stretch and loosen tight muscles, all the while trying to meditate as he always did before a fight. "All right, Iosif. First I'm going to go kill Jenson and then I'm going to get in the helicopter and fly away from here." He closed his eyes and took a few cleansing breaths.

"No big explosions or loud gunfire?"

"Pistols are silenced, for what that's worth, and my grenades are on the table." Trofim walked toward the door. "The road is lined with low buildings. It looks like most of the buildings are abandoned. They're parked single file on a narrow road, which leaves them open for an ambush. And that tells me either they're not regular military, or they're not very smart, or they aren't expecting anything. Or it is all of these things. Jenson is cocky. He acts like someone who can't be touched. I'm going to show him otherwise."

"Very well. Yulian speaks very fondly of you. And I can tell that you aren't a homicidal maniac. The back door is this way. But please, remember to try not to make a mess." Iosif took Trofim by the shoulder and led him away.

CHAPTER 51

Trofim followed a long tunnel which terminated at a stairwell, just as Iosif had said it would. He climbed the stairs, checking his watch. Thibaud would leave in three minutes. A large steel door greeted him at the top of the stairwell. He reached for the handle, which didn't budge. Trofim felt a twinge of anxiety rise up. He had a narrow window. If he didn't see Thibaud's signal, things would be much more difficult. He checked his watch one more time and jiggled the door handle. His lips pursed and he looked back down the stairwell. No time to get back. He searched his tactical vest for something to rap against the steel door other than his knuckle. He knocked again and the click of an internal lock echoed. Trofim stepped back as the heavy door swung outward.

He stepped into a low-lit room, weapon drawn, and saw men stationed at different tables staring at laptops. The building was anything but abandoned. The door closed behind him and Trofim stared at a wood panel wall. He rubbed his hand along the door seam, nodding his head in approval.

"The door is on the right, Tro," a woman's voice said from the darkest corner.

Trofim squinted. "Agnes? I haven't seen you since…Marrakesh."

"Yeah, it's been awhile. Thanks for bringing Keith in. A little late, but since when do things go as planned?"

"I would like to stay, but…"

"Go. I'll see you again sometime."

Trofim paused for a moment. She'd probably be gone when he got back. "Keith will be happy to see you," he said, and reached the door.

"I doubt it."

Trofim shook his head. The past weeks had been like a family reunion. People who he hadn't even heard from, some, like Agnes, who he thought might be dead, just kept popping up. It wasn't a surprise though. An event as big as the Antarctic disturbance was bound to draw a crowd; it would especially attract those from BioCon. He wondered if they were after Colonel Jenson as well. He checked his watch. Two minutes.

He ducked out the door, surveyed the near wall, jumped on top of a dumpster and pulled himself to the flat roof. Staying low, Trofim crept to the edge just in time to see Thibaud's headlights appear at the gate. He shook his head at seeing Thibaud rattling down the street in a beat up micro-van. He hoped Thibaud didn't have to make a getaway in the thing.

The black SUVs, parked in front of the next building down, remained in place with engines idling. Trofim stood and ran along the roof top, keeping pace with the tiny van. Thibaud brought the van to a sudden stop alongside the SUVs, moist brakes echoing against the barren walls of the abandoned buildings. Trofim timed his leap to match Thibaud's piercing stop and landed on the next building, barely keeping his balance on the hipped roof. He scrambled to the edge and waited.

Thibaud let the van sit in the middle of the road. Trofim could just make out his form in the dashboard light, behind a haze of fogged glass. He waited while the cars sat, unmoving with plumes of vapor billowing from exhaust pipes. It was obvious that Thibaud couldn't see through the blackened windows of the motorcade.

"Just go," Trofim whispered, not wanting Thibaud to put himself at any more risk. Several seconds passed by and he was about try a different strategy when the front and rear passenger doors of the lead and trailing

Suburbans opened. Six men dressed in generic military fatigues rounded the vehicles, walking with purpose toward the van. The micro-van jumped to life and sped away, its gears grinding in the night.

"I'm going to miss working with him," Trofim said. No passengers got out of the middle vehicle, making that the likely candidate for Jenson's car.

At that same moment, he heard a squawking penguin and Keith shouting, giving a good show of trying to capture the bird.

Trofim slid to the edge and let himself ease down while the men stood in the road watching the broken tail lights disappear around a corner. He crouched in the shadows, waiting. Two men slid into their seats, leaving the third to walk around the back.

Trofim pulled a flashbang from his vest pocket, pulled the pin, and waited until the last man opened the rear door. When the man slid in, Trofim rushed forward, tossed the stun grenade on the floorboard, and ducked away, slamming the door behind him. A half second later, a muffled explosion and bright flash sent the passengers falling out of the Suburban, half-blinded and partially deaf from a one hundred seventy decibel blast.

Trofim drew his sidearm and made his way around the back of the SUV. He came to the first passenger who stumbled toward him, holding his hands over his eyes. Trofim side-stepped and landed a strike to the back of his neck, sending him to the ground. The driver was on his knees, holding his ears. A snap kick to the jaw stole the man's consciousness.

Two men from the lead truck stepped out and shouted something in Spanish. Trofim jumped in the driver's side, leaving the door open. By the men speaking Spanish Trofim knew that they were most likely local thugs for hire. A spray of machine gun fire rattled against the open door, bullets making their way up until they flew over the top of the SUV. Judging by the way they handled their weapons, they were definitely amateurs. Trofim almost felt bad when the burst ended and he leaned out and fired four quick shots, dropping both men.

Trofim spotted a man poke his head around the right side of the truck ahead of him. He looked over and tried to gauge if he could close the passenger door before the man got to it. Probably not. He threw the SUV into gear, stomped on the accelerator, and slammed into the other, the impact jarring the doors closed. He threw the shifter in reverse and felt a thump. One more man down. He slammed it back into drive and in the next instant he found himself hoping the windshield really was ballistic glass when the rear window of Jenson's SUV opened and machine gun fire began to spray across the glass. The window held. He floored the accelerator once more, slamming into it again.

He leapt from the cab, leaving it in gear, hoping to repeat his flashbang stunt through the open window. He never got the chance. A bear-sized man slammed him against the fender. *Where the hell did he come from?* Trofim dropped his pistol and brought his arms up to protect his head before a barrage of punches began. He endured the blows and caught a brief reprieve when the sack of muscle reared back to throw a haymaker. The fraction of a second was all he needed. He threw a quick left jab, smashing the brute's septum. *Why do the big ones always do that?* he wondered.

The haymaker never landed. Trofim stepped in and delivered a front kick to create separation. He stepped in again and attempted two snap kicks to the groin which met a protective cup. It hurt the man, but not enough to stop him. Trofim took a few quick steps back, creating space to draw his other pistol. The bulk of angry muscle charged at him, half-blinded by the broken nose and rage. Tro side-stepped when the other got near, spun, and landed a palm thrust to the back of his skull, assisting the forward momentum. It planted the man's head against the window.

The brute stumbled back and threw a half-conscious swing at Trofim. Trofim responded by placing his leg behind the man's legs and grabbing his face, slamming his head against the asphalt. Trofim retrieved his dropped pistol and turned his attention back to Jenson's SUV. He took a step forward, and a large hand grabbed his ankle. He had to admire the beast's resilience, but some people just didn't know when to quit. Tro twisted back and kicked him in the head. He followed up by firing two rounds into the big guy's backside, one for each cheek, to make sure he stayed down.

The lead SUV screeched forward, forced to make a three-point turn in the narrow roadway. Jenson's followed suit. Trofim tried to grab the door of the one he left in drive, but it slid out of his grip and vehicle veered right and into a building. The Suburban had finished its U-turn and sped away, leaving Jenson's behind to complete its turn. Trofim ran toward the truck, firing a pair of rounds at the windows to discourage any ideas of anyone lowering them to shoot at him. He reached the SUV as it was backing up from its three-point turn. He reached into his vest pouch, and pulled out another flashbang, regretting his decision to leave the frag grenades behind. He dropped his gun, pulled the pin, and jumped onto the hood as the driver put it into drive. With no other recourse, Trofim pulled back a wiper blade and wedged the flashbang against the window.

The Suburban lurched forward and Trofim rolled off the hood. A second later the grenade exploded and the SUV swerved back and forth until it rammed into the stoop of the next building down. He became dimly aware of sirens wailing in the distance. He hesitated, trying to gauge the distance of the sirens. The vehicle backed up and raced away, taking away any chance of catching Jenson while in Argentina.

Trofim quickly retrieved his weapon and began trotting toward the Russian compound. He desperately wanted to question some of the downed men, but didn't have the time. The sirens were close. He ran through the partially open gate, drawing a disapproving look from Iosif while walking by. He continued past Keith, who was shaking his head with a smile; he looked down at Leepoh who ruffled his feathers.

"Remind me not to upset him," Leepoh said to Keith.

"I'll be too busy reminding myself," Keith said, nudging Leepoh back toward the helicopter.

CHAPTER 52

"In light of your escapades, my commander believes it is time for you to go," Iosif said, his voice loud and echoing in the institutional green hallway. He looked down the hall, closed the door behind, and lowered his voice. "But he is not aware of the work you do. Nor can he be. Keeping that in mind, I will let you stay until your partner leaves."

Trofim sat in a wooden chair, with his arm resting on a steel table. "I did as you asked; I was silent. They made the noise." He slipped off his tac vest and returned to resting his arm on the table.

Trofim's motions didn't escape Iosif's notice. "Is it broken?" he asked, motioning to Trofim's left arm with his head.

Trofim shook his head, wiggling his fingers rather slowly.

Iosif gave him a doubtful look. "You killed two Argentines this evening. I believe the dead men were wanted criminals, so they were willing to believe what I told them."

"One was a rushed shot. I didn't mean to hit an artery. The other…I didn't see him behind the truck."

Keith burst in the room with his usual liveliness, but curiously out of breath. "That penguin friend of yours really makes a mess. The helipad looks like he lost a paintball fight. He's crappin' every four minutes; I timed him."

Trofim stood and examined his friend. No sweat or blood on him, so he dismissed it. "As long as he gets it all out of him before we leave."

"Here's yer goodies," Keith said, dropping a metal briefcase and a satellite phone on the table. "It's not a lot, but it'll do ya."

Trofim opened the case and thumbed through various forms of currency and passports. "Did you talk to Agnes?"

Keith looked at Trofim sideways. "Yep. Speaking so, I have to go. Come here, ya minger." He took Trofim in a tight embrace, and then slapped him on the shoulders.

"I will see you soon, in California, *ublyudok*." Trofim smiled.

"Did ya jus' call me an ugly duck?" Keith asked, before he walked out.

"I wouldn't have been wrong if I had," Trofim laughed, watching the door close.

The door swung back open before Trofim had a chance to sit and in walked Agnes. Standing near to Trofim's height, with cropped dirty-blonde hair, and a perpetual determined look in her eyes, Agnes had an aura that some said reeked of authority, but her slightly crooked smile betrayed some form of mischief. She glanced at Iosif. He nodded and stepped out of the room. When the door closed, Agnes' expression softened and she gave Trofim a tight hug. "We thought you were dead," she said, stepping back.

"Close," Trofim said, turning away.

"I only have a minute. You're officially off the grid, so to speak. And I know you don't need it, but BioCon has given its blessing to go after Jenson." Trofim turned back toward her, carrying an inquisitive look. "This guy isn't a real colonel. He is, however, working for the U.S. government. They used us. We weren't told the full extent of what has been taking place in the southern hemisphere. We're not in the war business."

Trofim opened his mouth to speak, but caught himself. He let out a tired breath instead and then began. "A lot of good soldiers died. Some of the best in our business were killed. We were sent in underequipped and with bogus intel." He turned away, trying to keep his anger down.

"I know. We're flushing the system to make sure it doesn't happen again. Millerton was playing both sides."

"Millerton's dead."

"I know. Tro, look at me," Agnes said. "Jenson is in deep with a company called GT. They're spearheading the Antarctic campaign. A man by the name of Bryan Collin Turlock is the one calling the shots. His company will be the one reaping the benefits of this catastrophe. His brother, Edwin Turlock, is a U.S. senator from Arizona. Some say he could be the president in two years, should he decide to run." Agnes waited for Trofim to digest the information. "Keep in mind, Turlock makes Jenson look like a ball of fluff, and he'll stop at nothing to clean up Vance Lyons' mess; including eradicating the species as a whole."

"So why not go after this Turlock? It seems he's the problem." Trofim wiggled the fingers of his injured arm.

"He's heavily connected with the U.S. government, even above and beyond his brother. He's making a lot of politicians very wealthy."

"So. Again, why not just kill him?"

"BioCon isn't in the assassination business either. Speaking of business…I hate to see you go, Trofim. Not just because of your skill, but also as a friend." Agnes waited for a reply, but knew she wouldn't get much of one. She opened a satchel, pulling out a stack of folded papers. "You're officially retired now. Take these as a token of appreciation."

Trofim thumbed through them. "Maps?"

"Coordinates are marked for safe zones. Places where you can't be touched, regardless of who you piss off."

Trofim pulled off the rubber band from around the bundle and pulled out several photos. He lifted them toward Agnes with eyebrows raised.

"The handsome man getting into the limo is Bryan Turlock. His business and home address are written on the back." Agnes answered Trofim's question with a slight cock of her head before he asked.

Trofim smiled, imagining a bull's-eye on Turlock.

Agnes continued. "The others are of Randy Lee and Gina Rosedale, sole survivors from the so-called purge in Antarctica. Gina is being encouraged and monitored by BioCon. She has potential. Aside from that, Jenson might be going for them. Maycotte was our insider in Antarctica. That's the only reason they're still alive. But Jenson had Maycotte killed, which is just as well, he was playing both sides…three sides, actually. Jenson might try to tie up those loose ends. Randy and Gina live San Luis Obispo, California. You might want to go there, Jenson is extremely difficult to track, and he might show up there. No time soon though, we *do* know that the colonel will be overseeing operations in Costa Rica and Peru. And you need to trust me when I tell you this: don't touch him while he's there. Other than that, your pension will waiting for you at our predetermined position." She reached for the door.

"Thank you, Agnes. Take care of Keith," he said with a wry grin.

"Tro, has anybody ever told you that you talk too much?" Agnes said, letting the door swing shut as she left.

Trofim snorted a laugh, he would miss these people. A few months earlier he didn't think he would, but now he knew better. He gathered his maps and photos, stuffed them in the case, and leaned against the table, waiting for Iosif. After half a minute, he figured his instinct had been wrong and stood to leave, but was proven correct when the door flew open and Iosif rushed in. "I need to go," Tro said, walking to the door.

"I wish I could say that I am sorry to see you go, but after this evening…" Iosif pulled open the door and escorted Trofim down the hall. A few steps in to the walk, Iosif looked at Trofim. "You know, the American offered me a large amount of money to betray you. After witnessing what I did this evening, I'm glad I kept my honor."

Trofim looked down at a roll of duct tape in Iosif's hand. "I'm glad you did, too. How much did he offer you?"

"Five hundred thousand…rubles, not dollars. He would really like to see you dead, and I can see that the feeling is mutual."

Trofim cracked a smile in response.

"However, my commanding officer was not so honorable. Your friends have neutralized him. They didn't kill him," Iosif answered before Trofim could ask. He opened the door to a broom closet and handed Trofim the tape. "I do need you to do something for me before you leave."

Trofim nodded his head, but looked at the bubble camera in the corner of the hall.

"They're deactivated. Your helicopter has been fueled and prepped." Iosif extended his hands to be bound.

Trofim wrapped Iosif's hands, and then ripped off a small strip, and held it to the other's face.

"Safe journeys, my friend," Iosif said, before Trofim pressed the tape against his mouth.

Trofim pulled Iosif's side arm from the holster, emptied the chamber, and slid the gun down the hall. "Thank you," he said, closing the door with a click.

Trofim walked across the pad with all casualness. He thanked the flight crew, climbed up, and closed the door. He went to the back and let Leepoh out of the box. The Gentoo gave him a sideways look and followed him to the cockpit. Trofim lifted him to the co-pilot's seat. "You can ride up here with me; just promise not to crap all over chair."

Leepoh's shoulders fell. "You ask too much of me, Trofim Lagendander Geekov, too much."

Trofim shook his head and engaged the rotors. Maybe bringing the bird up there wasn't such a good idea.

CHAPTER 53

"We need to land," Trofim said, speaking more to himself than Leepoh.

"I think we need to land," Leepoh mocked.

Trofim checked his coordinates, one of three or four islands marked on the map lay a thousand feet below his position, hidden in the darkness of the night sea. "You're starting to sound like a parrot. Damn this wind!" He fought the yoke, trying to stay on course in the strong gale.

"I've been told that before. Are these parrots like us? Or are they like skuas, mindless primitive feathery beasts?" Leepoh stood on his seat, looking out the window expectantly, like a child going to a toy store.

Trofim ignored the question, focusing on his task. Once he caught sight of the strand of an island, he relented. "Yes, they're just as irritating as you. They scream and squawk all day in their cages, demanding crackers of their caretakers." The landing struts hit the ground a little too rough, but given the circumstances, Trofim was happy with the landing.

"What's a cracker? Is it for eating, or is it a weapon the parrots want to use against their captors?" Leepoh hopped on the seat, trying to see what was outside. The further over the sea they traveled, the more energetic he had become; or, as Trofim called it, *annoying*.

Trofim pushed the cockpit door open and grabbed one of his many bags. Leepoh watched, curious about what was to come. Tro dug a cracker out of a box and showed Leepoh. "This is a cracker. You eat it." He took a bite. "Mmmm."

Leepoh leaned close to the cracker and snatched it in his beak. A moment later, he spit it out, hacking and complaining. "Parrots eat that? It tastes like sand. Worse than sand; it tastes like kaaykakikkik."

"I don't know what kayakiks are," Trofim said, doing his best to pronounce the squawk Leepoh had said the cracker tastes like.

Leepoh thought about it for a moment. "They're those things that walk on the bottom of the water and on the shore."

"Crabs?"

"Bah! Not crabs. I know what crabs are. Kaayakikiks have the things on them. They look like little stones. If you've ever eaten one, you'd know it tastes like crackers. They're like crabs, but not."

Trofim pushed the air stairs open. "That doesn't help. I don't know what you are talking about, and I really don't care." He stepped out into the icy south Atlantic wind, letting it reinvigorate his senses after a tense flight.

Leepoh hopped down behind him, and was still going on about the cracker when he stopped talking. "I know this place," he said. He stepped out and looked northward. "We're not far from where I nested once."

Trofim took out his compass and clicked on a LED light to illuminate the situation. He followed Leepoh's gaze, noticing he seemed transfixed by something. "Hey. Hey, penguin, are you all right?"

Leepoh remained silent for a few more seconds and then slowly turned his head to Trofim. "Can't be all right, or all wrong for that matter," he spoke slowly, as if he were only partially awake.

Trofim furrowed his brow. "So your home's that way?" he asked, pointing to where Leepoh had been staring.

Leepoh shook his head vigorously. "Bah! It's not anymore. I need to eat, and not that cracker thing either. I will return." He walked toward the shore like a penguin on a mission.

Trofim followed him to the water's edge. "You are coming back, right?"

"You are taking me to see my son, right?"

Trofim hesitated. In his quest to escape and then to kill Jenson, he had completely forgotten the promise he had never intended to keep. "Of course I am. Yes."

"Then I will be back when my belly is fat." Leepoh looked at the cloud covered sky. "Bah! No squid tonight."

Trofim watched him jump into the surf, turned his collar against the wind, and set out to explore the island. At roughly five hundred meters square, there wasn't much to explore. A few rocky outcroppings and patches of tusset grass were the only distinguishing features on the windswept island. He let out a long, bored sigh, and walked back to his ride. He grabbed a tablet, shut off the lights, and scrolled through maps and coordinates installed by Agnes.

A small island, highlighted in red, caught Trofim's attention. It was almost directly north, the direction Leepoh had been looking. He wondered if that was where the Gentoo was headed. Maybe there were more Gentoo there, or even his mate. It was less than fifty kilometers away, he didn't know how fast a penguin could swim, but he was certain that Leepoh could make it there and back by daybreak. He tapped the red island and a paragraph about it popped up.

Trofim scanned the text, learning the unofficial name of the island, La Isla de los Pengüinos de la Muerte. He wasn't good at Spanish, but he knew enough to know it said something about an island, penguins, and death. "No wonder it's marked in red." The text also let him know it was uninhabited. It cross referenced as a 'safe' spot, though he doubted how safe a place could be with death in its name.

He closed the door and collapsed back in the bench seat. The warmer air made his eyes grow heavy. He couldn't remember the last time he had slept. His head fell forward, making him snap his eyes open. He clutched his knife, laid his head back, and instantly fell asleep.

An odd noise made his eyes snap open. He looked out the portal window, squinting from the bright gray morning. He threw open the air stairs and stepped down, wooden steps creaking under his weight. He looked back, finding it strange that they made the steps out of wood. The sun broke through the overcast, wind rustled leaves high up in the tops of eucalyptus trees. He walked, strips of yellow-brown bark littering the ground crunched underfoot. Light waves lapped against a rocky shore. Calls of gulls and crows filled the cool morning air.

He turned back toward the helicopter to find it gone, replaced by a small house, far away, but close enough to see a woman leaning against the patio door. He began to walk toward the figure, but his steps never took him any closer. He stopped, feeling suddenly tired. The crows took flight, hundreds blackening the sky. His eyes followed them to the northern horizon. He looked back to the house and the woman. He hoped it was Alyssa, but he knew it wasn't.

The morning changed to late afternoon and the woman still stood on the patio. He had to get to her. For whatever reason, he knew he had to. The sun disappeared behind clouds so dark they swallowed the light. A wave appeared in the distance. Panic set in when the wave rose behind the house. Large, coal black, the wave raced toward the house and so did he. He ran hard, the ground sticking to his feet, holding him in place. He couldn't break free. He wouldn't be able to save the woman and she had no idea what was coming. He took a sluggish step forward and a Chinstrap penguin walked out of the trees. Trofim knelt, knowing the penguin would ask for help, and would die, just as it had in Antarctica. The events unfolded just as he knew they would. He thought of Leepoh. "Where was that damned bird? He could warn her." The wave approached, the house disappeared beneath its enormity and Trofim stood, staring up at the tsunami's crest, as high as any skyscraper he had ever seen. The wave crashed down.

Trofim sprung up, catching his breath. He looked around, shaking through the adrenaline of snapping awake. He looked outside at the first gray light of morning and checked his watch. "Six hours?" he said, surprised by how long he slept. He tried to remember the details of his dream. He learned long ago that sometimes the subconscious mind could solve problems the conscious could not. But then again, sometimes dreams were just a collection of nonsense and there was no oneirocritic nearby to tell him otherwise.

The crisp ocean air surged in when Trofim opened the door. He hopped down the steps, stretched, and found a good spot to take care of morning business. When he returned to the front of the helicopter, he spotted Leepoh sitting on a rock staring north again. "How was hunting?" he asked, removing his outer layer of shirts and finding a patch of earth to begin his exercises.

"It was a feast. Those fishes and things never knew what hit them. I swam here and there, catching everything my beak could take. I came back and guessed you were asleep, so I went and ate some more. Which reminds me, I brought you a cracker." Leepoh indicated the nearby rock.

Trofim began his sun salutations, moving from one yoga pose to the next. He looked where Leepoh had pointed. "A rock?"

Leepoh snapped his head toward the rock. "Bah! The cracker has escaped!" He began hopping from rock to rock in search of the cracker creature.

Trofim continued his meditations, even while listening to Leepoh squawk and complain. After several minutes, he heard Leepoh say that he would find another, followed by a splash. Cold air threatened to stiffen loosened muscles, so Trofim switched his routine to a more vigorous workout. After twenty minutes of calisthenics, he began sprints up and down the length of the island. When his lungs burned for air and his knees told him to quit, he pushed on for several more minutes until he finally fell against the helicopter. He grabbed his canteen and walked his cool down.

Leepoh came bounding back from the water still grumbling. "Leave it to a cracker to not stay put where you put it."

Trofim spat a mouthful of water and walked to the shore. "How deep is the water?" he asked, standing on the water's edge.

"How am I supposed to know that? That's like me asking you how high the clouds are."

Trofim looked up. "About one hundred fifty meters."

Leepoh narrowed his eyes. "What's a one hundred fifty meter?"

"Never mind." He pulled off his boots and stripping down to nothing, he plunged into the surf. He stood and braced against a wave, grunting in the frigid water. He crawled out and grabbed his gear, looking down at Leepoh who returned his look with a curious stare. "Have a cracker," Trofim said, and dropped a sea snail at Leepoh's feet.

"Hah! You found it. Now give it a taste. If you like crackers, you'll like these crackers."

Trofim shook his head. "No thank you." He climbed inside the helicopter, rummaged for a blanket, and fell into the seat. Leepoh hopped up the steps and Trofim closed the door behind him.

Leepoh crawled inside his carrier while Trofim got dressed. "When are we going to Califorka?"

Trofim extended his fingers then made a fist, shaking his head. He fished a wrap out of the med-pack and reluctantly wrapped his injured wrist after getting dressed. "Not anytime soon." He grabbed binoculars, threw on a wool cap, and headed back outside. Leepoh dutifully followed.

Trofim scanned the gray horizon, not really sure what he was looking for, but doing something was better than sitting. He blew through his mouth, letting his lips flap, and looked at Leepoh who was watching him, as he often did. Trofim had to chuckle at the Gentoo's curiosity. He was always watching. "What?" Tro asked, when Leepoh continued to study him without falling into an exhaustive diatribe about crackers or something else equally banal.

"Is that thing you're carrying the thing that makes pictures?" Leepoh stepped closer, looking up at the binoculars.

Trofim blurted a laugh. "No. They are called binoculars. I can see things that are far away with these."

Leepoh shrugged. "Randy told me about a thing that makes pictures. I don't know what a picture is."

Trofim scrunched his brow. "Randy?"

"Yes. The human who took my son. Remember?" Leepoh turned his attention back to watching the waves.

"Wait here. I'll show you a picture." Trofim jumped inside the helicopter and returned holding the bundle Agnes had given him. "Look at this. This is a picture. Can you tell me who the man is in this picture?"

Leepoh studied the photo for a moment. "Hah! That's Randy. I met him when that fat, bloated, half-smarted, whale's guano hole of an Overlord had him as a prisoner." Leepoh went into an exhaustive tale about how he had seen Randy on several occasions. Trofim showed him the photo of Gina. Leepoh confirmed that she was Randy's mate.

"That's some coincidence; you meeting him. Some would call it fate or destiny," Tro said after Leepoh's recitation.

"Bah! Destiny is just a series of coincidences that we try to give a reason for." Leepoh looked at sky. "There's a storm coming this way. This isn't the best place to be when that happens."

Trofim looked at Leepoh doubtfully. He was about to express it when the wind picked up strength. "If you knew this, it would've been good to know a little sooner." He surveyed the small island; there definitely wasn't any shelter.

"Us penguins know where to go in a storm. This place is not one of them."

Trofim rushed to the helicopter and immediately began his preflight check. Leepoh followed and assumed his position up front. Tro looked at him. The Gentoo never showed any sign of fear, no matter the situation. But then again, he didn't know what a scared penguin looked like. He closed the stairs and fastened down his supplies. He slipped back into the pilot's seat and peeked at Leepoh. "What do you think about going to your former home?"

Leepoh stayed silent for nearly a minute. "I think it's time."

Trofim thought about the unofficial name of the island. "Is it safe?"

"It is for me. Just try not to upset those daisy-headed Rockhoppers."

CHAPTER 54

After flying around the island to approach from the north shore, and after being buffeted by nearly gale force winds, and after Leepoh's earnest, yet noisy and repeated calls of excitement at seeing the island from a 'gull's view,' Trofim managed to put the helicopter down in a relatively easy manner on top of one of the many low hills which comprised Gentoo Rise. Leepoh bounced from his seat, waiting impatiently for Tro to make the helicopter stop helicoptering, as he liked to say. Once Trofim completed his task and opened the door, Leepoh bolted outside and ran to the top of the next highest hill to scout the area. Trofim armed himself and followed after him.

Trofim pulled his hood up against the wind and drizzle, and slipped along the slopes until he finally caught up with Leepoh, Trofim squatted next to him, following his gaze to the shore. "What do you see? Do you have family here?"

Leepoh met his eyes. "Come with me." He led him across slopes and hills until they reached the summit of Gentoo Rise. Months of weather erased most of the destruction, scavengers had picked away flesh from bones, but the story of what had happened there still remained.

Trofim looked at Leepoh, then at the hillsides and spotted detonation sites. He walked through the zone, checking for traces of explosions left imprinted on the dirt. He kneeled alongside the large opening of what used to be a burrow. He stood and faced Leepoh.

"I knew every one of these Gentoo by name. They were nearly all fledglings and their mothers, and elderly."

"Is this why you started fighting back?"

"No, it's why I stopped." Leepoh walked around a burrow and stared at what remained. "This happened while we were at the islands you call the Falklands. While we were being slaughtered there, a small band of men slaughtered us here."

"Were they military? Organized fighters?" Trofim asked.

"No. Before this happened, the Gentoo joined the Rockhoppers to attack, what I believe you call 'poachers'. We defeated them and we thought we had provided peace for the island. This place is where we come to raise our chicks. Rockhoppers, Gentoo, and not long ago, the Magellanics did too. Now there are only Rockhoppers. Stubborn, angry, daisy-headed little Rockhoppers."

"What happened to the people who did this?"

"There still might be some pieces of them further inland. It was a good release of frustration after our defeat at the Falklands. We had the entire…" Leepoh's words trailed away. He looked toward the shore and spotted a large group of Rockhoppers porpoising just beyond the surf. "You should probably go back to your helicopter. Remember those stubborn, angry, daisy-headed little Rockhoppers I told you about?"

Trofim nodded and followed Leepoh's eyes to the sea.

"There's a group coming here. They'll come from inland too. They're tricky like that." Leepoh waited for Trofim to leave. "Go. They don't like your kind so much."

Trofim squinted against the rain. "What about you? Will you be safe?"

"Bah! They can't touch a spirit returned from the underworld. Go. Run along. And don't go shooting anybody."

CHAPTER 55

Leepoh found a burrow dark enough to hide in and scooted to the back, hoping it wouldn't cave in. He sat and waited. He hoped the one he waited for would be part of the advance group. He wasn't disappointed when he heard Nok's voice grumbling about something.

"If it comes to a fight, I hope you know I'm retired, Colonel," Nok said, his tone betraying his lack of sincerity.

Colonel Kairg barked a laugh. "Ah come on, General. You know you'll join in. It's just too much fun."

"Sergeant Kuk-kek, tell your commanding officer that I am no longer an officer in the ministry."

"Sir, if you don't mind I would prefer to stay out of this spat." Kuk-kek stretched his neck to see if he could spot the flying machine.

"You see, Colonel? That proves my point. I can't even get a lowly sergeant to follow orders."

Commander Trarck chirped a call, and the group went silent. "There it is. Kairg, take a squad and move around to the south. Kuk-kek, take a squad and come in from the north. Trasik-lon and his squad should be coming in from the east at any moment. Nok, you're with me."

"Are you sure putting Trasik-lon in command of a squad was a good idea?" Nok asked.

"He wanted to prove his loyalty after what happened. What better way to prove it than a potential combat situation?"

"That's why I selected you as my successor; I probably wouldn't have been so forgiving."

"You always did abuse your power," Trarck said in his usual stoic manner.

"I probably should've had you flogged," Nok said, knowing Trarck's sense of humor.

"You could've tried." He looked at his longtime friend. "Lydeck is gone and we both know how he manipulated others to get what he wanted, Trasik-lon not the least of them. Besides that, Tearsk is with him."

"I feel better already. That young Rockhopper can talk the beak off a Gentoo." Nok looked back down the slope and let out a heavy breath. "Remember the last time you and I made this climb? Seems so long ago, but it really hasn't been, has it?"

"I was wondering when you were going to say something. We lost a lot of friends and family during the war, and to be honest, I'm kind of surprised that his death has affected you the most."

"You're right. I know you're right. We went through a lot together, and the friendship was genuine; not circumstantial. I think it's because of how I left him. He fought on even after he had been wounded and if it weren't for him, I doubt we would have survived. And then I just left him there. He told me to leave; there was no way to get him out, but still… I don't know how long he lived afterward. He could've been gone by the time we left; in fact, I'm sure he was." Nok stared at the ground, his eyes shifting in thought. "Maybe it's time to let go, though I feel like I'm not honoring him if I do."

"We all feel that way about the ones we lose, Nok. You know as well as I do that the living can never hope to be exalted like the dead are. But the choice is yours to decide when to let go." Trarck studied the helicopter not twenty meters ahead. "Back to why we're here; there doesn't seem to be any movement. The machine looks big enough to hold several men though. We need to stay alert."

Leepoh listened to Nok's conversation. He almost felt bad for what he was about to do…almost. Once Nok passed the burrow, Leepoh crept out, standing just out of sight. "Nok," he said in a long, drawn-out whisper.

Nok jolted to a stop. "Did you hear that?" he asked Commander Trarck.

Trarck looked at him curiously. "Hear what?"

"My name. Someone said my name; quietly, like a whisper."

Trarck shook his head. "I didn't hear anything. It's windy and rainy. I'm sure it was the wind."

Nok stayed still a moment longer. "I was sure I heard my name."

Nok started to walk again, and Leepoh called his name a little louder.

"There!" he said. "I heard it again."

Trarck turned back to Nok. "I think I heard it too," he said, scanning the hill.

Nok and Trarck narrowed their eyes. "It sounded like…" Nok stopped himself from saying more.

"Like what?"

"Nothing," Nok said.

Leepoh took it a little further. "Nok, Nok," he said, letting the second *Nok* trail away.

"Who's there?" Nok asked.

"Hah!" Leepoh couldn't help but blurt a laugh. With his cover blown, he stepped out of cover. "It is I, Leepoh. Mahak-chig-rantoo has allowed me to cross over with a message."

Nok screamed out in alarm, back-pedaled, and fell over Trarck. "No, it can't be. The keeper is just a legend."

"Bah! And yet I am here, and I have a message from the Great Sea."

Nok got to his feet. "How can…how? W-what is your message?" he stammered for more, but couldn't find the words.

Trarck looked at Leepoh suspiciously and stepped closer.

"The message I have been told to bring you is…stop being a daisy-headed cracker-cruncher."

Nok looked at Trarck, confused, and Trarck returned the look. "What's a…wait, you came back for that?" Nok asked in disbelief, with tinge of anger in his voice.

Trarck stepped up to Leepoh, looking up at his face. "Wait a second."

Leepoh looked at Trarck for a pair of heartbeats, until he couldn't hold back any longer. "Hah! What a couple of Kelp Gooses you are. Mahak-chig-rantoo, phhht. I'm not dead, you seal-fluke."

Nok stood with his beak open, uttering noises, not being able to articulate anything more.

"Well, are you going to say something, or stand there with your beak open until your tongue dries out?"

Trarck just looked at Leepoh and shook his head. "Figures," he said, and walked away.

Nok finally found his voice. "I don't know if I should rub your beak or kill you for real."

"How about neither. Rubbing beaks with a Rockhopper…blah."

Nok rushed to his friend. "How can you be alive? When we left, I thought you were dead. And the explosions…"

"A series of fortunate events, I guess you'd say. I really don't remember much. Just the boom and falling, or more sliding. Then there was a big ugly penguin looking over me in the darkness. The next thing you know, I woke up in a place under PIC, and with a human roommate, if you can believe that."

Nok fell into Leepoh. "I can't believe you're here. So much has happened since the war." He pulled back and looked at him. "I can't believe this. How?"

"I thought we went through this already? I got pecked by a big ugly penguin, booms, waking up next to a man; bigger, uglier penguin. Remember?"

"Yeah, yeah. It's just so…I'm so happy. I can't even say." Nok looked to Trarck, who lifted his flippers to say he wasn't as surprised. "We have a lot to discuss. You have to meet my son."

"Hah! I remember; you and Keerka. Is she still tolerating you?" Nok opened his beak to reply, but Leepoh interrupted. "Before we get to that, you might want to call off your Rockhoppers. There's a man in that helicopter who you don't wanna upset. Plus, he pretty much got me here. Oh, and he's on our side…sort of. Maybe not sort of; more like completely. He doesn't care too much for Royals either. In fact, I don't think he likes a lot of peoples. But he likes me."

"That's saying a lot. I commend him," Nok said, deadpan.

Leepoh did a double take. "I'm back from dead less than a day, and already with the insults."

"Oh I have plenty of those waiting for you," Nok said. He turned back to Trarck. "It's up to you, Commander. Leepoh asked to call off the attack."

Trarck stepped forward and eyed Leepoh for a moment. "All right. Leepoh did help save our colony, so I guess I'll trust him." He turned away from the Gentoo and gave Nok a look that wasn't entirely serious.

"Commander, huh? What about you, Nok? What's your position these days? Emperor? King? Potentate?"

"What's a potentate?"

"Exactly."

Nok shook his head. "Trarck's a good Rockhopper. He's a good leader. Me, I'm just a figurehead now. I don't want anything to do with leading or commanding. We had an incident with some Shadow Warriors not too long ago. It kind of soured me on the idea of politics."

Leepoh studied his friend. "We do have a lot to talk about then. Especially if there's those Shadow thingies swimming about still."

"Usually I would ask if you knew something I didn't, but there are some things you might be interested in."

"Like?" Leepoh's eyes shifted between Nok and Trarck.

Nok looked at Trarck before answering. When he gave his nod of approval Nok continued. "Like an Oracle."

Leepoh remained oddly silent for a few moments. "Visiting or born here?"

"Born. But she can't stay. I'll explain later."

Leepoh nodded his head, acting sullen. He straightened his body. "Before we get to that, let's get that human out of his machine. No attacks, right?" he said, looking at Commander Trarck.

"As long as he doesn't attack first." Track began barking out orders, telling the Rockhoppers to stand down, but to stay alert.

Leepoh led Trarck, Nok, Kuk-kek, Kairg, and Tearsk to the helicopter and called out to Trofim.

"This is as fool of a thing as I have ever seen," Colonel Kairg said. "We're just going to wait for the beast to come out and kill us all?"

"Leepoh assured us that this man won't kill us. He saved Leepoh," Nok answered, keeping his eyes on the door as the stairs slowly opened.

"Then I really don't trust it," Kairg said, drawing a look from Leepoh.

Tearsk pushed in between Kairg and Nok. "I've never seen one up close," he said when both gave him a disapproving look.

Trofim peered out the doorway and took a cautious step down. He lifted his hands to show the Rockhoppers that he was unarmed. "These are your friends?" he asked, checking the positions of every visible penguin.

"Yes. Except for Kairg," Leepoh answered.

"Wait. Did he say my name?" Colonel Kairg said, alarmed. "That sounded like my name. The Gentoo said my name, didn't he? What's he up to?"

Leepoh faced Trarck. "Commander, do you speak humanish?"

"A little. Not as well as you."

"It'll do." Leepoh stood between Trarck and the stairs. "Trofim, this is Trarck. He's the top Rockhopper in these parts."

Trofim descended the steps and the Rockhoppers took a few steps back. "Hello," Trofim said. "I'm not here to hurt any of you. I promise you that."

Trarck looked at Leepoh and then back to the man. "Hello. Forget our caution. Mans have been danger, much time," he stammered, trying to remember the words he had been taught long ago.

"Did you get that? Rockhoppers can be a little thick," Leepoh said, always doing his best to irritate others.

Trarck glared at Leepoh.

Leepoh looked at Trofim and stepped a little closer to the man. "I guess he understood that."

"It's okay," Trofim said. He sat on the bottom step to get closer to eye-level. "I know the difficulty of learning new tongues and I understand your lack of trust. With your permission, I would like to stay here for a while. There are men who would like to kill me as well and I need someplace to stay."

Trarck stared at Trofim, trying to understand what he was told. Leepoh jumped into his attempts to understand and explained what Trofim had said. Trarck gathered the others. "What do you think? I don't see how it could hurt. But then again, he is a human."

"And humans can't be trusted," Kairg blurted.

Tearsk jumped in the conversation. "If he wanted to hurt us, he could have killed all of us the moment he stepped out." All eyes turned to Nok.

"Why is everyone looking at me? I hate humans. But...he did help Leepoh."

"I've seen him fight other men more than once. And he could've left me to be killed by them and didn't. Remember the ones who helped Meuseaux? He's like them." Leepoh looked at Trofim. "Except a little meaner...and a little uglier."

Trarck let out a heavy breath. "Yes, Trokeem. You can stay. Here but. No where us are."

Trofim nodded. "I understand. I'll stay on this side of the island. Thank you."

Leepoh watched Trarck join the others. "I've heard better speech come from a toothless toothfish."

"I can't believe you missed this," Trarck said, lifting his beak toward Leepoh.

"Once you get to know him, he's much worse." Nok laughed at seeing Leepoh struggle with the proper insult to follow up with.

Leepoh decided that there would be plenty of time to insult Nok later. He stepped up to Trofim and stared at him blankly.

"What?" Trofim asked when Leepoh didn't immediately speak.

"I'm going with these daisy-heads. I'll come back when I wear out my welcome."

"Then I'll see you soon."

Leepoh grunted. "Everybody having fun at my expense. Don't get eaten, Trofim Geekov." Leepoh hurried away to catch up with the others.

CHAPTER 56

Keerka stood with Leeg and Kicki at the base of the rocky cliffs known as the Warrens. Leeg spotted Nok and the others and rushed off to meet them at the base of Tusset Grass Slope. Keerka stayed behind with Kicki, watching. She knew there had been no real danger; Kicki would've warned them about it and precautions would've been taken. But still, a sigh of relief found her beak when she saw them come ashore. She counted the Rockhoppers; all had returned. She scanned the group and spotted Leeg meeting his father. Her sense of relief was soon replaced by curiosity when she spotted a taller penguin talking to Leeg and squawking back and forth with Nok. "A Gentoo?" she said, looking at Kicki.

As she had been doing more often than not recently, Kicki said nothing.

"Is this the messenger you spoke about?" Keerka asked. "The one you said Nok would go with?"

Kicki stared blank-eyed at the scene below. "Yes. But the choice is still yours to make."

Keerka pressed against Kicki, reassuring her. "I wish you still talked like a fledgling. You grew up too fast."

"I'm still a fledgling, Miss Keerka. I really would like to go back to roaming the caves and having adventures with Leeg, but there aren't any adventures if you know what you're going to find." She leaned her head against Keerka.

"C'mon. Let's go see who this messenger is." She nudged Kicki forward. "I don't know who it is, so don't tell me."

Kicki suppressed a giggle. "How am I supposed to know who it is? I can't read minds. But I think you know him, Miss Keerka."

Keerka grunted a not so serious grunt, happy to see a little of Kicki's sassiness showing through.

^^^

Nok spotted Keerka and Kicki hopping down the slope. "Just give me a moment and let me tell her about you."

"Bah! You don't want me to act like a spirit again?"

Nok gave Leepoh a warning glare.

"Some penguins really don't have a sense of humor, do they?" Leepoh said, nudging Leeg.

"Especially that old Rockhopper," Leeg said.

"Hah! You sure bit the squid on the beak there, kid."

"I can hear you, you know?" Nok said, looking back from the slope.

Leepoh and Leeg looked at each other, shaking their flippers as if frightened.

Nok ignored them and raced up the slope. "Keerka, I have something to tell you."

"If it's about the Gentoo, I already know."

"What? How could you?" He looked at Kicki. "Oh. I didn't think she would know him. Isn't it amazing? After all of this time too. He tried to scare me at first, but what else would you expect? Now I'm just happy about it."

Keerka shook her head. "How could you be happy? This changes everything now. Now you have to decide to either stay or go with him."

Nok stammered, trying to mask his disbelief. "But…but, how could you do that? Why? Why would you make me choose between him or you? I thought you'd be happy."

"Happy? How could I be happy, Nok? I'm surprised you are."

"How could I not be? I thought Leepoh was dead, and to find him here…alive!"

"Wait, wait, wait. Leepoh? That's Leepoh?"

"Yes. What did you think I was talking about?" Nok looked at Kicki.

"She told me not to tell her," Kicki said with a hint of humor hiding amongst her precociousness.

Keerka fixed Kicki a stern look and then looked down the slope. She saw Leepoh, flapping his flippers, probably regaling Leeg with tales of daring and eating. "That's him, all right."

Nok, Keerka, and Kicki hurried down the slope and were met by Trarck and Kuk-kek. "We're going to open the Council. Bring your friend along when you get settled."

"All right. We'll be there in a little while."

Colonel Kairg walked past Nok. "Exhausting," he muttered, and continued on his way.

"It's good to know he still has that effect on others," Keerka said with a laugh.

"Leepoh," Nok called. "You remember Keerka."

"Hah! How could I forget? Hello, Keerka. I admire your resilience for tolerating that curmudgeon for all this time."

"It's not as hard as it looks. I'm astounded. I'm happy. Nok had a hard time." She moved next to Nok, sharing his happiness. "But how?"

"I'll explain later," Nok said.

Leepoh stared at Nok and refrained from making a remark at his expense. "I'm happy, too. He was the first penguin I thought of when I found out I wasn't dead. And then I thought about that big one sticking me with his beak."

"I see you've met Leeg," Keerka said. "He was named after you in a way. Nok couldn't decide between your name and General Treeg's. So…Leeg."

"I guess, in a strange way, you're part of my family." Nok puffed his chest immediately after speaking, so not to appear too sentimental.

"This is Kicki." Keerka presented her by ushering her closer.

Leepoh cocked his head and stared at Kicki, his body language losing all humor. Kicki returned the look, not flinching beneath his heavy glare.

Nok and Keerka exchanged puzzled glances.

After a several moments, Leepoh straightened up. "I'm pleased to meet you," he said with all seriousness.

Kicki didn't reply, so Keerka answered for her. "I'm sure the feeling is mutual. She's been through a lot recently."

Leepoh spun toward Nok. "Where's Packt? I need to speak with her."

"You knew her?" Nok said, sounding more than a little surprised.

"She's dead," Kicki said. "You knew her well. For many, many moons."

Leepoh stooped to Kicki's height. "And Lapasia is as well." Kicki nodded, even though Leepoh didn't need affirmation.

"You're kinda spooking me, Leepoh. Did you come back from the Great Sea with the Seeing?" Nok joked, trying to hide his nervousness.

"I didn't die," Leepoh answered, as serious as Nok had ever seen him. "She can't stay here. It's not safe for her…or you."

Keerka stepped in. "We know. You came here just in time; a few more days and you would have missed us. So tell me, how do you know this?"

Leepoh hesitated.

Nok rested his flipper against Leepoh; a rare sign of affection for a Rockhopper. "We're your family now, Leepoh. You're acting like a squid bit your tongue. Tell me what's bothering you."

"I'm the last one alive. With Lapasia gone, I have to assume Cryftin is gone too. We were the last members of the Council of Thrace. When Antaean dissolved the Council, we went our own ways. He didn't want our authority to get in his way, but he also needed us. When he began uniting the clans, I came here to discuss the situation with Packt. We should've known he would mislead us, but without the Oracle, we didn't know where we were being led." Leepoh met each Rockhopper's serious eyes. "But that's an old story for old penguins. Are you going out to sea to fatten up, or leaving for good?"

"For good, I'm afraid. Commander Trarck will lead the colony to a safe haven, and somebody will escort Kicki and Leeg to someplace remote." Nok looked to the ground; the weight of never seeing his son again, was something he almost couldn't bear.

Leepoh stared at the same patch of ground. "You know what that means? If Leeg goes with her—"

"I'll never see him again. I know. We know," Nok waved at Keerka.

Leepoh remained unusually stoic. "I know what you're going through."

"Is that empathy I hear coming from the Gentoo?" Nok said in his most sardonic tone, trying to break up the seriousness.

"Bah! Well don't get used to it, daisy-head. There'll be less than little more of that where that came from."

Nok stared at Leepoh. "I have no idea what you just said."

"Is this what I have to look forward to now?" Keerka said. "Because if it is…"

"There's plenty more of it, Miss Daisy-head," Leepoh said, nudging Nok.

"Call me daisy-head again and I'll finish what Liutites started," Keerka warned.

Leepoh snapped his head toward Nok.

"Don't look to me for help," Nok said. He began walking toward the warrens. The others fell alongside of him. They walked in silence, each happy, but feeling the weight of knowing what would come all too soon. Nok glanced to Leepoh and broke the silence. "By the way, what's a daisy?"

CHAPTER 57

Leepoh exited the chamber of the Council of Order before they closed the assembly. He had quietly sat in on the meeting, avoiding making a spectacle of himself for a change. Listening to the final debate over abandoning the island and about the inevitable return of the Royal Emperors set Leepoh's thoughts down a path he no longer wanted to take, but knew he had to. The Alliance of Independent Colonies had fallen under the control of Mearna, the one-time leader of the Resistance against the Overlord's reign. He took a heavy breath, torn between what he wanted and what he knew needed to be done.

Nok, Melk, Colonel Kairg, and Seck walked through the dimly lit corridor, seemingly upbeat in spite of the solemnity of the meeting.

Melk spotted Leepoh and rushed toward him. "Leepoh, I must say upon hearing the dissemination of your survival, and ascertaining the validity of such promulgation—being that hearsay, quite often proliferates at greater speed than veracity—I am pleased beyond common measure that you did not meet your end in that horrific war. War being the answer to questions pondered only by the weak-minded among us who, more often than not, find their way into positions of influence, attempting to gain some manner of control over the inequities which we all face, whether perceived or real, and to a lesser extent, or perhaps greater, hide their own shortcomings through falsehood and misdirection. Present company excluded, of course.

With that being said, I would be reticent if I did not express my gratitude, and I'm certain Seck feels as I, in no less equality, for your part in securing our freedom, and our very lives from that awful human vessel."

Leepoh stood silent, blinking his eyes.

"He's glad you're alive and thanks you for helping to save his life," Nok said, breaking the silence.

"Well why didn't you say so?" Leepoh barked.

"I believe I just—" Melk began before being interrupted.

"Mearna, huh?" Leepoh said to Nok. "I never trusted her. Royals always have an ulterior motive."

"The only good Royal Emperor is a dead Royal Emperor," Colonel Kairg said. "And even then, not until the scavengers pick their bones."

Leepoh paced around the Rockhoppers, who were soon joined by Kuk-kek and Trarck. Trasik-lon stood in the background. "Are Lavour and Meuseaux with her?"

"No," answered Nok. He looked around and spotted Keerka coming his way. "They went their own way after…well, after you died."

Leepoh looked at the Rockhopper faces before him. They thought they were done with the war. But Leepoh knew better. "We're going to need Lavour. We need to wrest the AIC out of Mearna's control, and we can't do that without Lavour. He was their commander. They'll follow him."

"Where would you even begin to look for him?" Keerka asked when she arrived.

"There's only one ocean and two Chinstraps. I like our odds," said Leepoh.

Nok shook his head. "There's more than one ocean. And he made it pretty clear that he wanted nothing to do with this anymore."

"Bah! He'll rejoin us. He's like me; he does what's right, even if it costs him everything."

Leepoh started to walk away only to be stopped by Trarck. "The Rockhoppers are no longer part of this. We've suffered too much already.

Our colony is only a fraction of what it once was. I'm sorry, but you'll have to do it without us."

Leepoh nodded. "You're a good leader, Commander Trarck. You do what's best for your colony. If you ever need help…we'll find you. What about you, Nok?"

"What about me? My days of adventuring are over. I'm not going after Mearna and her band of Royal thugs. Let the humans deal with her, or better yet, let that Aperion have her. I didn't resign as Commander of the Colony just to go off trying to get myself killed on the other side of the world."

Leepoh looked at Nok. The war had been as rough on him as it had been to anyone of them. He hoped for more; it would have made the decision he was about to make a little bit easier, but he couldn't blame his friend. "I understand. I'll be back before you leave." He looked at various tunnels. "How do I get out of this monstrosity of a maze?"

"Leepoh…wait." Keerka called and faced Nok.

"Nope. No, no, no, no. I don't want to do it anymore," Nok protested, looking to the other Rockhoppers for help. They all found something of interest back toward the council chamber. Nok grunted.

"I think we should go." Keerka cut off his burgeoning adamant protest. "The Royals will come looking for Kicki, and so will Aperion. If they find her, they will kill Leeg and force her to do their bidding. They'll use her to keep watch over any attempts to finally be rid of them. We have to do what we can to prevent that from happening."

Nok relented. There was no changing Keerka's mind once it was made. "Will you be joining us, Commander? Colonel?"

"My primary concern is for the colony, my friend," Commander Trarck answered.

"I don't care about the Royals, or whatever the in the name of the accursed Ancients Aperion is. I just want to kill Lydeck." Colonel Kairg stepped toward Nok. "But I have to help the colony first. After that…if you're still out there, I'll see about joining up. In the meantime, if you run into Lydeck before me *or* Tretak, tear off a flipper or two for me."

Nok's shoulders slumped. He stared at the ground, nodding his head. "I guess you're the messenger Kicki prophesized."

"I've never been prophesized before," Leepoh said, back to form. "Does that mean I'm special? Am I going to be talked about for ages to come? Will I come to be revered?"

"Oh you'll be talked about all right." Nok stepped between Keerka and Leepoh. "I'm agreeing to this, but I have terms. We're not leaving until the colony and Leeg and Kicki leave."

"Done," Leepoh said.

"And we will escort them until we reach the straits."

"Yep," Leepoh agreed.

"And if everything turns into a floating heap of whale dung, we go back to Leeg and Kicki."

Leepoh raised his beak in salute. "As you wish, sir."

"All right. Now…where are Mearna and the alliance?"

"I don't know, sir," Leepoh said with precise military cadence.

"You don't know?"

"No, sir. I have no idea. But you have an Oracle nearby."

Nok gritted his beak. "True. I think I have a direction at least. We were supposed to rendezvous at Isla Fortuna. We'll start there."

"Very good, sir. Where is Isla Fortuna?"

"I was hoping you knew." Nok grunted in frustration again.

"It's on the other side of the strait," Kairg said. "Just head west. You're bound to find it."

"Thank you for the vague directions, Colonel," Nok headed toward his roost with Keerka, Leepoh followed behind. "Now we wait."

"Yes, sir," Leepoh said.

"And quit calling me sir."

"Yes, General."

"And I'm not a general. It's an honorific title."

"Yes, sir."

Nok's growling could be heard echoing throughout the warrens.

CHAPTER 58

Three days passed since the final Council of Order meeting. The colony got to the task of abandoning the warrens. They extinguished all but one of the remaining pilfered lights, leaving the last burning in the council chamber in remembrance of all who had passed through their halls. All caverns were searched and corridors were scoured to ensure nobody got left behind. When Commander Trarck received word that the last search party was clear of the mountain, he hopped off the last rock of the Warren. All three hundred thirteen surviving members of the colony watched in silence as Trarck declared that Rockhopper Colony Twenty-Three was no more and would be reconvened under a different name.

Nok walked with Keerka toward Black Sand Beach. They took pleasure in feeling the coarse sand crunch beneath their feet. As dusk approached, they stood together watching the sun set behind the rocky cliffs of their former home.

"I know they'll start again somewhere else; I just hate to see Treeg's vision die. He put so much into this colony, and the Royals killed it." Nok kicked at a small stone, suppressing a grunt when the stone didn't budge. "I'm getting that vengeful feeling again. I thought I left it behind. But to be honest, I wouldn't mind seeing every last Royal Emperor eradicated… for good this time, not like the old stories, where they were allowed to survive."

"We might get our chance. If we can convince Lavour to take command again, we will. Kicki did say he'll come back…at some point." Keerka walked along the beach, watching her footprints disappear in the surf. "I used to play in this very spot when I was a fledgling. I'm going to miss this place, but I'm glad to leave the bad memories behind."

"You can make some new ones, because there are plenty more bad memories in store for us."

"Don't be such a pessimist. We'll try to make some good memories too. Leepoh's alive, we're going to find Lavour and Meuseaux, and if it all goes right, we'll change the world for future generations."

Nok snorted a laugh. "You can show me an angry skua and try to convince me that it just has a shell stuck in its gullet. Speaking of Leepoh, did you see where he ran off to?"

^^^

Leepoh walked along the shore, staring up at Gentoo Rise. The last glow of the falling sun backlit the uppermost peak of the gentle hills, scattered wisps of clouds painted the sky in streaks of orange and violet. He braced himself and began the slow march up the rise, walking past the blasted burrows, he hoped to never see Gentoo Rise again except in memory.

Night had fallen by the time Leepoh arrived at the helicopter. He searched for Trofim, but couldn't find him inside or out of the chopper. "I wonder if got eaten?" He doubted that there was anything big enough on the island to eat a man so he decided to sit and wait.

His patience was rewarded when he heard the huffs of Trofim running up the hill. He watched him fall to the ground and do several push-ups, before making a noise to let him know he was there.

Trofim sprung to his feet, drew his knife, and was ready to strike before Leepoh could squawk an insult. "You're back," he panted.

"For the moment." Leepoh answered. "What are you running from? Did you see the Clarimeerkan?"

Trofim sheathed his weapon and pulled a towel off the railing and sat on the steps. "I'm conditioning. What's a Clarimeerkan?" he asked, wiping the sweat from his face.

"I don't know. I thought you knew."

"How would I know?"

"How would you know what?"

"What a Clari—" Trofim stood and dropped the towel along with the subject. "Never mind. Why are you back? I thought you'd be gone longer. Did you already wear out your welcome?"

Leepoh thought about the question for a second. "Well they are all fleeing the island. Bah! They're leaving because of the big scary penguin."

Trofim stepped inside and returned with a collapsible plastic cup. He walked to the back of the helicopter and took a stopper out of a makeshift cistern he constructed to collect the ever present mist. A trickle of water drained into the cup, all the while, Leepoh watching him curiously. He looked at Leepoh and lifted the cup. "*Za drujzhbu!*" He swished the water and promptly spit it out. "It's a bit briny."

Trofim grabbed a canteen and sat back on the steps. He studied Leepoh for a moment. "You're being quiet. I don't like you being quiet; it's not normal."

Leepoh parted his beak, but hesitated. Once he said what he was about to say, the words would be real. "I'm not going with you to Califorka."

Trofim looked at Leepoh over the edge of his canteen. He swallowed a little too hard, and his body deflated a little. "What about your son?"

"I... I can't. I see my friends making sacrifices; my daisy-headed friend will probably never see his only son again too. And that Randy said Mee'oni is doing really good. He even swims. He couldn't do that out here. The seals would've snatched him up in a day. I would be abandoning my friends if I went." Leepoh paced in a circle. "Just check in on him if you make it there."

"What are you going to do instead?"

"I'm going to chase down a big ugly Royal Emperor, kill her, and then we'll deal with this Aperion fellow."

Trofim stood. "When are you leaving?"

Leepoh looked at the sky. "Now," he said, letting his gaze shift to Trofim.

Trofim squatted and put both hands on Leepoh's shoulders. "You are my friend. I'm sorry to see you go."

"Hah! I knew we were friends." Leepoh turned and began to walk down the slope. "I hope you find what you're looking for, Trofim Grekov. Remember your dreams."

Trofim watched Leepoh until he disappeared from sight. He looked to the sea and called out. "*Bolshoe spasibo.*"

A moment later a reply came. "You're welcome, Trofim Geekov."

Trofim laughed, lowered his head, and sat alone.

CHAPTER 59

Lavour and Meuseaux hid against the dark stones on the shore of Isla Santa Maria in the Galapagos Islands. They stood, silent and still in the falling darkness, watching Aperion climb ashore not thirty meters away.

"Was he following us?" Meuseaux whispered.

Lavour shook with only the slightest of movement. "If he was, we would have known by now. We were lucky to come to shore when we did. Otherwise…"

"I don't like otherwise." Meuseaux lowered his head, trying to hide the white of his face. "Why is he here?"

"I don't know for sure. He's searching for his mate. That's all I know."

"I don't think he'll find her here…unless she's a Galapagos penguin." Meuseaux suppressed a laugh. "Can you imagine that? That'd be a pair."

"You have a strange sense of humor, Meuseaux." Aperion swung his head toward them. Lavour ducked his head. "Quiet."

Meuseaux did the same. "Why are we hiding? It's not like he knows we were there. I'm sure the Oracle didn't say we were."

"Maybe he saw us at some point. I don't know. I'd rather be cautious than dead."

"So it's safe for us to go then?" Meuseaux acted like he was about to stand.

"No," Lavour said a little too loudly. He shook his head at Meuseaux. "I swear, you're acting like a Gentoo more and more."

"Bah!"

The sound of a boat engine brought their attention back to what they were doing. Both Chinstraps watched the harbor cruiser coast into the bay. Aperion stood unmoving, as if he were contemplating his next move. For a moment, Lavour thought the beast would attack the boat. He was surprised to see the huge penguin quietly slink into the sea.

Lavour looked at Meuseaux. "I liked it better when I could see him. We should go inland."

"This place is infested with humans. Plus, it's a little warm on the beach. I don't like warm."

"Would you like to sit here and wait for Aperion to spring up and introduce himself to us?"

"Hmm. Humans on one side of us, big beastly thing on the other...I think I'd rather go home."

"That's not an option."

Meuseaux stared toward the southern sky. "I think it should be."

Lavour gave him an inquisitive look. "What about destiny, fate, and saving the world and all of that?"

Meuseaux closed one eye, and cocked his head. "We can't save the world if we're inside the belly of that thing," he nodded his head toward the spot Aperion had been.

"I seriously doubt that he will eat us."

"How do you think he survived for so long in the under realm of Pack Ice Command?"

Lavour gave him a dubious look. "Are you saying he's a cannibal?"

"Yes."

Lavour let out a tired breath. "I heard the stories while I was stationed there too. Are you suggesting he's the monster others spoke of? Because I'm pretty sure that story was invented by the Overlord to cover him making penguins disappear."

"All right, Commander. I won't try to persuade you." Meuseaux ducked his head toward Lavour. "Just don't get close to him when he's hungry."

Lavour laughed a little. "I don't intend to. But really, we're in this too deep to just turn around and go home now."

"Think about this: we can't hope to take him on directly. He'll swallow us whole in a second. We don't have the AIC to help and it could take who knows how long to wrest control of the Alliance from Mearna. And it will take even longer for Aperion to find his mate. And it will be even longer after that for him to gain enough power to be a real threat. I say we head back south and maybe even try to recruit Nok or T'Cuh-ka and ask them to send out scouts to seek out Mearna. You know…ask for help."

Lavour stared at his friend for a moment. "You should be Commander when the time comes."

"I don't want it."

"Do you think I do? Anyways, we'll stick around here for a few days; hopefully Aperion will just move on."

A voice coming from the rocks higher up the shore interrupted the conversation. "You are as loud as the waves crashing against the shore. I'm surprised that that creature has not returned and snatched you both into its beak."

Lavour snapped his head toward the voice, his heart pounding from surprise. "Who's there?" Meuseaux came to his side in an instant.

"Don't be so alarmed. If I intended you harm, I could've done so long before now."

Lavour looked to Meuseaux and back toward the speaker. "Who are you?"

The other sighed, followed by a slight pause, and stepped closer, revealing a two foot tall penguin with a black horseshoe stripe across its white breast and areas of pink skin showing on its face. "I am Pasillas. I am of the Humboldts, though I prefer for us to be called by the old name, Ank'ko."

"Captain Pasillas?" Lavour asked.

"Yes, the very same. However, I have relinquished my rank. Are you the scouts from the Alliance?"

Lavour cleared his throat, considering a lie, but changed his mind. "No. We're refugees from the war, so-to-speak."

Pasillas looked at Lavour sideways. "We are all refugees to some extent. And what may I call you other than refugee?"

Lavour hesitated, not so willing to give up his anonymity. He took a deep breath, letting the thick air fill his being with the final vestiges of freedom. "I'm Lavour. And this is Meuseaux."

Pasillas nodded his head. "I see you have dropped the designation of commander. News travels slowly this far north. Our brothers, the Galapagos, have received messages, but they said it was unclear as to whether you survived. And when we found out that Supreme Commander Kiley was returning, we hoped for the best."

The statement caught Lavour off guard. "Kiley is Supreme Commander, and he's coming here?" he said, giving Meuseaux a quick glance.

"You truly have been out of the current. Yes, Kiley is Supreme Commander and the AIC is headed toward us. But to be honest, I think it is a bad idea. We have been sporadically persecuted here, and I fear such a presence will bring unwanted attention…and not just human attention." Pasillas nodded toward the sea.

"I believe that is Aperion," Lavour said. "He's why we're here. He's dangerous."

Pasillas nodded and led the Chinstraps further away from the water. When they reached the top of the rocky shore he stopped and faced Lavour. "I could sense the violence dwelling inside of this Aperion. But, I…no, we will have nothing to do with fighting. The Ank'ko are near our end as a race." A splash nearby caused the three penguins to stop. "We should go inland."

Lavour stared back at the water. "I think you're right."

CHAPTER 60

Meuseaux stopped walking. "Is it safe?" he asked, looking toward an abandoned building.

Pasillas looked at Meuseaux. "I assure you, it's quite safe. With the southern current running north, you are in greater danger of starving than the humans causing you harm. We have had no acts of violence against us on this island in some time. The Galapagos leader, M'sha has offered us sanctuary, so long as we don't do anything to upset the balance."

Meuseaux resumed his walk, but at a slower pace. "Still, I don't like being this close to their settlements."

"It is a fact of life here, Meuseaux. They come to the shore and watch us. They study us and sometimes test our health, and we parade on the shore for their amusement. They have even taken to supplying us with food during these lean times."

The statement caught Lavour by surprise. He had never heard of such a thing. It didn't seem right. "But don't they find it odd to have Humboldt…I mean, Ank'ko here? You're a long way from home."

"As are you two." Pasillas looked at them from the corner of his eye. "Most humans cannot tell the differences between our races."

Lavour stopped to talk to Meuseaux. "This could be ideal for the time being. With the Alliance headed this way, we can nab two squid with one beak. And then we can go home and be done with this."

"I don't like it," Meuseaux said. "We should go find the Alliance tonight. They can't be too far away if he thought we were forward scouts or messengers."

"With Aperion swimming around out there? I think we'll do better in the light."

"This way, my friends," Pasillas called back to them. "The remainder of my clan is just beyond this shack. The humans have afforded us the opportunity of safety. We have colonized this abandoned town. It is much better than digging burrows and having our young picked off by predators."

"That's very…generous of them." Meuseaux made a motion to Lavour, telling him that they should go. Lavour shook him off.

They stepped onto a road nature had been trying her best to reclaim. Various forms of vegetation parted asphalt. Wood facings shed their paint in flakes of white and blue, and glassless windows peered out from skeletal frames. Pasillas lead them across a broken sidewalk and between a pair of crumbling plaster walls. He barked a sharp call, and Humboldt penguins began pouring from darkened doorways.

Meuseaux backed against Lavour. "I don't like this."

"Steady yourself. I'm sure they're just making a display of some sort," Lavour said, the confidence in his voice not matching his words.

The Chinstraps stepped backwards until Meuseaux bumped into a Humboldt. "Excuse me," he said. "But I really have to be going, and you're in my way." The other said nothing.

Lavour straightened to his full height of thirty inches and looked down at the slightly shorter Humboldt. "How about you tell me what's going on here, Pasillas? You're not doing a good job at putting your guests at ease."

"Commander Lavour," Pasillas began.

Lavour interrupted. "I'm no longer a commander. I told you this."

"Perhaps. But it matters very little." Pasillas raised a flipper to cut off any further interruptions. "We are doing our best to survive here, and I will not let anything get in the way of that. And Two Chinstrap penguins being followed by the Alliance will bring nothing but trouble upon us. We will do what we must to ensure our survival." Pasillas' eyes narrowed, gesturing to the penguins behind him. The mass parted to reveal several Humboldts dragging a large fishing net.

"What do you plan on doing with that?" Meuseaux asked. "You can't catch fish with your beaks? No wonder you're almost extinct."

Pasillas snorted. "It's true, the hunting is scarce here. But we are quite capable of gathering our own food. But…the humans have access to large catches, and they will value a prize such as two Chinstraps."

Lavour looked at Meuseaux. "I think it's time to go."

"What have you been waiting for?" Meuseaux said. He turned and butted his head into the nearest Humboldt.

The net wielding penguins rushed forward. "Go, go, go," Lavour shouted, but the Humboldts pressed in.

Meuseaux pushed and pecked, trying to make headway through the crowd. "I'm trying to be nice about this," he said just before giving one of his assailants a weak bite. "But they're not paying attention to my kindness."

"Do what you must, Meuseaux," Lavour said, after a group of Humboldts wedged their way between him and Meuseaux.

"If you insist," Meuseaux said. He gave the nearest penguin a vicious bite. He winced when he felt its flesh tear. The Humboldt fell away, giving him enough room to ram the next to the ground. Meuseaux looked back to tell Lavour he'd made progress, but he was nowhere to be seen. "Lavour!"

Lavour felt the weight of a dozen Humboldts attempt to push him to the ground. He knew he had been caught. There was no way out. He heard his friend's call, but he couldn't see him. "Run! Get out of here." Lavour fell to his back. He tried to roll over, but it was too late. The net fell on him, and every struggle ensnared him more. He heard Meuseaux call once more, but the weight of penguins falling on him kept him from answering.

CHAPTER 61

When Lavour didn't answer, Meuseaux knew his friend had been captured. He briefly considered going back to help, but knew if he did, he would probably end up the same way. He would help his friend, but not right now. He had to get to freedom first. But there were about forty penguins between him and the sea and more on the way. Now he had to fight.

The closest Humboldt took a sharp peck to its face, the next got one in the neck, and the one after that got a beak jabbed into his chest, followed by a slap to the head. When the third penguin fell, Meuseaux hopped on top of him to get a better view. The crowd pressed in. Meuseaux replied with a threatening hiss and dove into another fray.

He charged forward, slashing, biting, and slapping at each assailant. Four more Humboldts fell to the side, and a fifth, who wasn't smart enough to give up, took several pokes to the head, which were followed by a flurry of slaps. When the Humboldt finally fell, Meuseaux huffed, marveling at the penguin's stubbornness. Finding himself with room to fight, he chose his next target, a timid-looking male who appeared to want nothing to do with him. Meuseaux rushed forward, and the nervous male fled. His satisfaction at scaring off an attacker was short-lived. A robust female broadsided him, sending him skidding on his side on a rough patch of earth.

"Not good," Meuseaux muttered, trying to get to his feet. He could hear the rush of feet closing in, and knew his luck was about to run out. Without a second thought, he rolled sideways toward his attackers, causing the first to awkwardly fall over him. The awkwardness continued when Meuseaux attempted to stand and stumbled into the next Humboldt, causing that one to fall against another. After several seconds of tripping, tumbling, and squawks of frustration, Meuseaux found himself looking over several penguins slowly getting to their feet.

He looked around. He was out of the town, but still a good distance from the shore, with a larger group of even more determined Humboldt closing in. He began to run toward the shore, knocking over a Humboldt who had just found his feet.

The Humboldts began to close in from either side, attempting to cut off his escape. Meuseaux bore down, urging his feet to move faster than they ever had. He could see the rocky shoreline ahead. The Humboldts closed in. He ran, hopped, and skipped over the rough terrain. Escape was in sight, and no manner of penguin would keep him from freedom. He made it to the outcroppings and leapt onto the nearest rock. The sea and escape lay just below him. Before leaping, he heard Pasillas' call.

"If you attempt to return to rescue your friend, we will be left with no choice but to kill you."

"Many have tried, and many have failed. I'll see you soon, Captain." Meuseaux gave Pasillas a mocking salute and jumped toward the sea. He landed with a grunt on rock exposed by the low tide, and tumbled into the water.

CHAPTER 62

No less than a dozen Humboldt penguins dragged their netted prize across the broken pavement. Lavour endured the indignity in silence. He caught sight of Pasillas before being dumped in a back room of a decrepit building and fixed him with a glare that left no doubt in other's mind what would happen when he got free. The problem was getting free, and being tangled and twisted in the tortuous netting limited his options.

He tried to bite through the netting, but the sturdy nylon held. And for the first time ever, he wished he still had the metal tip on his beak. He rolled to his side, his fat reserve protecting him from the jabs of broken ceramic tiles. He squirmed, trying to figure out how to stand, but no amount of effort got him to his feet. He rolled back and listened to the clinking of the broken ceramic. His mind fell back on the memory of shattering glass during the fighting on the Falkland Islands. The images of flaming penguins flashed through his mind. The horror of it all was too much, and now he would die because of the war too. He almost preferred to be eaten by a Phocid; at least it was natural.

The sound of claws ticking against littered linoleum pulled him back into the now. He waited to see who or what had come to see him. He spotted a shadow just outside the door. "Are you going to talk, or stand there and admire your trophy?"

"Commander Lavour, you are not a trophy. Trophies are to be kept." Pasillas stepped into the room. Lavour twisted, trying to get at him. "Easy, Commander. The more you struggle, the tighter it becomes…or so I am told."

Lavour growled in frustration. "What do you hope to gain from this? You can't possibly think you can trust the humans."

"Actually I do. They have kept us sheltered and fed. The natives were not keen to help us when we arrived. But these people, they befriended us, and as long as we occasionally give them what they want, like say, a war refugee, they give us food. If you would've met the natives, you would have seen how they are starving and we are fat."

"So you speak their language? And you've made an alliance with them?"

"Let's call it an agreement. I suggest you rest. The men will be here at daybreak, and this may be your last time to enjoy your sleep." Pasillas spun to leave.

"You know, Antaean made *agreements* with the humans too. And in the end, they destroyed everything he built."

Pasillas abruptly turned back to Lavour. "That is where we differ. We are not a threat, while you and your Overlord were."

"If I get out of—"

"You won't, Commander. And if your friend foolishly decides to attempt to save you…"

"What, Pasillas? Say it, or remain a coward."

"Then I will protect my colony at all cost, even if it costs Meuseaux's life." Pasillas looked him over. "Rest Commander, Lavour. Tomorrow will be a longer day than this."

Lavour opened his beak to throw an insult, but the door shut, locking him in. "I've heard that before." He looked at what he could; there wasn't much to see in the vacant restroom. Light flowed from a high window. "I sure wish the Oracle would've warned me about this."

CHAPTER 63

"Supreme Commander," an Adélie penguin scout said, falling in and swimming alongside of Kiley.

Kiley slowed his pace to allow the other to speak. "Did you receive word from Captain Pasillas?"

"Actually, sir, he has sent messengers."

Kiley ordered the procession to come to a halt. Calls carrying the orders repeated themselves until reaching the rear line of the mass of penguins. "Where are they?" Kiley snapped, letting his irritation show. He knew all too well that messengers rarely carried good news.

The Adélie stiffened her body to attention. "I apologize, sir. It's just that the established protocol dictates that I inform the commanding officer before bringing unknown penguins to meet with him."

"If I wanted a lesson on protocol, I would ask a Macaroni penguin," Kiley said, trying his best to remain calm. "Now fetch them at once, Corporal."

After the messenger swam away, Commandant Welsy approached Kiley. "Sir, Corporal Mitsi is one of our best scouts. I hope I am not overstepping my rank, but experience has taught us that loyalty cannot be beaten into those who we command."

"Thank you for the lesson, Commandant. And yes, you are overstepping your rank." Kiley narrowed his eyes. "But…in this case, I will allow it."

"My apologies, Supreme Commander."

Kiley watched the horizon, anxiously awaiting the arrival of the messengers. The further north they went, the more tense he had grown. He needed to go south. The Order of Kings be damned, he needed to go back. "Commandant, I'm certain the messengers will bring more ill fortune. Therefore I've come to a decision. We will conduct one raid and then we will return south." Kiley watched Welsy turn the idea over in his head.

"Sir, are you certain that's wise? The Doyenne did give us specific orders."

"The Doyenne will cease to be before long. We will return home and take control of the Alliance once and for all." Welsy looked like he was holding something back. "Spit it out, Commandant. You may speak freely."

Welsy hesitated, clearing his throat. "I don't want to return home. There are many among us who want to find the northern paradise. I would like to go and be done with the war. We can establish a colony if we find it."

"Out of the question, Commandant. The war is far from over; in fact, it is only just beginning. I will not allow you to be released from your duties until this is over."

The call of Mitsi drew Welsy's eyes away. "Will it be over before we're all dead?"

Kiley felt his anger rise over Welsy's insolence. How dare he be so condescending? He nearly lashed out. He let his rage die off instead, remembering he had told Welsy to speak freely. But he wouldn't let Welsy retire, if for no other reason than spite. The Adélie arrived, cutting off further discussion.

Mitsi introduced the messengers to Kiley and drifted aside. "Mi Caudillo, Kiley. Pasillas has sent us to warn you of great danger ahead."

Kiley gave Welsy a brief look. "Let's hear it."

"Pasillas instructed us to tell you that even though he is indebted to you for the battle which cost us our breeding grounds, he regretfully cannot commit to the Alliance of Independent Colonies. Our population has fallen dramatically, and staying where we are, where the humans do no harm, is the only way we will be able to survive. Furthermore, food is in short supply, and the addition of a group the size of the Alliance would be detrimental. Your course of action is up to you, but he urges you to bypass the islands. If you choose to proceed, the humans will become aware, and it will cost us all. He also urges you to recall the large penguin who has been seen around the islands. He gives you the blessing of the Ancients and thanks you."

"What do you think, Commandant?" Kiley said to Welsy. "We know the current has shifted."

"While the islands may be an ideal place to strike, it may not be in our best interest. We had the Magellanics and other locals at the Falklands working in preparation for the assault, and we still were beaten rather badly. And we have even fewer resources now." Welsy looked to his right and spotted a crested penguin swimming nearby. There were thousands of crested penguins in the AIC. He ignored it and returned his attention to Kiley.

Kiley let out a heavy breath. "If Pasillas doesn't believe the timing is right, we will continue west and find a soft target on the mainland. Tell Pasillas thank you, and that I wish him well, in the name of the Ancients."

Commandant Welsy waited until the messengers were gone before speaking. "Do you think they were talking about Aperion?"

Kiley shot Welsy an incredulous look for even asking. "I have no doubt that it is. But, there's little we can do about it at the moment. If what we were told is true, Aperion will have to wait. And to be honest, I don't think he is the threat Mearna makes him to be. It's a war between their clans; a war that I wouldn't mind seeing the Royals lose." Kiley looked to the stars, quietly mulling over what the future might hold. He thought about the Order of Kings and coughed a derisive laugh. They had been too short-sighted. He needed to bring them into the fold and he would do it with the force of the AIC behind him. "Send the scouts west to find our target. We've already wasted too much time going north. One assault to grab attention, and then we're on our way."

"Yes sir." Welsy let a slow breath of resignation escape and swam away.

^^^

Lydeck swam as close as he dared to eavesdrop on the conversation. Although he heard only a little, he had heard enough. Aperion was near. Now all he had to do was find him. Lydeck guessed that a creature as big as the legendary Aperion was supposed shouldn't be that hard to find. He let himself fall beneath the surface and swam away, feeling both the excitement of seeing his plans come to fruition and the anxiousness of finding the beast.

CHAPTER 64

Meuseaux swam for nearly an hour, making certain he hadn't been followed. He drifted on the surface in a calm and secluded cove, trying to formulate a plan to rescue Lavour. He wouldn't leave him behind, even if it cost both of their lives. He slowly paddled, mulling over the possibilities. It would take a while to find the Alliance, and then he would have to convince them to help, which would take even longer. That wouldn't do.

He thought about beseeching the aid of the native Galapagos penguins, but he was sure Pasillas had struck a deal with them, too. Even if he hadn't, why would a group of starving penguins care about the fate of one Chinstrap? They wouldn't. There had to be another answer. Meuseaux kicked toward the shore, frustrated and feeling helpless. A light wind skimmed along the surface, threatening to lull him into sleep. The El Niño warmth of the equatorial sea, doused with the cold Peruvian Current, allying itself with the wind to make Meuseaux sleep.

"No," Meuseaux said, becoming suddenly alert. The quiet of the night was broken by the calls of distressed Fur Seals. Meuseaux's first thought was that a predator might be near. But since he was still alive to have the thought, he thought otherwise. He looked toward the noise and decided that it was in his best interest to go opposite of the disturbance. He took another look back before swimming away, and glimpsed the silhouette of

Aperion on the shore.

He quickly turned away, eager to not get eaten by either predators or a cannibal penguin. After a few short strokes, he stopped. He looked back at Aperion moving on the dark shore with surprising ease. Meuseaux lowered his head, remembering part of one the stories of the Ancients he'd heard in his youth. It was something about big problems requiring big solutions. He couldn't remember the story in its entirety; it had something to do with a penguin getting stuck in an iceberg, but he did remember the phrase. Meuseaux swam in circles, debating what to do. He couldn't hope to take on Pasillas and his clan alone, but there was a great possibility that if he did what he was contemplating, he would end up as Aperion's meal. Either way, the outcome wasn't certain, but he hadn't been certain of much for the past year.

He made up his mind. It would be dangerous, and probably one of the more stupid things he had ever done, but he could see no other recourse. He redoubled his resolve and quickly swam toward Aperion, hoping to catch him before he decided to quit harassing the seals.

Meuseaux jumped on to the rocky beach and marched with as much determination as he could find. His legs felt weak and his breathing came in shallow fits. He tried to convince himself of his bravery; that he had faced and killed Liutites, outsmarted Phocid and Royals; there were no obstacles he couldn't overcome. He squeezed past the upset seals and planted his feet firmly in the sand behind Aperion. *I am the killer of Royals. I have no fear.* He braced himself, and looking up at the enormous penguin's back, he called to him. "Aperion, I wish to speak with you." His voice remained unwavering and strong.

He watched curiously as Aperion lifted his head high and turned to face him. Meuseaux saw Aperion's massive beak pointing to the sky, and then he saw the tail of a young seal disappear down his throat. Meuseaux's legs threatened to fall out from under him. He had seriously miscalculated the Basileios, and wondered if he was facing one of the Ancients of legend.

Aperion's black eyes fell on Meuseaux while his head bobbed to swallow his meal. He clicked his beak together several times and stared down at the much smaller penguin. "You're a long way from home, Chinstrap." He brought his beak down and snapped it shut in front of Meuseaux's face so quickly that he had no time to react.

Meuseaux flinched, but stood his ground. "I'm here to ask you a favor."

Aperion let out a disturbing, almost guttural laugh. "A favor? The only favor I'll grant a Chinstrap is to end your pitiable existence quickly. Your sole purpose is for your young to feed the raptors, and your adults to feed the Phocids. Now leave, before I lose my patience." He turned away, nudging upset seals aside with his beak.

Meuseaux watched Aperion move through the throng of seals. He was larger than any penguin he had ever seen, save the Kaurochs, and he was also his only hope of saving Lavour. "I would return a favor, of course. But if you have no need for an army to destroy the Royal Emperors, including Mearna, then I will excuse myself" He braced himself for an outburst that never came. It surprised him. He expected Aperion to react the same way Liutites might have. But he found the calm much more disturbing.

Aperion turned back, taking slow steps, never taking his eyes from Meuseaux. "Who are you to offer me, what is it called, the Alliance?"

"My name is Meuseaux, and if you help me free my friend Lavour, you will have your soldiers."

Aperion laughed once again, this time sounding almost sincere. "You are the penguins who killed Liutites? This is funny. I expected you to be at least slightly formidable. You have made my day, knowing that the great Liutites was killed by a penguin such as you. It's quite pathetic. Now go away, before I lose my good humor."

Good humor? Meuseaux thought. If threats of killing and laughing at another's death were his good humor, he didn't want to know what made him angry. "Lavour can rally the Alliance against Mearna. They would follow him to the stars if we could go there. They would be a valuable asset in you search for your queen." The next thing Meuseaux knew, he splash-landed back in the cove. He had no idea how he had got there. He felt a burning sensation across his body and remembered that he had been slapped. He shook his head clear and climbed back to the shore.

"You've come back for more." Aperion loomed over him, black coat against the night sky poised to strike the killing blow.

"Actually, no," Meuseaux said, making sure to stand out of reach of Aperion's flippers. "I've come back to once again ask for your help."

Aperion stood motionless and silent for nearly a minute, gauging Meuseaux's resolve. When the Chinstrap didn't waiver, he relaxed his posture. "Can you guarantee me control of the Alliance?"

Meuseaux figured that honesty might serve him better in this situation rather than an empty promise. "No, I can't. But it is a great possibility."

Aperion hissed a laugh. "I commend you, Chinstrap. Most penguins would falter and lie to tell me what I want to hear. If you cannot guarantee this army, I demand something else only you can promise. And if you do so, I will save the great leader, Commander Lavour."

Meuseaux braced himself for whatever would come next. He knew no good would come from it, but he would do whatever it took to save Lavour. "What do you demand?"

Aperion's eyes narrowed with a glee only a demon could feel. "Swear your allegiance to me. Obey my commands; do my bidding; spend your days in my service. Agree to these demands, and I will grant your favor."

Meuseaux closed his eyes. He fought through the murkiness of his mind, trying to find another solution, anything that would keep him from doing what he was about to do. Nothing came forward; no great enlightenment shone the way to another possibility. It was either this or let Lavour die. He lifted his head and met eyes so dark they seemed to steal the light from the stars. "I will swear allegiance to you, Aperion…my lord."

Aperion walked to the shore and leaned his head down to Meuseaux. "I hope your friend's life is worth your servitude."

Meuseaux wrestled with the answer. Lavour is needed to set things right, not him. There were no other options. Meuseaux the escapist had finally been caught.

CHAPTER 65

Aperion followed Meuseaux to the edge of the abandoned town. Having the monstrous penguin at his back made Meuseaux more than a little nervous. He didn't put it past the beast to change his mind about the deal and swallow him whole like he had the seal pup. He made a special point to stay a few steps out of reach of Aperion's beak, just in case.

Meuseaux slowed his pace to a creep. The outline of a ram shackled one-story building revealed itself from the mist and darkness. He saw a Humboldt round the corner of the building. Meuseaux motioned for Aperion to stop. "It looks like a sentry," Meuseaux said.

"Sentries don't concern me," Aperion said, making a motion to go forward.

Meuseaux jumped in front of him. "No, no, no. What are you doing? We can't just rush in. We have to be quiet. We sneak in, find him, and get out before they know he's gone." Aperion fixed him with a look that told the Chinstrap that he was considering biting his head off. Meuseaux had no doubt that the head removal would be literal, not a verbal reprimand.

"And if your friend is already gone or dead, what then?"

Meuseaux looked at the sentry; he hadn't considered that option. He had taken Pasillas' word that they were capturing Lavour, not killing him. "If he's dead, then we take his body and leave it to the sea. If he's gone...

then there's nothing we can do."

"It would be a shame to waste a fresh kill on the sea."

Meuseaux spun toward Aperion. "Listen to me. You are not buried under Antaean's feet any longer. As long as we're in this arrangement, you will not cannibalize anyone. You're not scavenging for food anymore. There's plenty of catch for you to eat other than penguins." Meuseaux stood firm, unwavering beneath Aperion's glare.

Aperion leaned in, his beak nearly touching Meuseaux's. He let the silence hang in the air for several breaths. "I like the taste." Aperion raised his head, looking like he was about to strike. Then he turned his attention back to the sentry.

Meuseaux tried to hide his relief, letting the breath he had been holding slowly escape. "Now here's the plan… I'll skirt the first building you see there and try to gauge where Lavour is being held. There should be guards wherever they're keeping him. Shouldn't be too hard to find. When I give the signal, you make your way toward me. Make slow, but steady movements. We don't want to be seen."

"Why would I care about being seen?"

Meuseaux was surprised Aperion even had to ask, especially for someone who had spent his life hiding in the shadows. "Because if we're seen, it will become much more difficult, and we'll have to fight our way out."

Aperion raised himself to his full height. "Your timidity sickens me." Without warning, he rushed toward the nearest building. Powerful legs pushed him forward with such strength that his body became nearly parallel to the ground. His claws dug into the loose soil while he swung his wings forward in a galloping motion.

Startled by the outburst, it took Meuseaux a moment before he realized what Aperion was about to do. He shouted for him to stop, but the enormous penguin paid him no mind. He ran to catch him, but the Basileios outdistanced him in no time. He could only watch when the sentry, alerted by the disturbance, came back around the corner and met the tip of Aperion's charging beak.

Meuseaux reached the building without a glance toward the Humboldt. He was dead; Aperion's beak had gone clean through his body. No need to check. He spotted Aperion walk onto the crumbling road, spinning his head, looking for the next challenger. When no penguin challenged him, they became victims.

Alarm calls echoed through the heavy night air, and several more Humboldt rushed out to meet the emergency. Meuseaux tried to yell to warn them to stay hidden, but it was too late. Aperion began tearing through penguins with a sadistic glee. They didn't try to fight. They tried to run, but Aperion caught them, bit them, stabbed them, and in some cases, tore off their wings and watched them stand frozen in shock before finally taking them into his beak and snapping their necks.

The Humboldts tried to hide in their buildings, but he found them. They fled from dark rooms, chased by the specter of death, who snatched them up and tossed them against walls and into the ground. When one eluded him, the next one would suffer twice as payment for the other's escape.

Meuseaux became ill from the violence. The horror Aperion was capable of stole the strength from his legs, and he nearly fell to the ground. "What have I done?" he whispered. Pasillas was guilty of treason, of betraying trust for his own good, but this was too much. He had to find a way to stop the carnage he had unleashed. He found his wits and ran to the buildings Aperion hadn't yet come to. He told the fear-stricken Humboldts, hiding in the shadows, to run, to get out before death arrived. Very few listened, believing they were safe in the sanctuary provided to them.

With no other recourse, Meuseaux called on his anger to overcome his fear and marched into the street. He demanded to Aperion that he stop immediately. Aperion let a Humboldt fall from his beak and walked directly toward him. Meuseaux didn't budge when the brute stood before him, letting blood and gore fall from his beak at his feet.

"Do you not want me to rescue your friend?" Aperion said, his voice sounding like the whisper of Cuasan.

"Not like this." Meuseaux's voice quivered, but he held firm. "No more."

Aperion turned his attention to the sound of Pasillas emerging from a doorway.

"I did not expect a Chinstrap to unleash such barbarism on my colony. Is this my punishment for my sins, Meuseaux; to see my kind brought to extinction before my very eyes? We are gone. This generation is indeed the last." Pasillas' voice sounded small and resigned.

Meuseaux looked at Aperion, who didn't move. He hoped he stayed that way. "It wasn't supposed to be this way. I simply wanted to free Lavour. I didn't want this." He motioned to the carnage in the street.

"That is what happens when you seek the aid of demons. Death comes to you, death follows you. I sought the aid of demons myself, and it has led to this."

Meuseaux lowered his head. He had no doubt that he had saved Lavour's life, but he was certain that Lavour would say the price was too high. "Just release Lavour, and we'll leave."

Pasillas shook his head. "No. We will all pay for our deeds. The men will be here by morning, and you and this beast, along with Lavour, will die."

Meuseaux felt his frustration rise. All of this would not be for nothing. Pasillas was mad; he was certain of it now. How could he refuse with death standing so close? "Tell me where he is," he said with deliberation. Meuseaux motioned for Aperion.

"Death does not hold sway over me, Meuseaux. Your pet may take me to the Great Sea, but I have no fear."

Aperion stepped toward Pasillas. "He didn't say I was going to kill you. I can leave you alive for a very long time."

"You do not scare me, beast," Pasillas said, stepping back.

"What am I doing?" Meuseaux said, shaking his head. He lifted his beak and called for Lavour. A second later, Lavour replied. He looked at

Aperion and started walking toward the call. "This way."

Pasillas followed close behind. "It will do you no good. You cannot get to him. He is sealed in his prison until the men arrive."

Meuseaux rushed into the small outbuilding holding Lavour and called once again. "Are you in here? Where are you?"

"I'm in here," Lavour answered. "I'm trapped. I can't stand."

"You see, Meuseaux?" Pasillas motioned toward the doorknob. "Only the men can open this dungeon. We can't."

Meuseaux started scratching on the wooden door. "Lavour, can you reach this…this door with your feet? It will take too long for me to dig through. It sounds hollow, but it's strong." He heard Lavour make grunting noises on the other side.

"I can't. Just leave before they come. Save yourself, Meuseaux."

Aperion stepped up to the door and tapped on it with his beak. He fumbled with the round doorknob and stepped back.

"You see as well, beast. Your efforts were for nothing. I will stay here and laugh when the men arrive and kill you."

Aperion reached down and took Pasillas in his beak.

"Kill me if you will. It will still not save your friend."

Aperion reared back and hurled Pasillas against the hollow wood door, splintering it slightly. The Humboldt fell to the littered floor, and Aperion grabbed him once more and repeated the throw. Pasillas crumpled in a heap. Aperion took him again, threw him, and this time Pasillas crashed through the door. Aperion looked inside the room, ripped away the remaining door, and grabbed the net, dragging it and Lavour out of the small restroom. He took the net in his beak and shook until Lavour fell out.

Lavour scurried away, terrified by the massive form of Aperion standing over him.

Meuseaux stepped between the two. "It's all right. I'll explain on our way out of here."

"Is that—?" Lavour stammered.

"Yes." Meuseaux said. "But we have to go, now."

"I've upheld my part. Now take me to your alliance," Aperion said in an odd, yet calm voice, as if the violence had temporarily quelled his rage.

Lavour looked at Meuseaux through narrowed eyes. "What have you done?"

CHAPTER 66

Lydeck floated just off the coast of Isla Santa Maria, discouraged over his prospects of finding Aperion. The islands were much bigger than he imagined, and there were several. He realized it could take a long time to find him, and he didn't have a long time. He needed to get back to RHC23 before Mearna could consolidate her power, or worse, destroy the Rockhoppers who resisted her. There was no point in being Commander of the Colony if there wasn't a colony.

He scanned the horizon of the nearby island, spotted the lights of towns. He was relatively certain that Aperion wouldn't step foot in a place so inhabited. In the midst of his labored deliberations, Lydeck heard a curious sound from somewhere ahead of him. It was an odd sound, a sound he couldn't remember hearing before. He swam toward the noise.

The closer Lydeck got, the more he realized it wasn't a natural sound. It was the sound of man. His mind flashed back to being taken aboard that terrible ship. He remembered the clank of chains and the odd resonance of their claws on the metal stairs as they climbed to freedom; the slamming of steel doors. And then he remembered the scene in the bridge; the men dying, penguins dying, the blood and carnage, and standing in the deepest part of the room, hiding from the fray. He shook away the memory. That was a different time. His fear had begun to fade.

Lost in his reveries, Lydeck didn't realize that he had drifted within sight of what made the clanging noise. A strange object floated on the surface. With each rise and fall of the water, the tall object rang out. Keeping his distance, Lydeck circled the noisemaker and concluded that it was too small for a boat. He dove below to get a look and found that it was tethered to the seafloor. Curiosity got the better of him, and he decided he needed to see the object close up. Lydeck dove and swam toward it, and surfaced only a meter away. When he finally got a good look at it, he spotted a seal sleeping on board. Thinking it was a sea lion, Lydeck fled as fast as he could.

When he was a good distance away, another odd sound caught his ear. This was a sound he did know. It was the sound of penguins. Though he didn't recognize the calls or know which clan they belonged to, he did know they were calls of distress. Something was wrong. That meant going the opposite direction.

He got no more than two or three strokes away before a thought flashed in his mind. It fled as quickly as it had come. He began again, and the thought returned. *What if Aperion is causing the ruckus?* Proud of his brilliance, he swam toward the disruption.

Lydeck found an easy shore to climb up and hobbled toward the sound. A misty fog disguised the landscape, muting the sound slightly. He continued across unfamiliar terrain, warily at first, but gaining confidence with each step. His progress came to a sudden halt when a skeletal building appeared in the mist. Its broken posts and beams intimidated Lydeck enough to make him take a few steps back, but the squawks of dying penguins planted his feet to the ground. He couldn't move; whether from fear or morbid curiosity, or both, he felt compelled to stay.

The sound of death entered his mind and he drifted back to the colony, imaging it was Nok and Trarck's screams of agony. And Tearsk, that inept little waste of a penguin, he would suffer a long and excruciatingly painful death. Lydeck laughed at the thought of it all. Then he would enter the warren and put an end to the suffering by controlling the beast. "They will worship me as their savior."

The sound of a Chinstrap's call brought Lydeck back to reality. "Why would a Chinstrap be here? Unless…" Lydeck felt his pulse race. The Alliance had gotten here first. How did they beat him? They couldn't have. It had to be a scout, nothing more. He could deal with a scout or two. He listened to calls between the Chinstraps; they spoke in their native tongue, and he only spoke Common and Northern Rockhopper. He would have to wait to see what they were up to; he couldn't imagine a Chinstrap, or even two Chinstraps, could cause the amount of damage he'd heard.

The sound of killing had gone silent, allowing Lydeck to find his feet. He took a cautious step toward the town and lost the strength to take a second. A large black figure emerged from the darkened street, highlighted by vague moonlight and distant street lights seeping through the fog. The mist swirled around a form as big as a man, but with the shape of a penguin. It moved quickly, quicker than any penguin he'd ever seen, and it headed straight toward him. His heart raced. This thing could kill him, it would kill him. The creature loomed closer; no time to move. It took all of Lydeck's strength just to open his beak. "Lord Aperion," he said, bowing his head.

Aperion stopped and lowered his head to inspect the Rockhopper. He snorted and went on his way.

Once again, Lydeck's feet felt planted in the ground. They were heavy and unyielding. His breath came in rasping fits. When at last he realized that he hadn't been killed, his paralysis subsided. He looked back and saw his hope begin to fade into the mist. Two Chinstraps followed Aperion, looking back at him. He shook his head clear and called out. "Wait, Lord Aperion, I have important information." He felt a mix of relief and fear when Aperion turned back and rushed toward him.

The Basileios drew himself to his full height, looking down his beak at the diminutive penguin. "What information could a Rockhopper have for me? Spit it out, before I remove your head for delaying me."

"My apologies, my lord. To be honest, I am only guessing that you will want this. But I know where the Oracle lives." Lydeck bowed his head.

"The Oracle does not live anywhere. I killed her," Aperion growled and turned away.

"I was with Mearna and her Alliance at the atoll. I am aware that you killed an Oracle, but there is another."

Aperion spun around and struck Lydeck, sending him flying several feet away. "Lies will get you killed, Rockhopper."

Lydeck stayed on his back. Even if he wanted to, he couldn't stand. "I am aware of the danger, Lord Aperion. And I am not willing to die for a lie. I tell you, there is an Oracle and I know where she is." For the briefest of moments, Lydeck thought he saw uncertainty in Aperion's eyes. The uncertainty vanished when Aperion leapt toward him, landing inches away.

"Tell me where she is." Aperion's voice carried a darkness that made the other begin to quiver.

Lydeck stood and steeled his nerves. He looked at the two Chinstraps, who were watching the display with both apprehension and curiosity. "I will lead you to her…if you help me."

"You will tell me or I will tear your flesh from your bones," Aperion bellowed. He took Lydeck in his beak, swallowed him up to his feet, and spat him to the ground.

Lydeck stood, the smell of penguin flesh clinging to his feathers. He knew if he told him, he would die. He also knew that even if he didn't, he still might die. He shook the bits of Humboldt from his coat and stood firm. "If you kill me, you will never know where she is. And Mearna, who is on her way to find the Oracle, will use her to hunt you down and destroy you."

Aperion laughed. "She will die trying."

"I only say what I heard. She fears you and wants to kill you. She has enough support to do it."

Aperion stood silent for far too long, studying Lydeck. "The Oracle is a

Rockhopper," he said. His eyes glinted with satisfaction when Lydeck tried to mask surprise at hearing he knew. "I think I will kill you now."

Lydeck scrambled to get away. "There are a thousand islands in our region, and it will take you a thousand moons to find her. And in that time, Mearna will find you through the Oracle and send her army to destroy you. I know where she is. I will lead you to her. All you have to do is kill a few Rockhoppers, and you can do with her as you wish. Eat her, drown her, feed her to the Petrels; I don't care. She has already caused me enough trouble and she is only a fledgling."

Aperion watched Lydeck for any signs of a lie. "Why not kill her yourself? Surely a young Oracle's power is not enough to stop an adult," he said through a sinister hiss of a laugh. He began to walk away again.

"I tried," Lydeck grumbled, circling in front of Aperion. "But Mearna and her Shadow Warriors betrayed me, and Commander Nok and his cronies thwarted me. They're the ones who need to die."

Aperion looked at a distant light through a break in the fog, no longer paying attention to Lydeck. "I doubt that Mearna aims to destroy me. She has tried in the past, and she has tried other means to coerce me to her side as well. She is a fool, like every other K'tha."

Lydeck stared at Aperion blankly. He didn't know what a K'tha was, and he didn't care. He only cared about killing Nok and the others. This centuries-long feud had nothing to do with him. He waited for Aperion to finish his internal struggles and saw the two Chinstraps glaring at him. Lydeck couldn't distinguish one Chinstrap from the other, but something about them seemed familiar. He returned their glare. Why would they glare at him? He had never crossed a Chinstrap.

"Take me to this Oracle," Aperion said.

"Huh?" Lydeck said, snapping out of his stare down.

"The Oracle. Lead me to her. And know this, if I find you have mislead me, you will pray for death every day for the rest of your life." Aperion turned to Meuseaux and Lavour. "But you will take me to the Alliance first.

I may have need of them."

Lavour looked at Meuseaux with accusation burning in his eyes.

He nodded to Aperion without speaking.

Aperion noticed the exchange between the Chinstraps and Lydeck. "Have you met Commander Lavour before?" he asked Lydeck.

The Rockhopper jerked in surprise. That's where he had seen him; at the colony. He was friends with Nok—he had talked about him frequently. If he said something now, he'd be dead. Aperion would rely on them to show him to the island. "Only by reputation."

Aperion watched for Lavour's reaction. When nothing came of it, he walked to the shoreline. "Chinstrap, we leave now." Meuseaux looked at Lavour and rushed away, leaving Lavour alone with Lydeck.

Lavour stepped in close to Lydeck. "You won't get away with this. I'll kill you before I let that beast harm Nok."

The venom in Lavour's voice was apparent, and Lydeck believed the threat. "You had your chance. In fact, if you hadn't abandoned the AIC, Mearna wouldn't have control, and Nok wouldn't get murdered. Your chances are over, *Commander* Lavour."

Lavour stepped back. "I haven't taken my chance yet. It's a long swim back; keep an eye on your wake." He turned and rushed toward Meuseaux.

"Watch my wake," Lydeck said to himself, making a derisive snort. He watched Lavour's back, fantasizing about putting his beak in it and a thought occurred. *He was the one who killed the Supreme Commander.* Whatever confidence Lydeck had gained vanished the moment he remembered that fact. Lavour could probably uphold his threats with ease, but not if he got to the Chinstraps first. Lydeck limped to the shore, his mind brewing a plan. "He's right, I do have a long swim ahead of me. I'll figure out how to kill him along the way." Lydeck looked around, wondering if he had said that out loud.

CHAPTER 67

Pin watched the waves from the beach of the lonely atoll, the sun warming his body just enough to be comfortable. He had settled into a daily routine of hunting at midday, when predators would be the least likely to be on the hunt. Today was no different than the numerous days before. He had finished his meal and enjoyed the solitude. The occasional gull would swoop in and figure out that he still wasn't a meal after weeks of trying. He had tried to tell them, but they only squawked when he tried. This led to him naming each stupid gull a vulgarity of one form or another.

Bored of the sea, he walked back toward the cave. When he reached the apex of the low dunes, he looked across the waves and spotted a penguin porpoising toward the shore. It headed in from the south. He thought it must be a scout from the Alliance who had gotten turned around. They should be coming from the north. He scurried to the cave, hiding in the shadows to see who had arrived.

A Rockhopper came ashore and immediately began inspecting the sand. Pin had no idea what it was doing until it put its foot against one of his footprints. The Rockhopper was looking for someone. He hoped it was the one who had tried to kill him. He wanted to get his revenge.

Pin watched a little longer and saw the Rockhopper begin to follow his tracks. It couldn't follow them through the softer sand, so he wasn't concerned. He noticed that the Rockhopper didn't limp like the one who attacked him. It could've healed. He saw the penguin look toward the cave and remembered he was in the only shelter on the island. Then he saw the holes in his ambush plan. He dismissed his doubts; whoever was out there still wouldn't know where he'd hidden.

The shuffling of feet through sand came nearer, and Pin backed against the nearest wall. He saw the yellow plumage pop through the mouth. Deciding not to let his foe's eyes adjust, Pin sprung his trap, charging at the Rockhopper with all of his might. The Rockhopper heard the attack coming and ducked back outside. Pin raced outside; he had the enemy on the run. The bright sun obscured his vision. He ran into the Rockhopper's stomach and fell backwards.

"Hey, watch yourself, little fellow," the Rockhopper said, looking past him into the cave. "What's got you so spooked?"

Pin stayed lying on the ground, looking up, giving the Rockhopper a verbal what-for. He stood, still spouting a long list of reasons why he hated being called *little fellow*.

The Rockhopper endured the assault, patiently waiting for Pin to stop. He lobbed one more insult about the Rockhopper's parents, and the Rockhopper put an end to it. "That's enough. Don't talk about my parents like that."

Pin blinked his eyes in surprise and chirped some more.

"Yes, I understood most of what you said. Did you really call me a sea urchin's…well, you know?"

Pin lowered his head and chattered an acknowledgement. He followed up by asking the other's name, and how she knew Blue speak?

"My name is Tretak. What's yours?"

Pin answered and asked a series of questions in rapid succession.

"Slow down. I know your language, but you have to go a little slower," she said, looking around the atoll.

Pin asked the same questions with exaggerated slowness and somewhat sarcastically.

"I've been a few places in my life, and I picked up Blue, but I can't speak it. I come from RHC23, and I'm hunting another Rockhopper. Maybe you've seen him."

Pin rambled about how a Rockhopper had tried to kill him and how he thought she might've been him.

"You need to work on your attack," she said, eliciting a comment about what she could do with her opinion. Tretak chuckled at the insult. "But it seems you've met Lydeck, too. I've been on his tail for some time. But I lost the Alliance around Isla Tenquehuen. Was he still limping? I did that, you know? Wish it was more than his toe."

Pin chattered to her about how the Alliance might come back and how they were going to overthrow Mearna. After careful consideration, he also decided that Tretak would be a welcomed guest on his atoll.

Tretak laughed a little. "Your island, huh? Are you sure they're coming back?"

He told her nothing was certain, but if they did, this would be the way they'd come.

Tretak walked to the north shore and stared across the sea. She turned back, squinting her eyes as she thought about the offer. "You know, I could use a rest. I've been at sea so long, I almost forgot how to walk."

Pin looked at her feet, telling her if he had feet that big, he wouldn't want to remember how to walk.

"What…an insult with no swearing? I'm already a little disappointed in you." Tretak laughed.

Pin made up for it by lavishing her with an extended tirade of profane insults that carried on as they walked the length of the beach.

CHAPTER 68

Santa Monica, California. An obtrusive, gleaming glass building transformed the easy morning sunlight into harsh penetrating rays, blinding the occupants of the neighboring buildings. The employees stationed near the windows of the victimized structures yanked the plastic chains of solar-gray screens, diffusing the redirected stellar light to a tolerable level. Every year, at the same time of year, the sunlight came like an unwanted equinox. And every year, the occupant of the top floor of the glass edifice, with a logo consisting of the letters GT resting on a compass placed on each side of the building, didn't give a damn.

The elevator dinged at the fifteenth floor, doors parted, and a man no older than twenty-five stepped into the foyer on the top floor of Global Threat's west coast office; the division with the pretty face, which Global Tech presented to the public. The man walked past the empty receptionist desk and looked at his watch. Six-forty A.M. He shook his head and swung open the door of Bryan Turlock's office.

Turlock stood behind a custom lacewood desk, fastening his cuffs. He looked up at the uninvited guest with an annoyed expression and cinched his tie. "If you showed up seven minutes earlier, I would have been upset," he said, looking at his watch.

A door on the north side of the neo-industrial designed room swung open, and a dark-haired woman, dressed in what would be considered anything but appropriate work attire sauntered toward Bryan. "Is there anything else, Mr. Turlock?" she asked in a breathy voice.

"No. That's all I need for the moment," Turlock said, putting his arms through his coat. "And Missy, please hold my calls."

"Yes, Mr. Turlock," Missy said. She passed by the young man, who kept his disinterested eyes on Turlock. She flipped his tie and smiled. "Hello, Trevor."

When the doors closed, Turlock turned his back on Trevor, swore, and removed his coat. He pulled a shoulder holster from the credenza and slipped it on. He checked the safety on his 9mm and holstered the weapon. "What is it, Langston? It's too early to see one of you."

"We have contact, Mr. Turlock," Trevor said, his voice free of emotion.

"Contact? With who?" Turlock asked, walking to another desk on the north side of the room. He flipped on a monitor and turned back to Trevor, impatiently motioning for him to continue.

Trevor looked back at the door.

Turlock's shoulders dropped. "The room has been swept. There's no one listening."

Trevor looked at the door once more.

"Missy is fine," Turlock insisted. When Trevor didn't budge, he tapped the intercom. "Miss Baker, could you go to the commissary for me? I'm really in the mood for a breakfast burrito. Thank you, doll."

Trevor waited until Turlock showed him the feed from the surveillance cameras. "We have satellite contact with an extremely large group of spheniscidae."

"English, please."

"Penguins."

"That's good news for once."

"Yes. Our contact on Isla Santa Maria gave us an indication of their whereabouts."

"Great. Kill them. Poison their fish or something."

"They are still a valuable resource, Mr. Turlock."

Turlock slapped his hand on the desk. "I want them dead. We have what we're after. We kill them all now, before they reach the U.S., and we'll make Lyons' little miscalculation go away. Speaking of which, is Project Epsilon ready to be delivered?"

Trevor shook his head. "Preliminary trials proved to be too virulent. We're moving to Zeta."

"Goddamnit. I thought we wanted virulent? Isn't that the whole God damned purpose?"

"The delivery vessel has to survive long enough to make contact and spread the virus. If it dies within three hours, there would be no guarantee of it spreading the disease." Trevor sat down in an overstuffed chair and tried to maintain a strong posture. He gave up on it and stood again. "How would you like to proceed?"

Turlock rubbed his chin, pulling his bottom lip over his teeth. "We need Aperion. He's the only one that can survive long enough. Any sign of it?"

Trevor shook his head. "We have an indication that it may have been near the Galapagos, but we haven't been able to confirm the report."

"What about the other one? What do they call it—Season, Sieson?"

"Saeson. By all accounts, it's sterile."

"Yeah, yeah, I know. The virus can be passed to the egg, ensuring the permanent eradication over time." Turlock continued to think. "Is BioCon available to us?"

"Not since the debacle in Antarctica. They don't care to do business with either of our partners at the moment."

Turlock sat on the desktop, shaking his foot. "Jenson is an idiot. I should've killed him along with the press."

"That probably wouldn't have been in your best interests." Trevor looked at Turlock, his gaze cold and piercing.

Turlock coughed a nervous laugh. "If that Russian catches up with him, there'll be nothing you can do to protect him."

"That's between them. How would you like to proceed?"

"What is their heading?"

"Westerly, directly toward Costa Rica. There is a possibility they mean to attack."

Turlock nodded repeatedly. "Good. Once you know exactly where they aim to attack, get your contact there to clear the beaches. Recall Jenson's useless ass and tell him to eliminate them. I want the Nightlock choppers used. Use laser weapon systems. No detonations. I want the locals kept in the dark."

"Mr. Turlock, using the Nightlocks is a risk. If the technology is spotted…"

"What is the purpose in developing a silent helicopter with a silent weapons platform if we can't use it?"

"The penguins' e.t.a. is thirty-two hours. We can have Apaches waiting for them," Trevor said, avoiding an answer.

Turlock stared at the other man. He looked as if he was about to argue, but changed his mind. "Good enough. Dust the locals then. I want them asleep until the beach is clear. I can't keep making reporters disappear."

Trevor pulled a small mic from his shirt pocket. "You heard the man. We are green. I want Jenson in San José by thirteen hundred hours." His eyes narrowed in a smile.

"I hate that. Next time, Trevor," Turlock said, straightening his jacket.

"You can release the woman," Trevor said into the mic, placing a receiver in his ear. "Really, Bryan, sending your mistress to plant explosives on my car? It's amateurish; I expected better from you."

Turlock grinned. "I'll make sure not to disappoint you next time."

Missy was escorted into the office by a pair of men wearing navy blue suits, with matching ties and haircuts.

"And I'll make sure to remember that. Gooday, Bryan." Trevor walked by the woman and flipped her hair back over her shoulder. "Goodbye, Missy."

CHAPTER 69

The Northern Alliance of Independent Colonies floated two miles off the coast of a quiet Costa Rican beach. For expediency, Commandant Welsy took to calling it the Northern Alliance. Supreme Commander Kiley couldn't care less about what the group called itself, so long as they performed when the time came. In the days since leaving the Galapagos, Kiley had become increasingly agitated. He wanted nothing more than to be done with this token assault and head south. He hoped that by the time he made it back, that Ceocilus would have found the courage to take control of the Southern Alliance. Having the backing of the AIC would make controlling the Order of Kings that much easier.

A Rockhopper surfaced in front of Kiley and Welsy, shook his head plume, and saluted. "Supreme Commander, we have completed reconnoiter of the coastline," the Rockhopper said with a precise voice.

"And?" Kiley asked, not bothering to mask his impatience.

"There is very little activity on the beach. We were only able to spot two humans."

Kiley stared toward the coast, wondering if it would be enough to turn the human's attention their direction. It had to be. He wasn't going to waste any more time seeking out a more populated beach. He rode the rise and fall of the sea, not wanting to give the go ahead. "Commandant Welsy, opinions?"

"If it's sparsely populated, that's all the better. We'll have fewer casualties."

"True, Commandant. Still, keep a third of our forces in reserve. If we hope to oust the Doyenne, we'll need to bring as many home as we can." Kiley watched Welsy stare toward the coast with a burgeoning grudge in his eyes. He'd get over wanting to go north. Kiley waited a minute longer, watching and wrestling with the final decision. He nodded his head and let out a short breath. "Order the attack, Commandant."

Welsy barked a call. The call was echoed by several other penguins in both directions. The water churned as the penguins fell into ranks. More than one hundred thousand penguins rested on the surface, awaiting the final call. When Commandant Welsy felt the time was right, he looked at Kiley, who only nodded.

^^^

Line after line of attackers porpoised through the sea, forming waves of black and carrying deadly beaks bent on destruction of the enemy. These penguins were the survivors. Veterans of the Falklands and both Antarctic campaigns, they knew what needed to be done. Each beat of their flippers in perfect synch with the others, diving and breeching, they sped toward the beach intent on carrying out their orders.

They made first contact with the beach in short time. Thousands came ashore and moved up the beach head, looking for targets. They arrived at the water's end, hesitated briefly, and marched onto the dry white sand. The leading wave of attackers reached the edge of the lush Costa Rican jungle. The jungle greeted them with silence. No calls, no squawks, no chirps from anything. Only the breeze rustling through the trees greeted them.

A Rockhopper lieutenant called a Gentoo sergeant forward. "Take a squad and investigate the vegetation. Something's isn't right."

"I'm not going in there," the Gentoo said firmly. "Something might get me ate."

The Rockhopper lowered his head, muttering about Gentoo. "Sergeant, we've been through worse. The scouts said there were only a pair of humans on this beach. Now let's just take a look around and call it good. I heard we can finally go home after this."

The Gentoo studied the brush. "There's not much home to go home to," he said, calling a mix of penguins to join him.

The Rockhopper lieutenant watched the Gentoo take his first step into the shade, then heard something. "Sergeant, hold on," he said, then looked around. He called for silence. Within a minute, the thousands of squawking penguins became oddly quiet. He waited another second and finally caught the sound. He looked at the Gentoo with horror in his eyes.

"What?" the Gentoo said, then heard it too.

"Off the beach! Retreat," the lieutenant cried.

His orders took another minute to reach the back of the lines, and by then, the thumping of helicopter blades could be heard by all. Panic set in when the first Apache Longbow cleared the tree line. When the first barrage of Hellfire missiles impacted the beachhead, hundreds died. And when nineteen ten-pound warheads were launched from both the port and starboard weapons system, it seemed like overkill. A dozen other similarly armed helicopters followed suit, pounding the penguins mercilessly. Less than ten minutes later, the Northern Alliance ceased to exist. And to make certain of the fact, all thirteen helicopters emptied their 30 mm cannon into the surf, hoping to eliminate any escapees.

Smoke, dust, and pinfeathers swirled in the air after the helicopters disappeared back over the tree line. Silence descended. No calls of agony from the dying could be heard. There were no survivors. Within minutes of the carnage, the creak of treads and the rumble of engines pounded through the silence. The dozers had arrived to clean up the mess.

^^^

A half mile offshore, Kiley watched the aerial killers disappear. It was over. The Northern Alliance was done. He watched the events unfold, powerless to do anything about it. When it was finally over, he was angry, weak, and beaten.

Commandant Welsy drifted to the Supreme Commander's side. Kiley lifted his head. "How many survived?"

Welsy cleared his throat. "We had approximately eighty thousand in reserve. By all accounts, over a hundred thousand lost. A few survivors are straggling in. I have scouts searching for them. We'll hold here until the last of them arrive." He tried to continue, but his voice failed him.

Kiley looked at Welsy. He watched the other in silence for a few moments. "No, Commandant. Take them north. Find their paradise, if it exists. Take them away from this. I'll wait for any survivors and send them your way."

Welsy lifted his head, nodding it slowly. "And what will you do?"

Kiley looked to the sky, and followed the flight of a gull. "They knew we were coming. I don't how, but they knew. And I believe Mearna knew what would happen to us. She'll pay, I promise you that. And then I'll follow Lavour's lead and fade into the sea, and hopefully be forgotten. May the Spirit of the Ancients swim at your side."

Welsy nodded once. "And may they swim at yours."

"I should hope not, my friend. I should hope not."

Kiley watched Welsy disappear below the surface and turned his eyes back toward the sky. He watched the gulls circle in toward the shore, hoping to get scraps of what used to be those he commanded. He waited until sunset, redirecting only nine survivors during that time, and when night finally came, he went south alone.

CHAPTER 70

Climbing a loose hillside, Ceocilus watched the Southern Alliance pass through a narrow channel near the Pacific side of the Strait of Magellan. Gravel trickled from beneath his feet. He dug his beak into the loose soil to stop his slide. Twenty dark forms glided just below the surface. Any more would have posed the risk of a bottleneck. Looking across the waterway, Ceocilus spotted Adikos. The hate he felt for the Shadow Warrior seemed to multiply every time he laid eyes on him. In the six weeks since they'd left the atoll, Adikos had become Mearna's enforcer, and Ceocilus had been pushed even further away. He wasn't jealous, he just hated him. Ceocilus turned away, no longer able to look at the Shadow Warrior without wanting to tear him apart.

He continued his climb up the hill until he reached the top and fell to his stomach. He spotted the naval formation entering the strait headed for Punta Arenas. That was why a daytime crossing was a bad idea. Ceocilus knew that these ships were dangerous. It would only take one set of eyes to spot them, and the Alliance would be finished. The Chilean Navy had stepped up its patrols since the beginning of the Antarctic conflict and the second Falkland Islands war. To Ceocilus, crossing to the Atlantic meant they would have to go through the archipelagos and south through Beagle channel, or around Cape Horn completely. To Mearna and Adikos, it meant putting the entire Alliance at risk and crossing through the straits.

Ceocilus watched a patrol vessel cruise by. He looked back to see Adikos' reaction when the boat came into view. Adikos had no reaction. He stood there, trying to show his boldness to anybody who would look. *Idiot.* He constantly seemed to confuse bravery with stupidity. Ceocilus hoped his stupidity wouldn't cost other penguins their lives. No sooner did the thought cross his mind than Ceocilus heard the patrol vessel cut its speed. He watched a second vessel come in and saw the turret swinging into firing position.

He looked back and saw Adikos still standing in place. He needed to die, really needed to, but Ceocilus wouldn't risk the lives of the other penguins. He called to Adikos, warning him about what was going to happen. The other stood in place. Ceocilus knew that as soon as the other ship cleared the spit of land, Adikos would become dust, and so would a lot of other penguins. Ceocilus slid back toward the water. As predicted, the patrol vessel cleared the tiny island, but just before it fired, Adikos disappeared into the water. Ceocilus watched, mesmerized by the power of the weapons, destroying the embankment in a single shot.

The dust began to settle, and Ceocilus took a breath. He turned his attention back to the ships. When the first boat came into view after the second one passed, he saw the gun aimed toward his position. He swore and slid toward the water. He hit the surface and swam to the bottom, the concussive sound of the gun muffled above him. Debris splashed the surface, thousands of pieces of earth left trails in the water, like an underwater rainstorm. Ceocilus didn't take the time to admire the destruction. He swam until his lungs burned for air. Finally coming up for a breath after ten minutes, he saw Adikos resting on the surface, not far from him. His rage finally came through. Adikos would pay; he didn't care what the Doyenne said.

The water churned behind Ceocilus. His rage was matched only by his speed. He saw Adikos look his way and drop below the surface. Ceocilus dove, trying to pick him out among the background. He dove deeper, slowing his pace. The Shadow Warrior had gone deep, concealing himself in the darkness. Ceocilus slowed to a cruise, a predator looking for his quarry. He spiraled downward until he, too, was a part of the darkness. Looking up, he saw the silhouettes of hundreds of penguins against the diffused light. None were Shadow Warriors.

He skimmed the seafloor, eyes scanning, trying to pick out his enemy in the black. Adikos was his enemy now; not a rival, nor annoyance, he was his enemy as much as any human, if not more so. A depression in the seafloor added to the darkness. Ceocilus hesitated. From where he swam, he could see a labyrinth of rock. Adikos could be anywhere. Ceocilus felt a flush of satisfaction; if he was hiding, he was afraid. The satisfaction ended quickly when Adikos darted from between the first rocks, beak forward, ready to deliver the killing blow.

Ceocilus reacted swiftly; twisting sideways, making Adikos miss entirely. Now it was his turn. He arched back in a corkscrew and got in Adikos' contrail. He could almost reach out and peck his foot, but he didn't dare take the chance just yet. He was surprised he had caught up so quickly. These things were supposed to be fast. It didn't matter; he would be close enough to strike in a moment.

Before the moment could come, Adikos angled back and shot straight up, leaving Ceocilus behind in a blink. All right, the Shadows were as fast as he had heard. Actually, they were faster.

He saw Adikos breech, becoming a shadow above the surface—a mistake Ceocilus hoped to exploit. He pulled his flippers back, hoping to be in the right place. Adikos reentered the water with nary a splash, torpedoing downward, straight into Ceocilus' path. The collision spun the Shadow Warrior end over end, and Ceocilus went for the kill, aiming his long beak straight for Adikos' throat. The Shadow reacted, ducking before the impact and attempting a stab of his own. Ceocilus parried the beak with his own and pushed his body against Adikos. He couldn't match his speed, but he knew he could outmatch him in strength.

The water churned, the combatants twisting, trying to find the opening to deliver the killing strike. Adikos twisted. Ceocilus answered by sticking close, hoping to use his size and strength to push him to the seafloor and end his life. The Shadow Warrior spun, rolling through the water until he finally put distance between himself and Ceocilus. Ceocilus saw his quarry heading toward the surface once more. He followed, stretching his neck outwards and snatching Adikos by the foot, holding him firmly in his beak.

Ceocilus held tight and let his body become dead weight, dragging Adikos to the depths. Adikos struggled wildly, gyrating and thrashing, trying to break free or wound his assailant. Ceocilus was sure he had him. His nemesis would die. A flash of movement caught his eye, and a moment later something smashed into the two penguins. Adikos swam to the surface, while Ceocilus had to take a moment to get his bearings, taking the brunt of the impact to his head. His vision cleared, and he surfaced to find Adikos waiting for him, along with his mother.

"What is the meaning of this?" Mearna rumbled. "My officers, trying to kill one another? This is not acceptable."

"Doyenne," Ceocilus said, mustering as much patience as he could. "Your *officer* put the entire alliance at risk by letting himself be seen by the humans. I only just survived."

"Is this true, Adikos?" Mearna asked.

"I was merely supervising the procession as ordered, Doyenne. I didn't see the human vessel until Ceocilus warned me," Adikos said, glaring at Ceocilus with smug eyes. "And a tardy warning at that. I was nearly killed."

"Lies," Ceocilus said. "Your stooge will be the end of us. He takes unnecessary risks."

"Did these risks, as you call them, warrant an attempt on my life?" Adikos said. He turned to Mearna. "An unprovoked attack."

Ceocilus growled. "You almost got me and a lot of other penguins killed. You knew what you were doing. It was far from unprovoked."

Mearna looked around the penguins gathered nearby. "Did any of you see what happened?"

An Adélie came forward. "We were attacked by the humans, Doyenne. As far as I could tell, the commander struck first." She looked at Ceocilus with apologetic eyes.

Ceocilus shook his head. He couldn't blame her for telling the truth. The attack had been unprovoked. He would watch Adikos; he would make a mistake soon enough.

Mearna looked at Ceocilus. "I have to take Adikos at his word, Commander. I can see the animosity between you two rising. Jealousy for attention does not make for good leadership."

Ceocilus used every bit of self-control to keep from lashing out. Jealousy for attention? She was a bigger fool than even the Overlord had been. *Delusional even, with visions of grandeur she'll never attain.* Egomaniacal fools were a danger to not only themselves, but to everyone associated with them. Something would have to be done…soon. He waited for whatever decision her lordship made.

"I have no choice but to demote you from Commander, Ceocilus. You will be lieutenant of the rear guard. That should keep the both of you separated well enough."

Ceocilus didn't react. He stared at his mother with emotionless eyes. "Do I have to ask who will take my position?"

Mearna titled her head. "Adikos is the best candidate."

"How very Antaean of you, mother." Ceocilus didn't stay around to listen to her diatribe about respect and order. He saluted the both of them and swam away to his new position. There was work to be done now.

CHAPTER 71

Ceocilus hovered near the trail end of the procession. A day into the journey through the strait, and there had been no more encounters. If the humans knew they were there, they didn't seem to care. In the first hours of his new position, he enlisted several penguins to help him in his bid to overthrow Mearna. All of his recruits were those who had witnessed her brutality and the sadistic glee the Shadow Warriors and many other Royal Emperors took in reprimanding the other clans. There was plenty of discourse in the ranks to incite rebellion and there seemed to be a movement towards it already. The trouble was, most of them distrusted Royal Emperors.

He swam among the Chinstraps, looking for a penguin to send on a special assignment. No luck. He fell into a crowd of Gentoo and hoped his luck would change. "I've heard that the Gentoo are the fastest penguins of the seas."

Several Gentoo squawked their approval of the statement.

"Who among the Gentoo is the fastest?"

A chorus of the name 'Jasper' rang out.

"Jasper?" Ceocilus asked the closest Gentoo to him. "What's his rank?"

"Oh, Jasper doesn't have a rank. Doesn't believe in them," the Gentoo answered.

Ceocilus didn't understand. "But if he's in the Alliance, he had to have been given a rank."

"He was given a rank. Private, ensign, or colonel, or some other name. He just doesn't believe in ranks." The Gentoo looked at Ceocilus as if he couldn't fathom him not understanding what he had said.

"I know. You said that. Are you saying he rejected his rank?"

"No. I'm saying he doesn't believe in ranks. He doesn't think they're real. They're just made-up names to him. You know, like the invisible squid."

Ceocilus looked away in frustration. "All right, so names aren't real to him."

"Names are real, ranks aren't."

"Right. Ranks aren't real. I think I get it. He doesn't…wait. Invisible squid?"

"Yeah. You know the story. The invisible squid you can never catch."

"No. I have no idea what you're talking about." Ceocilus had never spent much time in the company of Gentoo. It was something he didn't regret. "I hate to ask this, but how do you catch something you can't see?"

"You just gotta be fast." *Gotta be fast* echoed throughout the group of Gentoo.

"It doesn't matter how fast you are if you can't see the squid. How are you supposed to catch it if you can't see it?" Ceocilus asked, his voice beginning to rise.

"Exactly," the Gentoo said.

Ceocilus closed his eyes and lowered his head. Gentoo. What in the name of the Ancients was wrong with them? "All right, never mind that. Where is Jasper? I need his help."

"I'm Jasper," the Gentoo said.

Ceocilus ducked his head below the surface, wanting to scream. "Why didn't you just tell me that?"

"You didn't ask. I don't think you asked. Did you ask?"

Ceocilus struggled to stay calm. Why couldn't Adélie be the fastest? He was curious as to why Jasper was referring to himself like he was somebody else, but thought better of it. "I don't remember anymore. You're the fastest of the fast, huh? Do you think you can outswim a Shadow Warrior?"

Jasper looked at Ceocilus out of the corner of his eye, becoming serious. "I can out-swim an Orca. And Shadows can't outswim Orca. What do you need from me?"

Ceocilus looked around and then swam in close to him. "I need to get a message to RHC 23."

"Aren't we going there?" Jasper asked, mimicking Ceocilus' movements.

"Yes, but they need to be warned about the Doyenne. She's not going there for a polite visit. She intends to overrun the colony and claim one of them as her own. Do you know the island? Can you get there ahead of us?"

"Hmph. This parade is moving as fast as a sea slug. Of course I can get there first. And I know where the island is. It's just a gull's flight from where I was hatched."

"Gulls can fly a very long way."

Jasper looked at Ceocilus, his eyes steady and unblinking. "A short-winged gull."

"There's no such thing." Jasper looked like he was about to argue, but Ceocilus spoke first. "When can you leave?"

"Now is good. See you later."

He swam away before Ceocilus could say another word. He listened to the Gentoo saying bye to Jasper, even though he had gone. He didn't have the chance to give him any warnings about the other Royals. Worried, he swam next to another Gentoo. "I'm going to make sure he gets away safely." The Gentoo just stared at him without replying. Ceocilus stared back until giving up on waiting for a reply.

Ceocilus dove below and hugged the seafloor, watching for any potential dangers to Jasper. It didn't take long to find one. A blur of darkness fell beneath the surface and darted ahead. There would be no way to warn him. It wasn't Adikos, but it didn't matter; the Shadow Warrior would eventually catch him and kill him. With no other options, Ceocilus followed the

Shadow. He wouldn't allow the Shadow Warrior to harm Jasper. He'd make sure of it.

CHAPTER 72

Nok, Leepoh, Keerka, and Colonel Kairg climbed the rocky shore of Isla Sola, the midway point between the straits and RHC23. The persistent wind swept across the tiny island, buffeting the quartet of penguins, nearly pushing them over. "This is probably your last chance, Colonel. Are you sure you want to stay the course?" Nok yelled against the wind.

Colonel Kairg looked around the barren landscape. "Of course I do. I promised Tretak that I'd help her track down Lydeck. Kuk-kek can more than handle the job. You should've seen how straight he stood when Trarck gave him the promotion."

"I bet," Nok said. He looked back toward the water, following the surface until the gray sky and sea became one. He let out a heavy breath.

"They'll be fine," Kairg said.

Keerka stood by Nok's side. "Leeg is like you. He's strong, he's devoted."

"They're so young. He was scared. He wouldn't say it, but I saw it in his eyes." Nok turned away from the view.

"Kicki chose the island. She knows it will be safe there," Keerka reassured.

"I know, I know, I know. We've been through it already. Still…they're too young for this." Nok climbed over another rock, and what little landscape there was came into view. "This place seemed bigger the last time we were here."

Keerka walked ahead of the group. "I don't like this place. The Shadow Warriors, Treeg's death, getting captured. A lot of bad things in a short amount of time." Stepping away from the waves, she found she didn't have to yell as loud to be heard.

"I rescued you here. That wasn't so bad," Nok said, closing the space between them.

"Hah!" Leepoh barked. "You saved her? I saved her, my friend."

"No you didn't."

"Yes, I did."

"No you didn't," Nok said adamantly.

"Yes, I did. Who talked to the man on the talkie thingy?" Leepoh asked.

"You did. Who rallied the troops and organized the attack?" Nok countered.

"Lavour?" Leepoh asked, unsure.

"What? No, I did," Nok said, affronted.

"Are you sure? Because I thought it was Lavour. Or maybe even Natoo."

Nok was about to answer when Keerka intervened. "Can we just say it was a group effort? Seriously, I'm about ready to crack some beaks."

Leepoh opened his, and Keerka gave him a warning look. He averted his eyes, keeping his head forward and stiff. "She scares me," he muttered to Nok.

"I'll do a lot more than scare you," Keerka threatened.

"Bah! Penguins a lot smaller than you have tried."

Keerka looked at Nok, who was at a loss to explain what Leepoh meant.

"Look," Kairg said before anyone could say anything else. He pointed to bare patches of earth, too smooth to be natural. "Looks like they cleaned up the place."

Nok examined the ground. They had left the island in such a hurry the last time they were there; he had hoped to do Treeg the honor of putting his remains in the sea now. He didn't have to look to know they were gone.

"We should rest here overnight. We'll make the push for the strait in the morning."

"There's a storm coming," Colonel Kairg said.

Nok shrugged. "All the better. Less ships."

"I'm checking the pools for something to eat," Leepoh said, he walked no more than a couple of meters and stopped. "Hey, Rockhoppers. We have a visitor."

The three Rockhoppers, spotted the newcomer and rushed over.

"Hello, Jasper," Leepoh said.

"Leepoh," Jasper replied.

"Jasper," Leepoh said again.

"Leepoh," Jasper said with a sharp tone.

Leepoh eyed the other Gentoo. "Jasper," he said, drawing out the name.

Jasper squinted his eyes. "Leepoh."

"Jas—"

"Will you shut up please?" Nok said, finally having enough of the exchange. "What are you doing?"

Both Gentoo looked at Nok, surprised by the outburst. "We're name calling," Leepoh said, like Nok should know.

"This is why I always avoided the north side of the island. If you spend too much time with a Gentoo, they start to make sense. And that isn't a good thing," Kairg said with his back to Leepoh and Jasper.

"Trust me, that's not even close to the truth. They never make any sense," he said, then stepped around Kairg. "Your name is Jasper, I presume."

"You presume rightly," Jasper answered.

"What brings you out here? There aren't any Gentoo colonies nearby that I know of. Are you lost?"

Jasper studied the trio of Rockhoppers. "I'm a messenger. I'm messaging a message to some Rockhoppers on RHC23."

Nok snorted. "Well, you're going to have a hard time; we abandoned that island some time ago."

Jasper didn't say anything.

Nok looked to Leepoh for help.

"Wait for it," Leepoh said. "It'll crack open here in a moment. Ah. There it is."

Jasper blinked. "Are you from the colony?"

Nok rolled his head, loosening tense muscles. He watched Leepoh turn away and walk toward the rocks. "Yes, we're all from that island. My name is Nok."

Jasper's eyes seemed to light up. "Oh. Captain Nok. I can tell you, then. The Doyenne is going to the island and she intends to overrun the colony and claim one of them. It is not a polite visit."

Nok looked at Keerka. "What's a Doyenne?" Nok looked to the others for answers.

"It's Mearna's title," Jasper said.

Nok turned to Keerka. "They're going after Kicki."

"She's safe, Nok. When Mearna arrives, she's not going to find anything. This is why we left. We knew they'd come looking for her."

"Still, I can't help but worry." He turned to thank Jasper, but the words got caught in his throat when saw Leepoh backing away from the shore.

"We have another visitor," Leepoh said, picking up his pace away from the rocky shoreline. "This one is worse than the first."

A dark penguin head peered over the rocks. The beak dug into the ground like a climber's pick as it crawled over the small escarpment. The solid black feathered coat gleamed, wet with seawater. The Shadow Warrior calmly walked forward with an air of imperiousness so strong it could be felt.

Jasper turned and saw the Shadow Warrior. He looked back at Nok, who had moved close to Keerka. "I'm glad you don't call yourself Captain Nok any longer. You've learned that a rank isn't anything but a word. You can't see words. So ranks aren't real."

"What's real is that you're insane," Nok said. "Now stick close. We've dealt with their kind before."

"Jasper," Leepoh said quietly. "You can't see the air, but it fills our body. Things you can't see *are* real."

Jasper scanned the ground, looking for a response he couldn't find.

"Leepoh, what are you doing? We need a plan to kill this thing, and you're sending Jasper on an internal quest."

"Bah! The beasty will die soon enough."

The Shadow Warrior approached and stared down at Jasper. "Are you a defector or a traitor? Hmm. Perhaps both. And you know the punishment for treason," the Shadow hissed.

"There's always something near. We're never alone," Jasper replied, looking up at the Shadow Warrior.

Leepoh leaned into Nok, his beak close to his ear. "Here it comes. Watch, it'll be fun."

The group watched a large Royal Emperor climb over the rocks behind the Shadow Warrior and move toward him. Unsure of what was going on, nobody moved.

"Are you trying to delay your execution, Gentoo?" the Shadow asked, with a sadistic amusement in his voice.

"No, I'm trying to make sure you die."

The Shadow Warrior narrowed his eyes and laughed. "And are you going to do the killing?"

Jasper looked to the darkening sky in thought. "No."

Before the Shadow Warrior could open his mouth to speak, Ceocilus drove his beak into the back of the Shadow's neck. It howled as it fell, and Ceocilus stabbed again. The Shadow Warrior tried to squirm away, and Ceocilus stabbed once more, and then one more time. He stabbed it again for good measure and then another out of spite.

"Are you all right?" Ceocilus asked Jasper.

Jasper nodded. "You can't be all right...all wrong either."

"Hey! That's my line," Leepoh accused.

"The message has been messaged, sir." Jasper looked at the Rockhoppers who were staring at the dead Shadow Warrior. "I'm going now. My part in this story is over."

Ceocilus and the others watched Jasper disappear down the shore. "That was one odd penguin," Ceocilus said.

"You sure got that right," Leepoh said, drawing looks from the Rockhoppers. He returned their stares. "What?"

Ceocilus began rubbing his beak on the ground. "This is disgusting. I'll be back." He scrambled over the rocks and out of sight.

"What just happened?" Colonel Kairg asked.

Leepoh shook his head. "A Gentoo named Jasper brought a message and a black shadow whatever followed. The shadow whatever tried to act really scary, and Ceocilus killed the shadowy Shadow Warrior soldier thing."

"You know the Royal Emperor?" Keerka asked.

"Hah! Haven't you figured out that I am a surprising fountain of knowledge? Ceocilus is, or used to be, a member of the Resistance back at Pack Ice Command. His parentage is questionable, his mother being the doynan or goynan, or toyan. What is Mearna calling herself again? She was the leader of the Resistance, but apparently had her own ideas and bailed out during the assault on PIC; the battle where I eventually died."

"Thank you for the exposition," Kairg said.

"That's why I'm here." Leepoh looked toward the far end of the island and started walking. "This is a busy little place."

Nok let out a long, exhausted breath. He laid his head against Keerka's chest and repeated the long breath. "I just wanted a place to rest. That's all." He waved his flippers at the dead Shadow Warrior.

"This island *is* half way between here and there," Kairg said, followed by a string of profanity. "I warned you it would happen. I'm sounding like a Gentoo now."

Nok laughed at the colonel. "At least you're not making sense to me, so I'm safe."

CHAPTER 73

Ceocilus returned to the others, his face clear of the Shadow Warrior's blood. He examined the body, wishing that it was Adikos. The other Gentoo had gone, but the three Rockhoppers remained, keeping their eyes trained on him when he approached. He stood before them. Nobody spoke. When it became obvious that they were waiting on him, Ceocilus took a breath. "My name is Ceocilus. I'm with the Alliance of Independent Colonies. I understand you received the message I dispatched to RHC23?"

Nok scrutinized the Royal Emperor. "How do I know you weren't sent here by Mearna? She abandoned us at PIC and she sent her minions to try to overthrow my colony."

"You don't know. You can't know. I can assure you I'm no longer under her command, but it is your decision to believe me."

Keerka stepped back by Nok's side. "He did kill a Shadow Warrior. You know how I feel about those things."

"He's a Royal," Kairg barked. "None are to be trusted. They're avaricious, deceitful; they're born with a lust for power. They'll betray and kill anyone to attain power. They say anything to get what they want."

Ceocilus nodded in agreement. "Royal Emperors are all of those things and more. My clan has gone too far. I plan to overthrow Mearna and end this madness once and for all. She wants the Oracle so that she can consolidate her power and find her enemies before they come for her. One of yours told her about the Oracle; I'm sure you know Lydeck."

"We should have killed him when we had the chance," Kairg growled.

"We tried," Nok reminded him. "It appears Tretak hasn't found him yet."

Keerka walked up to Ceocilus. "You were a member of the Resistance, yet you fled with Mearna and Kiley when the time came to oust the Overlord. Why would you want to be rid of your mother? What do you have to gain?"

"Mearna has become as twisted as Antaean, my father, was. She seeks absolute reign over the Southern Ocean and to subjugate all of the clans just as the Overlord did. If she finds the new Oracle, only the humans will be able to stop her. But before that, her one true threat would be Aperion, the Basileios. If either she or Aperion find the Oracle and if Aperion finds his queen and begins the line once more, then all will suffer. I will not let my kind be the blame for the loss of other clans, as it happened after the Great Auk War. Both have to be stopped."

Nok looked at his companions, then back to Ceocilus. "The Oracle warned us that this would happen. RHC 23 no longer exists. The island has been abandoned and the Oracle has been secreted away...far away. She won't find her."

Ceocilus nodded his approval. "Then my only concern now is to take control of the Alliance and end this. But I have a problem, and maybe you can help."

Kairg stepped next to Keerka. "Who's going to trust a Royal? Cuasan knows I don't. In fact you're the first one I've met that I haven't wanted to kill. Well, that wasn't true at first. But now...I don't want to kill you. Not much anyways. I don't want to kill you too much."

"You should be a diplomat," Keerka said, shaking her head at the colonel. "You're not going to be able to get any clans to follow you; which makes me wonder why they all haven't left the Alliance."

"Safety," Ceocilus said. "And I believe they've become comfortable with being led instead of thinking for themselves. Too many were lost at the onset of the war. The humans still take every opportunity against us. We've been fortunate; we've been on the move since we left Antarctica, and they haven't found us. Most of the clans no longer have their breeding homes to go to. The war isn't over."

"We're looking for a penguin who would be able to pull the Alliance from Mearna," Nok said. "Though we don't know where he is or if he's still alive."

"Lavour?" Ceocilus said.

"Lavour," Nok agreed.

Leepoh returned, made a squawking noise and interrupted any further discussion. "Do any of you know the whereabouts of that pile of Skua excrement known as Kiley? Because these guys would like to know." Leepoh waved his flipper in dramatic fashion at twenty King penguins walking their way.

Ceocilus took a heavy breath. Kiley's disobedience of the Order of Kings has come back to him. This could pose a problem.

CHAPTER 74

"Commander Nok," said the King at the head of the group. His voice carried a certain haughtiness, while also carrying a measure of loyalty, empathy, and stalwart drive, but with an undertone of threat. His magnetism could not be denied, and his passion for rightness burned bright. With all of his natures, one stood out among the rest: danger. His eyes portrayed the cheer of greetings. "I am Admiral Gregor, surveyor and commander to the Order of Kings, in service to Her Majesty, Queen Gelika."

Nok lifted his head at the newcomer. "I would say welcome, Admiral, but I have nothing to welcome you to, as this is not my home. In place of that, all I can offer is good evening. Leepoh tells us you're looking for Kiley." He did his best to sound formal, but Rockhoppers rarely welcomed dignitaries, and almost never from other clans.

"Your home, I'm glad you brought that to my attention. It's far too early in the season for the Rockhoppers to have gone to sea. Have you abandoned those amazing warrens of yours?" Gregor waved his company closer. "If you have, you wouldn't mind the Order securing them for the Kings would you?"

Nok snorted, giving up on his pretense of dignity. "The island is yours for the taking, Admiral. Though I have to warn you, the humans go there quite often."

Gregor clicked his beak, and two members of his group left immediately. "Now, back to why we're here. Yes, we're looking for Kiley, and I already know that neither you nor the Gentoo have seen him in quite some time. But according to an extraordinarily odd Gentoo we swam into, there is someone here who has been in contact with him." He strode forward and stood before Ceocilus, looking up, trying to read his face.

Ceocilus let out a bored sigh. Kings always seemed to think they were more than what they are. It was the same for Kiley, and the same for Gregor. But needing as many allies as he could find, regardless of their self-importance, Ceocilus put on an air of cordiality. "Admiral Gregor, you've come a long way. The last I heard from the Order, you had just become lieutenant-commander."

Gregor stared up at the Royal Emperor. "I don't seem to recall meeting you. But that doesn't really matter, does it? You know Kiley's whereabouts."

"Correct on all three counts, Admiral. We've never met, it doesn't matter, and I do have an idea as to where Supreme Commander Kiley is. And for courtesy's sake, my name is Ceocilus."

Gregor's bravado waivered momentarily, but he quickly regained composure. "The Overlord's son."

"One of many, I'm afraid. When you sire countless offspring, as my father did, maintaining a bond with one becomes impractical. Suffice for you to know, I am not following my father's wake…or my mother's. However, you're not here to discuss my parentage."

"Right, you're a different breed of Royal Emperor. Kimmer said as much, although he didn't have too many good things to say about your mother. Back to why we're here…Kiley, or Supreme Commander Kiley," the admiral said through a laugh, "I can't imagine how desperate Mearna had to be to give him that title."

"Kiley has been given orders to go north. The AIC separated into the Northern and Southern Alliance. However, it's been some time since there has been any word via messengers. It may have been that he didn't fare well up there." Ceocilus waited for a response. It seemed that Admiral Gregor was trying to gauge whether he was telling the truth. An idea sparked before Gregor could answer him. "Mearna aims to take control of the former Rockhopper colony. In fact, that's why I'm here. The island has been abandoned. So I believe we can work out an arrangement that would be mutually beneficial."

Gregor's posture dipped, his head slightly cocked. "What might that be? The Queen has sent me on a very specific mission, and it's not to make deals with Royals."

"We will attempt to liberate the clans from the Alliance, and if we're successful, Mearna will only have Royal Emperors left under her command. I'm sure the Order can defeat a force of two hundred Royals. You get the island and the glory of defeating her; I can pursue an enemy that needs to be stopped."

"What will become of the clans? I'm sure this enemy will not just surrender to you."

"They will be free to choose their own path."

Admiral Gregor paced in small circles, contemplating the arrangement. "Who is your enemy? The humans?"

"We're done with fighting humans. They have shown time and again that they are far too powerful to hope to defeat, or even concede territory. They will do as they wish to this world." Ceocilus hesitated. "It is the ancient enemy I aim to destroy."

Gregor's eyes widened. "I would have thought the Overlord had destroyed them himself."

"He had his reasons for not killing them. I don't, and I will. We can't afford another war like the Great Auk war. This ill-advised campaign has put us all in enough jeopardy." Ceocilus' eyes fell on Leepoh, who seemed to be trying with all of his strength to keep from talking. "Do we have a deal, Admiral?"

"How far out is the Alliance?" Gregor asked.

"At speed, maybe a week. But the strait has slowed progress. There are a lot of fighting vessels in that area. It could be as long as the moon's journey, perhaps longer."

"Very well. Make sure you reduce her force," Gregor said, nodding his agreement. "Once you do, I want a messenger line in place. We'll need as much information as possible."

Ceocilus agreed and joined the Rockhoppers, who had struck up conversation with the Kings.

The Admiral went to gather his company, but was stopped by Leepoh. "What is it, Gentoo? I have no time for arguments."

"The Council, Admiral," Leepoh said, his tone as serious as it had ever been. "We must restore the Council of Thrace. It's the only way to prevent this again."

"I doubt Queen Gelika will be keen on that idea, General Leepoh. The Kings will govern their own affairs. I will be going now."

Leepoh jumped in front of Gregor. "Kings doing what Kings do best, looking out for themselves. If King Elinthaw hadn't voted to allow the Royals and Basileios to live, serving his own interest, this war would never have happened. The vote needed to be unanimous."

"King Elinthaw is dead. The Council is a thing of the past, and it should be kept that way." Gregor called the other Kings and turned away.

"I'll reestablish the Council whether the Kings join or not," Leepoh said to Gregor's back. "You won't have a vote."

"Do as you wish, General," Gregor said, disappearing into the darkness.

Leepoh looked at Ceocilus. "You could be the first Royal Emperor on the Council since ancient times."

Ceocilus nodded. "Let's hope I live to see that day."

CHAPTER 75

Bryan Turlock rounded his desk and threw his brandy snifter across the office. Glass and liquor smashed against the ballistic window. "You're an idiot. I gave very specific instructions—quiet. That's all I wanted: a quiet operation. And what did I get?"

Colonel Jenson stood, looked at Trevor, who remained sitting, and took a calming breath. "I did what was asked of me. As it was, we had to blackmail several officials into silence before the operation began. The problem was eliminated."

"The problem was not eliminated. You said yourself that a portion of them escaped. Need I tell you what will happen if they reach the states and stories are corroborated? And Trevor, the virus? Is there any possibility of that actually being completed, or are we going to have to stick with conventional weaponry to kill a bunch of damned birds?"

"We are having trouble finding the carrier." Trevor stood, fished his phone from his pocket, and read a text. "We've secured our stake in Antarctica. Driving the species to extinction is pointless now."

"They talk, Trevor. When word gets out about their intelligence, we'll have half the world trying to shut down our facilities in Antarctica. We're talking profit in the trillions. We will control the greatest energy resources on the planet. The OPEC nations will return to their third world status, and GT will control the financial markets. This was our goal to begin with.

Vance nearly cost us that. I'm not willing to let some species that is already headed toward extinction hold me back from reaching those goals." When he finished, Turlock called Missy on the intercom. "Will you see to it that our guests are escorted to their vehicles, please?"

Trevor laughed. "You might be too late. It appears Mr. Lee has sold a series of photos to NPL. Why you tried to eliminate their identities is beyond me. What do you think they'd do when you starved them out?"

"Exactly what they're doing," Turlock said. "Lee will die not knowing just how fortunate he's been. And his father can't protect him now. The senator's bastard child won't be able to talk to anyone."

Trevor threw up his hands. "I don't think killing him will work to your advantage. But if that's your decision…"

"It is. Now, Jenson, do you think you can handle killing two unarmed civilians?" The office doors opened. Missy and four heavily armed men dressed in black fatigues walked in. Turlock waved them over and pointed to Trevor. "Thank you for pointing out my security weaknesses. And make sure you find the host. Get that agent delivered. You have one month."

Missy waved at Trevor and blew him a kiss.

Jenson watched Trevor get escorted from the office. "I'll get on that right away."

"Please deal with your *escapees* first. And when the time comes to kill those two, don't botch it like you did with BioCon." Turlock turned his back on Jenson. "Use the laser weapons system on the penguins, please. We don't need the same kind of attention you caused in Costa Rica. Good day, Mr. Jenson."

"BioCon wants Miss Rosedale," Jenson said before leaving.

"Wanting and having are quite different. Close the door on your way out." He waited until the doors actually did close and grabbed his phone. "This is Bryan. Jenson will be in San Luis Obispo…yes, California. He'll be there within a month. Yes, taking care of some work for me. Make sure the Russian finds out. I'm sure he would appreciate a reunion."

CHAPTER 76

Randy and Gina sat on the edge of a brickwork planter, enjoying a sandwich and watching people bump into each other in the busy farmer's market. The late afternoon breeze rustled hair and canopies, and brought the scent of a dozen vendors' wares wafting through each bite. The relaxed atmosphere, accented by the music of a nearby blues band, caused a lethargic calm, easy on the digestion.

"You know, in other parts of the country people don't even know what tri-tip is," Randy said, before stuffing another oversized bite of beef and French roll into his mouth.

Gina covered her mouth with a napkin, swallowing her food before talking. "Poor bastards."

"I know," Randy mumbled through a mouthful.

"What part of the cow does tri-tip come from?"

Randy took a swallow of water. "It comes from the third corner. Few people know that cows have three corners. Which is quite the feat for a quadruped. One would expect there to be four corners of a four-legged beast. But there be only three."

"There be? Did you just go pirate on me?"

"I'm a renowned swashbuckler, you know. The scourge of the ocean. Scurvy dog, and all of that."

Gina choked out a laugh. "Yeah, I think I heard of you. There was a news report about Red Beard, the buccaneer; tormenting coastal towns with bad music and false knowledge of beef."

"First of all, we no longer need to debate about my hair color, and second, you'll learn to appreciate the music I listen to *and* my treasure trove of information." Randy took his napkin and wiped a spot of sauce off of Gina's chin.

Gina's eyes shifted and she leaned into him. "Don't look, but there are a couple of men watching us." She kissed him to hide the conversation.

"Should I be jealous?" he joked.

Gina gave him a wry look. "I don't know; should *I* be jealous?"

"Probably," he said with a crooked smile. "Where are they?"

She watched the men watch them. They weren't wearing suits; they both wore loose-fitting khaki pants, with polo shirts, and light jackets, casual shoes. Nothing unusual about that. One, slightly taller than the other, Caucasian with short, layered hair, and sporting a van dyke which looked out of place, nodded to the clean-shaven other, who appeared to be of Middle-Eastern descent, with mid-length black hair. Both had muscular builds and sharp, alert eyes. Gina shook her head, having fallen into the habit of assessing strangers who looked her way. She had wondered if her growing caution was warranted, or if she was being paranoid. Today, she decided it was. "Walking toward us. Stepping on the sidewalk. Here."

Randy looked up. "Hi, if you're wondering where to find these sandwiches, it's right down the street beneath the sign that says Tri-tip sandwiches, seven ninety-nine." He pointed with his sandwich hand.

"Miss Rosedale, Mr. Lee," the slightly taller man said. He looked down the street, his face carrying a little humor. "Thank you, but we already ate."

Randy shrugged. "I hope it wasn't the Korean tacos. Those things, wow, they'll keep you up all night. And in the morning…phew."

The second man held his stomach and looked concerned.

"We'd like to speak with Miss Rosedale, if you don't mind," the first man said. His expression was serious, but not threatening.

Gina put down her meal and stood. Randy followed her lead, but stuffed the remaining sandwich in his mouth. "What about?" Gina asked.

The men traded glances. "Can we talk to Gina alone?" the middle-eastern man asked Randy with an unexpected modesty.

"He stays," Gina said, before Randy could answer. "I find it best to speak to strangers with witnesses present."

The two shrugged to one another. "Of course. First, so that we don't remain strangers, my name is Horace Gill. And this is J'ron Saad."

Randy scooted next to Gina, taking the last swallow of water from her bottle. "What can we do for you? I'm a photographer; she can tell you the weather."

Horace breathed a laugh. "We'll get back to your photography in a minute." He focused his attention back on Gina. "We're from an organization known as BioCon, sometimes referred to as BCU, or Biological Containment Unit. Gina, you've received some martial arts training recently. You've proven that you can handle yourself, and you're a willing student. We feel that we can use someone with your skill set. You graduated near the top of your class at Berkeley; an impressive feat."

"Are you offering me a job?" Now she was intrigued. With both her and Randy's identities having been practically erased, the past few months had been difficult, to say the least.

"In a manner of speaking, yes." He held out his hand to J'ron, who pulled a tablet from his coat pocket. "Before we go any further, first let me say that we know what happened in Antarctica, and we're impressed that both of you survived. Second, what I'm about to show you is restricted information, but it's necessary that you know what you're getting into before you agree to anything we're offering."

"So what are you, some kind of paramilitary or secret government agency?" Gina asked, trying to see what Horace was bringing up on the tablet.

"When I show you these images, you're going to think that they're manipulated…they're not," Horace said without acknowledging Gina's question. "After what you encountered, you're now aware that not everything is as you believed it to be. Here, sit next to me and don't react."

Gina sat and looked for her water bottle. She saw it in Randy's hand and gave him a scowl. Randy sandwiched Horace from the other side and offered J'ron the spot next to him. J'ron shook his head and walked away.

Horace brought up a slideshow and handed Gina the tablet. Randy quickly changed positions and squeezed beside her. Gina's eyebrows scrunched when the first image appeared. She studied it for a moment, shaking her head. "I don't know what I'm looking at. Is this an animal or a person?"

"Is it really red, or is that a camera issue?" Randy asked.

"This is what the indigenous people of Australia call Yara-ma-yha-who. And yes, it does have a red tint to its skin. It's only about three feet tall. According to legend, it's vampiric and hides in fig trees, lying in wait to ambush its victims and suck all of the unfortunate person's vital fluids. Stories tend to be exaggerated over time, but not this one. Actually, it was much worse. In most cases, we find a local population of harmless beings rooted out because of development, or sometimes an escaped lab experiment. And sometimes, like this, it's unexplained." Horace looked at both Randy and Gina who wore the same expression of disbelief. He tapped the screen. "Next."

Picture after picture, they scrolled through the unbelievable. Never in their lives did either think what they were seeing was possible. Gina tapped the screen once more, and her eyebrows rose. "Okay, this I know…sort of. Those are what they called Royal Emperors. Dead ones, thankfully."

Horace nodded his head. "This is the aftermath of our first encounter with them. One is known to have escaped, the others died, but not before killing about twenty well trained and highly skilled members of our unit. Only one of our people survived the encounter. It was one of the few times we let a formal military command our employees. Faulty intelligence was blamed. The commanding officer failed to explain exactly what we were up against. It's a mistake we won't let happen again."

Gina tapped the screen again and Randy sat up. "Whoa, what is this? Is this thing from the same…battle?"

"Yes," Horace said, looking at the image of a Kauroch. "We're not sure what they were. A hybrid of some sort, maybe a mutation. Regardless, they were used against us and were responsible for a majority of the deaths." He hesitated, taking a breath. "These images were not easy to come by."

After scrolling through pictures of the damage at the Falklands and Peru, Gina handed the tablet back to Horace. "It seems like a dangerous occupation."

"It can be. We have lost a few through the years, but never like Antarctica." Horace paused and looked away, seemingly lost in a thought.

"Can I see the big penguin, or whatever it is again?" Randy asked.

Horace brought the picture back up, locking the screen so nothing else could be seen. "This is what we do. We contain biological entities. BioCon." He paused and shook his head. "I sound like a television commercial."

Randy started pointing out the physical anomalies of the Kauroch to Gina. "Look, the beak is spade-shaped, like it's used for digging. Pronounced digits, probably used for digging or dragging itself along the ice, especially since it looks too top-heavy to walk upright. And the eyes; tiny eyes, it's probably blind or nearly blind, like a mole. But the flippers look like it's probably a strong swimmer, despite its subterranean adaptations." Randy looked up and realized all eyes were on him, including J'ron, who had returned with bottled water for Gina.

Horace nodded. "Yeah, that pretty much nails it."

Gina took a sip of the water after thanking J'ron. "This is a lot to consider. When would you need to know?"

"You don't have to decide today. But soon would be appreciated." He handed Gina a card. "This number is good for thirty days. After that, we'll take it your answer is no. You'll likely be used in a support role. So the danger will be reduced, but not eliminated."

Gina laughed. "What fun is that?" She put her hand in Randy's. "What about Randy? He was there too. He survived a long time without any help. I want him along, too. Surely you can use a photographer, or at least find something else for him."

"The offer is for you only." He looked at Randy, who was still absorbed by the picture. He took the tablet back. "Which reminds me, selling those pictures was a bad idea…very bad."

"What choice did I have?" Randy said, getting to his feet. "We're getting starved out. I mean, I might understand expunging our work history with GT, but all of it. That's just overkill."

Horace looked to J'ron, who returned a slight nod. "It wasn't just your work history that was supposed to be *expunged*. You're alive because of Colonel Maycotte. He was working both sides of a battle of ideals between certain government factions and GT's dual interest. Maycotte protected you."

"Why?" Randy and Gina asked in unison.

Horace let out a heavy breath, biting his lips in thought. "I don't know the whole story and I'm not really at liberty to tell you, as it could jeopardize your safety. One of the people Maycotte worked for has an interest in your protection, Randy. Don't you think it odd that GT contacted you for the Antarctic assignment? Your benefactor arranged that."

"I thought it was because of the work I did for NatGeo?" Randy said, sounding slightly demoralized.

"You're very good at what you do. You were put in place because of your skill, interest in the subject matter, and your strong sense of ethics. Then things didn't go as expected for GT or the other party. But…that's all I can say, and I really don't know a lot of it. I was briefed before coming here." Horace looked at the both of them. "I'll see what I can do about securing a position for you, Randy. If it proves to be for our benefit and if Gina decides to accept our offer."

"What is the offer?" Gina asked.

Horace handed the tablet back to J'ron and stepped back, and turned to go. "The offer is you get to see the world. You'll see unbelievable things that most will never know exist, and make a lot of money…a lot."

"I like a lot," Gina said quietly.

"Thirty days," Horace said, pointing to the card in her hand. "And I don't think I need to tell you not to mention this to anyone. But don't."

"What do you think?" Randy asked after the others left.

"I think life just took another unexpected turn." Gina watched the market goers milling around from booth to booth. The music seemed to return. She didn't know if it'd stopped or if she'd blocked it out. Stranger's faces changed from a backdrop of indistinguishable passersby and happily ambivalent shoppers to oblivious souls, not realizing they shared the world with nightmarish creatures and men. A chill crawled up her spine. She looked at Randy, seeing an uncertain future made more so. She took him by the hand. "Let's go home."

CHAPTER 77

Supreme Commander Kiley swam hard and fast. His hatred of Mearna fueled his rage while warring with the utter defeat gnawing at his spirit. Nabbing bits of food as he passed through shoals kept his body going. Passing predators watched him fly by, not bothering to pursue the streak of black and white. He had no plan other than killing Mearna. If Ceocilus had already taken care of it, then he would find her corpse and desecrate it out of spite.

Unencumbered by swimming masses of penguins, he sped down the Pacific coastline in half the time it had taken the Northern Alliance to get where it had all ended. Night and day passed in a haze. He refused to rest, for fear his enemy would be gone before he could get to her. He followed the current, which led him on a path back toward the atoll. He thought of the Rockhopper who had betrayed them, which added fuel to his fire.

After countless miles of swimming, he thought he spotted the form of a penguin somewhere ahead, swimming through the murk. He dismissed it as delusions of fatigue. But it showed itself again, and he had no doubt it was a penguin. Probably a defector or one lost along the journey. It didn't matter; he would swim past and not bother to stop.

Getting closer, he could make out the shape of a Chinstrap. There were so many in the Alliance; any number could've disappeared without being noticed. When he got closer still, he saw a Rockhopper ahead of the

Chinstrap. He surmised that they had to be defectors. Good for them, he was glad they had left; the path started by the Overlord had led to nothing but destruction.

He pressed on, not caring who they were. The next thing he knew, he was flying over the surface in a wild somersault. Something had hit him. Something big. When he splashed down, he quickly scanned his surroundings, searching for the Orca or whatever had attacked him. He spotted the likely culprit, but it made no sense to him. Floating on the surface was a penguin bigger than any he had ever seen. Kiley stayed on the surface as well, watching what could only be Aperion.

Aperion approached, and Kiley stayed. He had stopped swimming for the first time since his defeat, and his weariness took advantage. There was nothing he could do. He couldn't swim away, and he had no hope to defeat a penguin so large. He could only talk to the legend. "Lord Aperion, forgive my clumsiness. I didn't see you come up on me."

Aperion stared at Kiley, swimming a circle around him, doing his best to intimidate the King. Kiley was past being intimidated. He had been threatened by the Order, by Royals, and countless others, and at this point, he just didn't care.

Several moments later, Aperion laughed. "Your humor amuses me, King. Now, before I kill you, tell me why you were following us?"

It was Kiley's turn to stare down the other. He looked the Basileios over, checking for weaknesses. There was always the throat, but even that looked protected beneath layers of fat and muscle. "We were merely headed in the same direction. I have no need to follow you."

"We?" Aperion snapped. "Where are the others?"

Kiley squinched his eyes, cursing the Ancients for putting this stupid penguin on Earth and in his path. "We, as in, you're headed the same direction as I am," he said, trying not to sound too condescending. He spotted the Chinstrap arriving while Aperion tried to sort out the riddle of words. *Is that Lavour? Why would Lavour be in with Aperion?*

"Very well," Aperion said. "Now I'm going to kill you."

"Wait," Lavour called out. "That is Commander Kiley of the AIC. He might know where Mearna is."

Aperion looked at Lavour and Kiley. "Is this true, Kiley?"

Kiley looked at Lavour, wondering why he didn't let Aperion kill him after all he had done. "I have an idea. In fact I'm on my way to find her so I can kill her."

"Then we have mutual goals," Lavour said to Kiley, looking at Aperion.

"So it would seem," Aperion said. "Where do you suspect she is?"

Kiley hesitated. If he told him, Aperion might still kill him. If he didn't, he probably still would. "She is likely in the straits by now. Her son and I had planned to oust her, but that hasn't come to pass. I do know that she fears you, Aperion. She wants to destroy you."

"So I have heard," Aperion said, looking away. His head jerked and his eyes closed, and he nodded. "I must get to the atoll." He quickly circled around and swam away.

Meuseaux surfaced next to Lavour. "Kiley, I'm surprised to see you're alive, and a little disappointed."

"A sentiment shared by many, I assure you." He looked to Lavour. "I see Liutites' killers still live."

Lavour ignored Meuseaux's presence and approached Kiley. "A few of us do."

"Then there's hope," Kiley said, without explanation.

Lavour let out a long breath. "As much as I hate to say this, you should come with us. We have the same goals, for the time being."

Kiley considered telling him where to put the suggestion, but relented. He would have to travel slower, but he might need help when the time came. "Very well. Perhaps we can rid the world of Mearna together."

Lavour nodded. "And you can tell me what prompted you to abandon the fight at PIC and why the change in feelings toward Mearna."

Kiley almost reconsidered the offer. Explaining himself to a Chinstrap was beneath him. He caught his haughty behavior and had a change of mind. His way of thinking had gotten a lot of penguins killed. "Mearna is a Royal; I needn't say more. But Ceocilus and she don't agree. Ceocilus and I had decided to make a change in leadership, but we were outed by a Rockhopper."

"The Rockhopper's name wouldn't happen to be Lydeck, would it?" Meuseaux asked.

Kiley swam in beside the Chinstraps. "I believe it was. Yes."

"Then we have a surprise for you," Lavour said, leading the way to the atoll.

CHAPTER 78

Tretak hopped from the easy surf rolling against the atoll, carrying a fair amount of the local fauna in her stomach. Pìn emerged behind her, chattering at her back.

"I eat like a whale?" Tretak asked in surprise. "If that statement weren't true, I'd be offended."

Pìn chirped something about her being more Gentoo than Rockhopper and hurried off to assume his post on the weather-worn coral formation, to keep watch for any sign of the Northern Alliance.

Tretak scuffled along the beach toward the shade. Storms had reshaped the beach, washing away the remains of Cryftin and any signs that thousands of penguins had once been there. Every once in a while, an odd piece of debris would wash ashore, giving her something to occupy her mind during the long wait for something to happen. She would gather what she could carry, amassing a small collection of plastic containers, shoes, and various forms of clothing, representing fashion from four of the five surrounding continents. She knew enough to know that most of what she found came from the human realm, and ran theories by Pìn as to how men shed their outer layers with each new season. Pìn would refute most of her proclamations of discovery, leading to long debates, sometimes lasting for hours.

Life had become comfortable, and regardless of her reasons for being there, a certain peace had begun to worm its way into Tretak's soul. There were no humans to be found, and with the exception of an occasional airplane flyover, not even a ship had appeared on the horizon. There were no penguins trying to muster forces or attempting to rival man in their duplicity. It wasn't a half-bad life. She rested in the cool of the cave, examining her latest find of a rusted bottle cap, when she heard Pin's call. She knew at once that her days of peaceful existence were about to come to an end. She stared at her collection of artifacts and laughed at herself for hoping the calm would last.

Tretak walked out of the cave and looked at the gray horizon, waiting for whatever might emerge. She saw Pin waddling toward her, chittering in alarm. "Slow down."

Pin stomped in frustration, barked a couple of profanities, and started over.

"How far out?" Tretak asked in panic. Pin chirped, and Tretak issued her own curse. "How did you miss them?" She ignored Pin's angry retort and ran to the shore.

Pin came up behind her, and the two watched the sea until they spotted the first porpoising body. Tretak took a step back, followed closely by her Blue companion. He chattered in a low tone, turned, and began making his way toward the cave.

Tretak saw him scamper away. "Wait. What was that? Was that a penguin? It's too big to be a penguin. Penguin's aren't that big." She hopped to catch up and beat him to the entrance.

Pin ran in the cave on her tail feathers, explaining what they saw. He scanned the cave, spotted a nook, and urged her to join him.

Tretak followed, pushing and squeezing into the small space. "All right, so you're saying that big thing out there is a penguin, and it's not a Royal Emperor?"

Pin went on about what he had overheard between Kiley and Ceocilus.

Tretak peered into the cave beyond, waiting for something to show itself. "And what about the other penguins with the big one?"

Tirades of vulgarities were thrown at Tretak, while asking her how he would know who they were.

As if they weren't close enough already, Tretak leaned closer. "You're a grumpy little guy today, aren't you?"

Pin fixed her with a blank stare and didn't say another word.

Tretak tried to suppress a laugh. "I'm just joking. Don't be so short." She started to laugh again until she heard the sound of penguins outside of the cave. She pushed her body against Pin's, presenting her black back to the outside.

"Shut up, or I'll kill you myself," a voice hissed near the entrance.

Heavy feet and the swish of coarse tail feathers etched their way across the rubble strewn cavern. The footfalls stopped when they reached the collection of trinkets. Tretak dared to take a peek at who was examining her prizes. Daylight splashed on Aperion's back. He lifted his head with his beak parted, as if tasting the air. His head swung in her direction, and she tucked herself further in the darkness. Her heart raced, pounding in her chest and against Pin. A minute later, the sound of shuffling of feet resumed and disappeared down the narrow corridor. Tretak's body eased, and Pin spat a rebuke on her curiosity.

When she regained her courage, Tretak stepped back and went to the mouth of the cave to see how many penguins were outside. She peered outside, and spotted two Chinstraps, and a King gathered in a semi-circle with their backs toward her. The King stepped away, and Tretak's heart skipped a beat. There, on the crest of a small dune stood her prey, Lydeck. She didn't think; she reacted and sprung from the cave, dashing toward Lydeck.

The other Rockhopper looked at her, not realizing his danger. A second later, his eyes widened, and he tried to run. Tretak leapt and grazed him with her claws, causing Lydeck to lose his balance. The pair tumbled down the low dune, rolling to a stop, with Tretak resting on top of Lydeck. She stood and pecked at his neck. Lydeck yelped, trying to stand. Tretak was having none of that. She slammed her body into his, keeping him on the ground.

"No, please don't kill me. Aperion will kill them if you do," Lydeck begged, his voice whimpering.

Tretak looked at the three penguins, who stood watching the spectacle with interest. She pecked Lydeck once more, drawing blood, and backed off slightly. "Is this true? Will he?" she asked through heavy breaths.

Lavour stared at Lydeck for a moment. "He wants Aperion to kill my friend Nok."

"Nok is my friend, too," Meuseaux said.

She looked at Kiley, waiting for an answer.

Kiley walked toward Lydeck and stood over him. "I would very much like to see him die. In fact, I would like to assist you. But, we need him alive for the time being," he said, looking back to the Chinstraps.

"You see, Tretak?" Lydeck said. "They need me."

Tretak told Lydeck to shut up. She considered her options. She didn't know who the others were, but she didn't want to see them harmed. "Can I hurt him a little more, at least?"

"By all means," said Kiley. Lavour and Meuseaux nodded their heads in agreement.

Tretak raked her claws across Lydeck's face and bit into the side of his neck until she drew blood again, then reluctantly stepped away. "Now tell me why I can't kill him?"

Lavour stepped forward. "We're going to meet with the Southern Alliance, and Lydeck here is going to lead Aperion away."

Tretak gave Lavour a doubtful look. "Lydeck is working with you? I don't believe it; he only looks out for himself."

It was Kiley's turn to step forward. "We know that much. Lydeck told Aperion about the Oracle on RHC23."

"You're just going to let him destroy my colony?" Tretak said. She'd had enough of the nonsense, and moved toward Lydeck.

"No," Lavour answered. He motioned for Tretak to follow him. Once he was certain they were out of earshot, he explained Meuseaux's deal with Aperion and Kiley's plan to overthrow Mearna. "Lydeck is a distraction. As long as Aperion's eyes are focused elsewhere, we should be able to pull the Alliance from Mearna. I assure you, we have no intention of Aperion ever reaching the island."

"Let me tell you this…uh, you never told me your name." Tretak saw the indecision in the Chinstrap's eyes. He didn't want her to know who he was, which made her curious. If he was in the company of Aperion, a penguin whose reputation as a monster seemed to be spreading, maybe it was best that she didn't know. "Listen, you don't have to tell—"

"Lavour," he interrupted. "My name is Lavour, the other Chinstrap is Meuseaux, and the King is Kiley."

Tretak straightened her body in surprise. "Wow. Looks like I found the right group of penguins to get in with. Commanders of the Alliance of Independent Colonies, and you and Meuseaux; the way Nok described it, you're practically immortal. So what's your plan?"

"The Royals are still a threat."

"I know that. Your buddy Lydeck made a deal with them to help him remove Nok as Commander of the Colony. He even tried to have Nok's son killed. It was all for naught. Mearna changed her mind about the deal and left him to his fate."

"Is that why you want to kill him?"

Now it was Tretak's turn to be silent. She had lost everything because of Lydeck. She carried her loss with her. It had been her driving force to revenge, but she rarely thought about the event. Her hatred of Lydeck seemed to overshadow it all. She stared at Lavour, wondering what losses he had experienced to drive him to kill the Supreme Commander. She doubted that someone as important as the former commander of the AIC would share something like that with her. "He killed my mate, and I lost my eggs because of him. It was before the war. Funny how time doesn't really heal you."

"It does if you let it."

"Can I ask you something? Something personal."

Lavour looked at her suspiciously. "You can. But I might not answer," he said, not quite serious.

"What drove you to kill Liutites? From the stories I heard, the Royals at PIC had been defeated, and the place was under attack from those flying things the humans use. He probably would've died anyways." Tretak cringed, realizing she sounded awfully accusatory. "You don't have to answer. It's none of my business."

Lavour nodded his head. "I'm not so proud that I can't answer. It was revenge. The Royals had taken everything away from me. We were there to stop them. But it wasn't enough. Liutites targeted my colony because I was interested in the Resistance. His spies found out, and he made an example of my colony, my family, and my friends. He had every one of them killed. I wanted him dead. Meuseaux did as well. We hunted him down and killed him."

Tretak's body deflated. She hadn't expected him to answer, let alone be so candid. "Was it worth it?"

"No," Lavour answered without hesitation. "It cost my good friend's life, and very nearly all of our lives. It didn't change anything, really. Like you said, he was probably going to die anyways. And we're all still paying the price. I left after it ended. Mearna took control of the Alliance, and thousands more have died. Now I need to make things right."

"Commander Lavour," Tretak said, before he could walk away. She walked up close to him and leaned into his ear. "There's a chance that the colony will be gone by the time they get to RHC23. I don't know with any certainty, but they were talking about abandoning it at one point."

Lavour suppressed a laugh. "Then Aperion won't be too happy with Lydeck when they get there." He took a few steps and turned back to

Tretak. "Are you coming with us?"

She shook her head. "I have a few things to think about. And where better to think than an island in the middle of nowhere? Besides, the temptation to kill that loathsome piece of karnuckling snooker… I mean, Lydeck…might prove too much. And I don't think Aperion is the type to allow a merry band of followers."

"Karnuckling snooker?" Lavour asked, somewhat bemused.

"Huh? Oh, yeah…I was trying to be polite and all of that. You know, not use inappropriate language," Tretak said sheepishly.

"Then I won't tell you what 'karnuckling' means in Chinstrap." Lavour headed back to the others. "Good luck, Tretak."

"I won't be too far behind. I want to be there when Lydeck gets his," she called back.

CHAPTER 79

Aperion walked through Lapasia's chamber, snuffling his beak through the littered ground. The Oracle's body had to be there. It couldn't have wasted away so quickly. He needed it; his urge to kill the Rockhopper was overwhelming. If he could find the body and consume it, then he could find the new Oracle without Lydeck's aid. He would be able to rid himself of the Rockhopper. Where was her body?

With each passing moment, his urgency increased. He shoveled through sand and rocks and fragments of shells, finding nothing. He raised his head, the furrows of sand looking like a field plowed by a madman. He shook the sand from his beak and rushed toward the nook where Lapasia had lived. He passed by the whale vertebrae resting on a rock ledge. Aperion stopped and stared. The perch from which the old Hoiho stood and preached at the mighty Aperion teetered on the edge, ready to fall with the slightest movement. He should have consumed her entirely when he had the chance. Stupid and foolish. He raised his flipper to strike the bone from the rock, but stopped. How did something so large find its way so high? A penguin couldn't have done that. He snorted more wet sand from his nostrils.

Aperion twisted, looking around the room, his head spinning. Behind the furrows, the sand spiraled, leading back to where it merged with rock, to the vortex of rising and falling surf. It was gone. The storms had come and cleansed the chamber. He swatted the whale bone from its perch and shoveled through the debris, sand and gravel flying across the chamber.

You will disgust your queen. How can you expect to rule when you can't properly kill an Oracle?

Aperion spun around, looking at the voice in the wall. "No! I wasn't told about consuming her. If I had known…"

Excuses of the weak. If you would have known, you still would have failed. Your brother should never have saved you.

"I saved him. It was I who saved him."

Of course you did.

"He will never find his queen without me. I will find mine, and he will find his. Then we will destroy them all. The Royal Emperors will cry out for death as I consume their flesh. First the Rockhopper. He is useless for anything more than a meal."

Idiot! How will you find the Oracle without him? He knows.

Aperion twisted toward the voice behind him now. "He is lying."

If you believe that, then consume him. Why waste your time following a liar? Do it. Kill him. Tear his flesh from his bones. Feast on him. Prove yourself the idiot you are. Kill the Chinstraps and King. They're using you for their own gain. Kill them! Indulge on their meat. Feast!

Aperion followed the voice around the room. His head swiveled, chasing it with his eyes. "I need them. They will give me the Alliance."

If that is the course you choose, then follow it. Find the Oracle, devour her. Her knowledge will be yours and secrets will remain secrets.

Aperion waited for more, but the voices had vanished. He watched the water swirl, receding back down the hole. His body quivered with an insane rage. He screamed a horrible, screech. He followed the swirling water, disappearing into the black.

CHAPTER 80

Pin stood by the mouth of the cave, listening, trying to hear anything other than the constant breathing of the surf. He did hear Kiley, and he was sure he heard Lavour out there as well. He edged toward the gap to take a closer look and Tretak nearly knocked him to the ground when she entered.

"Are you still spying? I thought those days were behind you."

Pin refrained from using too many vulgarities in his response. He looked back outside and spotted Kiley. He couldn't decide if he hated the King penguin or merely despised him. Whatever it was, he was certainly glad to be free of servitude. He would stick by Tretak's side now, and hopefully, one day find a group of penguins headed back toward his home in New Zealand.

He tucked his head back inside and nestled in the loose sand. Lavour was out there too. He liked Lavour and the other Chinstrap too, even though him and that vexatious Gentoo had had some fun at his expense. But he didn't like them enough to go out there. He'd stay in this cave for days if that was what it took to avoid their company.

An unearthly howl crawled up the tunnel ahead of the surf, a lamenting yet murderous scream that made his feathers stand on end. Pin stood, watched the tunnel, waiting for the scream to stop. When it did, he wished for it to return. The silence was worse. Without a moment's hesitation, Pin ran from the cave, hoping to get free of whatever terrible, otherworldly beast was coming to make a meal of him.

He darted past Kiley, who watched him in surprise; he passed Lavour and Meuseaux, who looked at him curiously. Seeing Lydeck directly ahead, Pìn redirected his mindless fear into the animosity he felt for the Rockhopper. His path never wavered, and Lydeck, who looked as surprised as any of them to see the Blue penguin, took Pìn's charge full on in the stomach. Lydeck stumbled back, eventually falling, with Pìn repeating Tretak's earlier assault by jumping on him and delivering a few well-placed pecks on the already open wound.

Lydeck slapped the diminutive penguin away, stood, and was met by a ferocious slap from Kiley. The surprise and fear in Lydeck's eyes were evident, and he made no attempts to retaliate.

Kiley stared down at Pìn. "I'm happy to see you. I thought you were dead."

Pìn chattered the story of how Lydeck had attempted to kill him and why. He started to say more, but a second groan from the cave stopped him mid-chitter. The five penguins watched Tretak bolt from the cave. She gave the crowd a look of uncertainty and Kiley pointed with his beak toward an elevated outcrop. Tretak clambered up the coral stone, falling into a crag.

Mere seconds later, Aperion burst from the cave, huffing for breath. He stood still, scanning the atoll, looking for something. He ruffled his feathers, and in the next instant, he calmed. He walked to others and stood before them, as still as a stone.

The five penguins stared back, not knowing what to expect. After a minute of tense silence, Aperion closed his eyes and opened them slowly. The fits had gone. "What happened to you?" he asked Lydeck.

"I was attacked…assaulted. They want to kill me," Lydeck said, pointing to Pìn and the others. When he saw a spark of violence appear in Aperion's eyes, he shrank back, cowering beneath the heavy glare.

"I want to kill you, Rockhopper." Aperion looked at the others and spotted Pìn. He stared silently, unmoving. He leaned in close. "What is this? One of Antaean's spies out here?"

Pìn spat a few basic unpleasant words at the Basileios, standing his ground.

Aperion looked to the others. "What did he say?"

Kiley cleared his throat. "He said, he no longer works for the dead Overlord, and that he is free of Antaean's bondage." Kiley looked down at Pìn, giving him a silent warning to watch his tone.

Aperion leaned in so close that his beak nearly touched Pìn's. "Is that so? And were you the one who attacked my Rockhopper?"

"Yes," Lydeck shouted. "It was him and another Rockhopper."

"Shut up," Aperion barked, returning his attention to Pìn. "Well?"

Pìn chirped a few more choice words about Aperion's overall appearance and his close association with guano.

"He said yes. And that Lydeck deserved it, and much more," Kiley said, his eyes shifting toward Lydeck.

Aperion straightened. He scanned the group, waiting for one to flinch under his scrutiny. His gaze came to rest on Lydeck. After a few seconds of silence, he burst into laughter. Not a happy robust laugh, but a perverse, mocking laugh, dosed with a touch of insanity. The five penguins shifted nervously under the twisted outpouring of glee. "Don't kill him yet, little one. And you, fearless Rockhopper, would you like me to make a snack of your tormenter? How a creature could be so pathetic and live to maturity is beyond any reason. I should like to kill you now, but your existence is your bane. It provides me with entertainment."

Lydeck bowed his head. "Your words are true, Lord Aperion, but there is a Rock—"

"Shut up. Your wretched droning makes me ill." Aperion scanned the sea. "We leave now. There will be no more rest. Don't fall behind, Rockhopper."

The group walked to the ocean's edge. "Are you coming with us?" Kiley asked Pìn.

Pìn was surprised that Kiley had given him a choice. But he knew he didn't have one if he ever wanted to see home again. Pìn answered yes, with only the slightest of insults added.

Aperion turned to Meuseaux before they walked into the surf. "Prove yourself worthy to me. Don't let anyone lag behind. Drive them, push them, and if any are too weak for the journey, kill them. Do not fail in your duty to me, servant."

Lavour and Kiley passed by Meuseaux without saying a word. Pìn stopped and looked up. He hissed his disapproval at Meuseaux and ran into the waves.

CHAPTER 81

Welsy surfaced off the central California coast and scanned the sky, looking for the next attack. The blue sky stared back with the promise of more death. "I don't think we're going to make it," he said to a fellow King penguin. He continued to stare northward, waiting for another inevitable attack of drones, boats, or helicopters.

"We don't have a choice, Commandant," the other said. "We have to keep pushing northward. We've lost so many already in the south to the warmer water. And the sharks…I know we have to stay close to the shore to avoid attacks from the humans, but the sharks are feasting on us."

"I'm aware of what's happening to our ranks, Lieutenant Colby, but the fact is, if we push on, we'll be destroyed within a moon's time. Our scouts have said there's a large stretch ahead where there are no communities, and we both know the humans are less inclined to attack near their settlements." Welsy looked toward the shoreline, his mind wandering toward any possible future for his group of survivors. This really was the end of their journey. Kiley and his idiotic need for power had seen to their end.

"Welsy." Colby cleared his throat. "Commandant? You were saying."

Welsy looked at Colby, his mind still racing. "How many are left who are still tipped?" He thought back to the day they had all received their steel beak coverings at Pack Ice Command. Those who protested were forced into wearing them. And if they didn't fit properly, the Royal Emperors made them fit. *How come we didn't see it then? Fools. So caught up in the fervor of war, the Royals could have told us to eat sand and we would've done it.*

"It's difficult to say. A lot of us lost our tips along the way. I don't think they were meant to last for long. I for one am glad to be rid of the Overlord's weaponry."

"Give me an estimate, Lieutenant. I don't need precise numbers."

Colby shook his head. "I don't know; maybe twenty-five thousand; possibly more, likely less."

Welsy nodded his head in approval. "It'll have to do. Lieutenant, bring them to the front of the line. Dusk will be on us soon." His orders were interrupted by a messenger from the forward scouting party.

"Sir, the scouts report they have visual on several flying vehicles."

"What kind?" Welsy asked, looking at Colby with concern.

"The hoverers, sir. They have perched above the cliffs not far from here."

Welsy lowered his head. "It's as I feared. They're waiting for us. They seem to know where we are at all times and where we are heading. It's as if the Ancients have given them the power of foresight." He looked to the messenger. "Recall the scouts."

"Sir," Colby said with alarm. "What good will it do us if we're blind? The scouts have been our only warning."

"Don't you see, Lieutenant? It doesn't matter. Either way, we're dead. If we continue north, they'll be waiting. If we try to go home, they'll be waiting. If we head straight to sea, they'll attack us there. We can only hold our breath for so long. And like before, they'll be waiting when we rise for air. It's over. We're beaten." Welsy swam in a circle, frustrated. All he wanted was to live in peace, to be done with the war, to start over. But they wouldn't have it. The humans won't let it end. He looked to Colby. "It ends today. If they fear to attack us while we're close to their nesting grounds, we will attack them there. And we will die there, Colby, far from our homes, where none will know our fate."

"I'm not ready to die, sir." Lieutenant Colby tried to maintain his composure, but failed badly.

"None are, Lieutenant. But the choice has been stolen from us. If we don't make a stand today, the end will come tomorrow, when we are running like cowards, harried until there are none of us left for them to pursue. But we can take the fight to them, and our end will be remembered by the Ancients. We will force them to look up from the Great Sea and see that we died with honor. That we died taking the fight to our enemy rather than fleeing like fish from a beak. That we chose our day to join them in the Deep."

The sound of a helicopter passing over emphasized Welsy's point. Colby nodded his head. "Where is our target, sir?" he asked in a quiet voice.

Welsy looked to the shore. "There." He lifted his beak toward a small coastal town nestled in the San Luis Bay.

CHAPTER 82

The penguins flew from the surf, landing feet first on the warm California sand. At first, people were surprised. The surprise turned to amusement; the attack began, and fear and panic set in. Welsy's forces pressed their advantage. Initially, very few people fought back. When the first death cries were heard, some turned on their attackers. The defenders were too few, and soon any resistance on the beach was defeated. Children cried for their parents and were rounded up by the penguins, held captive in a circle of invaders.

The penguins stumbled and pushed their way up the beachhead, to the stairs on the seawall. They overran the boardwalk within minutes. Restaurant and shop owners took as many people inside as they could until they ran out of time. Floor to ceiling glass windows soon succumbed to the reinforced beaks, and the penguins flowed through the wreckage. The first penguins inside were met with heavy chairs and various dinnerware and pots. But the press of black and white overwhelmed the men, forcing the survivors to hide or flee.

The sporadic crackle of gunfire could be heard from around the town, but too few were armed to make a difference, and the penguins continued their advance. They charged up the narrow roads and into the public parking lot. Penguins were run over, but a traffic jam ensued. A hundred cars tried to leave the town at once, and the threat of moving vehicles ended.

A collision of panicked motorists blocked the main avenues of escape north of town, and the steel beaks tapped furiously against tempered windshields. The pecked glass gave way, and the penguins overtook the occupants. A fire erupted near the center of town, and flames began to spread.

^^^

Randy and Gina had been enjoying the day on the pier when the attack began. They tried to warn the beach-goers, but were mostly ignored. With no other option, they fled the scene. Gina reached the car parked on San Rafael Street on the high side of town. Randy followed, fishing the keys from his pocket. Gina pulled out her phone, but hearing the wail of sirens, put it away. Randy tossed her the keys and looked back. From their vantage point on the hill overlooking town, the attack seemed unreal. Like something out of a B-movie. But the screams were real. Sickened by the horror, Randy turned away.

A woman ran down the sloped street, headed toward the beach. Randy jumped in front of her. "Where are you going? You're headed the wrong way," he said, holding on to her, slowing her momentum.

"They're down there. My girls," the lady cried. "I have to get to them."

Randy stammered, not able to find the words to tell her it was probably too late. Thankfully, Gina stepped in.

"Ma'am, you can't go down there. Look," Gina said, pointing to the chaos.

The lady pushed them away. "I won't leave Hannah and Katie to die there. They're alive." She ran down the steep grade toward the madness.

Gina looked away when the woman fell into the throng of black. "I'd do the same thing if it were my children." She slammed the car door and turned the ignition.

Randy stood outside the car, still looking back. He heard Gina calling him, but he didn't move. The blast of sirens snapped him out of his stupor. Gina got out and pulled him out of the way of the approaching sheriff vehicles.

"The cops will take care of it now," Gina said. "There's nothing we can do."

CHAPTER 83

Randy sprang from the passenger seat, urging Gina to hurry up. She shook her head and followed him at a trot until they reached the door. She gave him the keys and he rushed inside, flipping on lights and began searching his closet. He found his duffle and threw it on the bed, stuffing clothes and knickknacks and anything else his hands touched into the bag. He looked at Gina, who stood watching. "Let's go. Get packed. We have to get out of here."

Gina took him by the shoulders and looked in his eyes. "Randy, we're safe here. We're a long way from the beach. They're not going to come this far inland."

Randy stepped back. "The Falklands. They had to go pretty far inland there."

"Those are islands," she said calmly.

"San Luis Creek…they can make their way up the creek." He started packing again.

Gina grabbed him firmly. "No, Randy, they won't come up the creek, a river, a canal or any other way. We're not in any danger here."

Randy looked at her, his eyes showing he was finally beginning to see reason. He flopped on the bed, grabbing the T.V. remote. "Those people. Those poor people. Why here? Why anywhere? How did they get this far north?" He sat up and began flipping through channels, trying to find news coverage.

Gina sat next to him, taking the remote from his hand. "This can't stay hidden now. Too many people saw it happen. I don't even think BioCon can conceal this one."

"Yeah, them. I wonder if your new employer will show up at our door."

"I haven't said yes yet." Gina stood, walked to the window, and peered between the blinds. She jumped back. "Why is there a car on the grass?"

Randy jumped up and looked for himself. "Did you pay the rent?" he joked, as he saw three men exit the black sedan. He popped back when one of the men looked at him.

Gina stepped into the living room, looking at the front door. A knock came a second later. She turned to Randy. "I don't like this. Have they been watching us, waiting for something like this to happen?"

"I told you we should've left," Randy said, coming to Gina's side. The knocking came again. "Maybe we shouldn't answer."

Gina raised her eyebrows. "Do you really think they don't know we're home?"

"One could hope," Randy said, reaching for the door. "You ready for this?"

Gina took a deep breath. "Maybe it's the boys from BioCon."

"I don't know. All three are wearing matching suits and ties. Looks like government or something."

Randy opened the door and a tall man filled the entry, framed by two men of similar stature. "Randall Lee?"

"I think you know that already. Who are you?" Randy said, blocking the entry.

"May we come in?" the man asked.

"Um, I don't usually let strangers in my home. So, good-day, sir." Randy started to push the door closed.

"I apologize. My name is Jenson, Tyler Jenson. I represent GT."

"That was quick. The attack happened thirty minutes ago, and you're already at our door. Almost like you knew it was coming," Gina barked from the middle of the room.

Jenson let a thin, humorless smile cross his lips. "Miss Rosedale, a pleasure to finally meet you," he said, stepping past Randy. He motioned for the two others to wait outside.

"Yeah, it's not mutual. What the hell is going on? First Antarctica, and then a dozen other places, and now here. You guys really screwed up, didn't you?" Gina took a breath. "And then you destroy our lives for whatever reason. I should just…"

"I do apologize for any inconveniences you have been through. I assure you plans are in motion to rectify the situation. But I am a bit pressed for time."

Gina stared at the man. Thin lips resting on a pasty pink face, highlighted with a slight case of rosacea, his face was as unpleasant as his condescending voice. She instantly found him nearly as detestable as Ferdinand Davis, the GT thug who'd attempted to kill her in Antarctica. "You have one minute."

Jenson looked at her through narrowed eyes. His expression changed back to fake kindness. "We have need of you. Both of you, actually. In light of the present situation, it has become quite urgent."

"Need of us?" Gina asked before Randy could open his mouth. "We don't have need of you, so goodbye."

"If you will give me just another moment. I wasn't there, but I understand you had verbal contact with…the indigenous life in Antarctica?"

"If you mean Weddell seals, then no. If you're talking about penguins, then yeah, you could say that," Randy said. He looked at Jenson's associates outside and closed the front door. "How do we know you are who you say you are?"

Jenson pulled his wallet from his coat pocket and showed both of them his ID and GT badge. "Satisfied?"

Randy looked at Gina and shrugged.

Randy was far too trusting, but Gina shook her head. "Okay. Let's say you are who you say you are; what do you want from us?"

"I need you to come with us…to Santa Monica and then to San Diego. Do you still have the gear GT provided you?" Jenson took a step back toward the door.

"We do. It's in storage, though. I don't remember southern California being all that cold," Randy said before Gina could answer, trying to keep things calm.

"We'll travel there first, and if the need arises, Antarctica may be in the plans," Jenson said, taking another step. When neither budged, Jenson took another approach. "We have what we call a talker. A penguin that can communicate. It wishes to speak with you."

The ever optimistic Randy looked at Gina. "Maybe it's Meuseaux. He would be the only one who knows us by name."

Gina shook her head, stepped forward, and looked Jenson straight in the eyes. After several seconds of silence, she snorted a laugh. "I don't think so. GT already tried to have me killed once, and you want me to leave with you so you can dump my body somewhere between here and who-knows-where? You need to leave…now."

Jenson mimicked her laugh and took the final step to the door. He took the handle in his hand and turned back to Gina. "You're making this much harder than I anticipated. Have it your way." He opened the door to let the others in. He stayed motionless for half a second. Both men were sprawled on the ground, blood oozing from their heads. He stepped back, and the space where his head had been a moment before erupted into splinters.

Randy flinched away from the shower of wood. The next thing he knew, Jenson's fist connected with his head. He shook the cobwebs from his head in time to see Gina land a palm thrust to Jenson's face, narrowly missing his nose. He tried to stand, but the room swirled and he collapsed back to the floor.

Jenson blocked Gina's next attempt and returned a backhand, which sent her to the floor, next to Randy.

Randy stood up, enraged, swinging his fist at Jenson. His first punch clipped the other's chin and his second fell short when Jenson slapped it away and connected with a cross to Randy's jaw. He stumbled back until his back met the wall and slid down, vaguely aware of the scuffle taking place.

^^^

Gina donkey-kicked from her hands and knees, landing her strike to the side of Jenson's groin, then rolled away. Trying to remember her brief martial arts training, she stood, keeping her feet light, waiting for the next move. The next move came when Jenson pulled pepper spray from under his jacket and sprayed her in the face. Gina fell back and began cussing and swinging wildly, trying to wipe her eyes while attempting a blind swing. Jenson rushed in, shoved her against the wall, and took her in a choke hold.

A bullet shattered the living room window, putting a hole through the drywall. Jenson drew his pistol and placed the barrel against Gina's temple. "You so much as twitch, and I'll put a bullet in your boyfriend's skull and then yours. You got that?"

Gina nodded in compliance. She could feel Jenson's breath on the side of her face, making her wince as much as the pepper spray.

"Good girl," Jenson said. "You're coming with me."

Good girl? Gina thought. God, she hated when people said crap like that. She resisted her urge fight back. She wouldn't let Randy die.

Jenson walked her to the door, pushing her over the threshold ahead of him, using her as a shield. Two bullets hit the planter to their right and Jenson stopped, watching the wooded grove of eucalyptus trees on the edge of the complex. He kept Gina between him and the trees, and sidestepped toward the car. Bullets sprayed dirt from the lawn in front of them. Undeterred, he kept moving until they reached the car. "Now, reach to your left, slowly, and open the door. Don't forget, I can still see your boyfriend."

Gina didn't move. She knew if she got in the car, her chances of getting away would diminish. She kept her hand up and in front of her.

"Do it," Jenson demanded. "I swear to God, I'll put a bullet between his eyes if you don't. Do it. Now." Gina let out a defeated breath and groped for the door handle and pulled the door open. Jenson kept her between the shooter and himself, backing toward the seat. In a quick motion, he fell into the driver's seat, pulling Gina on top of him. He pushed her toward the passenger seat, and she kicked madly at him. He landed an elbow against her chin and Gina slumped over. He slammed the door, pushing her limp body off of him, turned the ignition, and sped away, throwing clumps of turf against the stucco-walled apartments.

^^^

Randy stumbled out the door, watching the car's rear window get peppered with gunshots. The car bounced over the sidewalk and the taillights disappeared. Gina was gone. He had to do something. He looked at the bodies and realized the shooter was still out there. He ducked back inside, slamming the door. The door refused to close from the damaged frame and Randy gave up on closing it.

He patted his pockets, trying to find his phone. Running to the bedroom he found both his keys and phone lying on the bed. He snatched them up and turned to go, when he saw a shadow pass his window. Randy pressed his body against the wall, adrenaline helping to fight the disorientation of being knocked out. The front door creaked open. His heart hammered in his chest. The killer was inside; he could hear footsteps crunching on broken glass.

"Randy," the killer said quietly. "Randy Lee. I'm not here to hurt you. But we must go if you want to save Gina."

Randy scrunched his eyebrows in confusion. Why would he want to save her? The man spoke again, a little louder and with more urgency. It was a deep, husky voice, with a vague foreign accent. He stared at the ground. What to do? When the man spoke again, Randy stepped out of the bedroom. He saw a large man standing in his front room, straightening a lamp shade. He turned to face Randy. The muscular, bald man with a horseshoe mustache and several days' stubble, greeted him with a smile; a sincere but concerned smile.

"Hello, Randy. My name is Trofim. Trofim Grekov." He held out his hand in greeting.

Randy took the hand. "I'm…well, you already know who I am. Are you with BioCon?" he asked, guessing as to why he was there and not killing him.

Trofim raised his eyebrows. "Not officially. Not anymore. We can still catch Jenson and get Gina back for you. But we have to go now."

"Why should I trust you?" Randy asked. He berated himself in his mind after saying it. *Trust him, stupid. He said he can save Gina.* He wiped blood from his lip and walked to the kitchen. He wetted a towel and pressed it against his mouth.

"I'll explain on the way," Trofim said. "But please, every second we delay, the further they are."

Randy nodded. "Okay. Okay." He paused, looking around the room. "Let me get my jacket. And what about my place? I can't leave it wide open like this. And the bodies on the lawn?"

Trofim pulled out his phone and lifted a finger toward Randy. "Agnes, it's Trofim. I've made a small mess in San Luis Obispo. I need a cleanup… yes, I'm aware of what's happening in Avila, but Jenson took a shot at Gina Rosedale and her boyfriend…no, he got away, and he's taken Gina. I'm headed after him now." He motioned for Randy to follow him outside. He turned and slammed the door shut. "Two bodies. I'm not certain who they were. Probably GT. No sign of police yet."

Randy heard sirens in the distance and pointed to his ear, looking at Trofim.

"Scratch that. It sounds like they might be on their way…I know. I owe you a job then. Thank you, Agnes." He hung up and began trotting toward the parking lot. "Come on. We'll have to use your car."

Randy hesitated, took a deep breath, and followed after him. "My car isn't exactly a pursuit vehicle. And we're gonna need gas."

CHAPTER 84

"We are expanding our territory during a time in which others are falling away. Once we rein in Kiley's disobedience and bring our own back into the Order, we will see a kingdom which will rival Klakiduses' at its zenith." The King penguin calmly walked from the surf on the black sand beach of the former Rockhopper colony. Hundreds followed her, spreading across the beach as far north as Petral Landing, a large outcropping of rock dividing North Shore from Black Sand. Queen Gelika faced the sea, lifting her head high. "This place is our birthright, Admiral Gregor. Long before the Rockhoppers, before the Gentoo, and before the Magellanics, the Kings inhabited this island. Here was the original Council of Thrace. Fifty generations before that fool Antaean disbanded it, this was where the fate of the clans were decided."

Admiral Gregor cleared his throat, annoyed by Gelika's preamble. "Your Majesty, as much as I would like to continue this history lesson, our scouts have returned, and as of yet, there is still no sign of the Alliance."

"I doubt the *Doyenne* has the fortitude to claim this land as her own," Gelika said with the same pompous air of her former mate, the now-deceased King Elinthaw. "Besides, Admiral, you said the Alliance will be broken when or if they arrive."

"I said they might, Your Majesty. There are many variables in the plan. If they arrive at full strength, we will be considerably outnumbered." Gregor stood firmly before the Queen, awaiting a verbal berating for using a harsh tone. He was surprised by the lack thereof.

"Admiral, I've been thinking. In a situation such as this, why should we assume all of the risk? Surely there's another way."

Gregor looked at the gray sky, seemingly falling closer to the ground. *And here it is; she's going to suggest making an alliance with Mearna. Just as Elinthaw and her clutch mate Gelida predicted she would.* He could hear their voices, warning him of her treachery and her lust for power. And to think, he had assisted her taking the throne. "Your Majesty, what are you suggesting?" Gregor said, sounding defeated.

Gelika looked at Gregor, her eyes smiling. "It's not what you think, Admiral. Elinthaw and my sister only sought to maintain their power. If Gelida wasn't lost at the Battle of South Georgia, she would've taken my place at Elinthaw's side. No, my devoted friend, I will not seek an alliance with our enemy. However, I will ask that you send messengers to find T'Cuh-ka. I hope to make an alliance with our old friends, the Magellanics."

Gregor lowered his head, relieved by her words. How could he have ever doubted her? If others weren't around, he would have rubbed beaks with her then and there. He was more than half tempted to do it regardless. His trust hadn't been misplaced. Gelika was his queen, and his chest filled with pride. "Your Majesty, I will send messengers right away. And what will be their return if they should choose to accept your request?"

Queen Gelika's eyes fluttered. "Gentoo Rise will be theirs again."

Happy to be in her service, Admiral Gregor saluted and hurried off to see to the orders of the Queen, her eyes following him.

CHAPTER 85

PACK ICE COMMAND: In a cavernous room below the remnants, daylight flowed through an ice window high above the floor. To some, it looked like the moon had fallen toward Earth. To Lord Saeson, it looked like a promise of the future for his kind. More than one hundred Basileios warriors at various stages of development sparred, using their elongated beaks. Long flippers hanging to their sides, nearly touching the ground, were brought up for the occasional slap, knocking an unsuspecting opponent to the ground.

"Good," a voice shouted. "When your enemy falls to the ground, finish him. Drive that powerful beak of yours through his neck and sever the head. That's your only sure kill."

"Your training is unsurpassed, Warlord Talus. With your tutoring, none will match us in battle."

Talus spun around, a large knife slapping against his side, secured by a seal leather sheath. "My Lord, thank you for your praise, but they are still a long way from becoming true warriors. They'll have to kill soon, to get a taste for battle and blood."

"Soon enough, Warlord. My loves have captured a few men, but I'm hoping to find more."

"Let's hope they do. Cryzyrky, tell them to take a break. There's no need to exhaust them just yet." Talus stepped next to the much larger penguin and waited.

The one-flippered Adélie acknowledged the command and called out, and the room fell silent.

"You command them well, Warlord. I have no doubt they'll be ready when the time comes."

"They will, My Lord. I promise you they will fight without mercy. Your enemy's blood will stain the ice from here to Planarseae." Talus stood proudly before his trainees, who stood motionless at attention.

"Let's hope so, Warlord. There will be more for you to train very soon." The enormous penguin turned and left the room.

He lumbered down the dark corridor until he reached an end. Letting out a low, guttural growl, the door slid open, revealing another vast and well-lit room. Two penguins, with similar markings as him and the same elongated flippers and deadly beaks, turned to him. "Akronas, Koré, my queens, how are our offspring today?"

Her black crest falling forward, Koré bowed her head and spoke first. "Lord Saeson, the fledglings are strong. They are growing much faster than their predecessors."

Akronas bowed next, her golden crest matching Koré's movement. "Lord Saeson, the females have reached maturity. They are restless for mates."

"Very well, their restlessness will be answered soon." Saeson walked through the nesting area, accompanied by his queens. Ten Misshapen sat on their nests, incubating two eggs a piece. Further back, more Misshapen nurtured the young, taking turns on feeding runs below the pack ice. "The Kaurochs are protecting the gatherers well enough?"

"Yes, My Lord," the queens answered in unison.

"Good. Everything is proceeding as I desired. The K'tha will at last be destroyed and our reign will begin."

"Are you certain the Oracle is dead, My Lord?" Akronas asked. "Aperion has proven himself incapable in the past."

"If there is one thing my brother is capable of, it is killing. He has killed her, and he will die soon as well. Either Mearna's alliance will kill him, or the humans will. With Lapasia and Aperion dead, no one will know before it is too late. We will conquer all who oppose us. And we will retake our homeland."

CHAPTER 86

Leeg stood on the shore of the tiny island Kicki and he now called home. He watched Ceatak's dorsal fin appear and disappear in the surf as he circled the island, watching for any unwanted visitors. "I don't know, Kicki, seeing Ceatak out there kind of makes me a little nervous. What if he decides to make a snack of one of us when we go to eat? He's an animal, you know."

Kicki shook her head. "Ceatak is not just an animal. He's intelligent. Just because he can't speak like you doesn't mean he's mindless. And I think I'd know if he ever planned on eating you."

Leeg hopped on a rock for a better vantage point. "You're right again. I guess…hey! Why did you say eating me? So if he does get the idea to eat a penguin, it'll be me?"

Kicki laughed. "Of course he would. He's here to protect me, remember?"

Leeg hopped back down, his yellow crest bouncing when he landed. "Yeah, that's not very reassuring. Besides that, I thought I was supposed to be the one doing the protecting."

"Your job is to make sure any visitors are worthy and honest. That's a much bigger job than being a brute." Ceatak spouted his blowhole in the distance. "Sorry, Ceatak. I didn't mean anything by it; I'm just trying to reassure Leeg."

Ceatak slapped his tail on the surface and disappeared.

"They have such good hearing," Kicki said, looking at Leeg, who gave her a disapproving look. She slapped him playfully. "Don't be so sensitive."

"You're the sensitive one," Leeg said, looking up, feeling drops of rain begin to fall. "Let's get in the cave."

Leeg walked inside and got out of the path of the wind. He turned to say something smart to Kicki, but she stood in the rain, her body wavering. "Another vision. It's been a whole day since you had one."

Kicki swayed to the rhythms of the current she found herself in. She rocked forward and back, nearly falling, but Leeg was there to brace her up. He had done it enough now to know what to expect. He ran in front of her, in case she fell forward. Her body went rigid and her eyes closed. "This is different," Leeg said. Not knowing what to do, he stood and waited.

After several minutes, Leeg stepped closer. She had never done anything like this before. He knew better than to pull her out of a Seeing. He had made that mistake only once before, and vowed to never do it again. But he was starting to become concerned. She wasn't moving, and her breathing was shallow. He leaned in close and her eyes shot open.

Kicki stood, not seeing Leeg. "We have been deceived," she said, her voice cracking and weak.

"Who has?" Leeg asked nervously "Who's been deceived?"

"It is not him." Her eyes widened. "He is not the one. They will all die."